CODE OF HONOR

THE HONOR SERIES BY ROBERT N. MACOMBER

CODE *OF* HONOR

A Novel of RADM Peter Wake, USN,
in the 1904–1905 Russo-Japanese War

(Sixteenth novel in the Honor Series)

ROBERT N. MACOMBER

Naval Institute Press
Annapolis, Maryland

Naval Institute Press
291 Wood Road
Annapolis, MD 21402

Library of Congress Cataloging-in-Publication Data

Names: Macomber, Robert N., 1953–, author.
Title: Code of honor : a novel of RADM Peter Wake, USN, in the 1904–1905 Russo-Japanese war / Robert N. Macomber.
Identifiers: LCCN 2021059304 (print) | LCCN 2021059305 (ebook) | ISBN 9781682477847 (hardback) | ISBN 9781682478028 (ebook)
Subjects: LCSH: Wake, Peter (Fictitious character)—Fiction. | United States. Navy—Officers—Fiction. | Russo-Japanese War, 1904–1905—Fiction. | United States—History, Naval—20th century—Fiction. | BISAC: FICTION / War & Military | FICTION / Historical / General | LCGFT: Historical fiction. | War stories. | Sea stories.
Classification: LCC PS3613.A28 C63 2022 (print) | LCC PS3613.A28 (ebook) | DDC 813/.6—dc23/eng/20211207
LC record available at https://lccn.loc.gov/2021059304
LC ebook record available at https://lccn.loc.gov/2021059305

♾ Print editions meet the requirements of ANSI/NISO z39.48-1992 (Permanence of Paper).
Printed in the United States of America.

30 29 28 27 26 25 24 23 22   9 8 7 6 5 4 3 2 1
First printing

This novel is dedicated with great respect and appreciation to

Adm. James Stavridis, USN (Ret.)

Sailor-warrior, captain of ships, commander of allies,

scholar, diplomat, author, husband, father, mentor,

friend of many around the world, and dear friend of mine.

A man who not only understands and learns from history—

he's actually *made* a fair amount of it . . .

An Introductory Word with My Readers

When writing this sixteenth novel in the Honor Series about our fictional hero Peter Wake, it occurred to me that both new and longtime readers would appreciate a timeline of Wake's life until this point. It has certainly been far from dull. I've also included some special background for this book.

Timeline of Peter Wake's Life from 1839 to 1904

1839, 26 June—Peter Wake is born into a seafaring family on the coast of Massachusetts.

1852—Wake goes to sea to learn the coastal cargo trade in his father's schooner at age thirteen.

1855—Wake is promoted to schooner mate at age sixteen.

1857—Wake is promoted to command of a schooner at age eighteen.

1861—The Civil War begins. By 1862 his three older brothers—Luke, John, and Matthew—are already in the Navy and fighting the war. Two will not survive the war. The third will die of fever shortly after. At his father's plea, Wake remains a draft-exempt merchant marine schooner captain on the New England coast.

1863—Wake loses his draft exemption and volunteers for the U.S. Navy. He is stationed at Key West, commissioned an acting master, and given command of a small sailing gunboat, *Rosalie*. He operates on the Florida coast and in the Bahamas against blockade runners and is soon promoted to acting lieutenant. In Key West, he falls in love with Linda Donahue, daughter of a pro-Confederate merchant on the island. Irish-born boatswain's mate Sean Rork joins *Rosalie*'s crew, and the two men become lifelong best friends (as depicted in *At the Edge of Honor*—first novel of the Honor Series).

1864—Wake chases Union deserters from the Dry Tortugas to French-occupied Mexico. Later he marries Linda at Key West, with Rork as best man. Wake conducts coastal raids against Confederates in Florida (as depicted in *Point of Honor*).

1865—Wake's daughter Useppa is born at Useppa Island in Southwest Florida. After the tumultuous end of the Civil War in Florida and Cuba, Wake is sent to hunt down ex-Confederates in Puerto Rico (as depicted in *Honorable Mention*).

1867—When volunteer officers are dismissed after the war, Wake decides to stay in the Navy and is given a regular commission as lieutenant. He is one of the few officers in the Navy who didn't graduate from the Naval Academy. His son, Sean, is born at Pensacola Naval Station.

1869—As executive officer of a warship on a mission against a renegade American former naval officer off the coast of Panama, Wake relieves his own ship's drug-addicted captain of command and is charged with mutiny. He is subsequently acquitted of the charge, but his reputation is permanently tarnished (as depicted in *A Dishonorable Few*).

1874—Wake is involved in questionable activities in Spain and Italy when a beautiful French married woman enters his life, then is saved from further disrepute by Jesuits. He later rescues the woman and other French civilians in Africa, is awarded Legion of Honor by France, and is promoted to lieutenant commander (as depicted in *An Affair of Honor*).

1880—Wake embarks on his first espionage mission during the South American War of the Pacific and further cements his relationship with the Jesuits in the Catacombs of the Dead in Peru. He is awarded his second foreign medal, the Order of the Sun, by Peru. Before Wake can return home, his beloved wife, Linda, dies of cancer. He sinks into depression, then plunges into his work, helping to form the Office of Naval Intelligence (ONI) in 1882 (as depicted in *A Different Kind of Honor*).

1883—On an espionage mission into French Indochina, Wake befriends King Norodom of Cambodia, is awarded the Royal Order of Cambodia, warns Emperor Hoa of Vietnam about a coming battle with the French, and is promoted to commander upon his return home. Rork loses his left hand in the battle. Wake and Rork buy Patricio Island in Southwest Florida (where they served in the Civil War) and build bungalows there for use when they are on annual leave (as depicted in *The Honored Dead*).

1886—Wake meets young Theodore Roosevelt and Cuban patriot José Martí in New York City as he begins an espionage mission against the Spanish in Havana, Tampa, and Key West. His deadly twelve-year struggle against the Spanish secret police begins, as do close friendships with Martí and Roosevelt (as depicted in *The Darkest Shade of Honor*).

1888—The search for a lady friend's missing son in the Bahamas and Haiti becomes a love affair and an espionage mission against European anarchists. During a perilous escape, Wake's shadowy relationship with the Russian secret service begins. His lover having rejected his marriage proposal, Wake falls back into depression and focuses on his work (as depicted in *Honor Bound*). During a mission to rescue ONI's Cuban operatives from Spanish custody in Havana, Wake uses an introduction through Martí to forge a relationship with Cuban Freemasons and is designated a "Friend of Freemasonry." He manages to save the lives of the men he was sent to find and liberate, evades the secret police, and flees the island (as depicted in *Honorable Lies*).

1889—During the armed confrontation between Germany and America at Samoa, Wake is sent to the South Pacific on an espionage mission to either prevent a war or immediately win it. He is awarded the Royal Order of Kalākaua by the Kingdom of Hawaii and gains the gratitude of President Grover Cleveland but is ashamed of the sordid methods he felt forced to use in Samoa (as depicted in *Honors Rendered*).

1890—Wake learns that his 1888 love affair produced a daughter, Patricia, who is growing up in Illinois with her maternal aunt after her mother died in childbirth. Wake leaves ONI espionage work and thankfully returns to sea in command of a small cruiser. This same year, his son, Sean, graduates from the U.S. Naval Academy as a commissioned officer.

1892—Wake has a love affair in Washington, D.C., with María Ana Maura, widow of a Spanish diplomat. Brought back into espionage work on a counter-assassination mission in Mexico and Florida, Wake saves Martí's life and returns to sea in command of another warship (as depicted in *The Assassin's Honor*).

1893—In April, Wake is promoted to captain, and Rork to the newly established rank of chief boatswain's mate. In May, Wake marries María, and his daughter Useppa marries her Cuban fiancé, Mario Cano, in a double wedding ceremony in Key West, with Martí attending (as depicted in *The Assassin's Honor*).

1895—Wake's dear friend José Martí is killed in action while fighting the Spanish at Dos Rios in eastern Cuba on 19 May.

1897—Wake ends seven years of sea duty with orders to be the special assistant to the young new assistant secretary of the Navy, his friend Theodore Roosevelt. Together they ready the Navy for the looming war against Spain (as depicted in the first novel of the Honor Series trilogy about the Spanish-American War, *An Honorable War*).

1898, January to June—Roosevelt sends Wake inside Cuba on an espionage mission against the Spanish during the tense confrontation before the Spanish-American War begins. He is in Havana harbor when *Maine* explodes, and later that night kills his longtime nemesis, Colonel Isidro Marrón, the head of the Spanish secret police. After war is declared several months later, Wake is given command of an ill-planned coastal raid against the enemy in Cuba. Afterward he is shunned by naval and governmental leadership for employing shockingly brutal tactics against the Spanish troops to accomplish the mission, save the lives of his men, and get them all home. Wounded during the mission, he convalesces in Tampa, nursed by his wife, María (as depicted in *An Honorable War*, first book of the Spanish-American War Trilogy within the Honor Series).

1898, June and July—Recovered from the worst of his wounds, Wake is ordered back to Cuba as a liaison officer ashore with the Cuban and American armies, enduring the momentous jungle and hill battles against the Spanish at Santiago de Cuba. He then barely survives the climactic naval battle at Santiago while a prisoner on board one of the enemy warships. As all this is unfolding, María, a volunteer American Red Cross war nurse in the war zone, struggles with the horrors of the army field hospital and her own worsening illness. In the end, María is sent home and Wake begins a new sea command (as depicted in *Honoring the Enemy*, the second book of the Spanish-American War Trilogy within the Honor Series).

October 1901—While on his naval career's final tour of duty as a staff officer in Washington, Wake is called in and grilled about operational and personnel decisions he made while commanding the cruiser *Dixon* in the Caribbean during the 1898 Spanish-American War. Wake realizes this is a trap set up by his professional and political enemies to ruin his reputation and thwart his pending retirement and pension, but he proceeds to candidly tell his interrogators the surprising story. When he is done and all appears lost, he is summoned to the White House, expecting a demand for his resignation. But the new president, Theodore Roosevelt, instead convinces him not to retire but to accept a promotion to rear admiral and work in the White House as a special presidential aide conducting high-level missions around the world. Wake's career evolves into a new and exciting phrase (as depicted in *Word of Honor*, the third book in the Spanish-American War Trilogy within the Honor Series).

In *Code of Honor* we find Rear Admiral Wake in Europe in 1904 on an espionage mission to obtain the German plans to invade America. But the mission will unravel with Wake becoming a German target, inexorably embroiled in Russian turmoil and heading for the cataclysmic naval battle on the far side of the globe which will change world history forever, creating the daunting foe America will ultimately face thirty-seven years later.

My Research and Further Reading

So readers can understand even more about the people, places, and events in the story, I have included in the back of this book detailed endnotes arranged by chapter titles. For those whose curiosity demands more reading on the subjects within, I have included a bibliography of my research materials as well.

A Note about Wake's Writing Style

Like all of Peter Wake's memoirs, this volume is written with unusual candor and personal details, so family and friends would know the truth of what had really happened in his career. His descriptions and opinions of people may not be considered sensitive and tolerant in our modern age, but Wake was remarkably liberal for his time. His various grammatical mistakes, in both English and other languages (particularly Russian and Japanese, which he found quite difficult), are retained so the reader can appreciate the man and his limitations. His political assessments of personalities, policies, and events were frequently at odds with the norm back then but have proven to be uncannily prescient with our 118-year hindsight.

Dates Used in This Memoir

During the Russo-Japanese War of 1904–5, Russia still used the ancient Julian calendar, first implemented in AD 326. They didn't change to the standard Gregorian calendar used by the rest of the world until the 1917 Russian Revolution. In this memoir, Wake uses the standard Gregorian calendar understood by most of the Western world since AD 1572.

What Will the Future Hold for Peter Wake?

I am frequently asked what will come next for Wake. I can only say this: with a man like Peter Wake, under a president like Theodore Roosevelt, in a turbulent period like the dawn of the twentieth century, there are unlimited possibilities for both trouble and triumph. . . .

Robert N. Macomber
Distant Horizons Farm
Pineland Village, Pine Island
Florida

Rear Admiral Wake's Preface

I have long believed that brash arrogance about an adversary by a government or military leader is actually an indicator of that man's profound ignorance about both the foe and the realities of modern military operations. This oblivious egotism usually leads to disastrous consequences. Sadly, the cost is measured in the blood of thousands honor bound to carry out the orders of their profoundly foolish leadership, who are kept safely far from the grotesque sights and sounds of combat. Europeans have a long history of this sort of thing.

In 1901 a new president arrived in the White House as a result of the tragic assassination of President McKinley. Theodore Roosevelt has never been considered ignorant. By way of his own diverse life experiences, he deeply understands personal tragedy, the frailties of human nature, the aspirations of the American people, different world cultures and history, and how mortal combat really works. Most importantly, he has insatiable curiosity and constantly seeks information, digesting in-depth reports, listening intently to experienced opinions, and asking insightful questions. After weighing the options, he makes informed decisions, issues his orders, and speaks to the public with concise explanation and resolution. Roosevelt speaks in calm measured tones. He never blusters, never bluffs. His adversaries, domestic and foreign, have learned that the hard way.

And so it was in the summer of 1904. The president was dealing with a relatively minor issue in Africa that had been blown into an international crisis by the press. My role in the matter was minor and behind the scenes, and the situation was thankfully resolved without the use of force. I then returned to my main mission, a secret assignment in Europe to uncover a threat far more perilous to our nation.

Little did either Roosevelt or I comprehend at the time, but that secret assignment would lead me into the maelstrom of war on the opposite side of the world. There the new century's military machines of death were spewing forth human slaughter on a scale never before seen in human history. It was a war born of ignorant arrogance on one side and cold-hearted calculation on the other. The leadership of both foes used their own military culture's code of honor as an alibi for continuing the macabre insanity. The hundred thousand already dead or maimed over the previous year were beyond caring anymore, but the millions being lined up to take their places were absolutely terrified.

This is the story of that perilous mission, that war, and the unforeseen consequences of both. One of those consequences is the ominous rise of a new enemy, one whose arrogance is fueled not by ignorance but by something far more intoxicating for a country: overwhelming military success. I fear that my son's Navy will eventually face that daunting enemy someday.

I pray that when that time comes, our ships and men will be ready, our leaders wise and strong, and our nation resolute.

Rear Admiral Peter Wake, USN
Special Aide to the President
Washington, D.C.
3 March 1909

1

This War Ain't Even Ours

Tsushima Straits
Saturday, 27 May 1905

Hundreds of mangled Russian bodies silently floated among us in the oily water. Another swell washed over my head. All around us, burning ships cast hellishly eerie red and yellow glows in the smoke-laden night mist. Thunderous blasts erupted everywhere. I tried to think, *had* to think this out, but couldn't focus. Wailing cries of those still alive were incessant, negating any concentration.

Rork sputtered out some water and growled, "Damn that friggin' little fool Roosevelt for gettin' us into this mess."

"My eyes're swollen shut," gasped Law.

"They'll open up soon," I told him, hoping I was right. "Don't worry. I'm here right next to you, Edwin."

"There's nothin' pleasant to see anyways, Mr. Law," Rork muttered.

Rork awkwardly dog-paddled over to me, barely visible in the dark except for the white eyes in his oil-stained face. He looked like I felt—completely exhausted and in pain. One more wave slapped my face, filling my mouth with filthy water. After I vomited out what I could, Rork cast me a sarcastic look and muttered, "Well, what's the plan *now*, sir?"

I assessed our situation aloud. "Tsushima Island's sixteen miles southwest. Mainland Japan's sixty-five miles southwest. Tsushima Current's taking us north into the Sea of Japan, away from both." I gagged on water, then said the obvious, "We're in too bad shape to swim."

"Bloody friggin' right on that," said Rork.

"How's your legs?" I asked.

"Shredded from Nip shrapnel an' hurtin' like hell," he replied. "But I'll make it."

Debris were everywhere. Spotting a hatch cover floating not far away, I said, "Let's get up on that hatch cover. I'll go for it."

"The Japanese'll see us and rescue us," offered Law. "We're neutrals."

"Ha!" countered Rork. "With our bloody luck, the Nips'll think we're Rooskies an' shoot us on sight."

"Not if we yell in English," croaked Law hopefully, then added with a sigh, "Yeah . . . I guess maybe they will, Chief."

A searing pain abruptly shot through my left leg and I began to sink, barely making it to the hatch. A dead Russian was sprawled across it. With a curse and a grunt, I hauled myself up on it next to him.

Shoving the body overboard, I called out to them. "It's big enough for all of us. Swim over here."

It took a while. Once up on it, the three of us just lay there, desperate for breath, unable to move anymore. Waiting.

A hundred yards away, *Suvorov* was completely engulfed in flames but still moving slowly, a lone secondary gun still firing. A Russian torpedo boat steamed away from her into the black night, carrying a nearly dead Vice Admiral Zinovy Petrovich Rozhestvensky and his staff to another ship. We were supposed to be with them but had been hurled overboard by the blast of a Japanese shell impact.

From the east, a Japanese cruiser fired another salvo at *Suvorov*. They all hit. It wouldn't be long until she slid under. I heard a roar of steam turbines and knew the Japanese torpedo boats were attacking again. Four of them rushed out of the darkness toward us.

"Well lads, we're buggered now," Rork snarled. "Helluva way to die, after all these years. An' this war ain't even ours . . ."

In the glow of *Suvorov*'s flames, I saw him scowling at me, but he didn't say another word. He didn't have to. We all knew my decisions led to this.

The first one was in the president's office, a year earlier.

Part 1
The Mission

2

The Sheik, the Kaiser, and the Tsar

Temporary Executive Office of the President
Western Wing, White House
Washington, D.C.
Wednesday, 22 June 1904

"**A**dmiral, President Roosevelt wants you straight away. He's in the new office," advised the elderly presidential steward who knocked on the door to my hot, humid cubbyhole of an office.

Delay was never tolerated when President Theodore Roosevelt summoned one "straight away." I knew what he wanted: good news that the ridiculously overblown crisis in Africa was resolved and that military force wasn't needed. I left a quickly scribbled note on my assistant's vacant desk, gathered up my attaché case, and followed the steward down the hall. We ended up at the president's temporary office in the new wing being built on the White House's western end.

The steward opened the door and announced, "Admiral Wake is here, Mr. President."

The president didn't acknowledge my entry or even look toward the doorway. My own attention was drawn to two large electric floor fans in opposite corners, mechanical saviors on this hot summer day in Washington. Not many had them, but rank has its privileges: the fans filled the room with blessed air movement. I sidled toward the nearest one and tried to not moan with pleasure over the air cooling the sweat on my face.

Leaning back in his green-and-white cane swivel chair, Roosevelt intently inspected the white crown molding topping the dark green wall above the portrait of Lincoln over the fireplace. Jaw clenched, with narrowed eyes boring into the ceiling, he emitted a low rumbling growl at the molding. I knew exactly what that Rooseveltian look and sound meant—the time for waiting had ended. At the insistence of me and a few others, he'd waited three long weeks for the diplomats to solve the hostage crisis in Morocco. Now, he'd decided to use force. That meant the Navy.

He suddenly spoke, the words sounding like a judge doubtfully asking the condemned if they could conjure up any last words to mitigate the coming death sentence. "Peter, have you any message today from your man in Tangiers?"

For the first time in weeks, I could actually give good news. "Yes, sir. I was about to decipher the cable when I got word to come here. I brought my things and can decipher it now, if you wish."

The president swiveled his chair down and around toward me, put on his spectacles, and looked at me for the first time. "Yes, Peter, please do. I'd like to see how you do it."

Theodore Roosevelt is one of the smartest men I've ever met and has long been intrigued by methods of sending confidential messages. He's rather good at it, and we've used secret communications several times when I've gone forth on presidential assignments. Reaching into the attaché case, I brought out the telegram, then a paper containing a single line of Persian poetry in anglicized script. Next came a small revolving circle of letters, set within a larger circle of letters, both of rigid card stock, otherwise known as a cipher wheel. I laid them out on a small table beside the president's large desk.

That crowded desk had clues as to how he'd made his decision. Several books were stacked on the forward right corner: an English translation of the Koran; a French army officer's memoir of action in North Africa (published in French, which Roosevelt reads); and an atlas book of Africa, opened to the page on Morocco. The most notable was on the top of the stack, a syrupy 1888 novel about Morocco: *The Case of Mohammed Benani: A Story of Today*. It was written by none other than the senior hostage in the crisis that was unfolding, Ion Perdicaris. The other hostage was Perdicaris's stepson, Cromwell Varley.

On the other side of the desk was a pile of reports, including mine. Several had distinctive navy-blue Office of Naval Intelligence covers. Covering the center of the desk was a chart of the northwest coast of Africa, from the Straits of Gibraltar down to the Spanish Canary Islands. Roosevelt dropped his gaze down to the chart and stabbed a finger on Tangiers, epicenter of all the trouble, muttering to himself, "Thieves, the whole lot of them. Even your fellow Farid."

The president knew my informant was in the foreign ministry of Morocco's leader, Sultan Abdelaziz, but he didn't know his real name. Theodore and I had been friends for almost twenty years, but he knew better than to ask. Instead, I used a common Arab name as an alias: Farid.

I'd become a close friend of Farid's grandfather, an Islamic scholar, during my mission inside Morocco back in '74. The old man, adviser to Sultan Hassan I, had corresponded with me for many years before he'd passed on. Farid and I had continued that tradition for the last two decades. I'd last seen him in person on a port call in 1895, while commanding a cruiser in the Mediterranean. The acquaintanceship had yielded the occasional useful tidbit of North African–European politics.

Farid was an amiable fellow but not a man of honor like his grandfather. He seldom showed any discernible integrity in word or deed. In fact, in the current situation I assumed he was providing information to all sides, including the French, British, and Germans. Still, Farid was useful, for he communicated far more quickly and *accurately* than the usual diplomatic routes. Over the last several weeks his information had been at least a day ahead of the official reports out of Tangiers and considerably more factual—an extreme rarity. In the labyrinth world of Sultanate intrigue, Farid knew more than most, meaning I knew more than most in Washington.

I laid the telegram onto the desk in front of the president.

XRGTTAUPKTGJYIXFQXAIGPFJKTGFYOTSTAFTPFYGTMTXFTALXKXKX

He peered down at the message. "Hmm, let me study it a moment."

I did, knowing that Roosevelt possesses a phenomenal ability to read and memorize written words and numbers, and see patterns faster than anyone

I'd ever known. Completely engrossed in the message for a full minute, he then looked up at me with crafty satisfaction.

"An interesting conundrum, Peter. I do not see the letter 'W' and thus deduce it represents an infrequent letter of the alphabet. Perhaps 'X' or 'Q.' And the frequent letter 'A' in the telegram is probably a frequently used letter of the alphabet. Most likely 'E.' I see that 'T' is used ten times, meaning another frequently used letter."

"Good logical hypothesis," I acknowledged, then chuckled. "However, I must inform you that you are wrong, Mr. President. You haven't seen everything yet. You see, this method uses a simple cipher wheel, but the cipher changes every day based on the letters in a Persian poem. You must know the poem and also have the cipher wheel to solve the hidden message in the telegram."

I laid the poem before him.

Sar-i-chashma ba bayad firiftan b'a mil. Chi pur shud na shayad guzushtan ba fil.

As he looked it over, I explained, "It means: You can stop a spring with a twig. Let it flow unchecked, and an elephant cannot cross it."

"Well, I appreciate the import of that poem," he said. "But exactly how does it influence the cipher?"

"The poem was given to me in 1874 by a North African Islamic scholar who became my friend. Along with several other classical languages such as Latin, Hebrew, and Greek, he was also an expert in Persian, an unusual skill in Africa. He gave me this poem to use as a key to solving messages from him thirty years ago. Farid has this same poem in his possession currently, for the same purpose. Today is the twenty-eighth day since Farid's first message to me at the beginning of the hostage crisis. Thus, today's cipher is based on the twenty-eighth anglicized letter of the poem—which is the letter '*a*' in the word '*b'a*.'"

I put the cipher wheel on the desk and explained to the president, "The letter 'X' was designated the inner wheel alphabet's starting point. Therefore, I simply align the 'X' of the inner wheel under the 'A' of the outer circle of letters. The cipher is then solved, but only for today."

"By the way, sir, 'W' doesn't mean 'X,' it means 'B.' There is no 'B' in the message, thus no 'W.' The letters 'A' and 'Y' represent 'X' and 'Z' and are merely used to separate words in the message. You were right on the 'T,' though. It represents the common letter 'E.' Here's how it all works out." I twirled the wheel and wrote down the letters, which formed:

AGREE DINERO PASHA PRISONERS JEFE SEIS RELEASE MANANA

Roosevelt didn't get the meaning and cast me a perturbed look.

Shaking my head at Farid's sense of humor, I said, "He's combined Spanish into it as a joke, and maybe a subterfuge, but at any rate this is good news for us. Sultan Abdelaziz has agreed to Sheik Raisuli's various demands: the $70,000 ransom for the hostages is paid, the pasha of Tangiers has stepped down, Raisuli's tribal warriors are being released from prison, and Raisuli will have control of six districts. Farid sent this yesterday evening, so the last part means Mr. Perdicaris and his stepson will be released today."

The president visibly relaxed. "Brilliantly simple message, and the tiding of good news indeed!"

I let out a breath. "Yeah, we're damned lucky this thing ended the way it did. The French threat was what did it."

That was almost too candid but better than what I was thinking: it was an election year, and the Republican National Convention had just started in Chicago. A U.S. naval landing party ineffectually blundering about in Morocco would be a military and political disaster.

He raised an eyebrow and ruefully nodded his agreement. I quickly switched to another serious subject. "Now I can get back to the important matters. Mr. President, please remember on Saturday I'm embarking at New York for Hamburg and Saint Petersburg on the German mission. I'm still very concerned the Kaiser is so ignorant about us he might actually attempt it."

"It" was nothing less than a German invasion plan for the United States. We knew they had refined a prior theoretical plan with recent specific reconnaissance of our New York defenses. The Kaiser had openly disdained our army's capabilities, and said our navy was inferior to a modern European one. His arrogance had rapidly increased in proportion to the Imperial German Navy's expansion around the world. There was also the unknown factor of the Kaiser's influence over German immigrants in the United States—what would they do if Germany invaded? There had been disturbing signs of continuing fealty for the Fatherland.

Roosevelt tensed again. "Peter, this false-flag scheme of yours is ready to go *quietly*, correct?"

"Yes, sir. As ready as it can be at this point."

We'd prepared for two months, but I knew things could, and probably would, still go wrong. I just didn't know what. For a brief moment, Roosevelt looked disturbed at my less than totally reassuring answer.

Then the doubt cleared from his face, and he said, "Yes, well, in addition to getting the plans, and your personal appraisal of the personalities of Kaiser Wilhelm and Tsar Nicholas, I want something else—your assessment of the situation inside Russia. The army and the society. How long can they continue fighting the Japanese armies in the Far East?"

He held up a finger. "And I really need to know about the quality of their navy—can it actually go around the world and, once there, destroy the Japanese navy? Go on board their ships at Saint Petersburg and look into their eyes. Gauge the *attitude* of their officers and men. This is important. I need to know the answer. Can you do that?"

My trip to Europe was officially a goodwill professional visit. I hadn't anticipated this new burden and wasn't sure how to accomplish it. Our naval attaché had tried that very thing, but the Russians weren't allowing foreign officers on their ships. "Yes, sir. Not sure how right now, but I'll find a way."

"Good! We must know all we can and be thus prepared. If they defeat the Russians, Japan's next target may very well be our Philippines. The Kaiser would certainly enjoy *that*."

"That's my worry as well, sir," I said, thinking of my son stationed in Manila. I gathered up my papers to leave.

The president abruptly stood, gripping my hand hard. "Be careful. Europe is a Machiavellian snake pit these days, and the worst of the vipers have royal blue blood."

"Don't worry, Mr. President. I've faced vipers before. I'll be back in four weeks with the answers for you."

3

My Entourage

Hamburg, Germany
Wednesday, 27 July 1904

After journeying by train to New York, we began a stormy—and therefore much longer than anticipated—Atlantic crossing on board the Hamburg-America Line's new showpiece ship, SS *Deutschland*, to the bustling German port of Hamburg.

Two hours after our arrival I received an intriguing cable from a longtime trusted acquaintance in a little-known, and supposedly disbanded, section within French counter-espionage—the Section de Surveillance of the Deux-ième Bureau. Knowing the French keep close watch on German military and intelligence activities, a month earlier I'd sent him a vaguely worded telegram inquiring if he knew about German émigré conscript registration around the world, insinuating I was worried about Latin America and adding that I'd be visiting Hamburg soon. I didn't get a reply and forgot about it.

However, when we docked in Hamburg, a telegram was hand delivered to me by the French consular chargé d'affaires. It was from my friend, providing the tantalizing news that he had a woman informant possessing information about German staff officers in Berlin working on conscription registration of German immigrants not in Latin America but inside the United States.

She had just returned to Paris from Berlin and mentioned it to him. Could I come from Hamburg to Paris and meet her? I instantly boarded a train to France.

Over aperitifs at a café on the Boulevard des Italiens in Paris two days later, my colleague introduced me to the woman. She was a dowdy, vacant-eyed Parisian bookseller of Alsace background who didn't like the German government. I learned that she had lost both her husband and her home when the Germans invaded and occupied her area thirty-four years before, humiliating France and destroying the woman's comfortable life. She spoke both languages fluently and crossed between the countries frequently. Ostensibly, she'd been in Berlin to buy German-language books to bring back to her bookshop. I didn't ask why she was really there.

It turned out she had no specific or urgent facts regarding Germans in the United States, only some general information about émigré conscription, mainly in New York and Philadelphia, which I'd already known. She'd learned it secondhand in a conversation and didn't think she'd see the friend again soon. As we parted, she promised to be watchful for anything on the subject in the future and pass it on to me through our mutual friend.

I was disappointed. The entire thing had been a waste of several days, when we could little afford postponements. The next day we rattled our way back to Hamburg by train, hoping our target hadn't disappeared. Due to all these interruptions and delays, we were beginning the mission almost two weeks behind our planned schedule. President Roosevelt, informed by my periodic cables from Hamburg and Paris, was clearly not happy, unnecessarily admonishing me to keep my "eye on the real prize."

Of course, I wasn't alone. My entourage consisted of three remarkable people. My formerly Spanish (now a naturalized American citizen) wife of eleven years, María Ana Maura Wake, has the ability to charm the upper-class Europeans at soirées and banquets. Widow of a Spanish diplomat, she intimately understands the various manners expected and subtle signals exchanged among them. It helps enormously that at an age when other women are losing their looks, María is still disarmingly beautiful. She's also absolutely brilliant at instantly evaluating personalities in both men and women. Fluent in Spanish, French, and English; conversant in German and Italian; and with a smattering of Russian, María can entice the most reticent aristocrat to share thoroughly sordid gossip about who is doing what and to whom. At an operational level, this can yield valuable intelligence for subsequent inducement or coercion to reveal secrets.

María, however, is a reluctant operative. She quit the gilded life years ago when her first husband died and in the last few years has desperately wanted me to retire. Her dream is to live quietly with me and raise her flowers, with frequent visits from her step-grandchildren. Notwithstanding her dream, I know that once she's in the middle of a cocktail gathering of the social crème de la crème, she is damned good at getting useful information. Therefore, to secure her crucial cooperation on this mission, I had to promise to completely retire when our friend Theodore left the presidency. From that moment on, I suspected she was silently hoping for his defeat in the upcoming election.

My young aide-de-camp, Capt. Edwin Law, USMC, handles the mundane details of travel, meals, lodging, communications, and liaison. Quietly well-mannered in formal social situations, able to hold his drink in informal company, a combat veteran from Cuba and the Philippines, conversant in Spanish with some French, Edwin is also an excellent pistol shot and always armed with a Navy Colt revolver should the need abruptly arise.

Captain Law's only social drawback is his obvious shyness among aristocracy, especially the female type, a trait that makes him stand out from the surrounding bon vivant crowd. He dispenses a comfortable dry wit when around naval and military men but is quite timid in the company of ladies. Law's handsome face and unusually serious mien only seem to fascinate women, however. María explained to me these ladies feel challenged to get him to loosen up in speech and gesture. They usually fail.

Edwin also stands out because of his six-foot two-inch height, with a ramrod straight Marine Corps spine. The fellow is simply incapable of relaxing, slouching, or leaning against anything, and thus is entirely inept at blending in with common folk. This trait is impressive on the deck of a warship but a handicap for surveillance work.

Irish-born chief boatswain mate Sean Aloysius Rork, of the U.S. Navy, is my longtime best friend, shipmate on many vessels, partner in past intelligence missions around the world, and current personal assistant. As always for the previous forty-two years, Rork is in charge of keeping me, and the others we work alongside, alive. He is fully prepared to do anything to make that happen.

To accomplish this, he possesses some rare attributes. Unlike the tongue-tied Law, Rork can beguile any woman of any status in any culture by using his innate Gaelic humor and good-natured boyish appeal. He uses more than charm to get the job done, though. Rork's left hand is false; made of India rubber and able to unscrew from its leather stump surrounding what's left of his forearm. From that base protrudes a six-inch-long steel marline spike—a silent and extremely lethal weapon that is normally covered by the rubber hand.

Rork lost that left hand and forearm to a sniper in French Indochina in 1883, but its loss has never slowed him down. The India-rubber left hand's realistic looking fingers are configured into a grasp, and can hold an oar loom, a belying pin, or a bottle. His good right hand and arm have compensated by becoming incredibly strong, capable of crushing or punching anyone catastrophically.

And yet, with all that, Rork is not just some stupid brute. He is self-educated and very well read on history and philosophy. I've seen him hold his own in conversations with the best academics. Especially if they are buying the next round.

Still, Rork is not perfect. He is plagued by recurrent malaria, occasional severe arthritis in his feet and right hand, and phantom pains in the left arm. He also has a lifelong fondness for decent rum and indecent women. Both those failings often require some sort of fast remedial action on my part to extricate him—and me—from whatever mess he's gotten into.

Now, though, we were in Hamburg at last and ready to begin the second phase of the operation. Comfortably ensconced on the third floor of the new and quite posh Hotel Vier Jahreszeiten, we portrayed the beau ideal of sophisticated and entitled American society. A mile from the city's industrial cacophony, filth, and crudeness of the sprawling docks on the River Elbe, our windows overlooked the genteel parks and fountains of Lake Alster, an oasis of beauty and calm in Hamburg's center.

Officially, I was stopping in Germany for a brief social visit while in transit on a presidential diplomatic mission to Russia. Of course, everyone in Hamburg knew I was a special aide to President Roosevelt. This heightened

German sensitivity about my presence. I was sure some among the senior naval and military officers greeting me with hard-eyed smiles at the welcoming reception knew of my previous confrontations with the German navy in the Caribbean and South Pacific. Not one of them, however, said a word about the past. Neither did I. That sort of thing would be grotesquely vulgar, and we all knew professionals mustn't sink to that level. At least not in public.

Naturally, accomplishing my mission would require maintaining the delicate balance between performing my public persona's expected official obligations and initiating covert communication and rendezvous with a man literally putting his life on the line to sell out his homeland, my host country. This sort of dual lifestyle is quite stressful, especially when one considers the consequences should my real mission be discovered and made public. The consequences were especially enormous for President Roosevelt, particularly in an election year. I fully understood why he was increasingly anxious for me to get the damn thing over with.

4

Othello

Hamburg, Germany
Wednesday, 27 July 1904

Our target's actual name was known only by me and never spoken or written, even to Rork or Roosevelt. Instead, at the outset of the operation, I assigned the target a false name and rank and assigned him to a real regiment: Major Hans Kolhe, on temporary duty with the 45th (Lauenburg) Field Artillery Regiment stationed at Altona, near Hamburg. This combination of false and real is common in espionage and lends itself to confusing, and thus delaying, an enemy's search for the spy in their midst. Operationally, I simply used the whimsical code name, "Othello."

Othello was actually a midlevel army staff officer in the 5th Department (Operational Studies) of the Oberquartiermeister III Division of the Imperial German Army's General Staff in Berlin. That meant that Othello was in strategic planning for future war operations. For the last several months he had been staying in temporary quarters at the Hamburg barracks of the 76th Infantry Regiment (IX Corps), doing research on maritime transport mobilization for projecting a large army landing force across the sea. Since most of those transport ships would be civilian-owned and government-commandeered out of Hamburg, Othello was quite busy interacting with shipping company officials. Most of the businessmen he dealt with naturally assumed the army's destination would be the French, Belgian, Dutch, Danish, or Swedish coasts.

What did we know about our Othello? By all accounts he was an unassuming fellow with an apparently typical north German childhood who didn't stand out among his army peers. The product of the usual rigorous Prussian university upbringing—complete with a *Renommierschmiss* dueling-scarred cheek—he subsequently joined the Imperial German Army, along with many of his fellow students. Before long, he attended and managed to graduate from the grueling General Staff War Academy, which only 30 percent of entrants completed.

With that impressive pedigree Othello should have been one more dependably conformist and predictable army officer, completely immune to even the thought of besmirching his honor by cowardice in battle or divulging military secrets in peacetime. Other than colonial wars against natives in Africa and the Pacific, Germany had not been in a real war for thirty years. Army staff work was routine and boring, the perfect place for a comfortable conformist.

But Othello wasn't comfortable or a conformist. Nor was he immune to weakness. His personal life was a litany of profound sadness, and the perfect incubator of resentment against established authority. When his harsh-worded banker father had died three years earlier in 1901, Othello received no inheritance, did not attend the funeral, or even show any grief. The money went to his oldest brother, the first son. His mother, never much of a nurturing soul herself, married a wealthy Swede six quick months later and moved off to Stockholm.

Both of Othello's older brothers were successful bankers in Hamburg but estranged from their soldier brother because of their long-held perceptions of his "weakness." Their view was he was only bright and ambitious enough to handle an army career, not commerce. And as if all that wasn't bad enough for Othello, the poor fellow had no wife or children to console or cheer him, no political or personal connections to ease his career, no religious faith to lean on, and no money or social standing to make life more enjoyable.

The only thing middle-aged Othello had in life was the Imperial German Army, and that hadn't gone well lately, either. A year earlier, he had been told that further promotion had become a moot point because of his "peculiar personality" and "dilettante interests." Othello knew from that moment he would never feel the power of command, bask in the glory of fame, or enjoy the finer things in life.

But the overwhelming weight of his personal loneliness and professional frustration still wasn't the catalyst for Othello to betray the Fatherland's sacred trust. Passing that salient point of no return was stimulated by one of the most basic motives for traitors, even in the vaunted Prussian-trained military culture of Kaiser Wilhelm II's Germany.

Othello wanted simple, everyday revenge.

That vengeance was directed at precisely one person—Major General Johann von Sonnenblume, the pompous blowhard in charge of future war planning for the General Staff. Forty-seven years earlier, Sonnenblume had gotten his commission through political influence but never served in combat due to a purported foot condition. His career had advanced through mediocre staff work, Machiavellian backstabbing and maneuvering, bullying subordinates, and fawning over nobility, which Germany had in abundance.

Othello had a plan for Sonnenblume. The fat old general with extravagantly fluffed and bleached hair would be embarrassed by a breach of security for the highly secret German war plans. The embarrassment would be greatly enhanced because the plans would be obtained by none other than the barbaric Russians. Othello's need for revenge was ignited by Sonnenblume viciously embarrassing him in front of others at a very exclusive party, effectively ending his military career.

Othello's treachery did have limits though. He wasn't offering the Russians Germany's war plans against her traditional enemies, Russia or France. Those plans were far too serious, ready for instant use, and disastrously consequential if unveiled. Instead, he chose the war plans against a lesser and easier foe, one far away from Germany's borders.

This foe was Germany's new adversary—the United States of America. The Deutsches Kaiserreich (the Kaiser's Empire) had already confronted the United States directly or indirectly in the Philippines, Samoa, Hawaii, Cuba, Puerto Rico, Mexico, Panama, Venezuela, and Morocco. Kaiser Wilhelm II had backed down from President Roosevelt over Venezuela only two years earlier, and the humiliation still rankled him. In Othello's mind, the effect upon Sonnenblume's reputation would be the same, but without imperiling national safety from the Russians.

After all, he knew full well that the Russians, tricky Slavic bastards that they are, probably wouldn't share those plans with the Americans. It was well known that the popular American president couldn't stand both the Tsar and the Russian concept of autocratic rule and feudalism. It was also known that the Russians wanted Alaska back, especially now with the current gold rush. *No*, thought Othello, *they would take the plans and keep them quietly in reserve for the time they might ever need to use them for bargaining.* In fact, if Germany ever did attack America's East Coast, that would be an excellent opportunity for the Russians to retake Alaska, and *that* diversion would immensely help the German war effort.

What the Russians wouldn't know was that Othello, with Prussian thoroughness, would arrange for the Berlin press to learn a week after the transfer of information that undisclosed secret war plans were missing, that the despised Russians had them, and that Sonnenblume was responsible.

Othello and his scheming first came to my attention in December 1903, through the American naval attaché in Berlin. That officer spoke perfect German and frequently offered a friendly ear to middle-grade imperial army and navy officers, especially the disgruntled ones. Our man met Othello at a late-night diplomatic Christmas party at Berlin. Othello, persona non grata that he had become in the army, wasn't invited. But since no one he knew was there, and he was lonely that night, he entered and mixed in anyway. He was intrigued by the American naval officer who spoke such good German, and they began conversing about family and hometowns.

As the evening wore on, a champagne-overindulged and droopy-eyed Othello darkly hinted to his new best friend that he worked on invasion strategies in the war plans division. With a smug grin, he insinuated he was overworked with yet another quite difficult assignment, this one against a new overseas adversary. Gazing at the fireplace, Othello went on to say this plan involved an enormous effort in planning, for it was very complicated. He then lamented about how little anyone above him appreciated all his work, his career's waning future, and how much he heartily despised his loutish boss for ruining his life. Just as his friend was commiserating with him, Othello suddenly recognized the uniform the kindly American was wearing. Abruptly, Othello shut up and departed, plainly realizing he may have said too much already.

He certainly had. The German officer's information and potential usefulness were instantly recognized by the attaché and duly reported to the Office of Naval Intelligence in Washington. There, bureaucratic dolts duly filed the information away to gather dust for decades. But one veteran clerk, an old friend of mine, remembered a report from three months earlier that a German naval attaché in the United States had been seen walking around the forts guarding New York City. No one else at ONI cared when he told them, too occupied with their own mind-numbing assignments. The clerk passed copies of both reports on to me.

At the time, President Roosevelt and I discussed these two possibly related developments but couldn't draw any solid conclusions as to German intentions. The president wanted indisputable evidence, and he ordered me to provide it as soon as possible. The outline of a covert operation formulated in my mind. It centered around the unhappy German in Berlin. The first step was to know Othello in depth.

The best way to accomplish that was also the oldest way.

5

A Sympathetic Ear

Hamburg, Germany
Wednesday, 27 July 1904

A week later, an émigré Russian lady of the evening was discreetly hired by our naval officer in Germany, who was wearing civilian togs and told her he was a Canadian in the British service. The next evening the lady struck up a conversation with Othello in the bar lobby of the famous Thalia Theater during intermission. One thing predictably led to another, and over the next several frigid winter months she provided weekly sympathy and schnapps to the lonely gentleman.

The morning after each assignation she wrote a concise but thorough summary to our man in Berlin, who then encrypted it into a cable to me. Their friendship bloomed with sixteen rendezvous, and she got to know every aspect of the man's life and career problems. Most importantly, she learned of his obsession for revenge, which she was ordered to stoke. As winter turned into spring, Othello's initial hesitation in discussing details of his work dwindled. By the sunny month of May they were meeting twice a week, and he was gushing forth a cascade of information.

Notably, she reported that Othello never tried to consummate their relationship. He was content to merely cuddle, converse, and escape with her into the oblivion of drink. Of course, she wasn't nearly as much under the influence. Slowly at first, then more rapidly, her reports gave us a full picture of Othello. That she was experienced in this sort of work was obvious, and I suspected she worked for the French and worried she worked also for the Okhrana, the Russian secret service, with which I had many years of familiarity.

The attaché, however, assured me she was very much anti-Tsar—her Jewish family were victims of Russian pogroms under the Tsar's father, and she had been an Okhrana target in Paris for her vocal revolutionary comments. She had a prostitution arrest in Germany three years earlier but had since maintained a low profile, steering clear of revolutionary groups and criminal gangs. I wasn't so sure.

To protect against the lady potentially being a double or triple agent, the attaché told her his Canadian-British interest centered around Othello's banker brothers' connections with Blohm & Voss, the long-standing commercial rivals of British warship builders. We were careful to never *ask* specific questions about anything else.

In mid-May she reported Othello was in Hamburg trying to locate enough colliers to fuel the ships in his force projection plan. This was a significant clue. Large numbers of colliers weren't needed for landing an invasion force heading for the nearby Dutch, Danish, Swedish, or French coasts—but they would be crucial for a long-range operation.

Roosevelt and I had discussed this latest intelligence and realized that, while still entirely conjecture, it did point to a cross-Atlantic operation. It also raised some questions. The answers we arrived at were disturbing.

Did the Germans have a plan to invade America? Yes. *Had the German attaché been reconnoitering our defenses of New York as part of this plan?* Yes. *Why attack us?* Not to conquer us, certainly, but to follow the deep-rooted European strategy of capturing someplace valued by your opponent in order to trade it for someplace else you want to possess. In Kaiser Wilhelm's case, that would be a naval base and commercial colony in the Caribbean, from which he could influence global shipping through the canal being built at Panama. He'd wanted that base for many years, as I knew from personal experience.

Would Kaiser Wilhelm II actually be rash enough to try to attack the United States? Perhaps. He'd demonstrated no respect or fear regarding America, calling us "a land of mongrels," and had consistently been pressuring us around the world. He still resented us for making him retreat at Venezuela. His ignorance regarding the geography, culture, and industrial power of America was apparent in his comments and policies. *Where would the Germans attack us?* Obviously, it would be an Atlantic coast port. Probably a smaller-sized place like Portland, Maine, or Portsmouth, New Hampshire (nearest to northern Europe), which would then be occupied by German troops and held hostage until the United States gave away a suitable place for the naval base and colonial enclave, probably in Cuba or Puerto Rico.

Could the Germans really carry out such a large and complicated operation? Yes. It would have to be a surprise first strike, before we could mobilize and strengthen our coastal defenses. It would take at least 50,000 to 100,000 soldiers (which Germany had in more abundance than anyone else in Europe except Russia), most of their civilian shipping (which it also had in abundance), all of its navy (which was growing in size and lethality), and an incredible amount of planning and coordinating (which the Germans were known for). *When would they do it?* Other than Othello, we had no idea of how to tell except by keeping an eye on shipping buildups and troop movements at Hamburg. But that sort of intelligence might come too little, too late. What we needed now was that plan itself.

Then, in late May, the tension heightened. Othello asked his Russian émigré lady friend if she knew anyone in the Okhrana who might like to meet him and discuss some sensitive documents involving a transoceanic invasion. She blandly indicated that, yes, she had met some Okhrana men before at a party. They had been passing through Hamburg on their way to Paris, and one promised to look her up on their return trip. If she saw them again, she would pass along the offer.

That settled it. Clearly, America was the subject of the war plans. Othello was putting his scheme against Sonnenblume into operation. Roosevelt and I decided to act. The ridiculous African mess delayed us for a while but did not thwart us. This was far more important.

By the time my colleagues and I finally arrived in Hamburg in July, I understood Othello as well as one could from reading reports about him over six months. Now we had to meet him and set up the deal. I readied myself to be inserted into the situation and play my role.

Accordingly, two mornings hence, at the café Othello frequented for breakfast each day near the Gansemarkt Square tram stop, I would sit down at his table and quietly confront him. Camouflaged by spectacles, wig, waxed moustache, hat, long coat, and guttural faux-Slavic-accented English—our sole common language—I would introduce myself as a Russian Okhrana operative who *fully understood* about the *peculiarities* of his personal life. What peculiarities were those? The type most men would fight to deny, and some men would blush to admit.

Following that threatening insinuation, I would then commiserate over how Sonnenblume had destroyed poor Othello's budding career. My sympathy would be followed by a show of respectful trust, conspiratorially sharing the secret that we Russians despised the general also, for he had recently spread ugly rumors about our Tsar's beloved Germanic wife and her baby, soon to be born.

At this moment, Othello would be offered a simple way out of his misery, which would, coincidently, match his own scheme. I would get the German staff plans for operations against America. The press would not learn the details or target of the plans but would learn that the disappearance of secret documents was the fault of General Sonnenblume. Kaiser Wilhelm would dismiss the general, banishing him into impotent obscurity. Othello would get a sizable amount of money from "we Russians," revenge against his hated personal enemy, and guaranteed anonymity, and he would move forward professionally, with his personal life much more financially comfortable.

It was a good plan—simple, fast, appealing to the target, deniable by us, confusing to the enemy. In four days, it would be over and my entourage and I would be out of Germany on a ship bound for Russia.

This is not how it unfolded, however, for something came up that I didn't anticipate. An assassination nine hundred miles away in Saint Petersburg abruptly changed everything.

6
Repugnant Skullduggery

Hamburg, Germany
Sunday, 14 August 1904

On 28 July 1904, the day before I was to rudely interrupt Othello's breakfast in Hamburg, Russian interior minister Vyacheslav von Plehve was killed on the way to his weekly briefing of the Tsar in Saint Petersburg by a bomb thrown into his carriage. It was the fourth attempt in a year to kill Plehve, one of the most hated men in Russia. The "Combat Organization" subgroup of the Russian Socialist Revolutionary Party claimed the deed to the press.

In addition to running the regular police services, Plehve was the ministerial overseer of the shadowy Russian secret police—the extremely efficient, little understood, and widely dreaded Okhrana. They worked against anyone suspected of trying to undermine the Russian monarchy, including Russian émigrés in Europe and America. Back in 1888 I had come into contact with a senior man in the Okhrana while in the Caribbean. It turned out we had mutual interests—or, should I say, targets. After barely escaping with our lives, we had been maintaining a polite and mutually beneficial correspondence since then—always useful for intelligence professionals.

With Plehve's violent and public death, the paranoia of the Russian elite and other European monarchies, and their secret police organs, rose precipitously. Any nongovernment Russian in Europe was suddenly suspected of anarchist ties. This suspicion instantly affected our mission, for a Russian exile woman had befriended him and now an apparently Russian man would be confronting Othello in a public place. That could either scare him away or attract police attention. And it most certainly wouldn't do for the supposed Russian to be exposed as Theodore Roosevelt's personal aide. I didn't *think* the Germans would shoot me as a spy, but I couldn't be entirely sure. Therefore, I decided yet another delay of our mission was necessary.

I held a hasty council of war with my colleagues. We concluded that Othello was better approached by a less physically menacing, less expected Russian. A woman would be both disorienting and disarming to Othello. The rendezvous should be far more private than a café, provide a good cover façade, and have various routes of physical egress should things go wrong. A new plan was made. Rork came up with the location, Law with the false story, and María volunteered to be the Russian. "Volunteered" might be a bit inaccurate. After much persuasion on my part, she *agreed* to be the Russian.

On the evening of the tenth of August 1904, the new plan went into effect. Othello's Russian émigré lady friend delivered a sealed envelope to him at their favorite tavern. Before the astonished man finished opening the envelope, she hastily walked out the door into the crowded street. Poor Othello would never see his sympathetic lady friend again.

Inside the envelope was a brief note, containing an offer designed to intrigue him.

My dear Sir,

I am ready to assist you with considerable money and personal justice for the wrong done to you, entirely conducted in complete privacy, in exchange for some bureaucratic papers. Time is of the essence, so kindly meet me alone at 10 a.m. on this Sunday, the 14th of August, in cabin 221 on the German East Africa Line steamer *Kronprinz*, at the Seeschiffhafen dock number 3, before the ship departs for Douala, East Africa. At the

cabin you will receive further answers. For your anonymity, I will refer to you henceforth as "Othello." Destroy this note after reading.
Your new friend, "Bianca"

The following Sunday morning, my colleagues and I waited at cabin 221. It was actually an expensive first-class suite with bath, bedroom, and sitting room. Rork was posted as lookout on the promenade deck outside, standing in the throng of people at the railing having a last look at the city before departure in an hour. Law and I were in the bedroom, where María sat in a small cane chair next to the locked door. The outer door to the suite's sitting room was left beckoningly ajar for Othello.

The location was perfect for a clandestine meeting, for the ship was crowded and chaotic while loading passengers, baggage, and cargo. Across the wharf, the giant Hamburg-America Atlantic liner *Kaiser Wilhelm der Grosse* was embarking even more passengers, adding to the turmoil. Normally, she would have docked at the new Hamburg-America wharfs at Cuxhaven on the coast, but we had rare good luck when she came up the river to the city.

At ten o'clock precisely, Rork softly let out a bobwhite birdcall whistle. A moment later, we heard Othello enter and warily call out, "Guten Morgen. Bianca, bist du hier?"

María spoke slowly through the locked bedroom door, lowering her voice several octaves in a good rendition of Slavic-accented English. "Thank you for coming, Othello. Let us speak in English. Please sit down in the chair on your side of this door, but do not open it. That way, we will continue to be faceless. This will not take long. Would you like some tea? There is a pot with a cup, and milk and sugar, on the sideboard."

We heard him sit in the chair on his side of the door. "You really are a *woman*? I thought that was a ruse. You sound Russian."

"Of course I am Russian, just like your lady friend. You told her you wanted revenge against Sonnenblume. I can make that happen, without hurting Germany at all, and you will get enough money to make your future very comfortable. I just need those papers."

Now that he was actually committing treason, Othello's voice took on a nervous, scared tone. "What papers do you want?"

María was soothing. "The ones you told your girlfriend about, Othello. I have 15,000 marks to buy the file copies of the operations plan for the invasion of the United States, which are located at your staff office in Berlin. After Sonnenblume is humiliated and removed from service, you can impress his replacement and resume your career."

Othello's nerves were failing. "I may have made a mistake here. Perhaps we should think about this."

"You are obviously confused. The American plans are secondary to us, merely a tool to remove Sonnenblume. The peace of Germany and Europe are involved here. Sonnenblume has poisoned General Count von Hülsen-Haeseler's and Kaiser Wilhelm's opinion of our Tsar, the Kaiser's own cousin Nicholas. We want closer warm relations with Germany, not worse. Sonnen-blume is the obstruction not only for your career but for Germany. He wants to take Germany backward in time. When General Count von Hülsen-Haeseler and the Kaiser learn the American operation plans are missing, Sonnenblume will be dismissed, and your career will once again have a bright future. So will the amity between Russia and Germany."

Having dangled the carrots, she then brandished our stick in a stone-cold monotone that brooked no further debate. "And with Sonnenblume gone, you can also resume your *special* friendships with Prince Philipp of Eulenberg-Hertefeld and General Kuno von Moltke. Oh yes, we know about those too."

It worked. Othello lost his hesitation. Now he showed outright fear, clearly understanding that the Russians knew precisely what he had been doing and with whom. A low moan could be heard from the other side of the door. "Ah . . ." There was a pause, then his words emerged in a barely audible, almost childlike, voice. "When do you want the plans?"

María continued, still pitiless. "Three days from today, at noon on the seventeenth, you will send a cable to a man named Cassio at the Hotel Hamburg on Eisenmacherstrasse in the old city. Your cable will simply say, 'Hello, Mr. Cassio. Good to meet you.' Cassio will not be at the hotel, but your cable message will get to him. His reply cable the next day will tell you where and when to meet him to exchange the papers for the money. That will involve travel for you, but it will be authorized travel as part of your official duties. Do you understand your instructions?"

Othello obediently repeated them. María-alias-Bianca then announced her final words to Othello. "You will never meet me again, Othello. Follow the instructions and all will go very well for you. Violate our trust and your life will be forfeit—executed by your personal enemies in the German army. This ship is about to steam away, so you must leave now."

Othello was ready to flee. He made haste to get off the ship, with Rork following. I gave María a heartfelt embrace and told her very sincerely, "That was perfectly done, my dear."

She wasn't in a celebratory mood. "Yes, I did it perfectly, Peter. But I could feel his abject fear, and it profoundly saddens me to inflict that on someone. That is not who I am. Please remember that, and the fact you and Theodore *owe* me for getting involved in this and all the other repugnant skullduggery you two have cooked up for this trip. As for now, I feel dirty and want a decent bath back at our hotel. Then you will buy me a delightful and relaxing lunch overlooking the park and lake."

She let out a long breath. "And after that, we need to return to our room for me to get ready to meet this country's chief idiot, Kaiser Willy."

That evening, María in light blue gown and dark blue sapphire jewelry, and I in full dress white uniform with baubles and dangles, were escorted by Captain Law in his dress blue uniform into the Grand Salon of the newly built Hamburg City Hall, known as the Hamburger Rathaus. From the servants' area in the far corner, a plain-clothed Rork observed the goings-on while, I had no doubt, sampling the food and drinks—and possibly other things.

The major domo stamped his official rod, intoning in stentorian German, then in equally dramatic English, "Mrs. and Rear Admiral Peter Wake, Special Aide to the President of the United States of *North* America."

That little but important addendum was a long-standing German taunt to diminish U.S. standing among other nations in the Western Hemisphere.

María, still in a bad mood, quietly groaned, "Oh, this will be a lovely evening, won't it?"

7

The Biggest Pickelhaube

Hamburg, Germany
Sunday, 14 August 1904

After enduring a very long hour of inane female blather and ridiculous male posturing, the main show began. A hush went over the Grand Salon and all eyes turned to the foyer, where trumpeters blared out a prolonged fanfare. Seconds later, the major domo marched forward, thumped his staff seven times, and made a theatrical announcement in clipped German, translated by an unimpressed Brit diplomat standing beside me.

"Honored members of the Imperial House of Hohenzollern, dignitaries of the city of Hamburg, distinguished guests, ladies and gentlemen . . . His Imperial and Royal Majesty, Emperor of Germany, King of Prussia, Wilhelm the Second!"

The trumpeters blared another wailing note and every man in uniform, including me, stood at attention as Kaiser Wilhelm II entered. Without stopping, he strode to a reception line forming on the other side of the room. Once there, he waved his right hand and pleasantly mumbled something. His subjects instantly relaxed and applauded, showing him their best expressions of adoration. Another wave of the imperial hand ended that, and the attendees, having done their obligatory kowtowing, recommenced mingling and chattering among themselves.

María and I, with Edwin Law close astern, were guided by a self-impressed young court staffer to the middle of the slow-moving line to meet the Kaiser. This position was evidently according to my relative rank in the crowd, below German and foreign royalty but above Hamburg's commoner rich class.

I was surprised to see Albert Ballin, the well-known director of the powerful Hamburg-America Line of passenger and cargo ships, placed right behind us. Since he was a commercial giant and well known as a private acquaintance of the Kaiser, I thought he would've been well ahead of us. Reading my mind, María whispered to me it was because he was Jewish and was being kept in his place at a public event. Being of Jewish heritage in Catholic Spain herself, she instinctually understood this type of not-so-subtle prejudice.

With his pursed lips and frown, Ballin clearly had no desire to converse with us (I'd hoped for some bit of pertinent information from the shipping magnate, but alas), so we dutifully trudged silently toward our destination, a standing audience of perhaps ten seconds in front of the great imperial leader of Germany. I've had to do this tedious but politically expected duty in many countries. It's always the same, and I heartily despise it, especially on a warm summer evening in full dress whites with choker collar, surrounded by a mob of obnoxious posers loudly carrying forth in a gruff alien lingo. Though the social affairs are similar, at least Spanish and French are much easier on my ears.

I glanced at my companions to see how they were coping. Standing to the side near us, Law was clearly nervous he might do or say something wrong. María was the opposite, bestowing a confident and serene smile to all around us, which I knew to be a long-practiced façade. I tried to follow her example but was unsuccessful. We shuffled forward. Then, at long last, we stood before the Kaiser of the worldwide German Empire. He stood there solo, since his formidable wife, Kaiserin Augusta, was off cruising the Norwegian fjords on their imperial yacht, *Hohenzollern II*.

From photographs, I knew that the Kaiser of the German Empire was a man of average height and build. This was my first time seeing him in person, and he appeared much taller and wider. This illusion was accomplished by a huge, almost farcical uniform that could have been designed as a theatrical costume in a London musical. The image wasn't helped by Wilhelm's dour eyes, set over a down-turned mouth and wide moustache, the ends of which were flamboyantly swept up with thick beeswax, like little imitation boar tusks.

Topping the entire getup was the most enormous Pickelhaube—the Teutonic spiked helmet—I'd ever seen. It was a shiny black affair with silver buttons and inlaid patterns, but instead of being surmounted by a spike, it sported a giant silver eagle with wings spread for imminent flight. The thing added at least ten inches to the royal form but seemed seriously top-heavy to me. I wondered if it might capsize at any moment.

The white uniform tunic had similarly large gold and silver epaulets protruding from padded shoulders and long bejeweled sleeve cuffs. Two broad sashes crossed the front, and half a dozen medals hung on ribbons around his neck, with another half-dozen medals pinned in the few vacant spots left on the chest. Around his middle was a gold sword belt with a two-foot-long tasseled cord. From the belt dragged a golden sword every bit of four feet long. His withered and shortened left arm and hand rested on the sword hilt, and I noticed the length of its cuff was cleverly altered to help disguise the difference. Below the tunic were white riding pants tucked into black leather thigh-high boots so shiny they nearly glowed.

The entire rig must have weighed forty pounds and been excruciating to wear. I nearly felt sorry for the trumped-up fool—until I saw his face when he registered who had come before him. It showed undisguised disdain.

Without waiting for my de rigueur salutation of respects, Kaiser Wilhelm announced in perfect British English, "Well, I was told that an American rear admiral had stopped here on his way to Saint Petersburg. Did you know that my beloved late grandmamá, Queen Victoria, appointed me rear admiral in her Royal Navy? That is a *real* navy, and the finest in the world—at least for now. Have you ever seen it?"

"I had heard that, Your Majesty." I did not add that my British naval officer friends reviled Wilhelm and were humiliated to see him wearing their uniform. They also told me Victoria did it just to shut up his constant begging for the honor. "And I have had the pleasure of visiting Royal Navy ships many times."

He pointed to my chest. "What are those medals—and how did an *American* get them?"

My foreign medals actually are unusual for an American naval officer. Several were awarded during my clandestine missions for the Office of Naval Intelligence, so the details are confidential.

Swallowing my disgust of this petulant man-child, I provided suitably vague explanations, "Your Majesty, this one is the Legion of Honor of France, commander grade, for helping to rescue some French people from bandits in North Africa. This is the Order of the Sun from Peru, for protecting some innocent civilians during the War of the Pacific. This is the Royal Order of Cambodia from King Norodom, for my assistance to him. This is the Royal Order of Kalākaua from the Kingdom of Hawaii, for helping King Kalākaua on a foreign policy issue."

I watched the Kaiser closely when saying that last part, for the foreign policy issue had to do with my confrontation with Germans at Samoa. No sign of prior understanding showed on his face, though, and I went on. "This one is the Sampson Medal, for my service in the recent Spanish-American War. And this last one is the Cuban Liberator Medal, presented to me last year by the Cuban government for my service with the Cuban Army in that same war."

He allowed a slight nod of his head. "Ach, yes, that black Cuban rabble defeated the weak Spanish Bourbon monarchy." His eyes flared and he banged the sword scabbard down on the floor, making it rattle. "A king should *never* be weak!"

I amended my earlier evaluation. He wasn't just a man-child—Willy was a delusional and demented man-child. I curtly bowed and clicked my heels. "Of course, Your Majesty. You and Tsar Nicholas have demonstrated that maxim quite vividly!"

My comment could be taken two ways, but I knew he would take it as a compliment.

He positively glowed, saying, "Yes, we have both done that." The royal right hand waved dismissively as he lamented, "But my dear cousin Nicholas has problems we Germans do not. Peasant rabble, spoiled intelligentsia, ignorant workers. Slavs have no real sophistication and strength."

Behind me, Ballin and the others were showing impatience at my overstaying the usual allotted time with their Kaiser. I didn't care. My new friend Willy was warming up to me, this naïve American who thought him such a great man.

Giving him my most sincere look of veneration, I said, "So true, sir. Since you are so famously well versed on naval affairs, Your Majesty, I would like to hear your views on whether the Tsar's fleet can even make it around the world to the fight against the Japanese. Supply and repairs en route will be critical, I would think."

He puffed up, raised an index finger in the air, and began pontificating. "You are absolutely correct! It will be difficult, yes, but not hopeless with *our* help. We will provide colliers for his ships at various points on their voyage. Herr Ballin will make sure that happens. Isn't that right, Ballin?"

And that will provide invaluable experience in long-range logistics, I thought. I turned and saw Ballin recoil at the surprise question about what certainly must have been confidential information. Now the Kaiser was blabbing to an American! The businessman recovered quickly and replied in a low voice. "Ah, yes, Your Majesty. The colliers and cargo ships are already heading to their rendezvous points to help the Russian fleet."

"Excellent, Ballin . . ." By now, Kaiser Wilhelm was radiating self-assurance. He tutored me further. "Admiral, we Germans have the best naval general staff in the world, so later this very week I am sending a few of my navy and army experts in planning long-range fleet operations to Saint Petersburg to assist the Tsar's navy. I can fully assure you, Admiral, those little Japanese monkeys will never prevail over a modern European navy!" He then huffed, "Of course, many of Russia's naval officers have German family heritage."

I'd heard the rumor that the Germans were secretly helping the Russians with coal, and that there was a secret liaison between the German and Russian navies. Now I knew those supply ships would be from Ballin's Hamburg-America Line. And once the company had supplied a fleet on an 18,000-mile voyage around the world, a 4,000-mile transit across the North Sea and Atlantic would be relatively simple. In addition, I also had just learned when the German officers would arrive in Saint Petersburg. In a rare stroke of good luck, it coincided with our mission perfectly.

With real gratitude, I gushed to the Kaiser, "Thank you for sharing your valuable *wisdom* on this issue, Your Majesty. I will share it with President Roosevelt."

His mouth turned up at one end, evidently an expression of approval. "Any time your president needs my opinion on matters of world affairs, I would be delighted to provide it. We leaders of the *civilized* world must take time to help you in the new world. How long will you be in Hamburg? Perhaps we can meet again tomorrow."

Interesting. He doesn't know we are departing early the next morning. I mentally debated whether to reply in the affirmative and stay for an extra day. With a little further cheap flattery applied to Willy, I had no doubt I could discover even more operational intelligence. Yes, this was working out well . . .

That is when we were interrupted. My good mood evaporated soon afterward.

8

The Desdemona Decoy

Hamburg, Germany
Sunday, 14 August 1904

The chief of staff of the Imperial German Army walked up and, neatly elbowing me out of the way in the process, greeted his monarch. In addition to being rude, Field Marshal Alfred Graf von Schlieffen, the world-renowned strategist, also wasn't that impressive physically. His tired eyes and flaccid expression gave the appearance of elderly dim-wittedness. Close behind him were several senior and midlevel minions of the General Staff, all of whom clicked their heels and lurched to attention in unison for their cherished Kaiser.

To my surprise, among the heel clickers was Othello's boss, Major General Johann von Sonnenblume, head of the General Staff's plans division, who informed the Kaiser he was conducting garrison inspections in the area. I thought that odd. *Why would a senior staff planner inspect line regiments in garrison at Hamburg? That's a lower-level commanding general's function.* I wondered if that comment was a smokescreen because I was there.

"My dear Sonnenblume," said Kaiser Wilhelm amiably, still in English, obviously for my benefit. "Are you ready for your visit with your Russian colleagues at Saint Petersburg?"

Hmm, another clue, duly noted in my mind. The general was no slouch in the sycophancy department, instantly fawning, "I am *always* ready to be at your service, Your Majesty. But I prefer to be leading a regiment at the front line in battle to defend the Fatherland!"

It had obviously been a long time since Sonnenblume had last served in a line regiment, and, of course, he had never actually been in combat to defend the Fatherland. His belly showed decades of constant surrender to beer and heavy food, and his swollen red nose and runny eyes betrayed a daily addiction to strong drink. It also appeared he'd already had a few that evening, for upon his introduction to María, he ogled his inspection of her. I instantly understood much better Othello's quest for revenge.

María is used to men admiring her, though not as crudely, and simply ignored the uncouth general. Instead, she pleasantly asked the Kaiser and Graf von Schlieffen about Hamburg's gardens and cultural attributes. Glaring at an oblivious Sonnenblume, I noticed at the rear of the staff officers behind him was our man Othello. María was unaware of his presence. Behind us, Ballin cleared his throat with a growl. Our time with the Kaiser was up.

María got the hint and said, "I do not want to incur the wrath of the others in line, Your Majesty, so I fear we must leave now. I hope there will be another time."

My stomach tightened as Othello suddenly turned his head toward her, a quizzical look in his eyes. María had just said the same three last words she had spoken to Othello that very morning. *He doesn't know what we look like, but does he recognize her voice, even though she's not using a Slavic accent now?*

Othello started edging closer, his focus on María. I needed to do something fast before he could get close enough to María to confirm any suspicions. Admirals don't normally converse with midlevel staff officers in a foreign country, so my plausible options were rather limited. I was turning to Captain Law to quietly tell him to do *something* when good luck intervened.

A steward approached Othello and whispered in his ear. Othello nodded his understanding and whispered in another staff officer's ear. Then Othello turned and strode off in the direction of the foyer. Out of the corner of my eye, I caught sight of Rork in the far corner by a serving table. He grinned and briefly bobbed his head toward me. The same steward now tapped my elbow and handed me a sealed note. I stepped away from the reception line and opened it. The scratched note inside was in Rork's scrawl.

Saw things looking dicey, so I sent Othello word his Russian Desdemona was nearby. I suggest we depart before he returns.

It was quick and brilliant thinking on Rork's part, for he knew Othello was in love with the Russian prostitute who had befriended him. I returned to María and the people gathered around the Kaiser. The line of those waiting to see their monarch were now looking openly angry at María and me. I took María's arm, made profuse thanks to the Kaiser et al., and steered first in the direction of the bar, then altered course for the Grand Salon's back door. Law followed close astern. Glancing back, I saw the Kaiser's expression return to its dour norm as Ballin stepped up.

"Very well done, Rork," I told him when he met us in the passageway to the back alley.

"Thankee, sir. All in a night's work," he said brightly, emanating a waft of schnapps. "By the by, you notice the Abteilung IIIb agent watchin' you?"

"German army intelligence was surveilling us?" It wasn't completely unexpected, but still, it might portend a problem. Why army intelligence? Was naval intelligence—the Nachrichten-Abteilung—watching us also?

Rork nodded. "Aye, sir. 'Twas that fellow who guided you to the line an' then stood there a while. He's actually an army counterintelligence lieutenant. One of the waiters knows 'im an' told me, thinkin' it was silly they'd waste time on an American. Later, I saw the lil' bugger writin' notes while eyeballin' the three of you. Methinks he lost us when we made French leave out the back."

"Hmm, I *thought* that fellow was a bit over-attentive. Was he watching Othello too?"

"Nay, sir. Never looked that way. Too busy watchin' *you*."

"Good work, Rork. I presume the waiter thought you were Irish and not American?"

"Aye, that he did, sir." He grinned, his brogue getting thicker. "Irish as a misty day in Kilkenny!"

We quickly made our way out of the building and down the alley to the side street. Keeping a lookout for a perplexed or irate Othello returning, we found a landau for hire and climbed inside, pulling the curtains closed. Everyone leaned back and breathed a sigh of relief.

I leaned close to María, "What was your impression of the Kaiser?"

She shook her head with a weary sigh. "Little Willy is very afraid of what others think of him. He totally surrounds himself with yes-men who feed his delusions of strength. The fool can't see they consider him *their* pawn. I've seen his type before, in Madrid. The Kaiser is very dangerous, Peter. He will start a war just to try looking decisive."

"Yes, I agree, dear. Ignorant, insecure, and arrogant. A bad combination."

"There's something more, though. Did you see his expression toward Sonnenblume? It wasn't that of superior to subordinate. I think those two are close friends."

"Yes, I did notice that." I didn't say what else I was thinking. It was too far-fetched.

Exhausted by the tension, we each fell into our beds that night. Six hours later we met in the lobby and headed by cabriolet for the docks, scrutinizing the people around us for the intelligence lieutenant or anyone else who was watching us. None were obvious enough to be spotted, and we boarded the German Argo Line steamer *Falke*, bound for Saint Petersburg and the Kaiser's almost lookalike cousin, Tsar Nicholas II.

And for Othello's plan for the German invasion of the United States of America.

9

Undercurrents

Saint Petersburg, Russia
Wednesday, 17 August 1904

After an easy two-night voyage through the Baltic, we settled into the very comfortable Hotel Europa on Nevski Prospeckt in the magnificent city of Saint Petersburg. María had visited the city in 1889 with her Spanish diplomat husband, who died two years later. I had never been there and was stunned by the parks, architecture, and hospitality. Rork was speechless, a rarity for him.

Remarkably, for a capital city of a nation in the midst of a bloody war, the ambiance appeared quite gay. In fact, there was a celebratory mood at Hotel Europa, not for any victories in battle against the Japanese in far-off Manchuria (yet another bloody battle had just been fought) but for the birth five days earlier of the Tsarina's baby. After four girls were born in recent years, Tsar Nicholas now—finally—had a male heir. Russia had a certain future.

The rejoicing toasts in the hotel bar and gleeful conversations in the lobby rang hollow to me, though. They seemed more a desperate avoidance of the incessant catalog of disastrous war news coming from the Pacific coast. I'd seen such behavior in other countries losing wars: France, Peru, Vietnam,

Spain. It was the same story: high society continuing to enjoy their privileges to the end, unable to deal with the ugly truth and hoping it will go away.

It was not my place to lecture, however, but to learn. Opportunities sprang forth immediately. Local civic, naval, and military leaders sent their official welcomes to the American presidential aide. The scarcity of such an American visit made me a curiosity to everyone from the cabbies to the imperial court.

Even better fortune smiled upon us with a personal invitation from the naval commandant of nearby Kronstadt naval base to accompany him to the Rachmaninov symphony at the legendary Maryinsky Theater later in the week. I thought this would do very nicely for accomplishing two major objectives in one evening—a venue for obtaining the German plan from Othello and an opportunity for assessing Russia's naval and army capabilities in the war.

This final phase of our original espionage mission required an exchange of artfully nebulous cables from and to Othello in Hamburg—in reality, a summons to him to come to Saint Petersburg as part of the German-Russian staff talks. Once he arrived, he would get a handwritten note telling him exactly when and where to go in the city with the documents. All of the circuitous rigamarole would preserve our anonymity and security, and keep Othello convinced he was dealing with Russians. The morning after receiving the plans, we would board a ship bound for Britain. From there we'd be happily ensconced in a first-class stateroom on board a luxurious Cunard liner bound for Boston.

Late in the afternoon of our arrival, a messenger boy from the concierge desk knocked at the door of our suite. He had a cablegram from a businessman in Hamburg who sometimes did small favors for our naval attaché in Berlin—for payment, of course. That gentleman's small favor in this instance was to obtain Othello's cable to "Cassio" from the desk clerk holding it at the Hotel Hamburg and forward it under his name to me in Saint Petersburg. The message was exactly as instructed by María.

XXX—HELLO MR CASSIO—X—GOOD TO MEET YOU—X—OTHELLO—XXX

"Follows orders well," observed María. "Even though they came from a woman."

An hour later the messenger returned and was given my cable reply to the businessman at Hamburg. That man would then take it to the desk at Hotel Hamburg, where "Mr. Othello" would pick it up.

XXX—YOUR EXPERTISE NEEDED AT STF MTG IN ST PTRSBRG IN 3 DAYS— X—JOIN GROUP GOING—X—BRING INVOICES—X—MORE DETAILS ON ARVL—X—BIANCA SAYS HELLO—XXX

"And why is it that I am saying hello?" asked María when I showed her the message.

"Just a gentle reminder of your last words to him about what happens if he fails," I explained. She frowned and walked away.

Four hours later—far earlier than I expected, and a twist that made me suspicious—another messenger arrived at our door with Othello's reply.

XXX—WILL BE AT ST PTRSBRG MTG WTH INVOICES—XXX

The four of us discussed the timing. Either Othello already had the documents and had joined the staff entourage headed for Saint Petersburg or German intelligence had compromised him and was running him as a double agent. Ultimately, I decided to continue the scheme as planned, but we would be watching for any other unusual developments that might signal a compromise of Othello by either the Germans or the Russians.

As we strolled across the hotel lobby that evening to head out for a reception in my honor, my senses were on high alert. This stress was heightened when I witnessed a scene validating my earlier impression of Saint Petersburg's mood. A well-dressed businessman was bellowing at another gentleman, then went silent when he looked around and saw other upper-crust Russians in the lobby listening anxiously. Both men stormed out of the hotel; then the other Russians also suddenly left, whispering intently among themselves.

While we waited for a taxi, Rork walked up and explained what we'd just observed.

"Porter speaks a bit o' English, sir, an' just told me about the nasty row we saw. Seems the old gent doin' the rantin' is the director at the big Putilov artillery factory here in the city. The other bloke was deputy head of the city's police, walkin' out after a wee romp with a lady upstairs. The factory chief collared the copper in the lobby, wantin' to know how he's gonna stop the labor strike that's comin'—said he ought'ta just shoot the revolutionary leaders. Porter didn't fancy that sort o' talk one bit. His brother's one o' those leaders."

The Putilov factory was crucial to the war effort. A disruption of production would be calamitous. I asked Rork, "When is the strike?"

"Wouldn't say, sir. But he did say there's been strikes all over Russia this summer, especially down in the south. Hundreds o' thousands o' workers walked the hell out. Factory bosses're worried." He waved his India-rubber hand around the lobby. "The porter lad says all this opulent gaiety stuff is just a flimsy pretense coverin' up the reality—the war against Japan is a catastrophe, the revolutionaries're gettin' stronger every day, an' Tsar Nicky's oblivious to the whole damned mess. Aye, sir, methinks the rich class 'round here ain't showin' it, but they're runnin' bloody well terrified for what's comin' next."

"Looks like the menacing undercurrent in this country is much worse than I'd thought back in Washington. We're going to steer well clear of it all, Rork. Be careful around the servants tonight. Don't let them drag you into anything."

"Aye on *that*, sir," he said, then walked off to have his porter friend hail us a landau.

Only a couple hours later I would find out just how close Russia was to exploding from within. But little did I know that the antagonist wouldn't be a radical revolutionary.

It would be a man I knew.

10
A Siberian Tiger Can Never Be a Vegetarian

Saint Petersburg, Russia
Wednesday, 17 August 1904

The reception for us was put on by the city's high society at a private mansion on the Neva River. An hour after arriving at the predictably unintriguing soiree, I spotted a man from my past on the far side of the room watching me closely. His presence was no great surprise. Now I was intrigued.

Standing there by the wall, he looked like a harmless grandfatherly grocery merchant. But I knew better. That benign image was precisely what he wanted others to see. Pyotr Ivanovich Rachkovsky was not benign at all. He was an extremely shrewd, disarmingly elegant, courteous, utterly ruthless, and very dangerous man.

Rachkovsky was just one of his aliases—he also had Polish, French, and German names from decades of secret missions to protect Russia's Tsars. An expert at forgery and spreading anonymously conjured disinformation to incite suspicion and hatred against the Tsar's enemies, he maintained deep clandestine ties with both terrorists and secret intelligence agencies in Berlin, Geneva, Paris, the Vatican, and London. Now age fifty, Rachkovsky had become one of the senior men in the Okhrana. My French spy friend thought he would be the next chief.

He saw me recognize him and bobbed his head slightly in my direction. The ghost of a smile briefly flickered across his face. Then he turned back to the fat elderly lady insistently asking him a question.

Rachkovsky came over a few minutes later, his manner full of bonhomie. His voice still had the gravelly sound of doom I remembered from our initial encounter sixteen years before.

"Oh Peter! Our longtime correspondence has been too few and far between lately." He grabbed me in a Russian bear hug, kissing both my cheeks. "Finally, we get to meet again. I am delighted!"

This was his first lie—the Pyotr I knew was never genuinely "delighted" about anything. That would be exposing a personal weakness, and weakness exposed one to attack and death. Extricating myself from his embrace, I told him my first lie. "Pyotr, what a pleasure and honor to see you again." Then I added quickly, "This is my wife, María."

I turned to her. "María, this is Pyotr Rachkovsky. We met in Haiti, back in '88."

Rachkovsky's many years in Okhrana's Paris office had cultivated keen skills in French chivalry. Bowing deeply, he kissed her hand—for a bit too long, in my opinion. María dutifully smiled. When the Russian came back up for air, he suavely murmured, "Oh, Madame Wake, bienvenue a Russie. Je suis enchanté pour ta beauté."

María has heard many men compliment her beauty, and performed the expected blushing of cheeks before presenting her own compliments to him and the city. "Merci. Et je suis enchantée pour votre gentillesse et pour la gentillesse du la ville éternelle, monsieur Rachkovsky."

He rewarded her with a wide smile and deep bow. With María having passed muster with flying colors, Rachkovsky now gestured toward me.

"My dear lady, I must tell you that your husband is one of the bravest men I've ever known. Our last time together was much less pleasant than tonight. Sadly, a group of maniacal anarchists were trying to kill us as we escaped their jungle lair in an air ship, of all things! Peter was such an expert rifle shot, he held off the terrorists and saved our lives. Remember that night, Peter? I will never forget!"

María knew about that mission and my low opinion of Rachkovsky's trustworthiness. My recollection of the event was less romantic. "I do remember that night, Pyotr. But only in my nightmares."

He overlooked my tone and grinned again. "And your bodyguard Rork, how is he?"

"He is well. He still guards my body and is here with us in Russia. Probably making friends with the maids upstairs right about now, I imagine."

Rachkovsky laughed. "A true international diplomatist!"

I switched subjects. "I've never been back to Haiti. Have you?"

Rachkovsky's smile lost its luster. "Never. I go to civilized places now. Paris, Rome, London—"

I interrupted, "—and New York. I believe it was earlier this year, same month as the Japanese attack on Port Arthur that started your current war. Visiting a former paramour, perhaps?"

That caught him by surprise, indicated by a split-second pause, but he recovered quickly. By the look in his eye, I could tell he instantly assessed that I was fully aware she was really one of his female operatives in America. A very successful one, who had a rumored affair with a congressman on the foreign affairs committee. She'd also infiltrated the Russian émigré community in the area and distributed copies of Rachkovsky's propaganda monograph of lies against Jews, *The Protocols of the Elders of Zion.*

He accepted my gift of an alibi for his New York visit and continued it effortlessly, complete with an accompanying raised eyebrow. "My dear Peter, the lady in question is *very* charming. I am afraid I was irresistibly lured across the ocean and away from my duties for a wonderful week in New York. Really, what can a mere mortal man do when faced with such feminine allure?"

Rachkovsky's face took on a pained look. "You know, I cabled you to join us for a nice dinner at Delmonicos but got no reply. Not to worry, though. I imagine your presidential work keeps you very busy. By the way, I hear you recently enjoyed the company of a beautiful woman in Paris."

Touché, I admitted, though the woman was less than beautiful. "How did you hear that?" I asked, guessing the answer.

"The woman your friend in the Deuxième Bureau thought was *his* informant is actually *my* informant. And I'm afraid she is not from Alsace. She is from Kiev. I am sorry her information was not what you needed about the Germans." He gave a sly little imitation Gallic shrug. "Peter, please do not burst Monsieur Deuxième's bubble about her true background and allegiance—French egos are so delicate, and we must never gloat over their petty failures. Besides, she has gone on to greater things and is no longer in his employ. Can it be our little secret?"

I smiled at his sarcasm. "But of course, Pyotr. One of so many. I suppose Henri Bint was the local handler kind enough to loan her to the French. How is Henri these days?"

Bint was a long time Okhrana agent in Paris. Rachkovsky dismissed my question. "Like us all, getting a little rounder with age. He will be pleased you asked. By the by, I am told you have come from the very busy city of Hamburg to honor us with a visit. How are our dear friends the Germans doing these days?"

"Quite well, it seems," I said pleasantly. This next part was going to be fun. "And according to my new good friend Kaiser Wilhelm, they also are coming here, to show Russia how to win at war."

"Ah, yes, such true and devoted friends, the Germans," he countered. "I am sure they will instruct us thoroughly. But enough of Teutonic camaraderie and military proficiency. Let us speak of you. Exactly why are *you* here, Peter? Please be candid with your old Russian friend."

As I took a breath, my mind filled with questions. *He knows about what happened in Paris. Does he know about what happened in Hamburg? Did he read and understand the cables with Othello? Did the Okhrana get to Othello even before we did? Have they been running him all this time? Are they playing us now to expose me and curry favor with the Kaiser?*

I smiled. "I've always wanted to see this magnificent city, Pyotr. And you again, of course."

Rachkovsky chuckled softly in appreciation of my absurd little perjury. "What a very thoughtful sentiment, my friend. You've always been so good-natured. But others here are far less charitable about you, Peter. Should I presume those who tell me—quite adamantly, I might add—that you are here to spy are wrong?"

Suddenly, this wasn't fun anymore. I tried to look insulted. "Pyotr, really, I am far too old to be a spy anymore. And so are you."

"Ha!" He slapped my shoulder hard, making it look playful. María had been talking to a Russian lady but glanced quizzically at me. Rachkovsky nodded his head. "We *are* old men! Now fit only for *looking* at ladies!"

I seized on that relatively safe subject. "Well, Pyotr . . . I still like to do a bit more than just *look*."

He didn't play along with me. "Peter, may I be blunt? Our war is not just eight thousand rail miles away on the Pacific coast. It is here also—a shadow war of espionage, sabotage, and assassination by Japanese intelligence. As you well know, Colonel Akashi Motojiro and his European network are disturbingly effective at obtaining confidential Russian information and funding foreign and domestic Russian revolutionary groups, like the one that killed our interior minister last month. The colonel has evaded death so far, but we *will* find and kill him. We cannot take chances with anyone, anymore."

He exhaled, then plunged into his main point. "We know your cowboy president Roosevelt loathes Russia and favors the Japanese. Your personal detractors in Okhrana think you are here to gather intelligence that will be passed to the Japanese, like your cousins the British constantly do. The Japanese will then use that intelligence to attack our fleet when it travels around the world to fight their navy. I have been warned to not consider you as an old and valued friend but as a deadly enemy in our time of national peril."

He was correct on all counts—except the possibility of my sending intelligence to the Japanese. I viewed them as a potential enemy. I tried to quietly defuse the situation with a half-lie. "Pyotr, the truth is I am only a diplomatic envoy to tell Tsar Nicholas that President Roosevelt is neutral in the war and wants friendship with both sides, including the Tsar personally. No espionage on my part, just conversation. And hopefully, perhaps some nice Russian wine. I prefer red, by the way . . ."

It didn't work. Pyotr leaned close and spoke into my ear. Everyone else would think he was telling me a risqué joke, but there was no mirth in his words. "Even when he gets old, a Siberian tiger is unable to change his habits—he still *kills* and never becomes a vegetarian. You and I cannot change our habits, Peter. These are extremely dangerous times for Mother Russia and our beloved Tsar. Anyone, Russian revolutionary or foreign spy, suspected of being an enemy will be stopped, completely. Anyone . . ."

His dark eyes went cold as they locked on to mine. The next came out sadly. "Peter, do you understand *exactly* what I mean?"

I glared at those dead eyes and said, "Pyotr, never threaten me." Then I returned to being amiable. "Besides, I never was a tiger, just a sailor. And nowadays I really am just a champagne-drinking diplomat."

He took a step back and shook his head in disgust. "Diplomats started this damned war."

"I agree with that. Their ignorance of war made them arrogant about it. You and I have never been ignorant about war. So, maybe men like you and I can finally end this tragedy."

Rachkovsky looked at the people around us and sighed. "It is far too late for that, Peter. The code of honor in both Japan and in Russia demands even more blood be shed by our peasant sons. We must avenge those already dead." He wagged a finger at me. "But never forget that Mother Russia has many more peasants to feed into the machines of war than Japan. We Russians will drown all the Japanese in *our blood*, if it comes to it."

He walked away, soon lost in the chattering crowd of glittering posers and fawners. A chill went through me—Pyotr Ivanovich Rachkovsky was deadly serious.

11
Rork's New Friend and Old Vodka

The Imperial German Army staff officers arrived four days after my tense reunion with Rachkovsky. The officers were sequestered at their large embassy instead of a hotel. This was probably for operational security reasons, but I worried it was possibly another clue that Othello was compromised. We knew he was there with them, for Rork reported seeing Othello in a group of German officers embarking in carriages en route to Russian army headquarters.

Rork's surveillance paid off when he later followed them to lunch with their Russian hosts. It was held in a private room at one of the finest restaurants in the city, the Felicien in the fashionable Kemmeni Ostrov part of the city.

There Rork portrayed himself as a journalist named François and used his basic French to make pecuniary friends with the assistant head waiter. In exchange, the Russian agreed to surreptitiously slip a folded note into the coat pocket of the nervous-looking German officer sitting near the far end of the table from the generals. "François" told his new Russian friend that he and the German were old and dear friends, and that the note was merely a joke. The Russian plainly didn't buy that explanation and thought the fellow was a Brit pretending to be French, but he didn't care. The whole world knew the British and Germans were at odds these days, and if he really was French, they hated the Germans for how they had demeaned France back in 1871. Either way, he figured the note was actually an insult. He didn't care about that either—he was bribed by rich people to do things every day, and money was money.

The note was written on a small torn scrap of blank telegram paper from Hotel Hamburg, and, as the reader will by now have surmised, contained simple final instructions to Othello via his fictitious Russian handler.

Othello—Mariyinski tonight—intermission—latrine on right side—eat this note—Cassio

Rork, observing from a dark corner by the kitchen, saw Othello look up when the waiter brushed against him while placing a beer by his plate. A moment later Othello reached into his pocket, looked perplexed, and glanced down at his lap. He somewhat hesitantly placed his hand to his mouth and coughed, ending up choking a bit on the paper before washing it down with the beer. His fellow Germans said something humorous about his choking on beer, and Othello got an embarrassed look on his face.

Rork gave the assistant head waiter an extra tip for a job well done, making the fellow even happier. In Russia this kind of situation demands a celebration, which the Russian suggested. Rork, being his usual incorrigible self, then joined his new friend in a toast of high-grade vodka from the barman, cousin of the assistant head waiter. Fortunately, it was only one small glass, and Rork then successfully egressed the place with no further delay. Traveling a circuitous route, with stops at a grocery market and a museum to check for anyone shadowing him, he arrived in midafternoon back at our rooms at the Hotel Europa and reported his mission, ending with, "The whole bloody lot o' these Rooskies're for sale. Can't trust any o' 'em."

María was more wary. "I am still worried about German intelligence. We don't know if they have doubled back Othello on us. They could expose the handover tonight by alerting the Okhrana. That would embarrass Roosevelt, increase Russian distrust of America, and gain the German Kaiser's goodwill with his cousin the Tsar. And, of course, Rachkovsky's Okhrana is now watching us closely."

She had valid points. But there was no *definitive* sign of double-dealing by Othello yet. Also no indication the Okhrana knew what we were doing. Espionage is by its nature dangerous and fraught with unknowns. I decided to continue.

"We'll watch everything and everyone closely at the theater tonight," I announced. "If any sign of compromise is seen, we call the operation off and implement the escape alibi."

Heretofore, Law had fulfilled a minor supporting role in this mission. Listening to Rork and María voice their thoughts, he seemed pensive, no doubt because tonight his role would be crucial and somewhat perilous. Now he echoed the plan for our emergency departure from the Maryinsky Theater tonight and Russia's capital city in the morning.

"Just so I've got it, sir, if things on the exchange go bad, then María will claim a sudden attack of food poisoning, start crying and wailing while accusing the Russians of poisoning her, and we'll immediately leave the theater. But instead of returning to the hotel, we'll go on board the British steamer at the docks, seeking medical attention and protective asylum, then depart on the ship for England at dawn."

Law didn't sound very convinced our escape plan would work. No surprise there. Marines aren't histrionic; they are quite the opposite: stoic amid the chaos. To improve my crew's waning morale, I tried to sound quite convincing. "Exactly, Edwin. One way or another, tomorrow we are leaving Saint Petersburg."

"An' good riddance to the bloody place . . ." groaned Rork.

12

The Hope of All Russia

Saint Petersburg, Russia
Wednesday, 24 August 1904

Saint Petersburg's Maryinsky Theater is a magnificent, world-renowned theater that showcases the very best of the musical and dramatic arts. Fronting the expansive Theater Square, the building gives one an impression of cultured power. On this particular evening that sense was even more profound due to the remarkable convergence of three diverse factors: the legendary Sergei Vasilyevich Rachmaninov was conducting a rare orchestral solo performance away from his usual Bolshoi Theater in Moscow; it was the eve of the annual Feast of the Assumption, and Tsar Nicholas II himself was attending.

I have no ear for music, but María does and told me about the composer. Though only thirty-one, Rachmaninov had been struggling for years with periodic debilitating depression; with endless conjecture about marrying his first cousin, incurring the wrath of the Russian Orthodox Church; and with his mercurial temper, which alienated members of his orchestra in Moscow and visiting performers there. Lately, however, things were beginning to look better for him. His family had recovered from a serious sickness the year before; his latest major composition had received the famous Glinka Prize; and, among other pieces, he was performing his famous Piano Concerto no. 2 in C Minor for his Tsar in the capital of all Russia.

For days there had been gossipy speculation about the coming performance among the society matrons. *Would Rachmaninov have a mental relapse on stage? Would the Tsar, leader and guardian of the Russian Orthodox Church, really attend the performance of an incestuous man?* María also caught a whiff of whispered excitement about us—said in French, which they didn't know she understood fluently. *What embarrassing faux pas will that uncultured American sailor and his Spanish wife commit at the Maryinsky in front of our beloved Tsar?*

This aroused María's wonderfully humorous streak of contrariness. She suggested we do something really scandalous in front of the attendees, like kissing as if we enjoyed it. I thought it an excellent and pleasant idea but felt obliged to remind her we were trying to be boringly drama-free this particular evening—unless things went badly, of course. Perhaps another time.

We were greeted at the entrance doors by the honorable high theater director himself, a pudgy little man with a twitchy moustache, who was openly unimpressed by a mere Yankee sailor. The director rattled off a perfunctory greeting and rushed off to welcome some arriving nobility. One of the lesser functionaries was detailed to guide us to our seats, where we would meet the rear admiral commanding the Kronstadt Naval Station, who had invited us in the first place.

Led inside to the main hall, we were immediately struck by a feeling of humbling awe. Our guide rattled off his explanation in a drone: the interior was decorated in the French Empire style, with ornate architectural details outlining the multiple levels of boxes, the wall façade around the stage, and the ceiling. They were merely accoutrements, however.

All eyes were naturally drawn to the dominating factor—a massive, triple-layer, heavy French damask stage curtain in crimson and gold, which must have weighed tons. Below and in front of all this were 1,626 comfortable seats on the main floor and balconies. The stage was so many meters tall, so many meters wide, and so many meters deep. The lecture continued into the unique arrangement of the orchestra pit, the luxurious balcony boxes and private reception rooms, the multitude of refreshments available, the location of gentlemen's and ladies' rooms, the main bar, and so on and so on.

In an ascending passageway to the imperial balcony boxes, we met the Russian rear admiral. He had an unpronounceable name, a beet-red face, and a less-than-welcoming manner; and I got the distinct impression he was quite angry about something that had just happened.

That issue was clarified when he stunned us with the news that the Tsar had personally requested María and myself to be his guests in the imperial box. The rear admiral informed us he would not be accompanying us at the Tsar's seats, but the most famous admiral of the Russian Navy would be—Vice Admiral Zinovy Petrovich Rozhestvensky.

I couldn't believe my extraordinary good fortune. Rozhestvensky was the man all Russia, and the world, was watching.

The reason why was because he had an unenviable, many said impossible, war assignment. He was charged by the Tsar to ready a fleet of warships— almost the entire Russian Navy in Europe—and then steam the fleet 18,000 miles around the world to the Sea of Japan. Once there, they were to destroy the Japanese Navy and cut off the Japanese Army in Korea and Manchuria from supplies and reinforcements. European-based ships were needed because the Japanese had already wiped out Russia's Asia-based warships in several battles. In the last seven months of war, the Russian Navy had so far proved even more worthless than the Russian Army, which was quite an accomplishment.

The anticipated (by civilian armchair strategists) naval victory would allow the Russian Army time to eventually transport enough Europe-based troops along the almost 9,000-mile Trans-Siberian Railway to the front lines in northeast Asia to reinforce their beleaguered comrades. They would then crush the Japanese land forces, which had been cut off from their source of replenishment by the Russian navy.

In other words, Rozhestvensky was the last hope for Mother Russia to win the war, salvage what military honor she had left, retain her Pacific coast possessions, and save the Tsar's reputation as a competent commander in chief.

Now I had several hours to be with him and the Tsar—and in the process obtain an excellent understanding of Russia's capabilities and liabilities as well as the future of Asia just north of the American Philippines. And even better: all this would be achieved while clandestinely securing the secret German plans to attack my country. It was going to be a memorable evening, indeed, and I allowed myself a moment of internal optimism and self-congratulation.

In the passageway outside the Tsar's box, the unpleasant rear admiral departed us and a moment later the hero arrived. Except for staff aides, he was alone. Like me, he was attired in the de rigueur full dress summer whites. And, also like me, he seemed uncomfortable in it and our surroundings.

I noticed immediately his seaman's tan and crinkled eyes, his erect frame, and the steady gaze taking in everything around him. Both sides of his receding hairline were close cropped, and the large moustache and jawline beard were neatly trimmed. Before he even spoke a word, I knew this man was no royal martinet or sycophant, no soft bon vivant or cynical career manipulator. The admiral's facial expression alternated between serious, inquisitive, compassionate, and resolute. It was absolutely clear to me that more than anything else, Vice Admiral Zinovy Rozhestvensky was a *commanding officer* to be reckoned with.

We were formally introduced and went together into the large imperial balcony box, sitting down to await the Tsar. As the admiral and I conversed (he spoke excellent English), I realized he was notably well versed, and interested in learning more, about my experience at sea and in naval intelligence. That depth of information, I decided, must have come from Pyotr Rachkovsky, and I mentioned the Okhrana spy master to the admiral.

"No, I was told about you by a remarkable fellow who seems to know everything about everyone, Arkadiy Mikhailovich Harting. Okhrana man, like Rachkovsky. Do you know him?"

I did, indeed, by different names. Harting was his current name in Russia. He was Aaron Landesmen in Switzerland and Finland; and Aharon Hackelman in Germany, Belgium, and France. An accomplished chameleon-like spy, he was quite adept at changing his accent, image, and identity. His specialty was penetrating revolutionary groups in western Europe. Then, only hours or minutes before they carried out their attacks, he would get them all arrested. He also was good at assassinating revolutionary leaders by inciting a revolutionary underling to do the killing. For the last several months, Harting had been Rachkovsky's assistant in the Okhrana, with the main mission of finding and killing Colonel Akashi Motojiro and his network in Europe.

Obviously, it wouldn't do to make the admiral aware I knew all of this, so I blandly said to him, "Yes, I remember meeting Arkadiy in London years ago. Amusing gentleman. Nice Belgian wife. Say, is he here tonight?"

"Why yes, I just saw him in the passageway leading here," Rozhestvensky said affably, without a trace of duplicitousness. "He was looking at you like he knew you, so I thought he would come by and say hello. He must have been interrupted."

"Well, I hope to see him tonight, Admiral. Been many years," I replied while assessing why Harting would be there. Something didn't seem right.

A staff officer entered and whispered to the Russian admiral, who announced to María and me, "The Tsar has arrived out front. When he gets here, I will be pleased to introduce you to him."

I was still thinking about Rachkovsky's warning and Harting's presence when the passageway outside the box grew hushed and the staff officers rushed away. Guards suddenly appeared. We all stood up and faced the passageway. Rozhestvensky appeared calm, but María seemed abnormally nervous. I completely understood why.

The most powerful absolute ruler in the world was arriving.

13
The Tsar

Saint Petersburg, Russia
Wednesday, 24 August 1904

The guards stamped to attention and presented arms as a court chamberlain appeared and announced the Tsar was coming in the passageway. Mercifully, he used the short version of the Tsar's title.

"By the Grace and Aid of God, Nicholas the Second, Emperor and Autocrat of All the Russias is arriving! All stand and show respect!"

We performed as bid and a moment later he emerged from an entourage of uniformed men crowding the passageway. Interestingly, Tsar Nicholas, unlike Kaiser Wilhelm, was clad in a simple dress blue uniform with gold trim and sash, hatless and without ostentatious accoutrements. I noted he had hung only half the medals he was entitled to wear.

But similar to his Germanic cousin, Nicholas was solo. The Tsarina was still recovering from the birth of the Tsarevich and the young crown princess daughters had gone on an overnight yachting trip. He did have some elderly royal retainers, counts and dukes and such, but they were diverted to the next box as Admiral Rozhestvensky introduced me and María.

Nicholas was much handsomer than I'd expected after meeting Wilhelm. He was tall and trim, with a bearing that was regal but not pompous. His eyes were what surprised me. Unlike Wilhelm's coldly disdaining visage—Nicholas looked incredibly melancholy, as if he had seen something horrific and would never be able to smile again. The moustache was less upswept and arrogantly bees-waxed than his German cousin's. The Tsar's voice was deep but quiet, his words emerging with apparent sincerity and without a hint of condescension. The unhappy eyes didn't dart about accusatorially like Wilhelm's, but they did take in the surroundings and then focused on us. The total effect was that I got the feeling he didn't *like* being Tsar.

Nicholas did seem genuinely pleased to see his admiral, however, and quite interested in me. The beginning of a smile brightened his face when he took in María. Speaking in very good English—the mode he used in communications with Wilhelm—he welcomed us to Russia, to Saint Petersburg, and to the theater. I thanked him for the invitation to join him and said I had a confidential message from President Roosevelt. He suggested that during the intermission would be the most appropriate time for a private conversation.

I could see that María, no stranger to royalty and no fan of most, liked him from the start. Her anxiousness disappeared, and that wondrous charm of hers began its subtle work on the Tsar when he inquired about what she thought of the city his ancestors had created.

"It is the most beautiful and thoughtfully laid out city in the entire world, Your Imperial Majesty." María glanced shyly at me. "I find it *very* romantic."

That did it. Nicholas was smitten and the tone for the evening was set. We all walked into the imperial box and out into the view of the multitudes below us. Instantly the crowd stood, and a roar of applause filled the massive hall. When it fell away, the chamberlain, now on the stage and in full bellow, announced the impossibly long version of Nicholas's vast pedigree of total autocratic power over various peoples and cultures inhabiting a huge swath of the Earth.

During this rousing recital, we three mere mortals stood behind Tsar Nicholas. As Rozhestvensky unobtrusively translated for María and me, I learned new things about the man standing in front of us. It turned out that he was also Tsar of Bulgaria, King of Poland, heir to the Crown of Norway, and possessed another two dozen royal titles and authorities over numerous nationalities on two continents. It took a full ten minutes for the chamberlain to declare the entire thing, after which the orchestra played the Russian imperial anthem, which also proved long-winded. The Russian patrons weren't faint-hearted, however, and every one of them sang lustily along as they faced the Tsar above them. He stood at attention during all this, his eyes fixed on the huge imperial Russian flag (much bigger than any other national flag I've ever seen), which was lowered down from the ceiling to hang over the stage.

When it was finally over, the Tsar humbly titled his head down, then gestured to everyone around the hall, acknowledging his subjects' show of loyalty. Protocol having been satisfied, the Tsar sat down and everyone else in the place followed suit. Many knew and admired Admiral Rozhestvensky, of course, but I was an unknown for most. I noted quite a few curious examinations of the foreign admiral sitting next to their Tsar.

The massive curtain rose, and the theater hushed. Rachmaninov's entrée onto the stage was greeted by polite applause. Nicholas applauded loudly. The musician bowed to his Tsar, who smiled back graciously. A very stern-looking Rachmaninov sat down at the polished grand piano with a flourish of his coattails. His hands rose, fingers like talons poised over the keys. The orchestra conductor raised his baton and swung it down, beginning the concert with a quiet lilting violin-cello melody, with which Rachmaninov eventually joined his piano as the lead part.

María pointed out to me in the program that the famous award-winning piece would be played after the intermission. I dutifully nodded. Musically deficient, especially in the classical variety, I took a moment to survey the crowd of mesmerized faces for Harting, but the Russian spy master-assassin wasn't in sight.

I did see Edwin Law in his dress blues, sitting right where he was supposed to be: seat 22 in the middle of the ninth row. In the rear of the main floor was Rork in civilian clothes, sitting at the far end of the last row, near the lobby exit. In the center of the seventh row there was a line of seated dark gray uniforms—the German officers. At their far end was Othello.

Everyone was in place.

14
The Surprise Offer

Saint Petersburg, Russia
Wednesday, 24 August 1904

Intermission arrived. I observed Rork, Law, and Othello get up and head for the lobby. As he walked, the German glanced nervously around at people—completely unaware of what any of our group looked like. The Tsar, Rozhestvensky, María, and I were escorted to the imperial reception room where we were refreshed with champagne and caviar, neither of which I enjoy but felt compelled to partake.

The elite patrons (you had to be somebody special to be invited into that room) clustered around us, trying to get the Tsar's eye or ear. He was polite to them as his retainers edged in to engage the intruder in deep conversation and lead them away. My own conversation with His Imperial Majesty centered on lightweight social topics, reliably safe from politics, religion, or war.

I eventually reminded him of my request, and he gestured toward a small room on the side, which his staff instantly made sure was empty. We entered and sat on simple chairs at a table under the light of a single wall sconce.

"I am sorry for the lack of decorum here, Admiral Wake, but any port in a storm, right?"

"Exactly, Your Imperial Majesty. And now to my message from President Roosevelt, which he directed me to tell you personally. First, he wants to maintain a sincere friendship, both personally and nationally, for Russia and for Japan. Second, he particularly would like to be personal friends with *you*, sir. Third, as a strictly neutral friend, he hopes that for the sake of both Russia and Japan, this war will soon end with honor for all concerned. If America can help in that endeavor, then we stand ready to assist the peace process."

Nicholas didn't say anything for several minutes, evaluating me with those sad eyes. His face grew grim, his tone determined. "The world knows we have suffered defeats on land and sea in the last seven months. I admit the Japanese are an efficient enemy, but they are not undefeatable. They have not yet faced our best forces. We are moving those forces by land and sea into positions to attack and overwhelm the Japanese. I cannot provide confidential details, of course."

It was what I figured he'd say. Now I had to say words he wouldn't want to hear, especially from an American. "Your Imperial Majesty, that will take time. And time appears to be on the side of the Japanese, who have a very short and secure line of supply and communications to fuel their large-scale offensives. It might be better to negotiate now, before the situation becomes worse."

His left hand clenched. "Admiral Wake, the Japanese are also running out of men—and money in their treasury. They completely underestimated us. They thought we would tire of losses and negotiate away our land long ago. But the men of Russia fought bravely and will continue fighting. Russians *never* give up."

His next came out in a decidedly more diplomatic manner. "If the Japanese want the peace of ante quo, let them tell *us*. And please tell President Roosevelt this: I would be happy to be personal friends with him. But I do not need his help in ending this war. I have the help of God, who ordained me with the authority and responsibility to perform this life of duty to my people and land. Mother Russia will emerge from this war victorious, and stronger than ever."

There was nothing more for me to say except, "Yes, sir, I understand. I would only ask that you please keep President Roosevelt's offer to help in your mind. Peace with honor is our goal."

Nicholas leaned forward across the table. "You need to be better informed, Admiral Wake. I want you to see our navy's headquarters at Kronstadt. Better than that, I want you to be the neutral international naval observer on board our flagship for her journey around the world. The fleet will be departing soon, and this way you can see for yourself, and for your president, the pride and strength of our nation."

That was something I never anticipated in my worst nightmares about how things could go wrong. The Tsar followed it up with another bombshell. "I sent a telegram today to your president to ask his permission for you to go with the fleet. He has replied to me with enthusiastic approval and has sent your orders to your embassy here. What do you say, Admiral? I know full well President Roosevelt wanted you to see Russia and her Tsar and to evaluate our strength. What better way than going to sea with our fleet? No American has ever been offered such access."

Damn all to hell and back! He had me in a fait accompli. Roosevelt said yes? Now I couldn't say no! Who the hell set this up? That bastard Rachkovsky—it must have been him. I tried to take it in stride, but I needed a moment to come up with a reply suitable for a Tsar.

"Ah, Your Imperial Majesty, you have me at a disadvantage, sir. I was not prepared for this . . . magnanimous . . . gesture of international naval goodwill. Of course, I have duties back at home, so I can only do part of the voyage. Perhaps to the area of the Mediterranean."

"No, no, Admiral. To get a proper appreciation, you must be with the fleet until the Red Sea, or Buenos Aires, or South Africa—whichever is chosen as the route—at least. Don't worry about things back home. This is the chance of a lifetime, and I will insist on such to President Roosevelt."

I thought South Africa the probable route. There was steamer service there. "Well, thank you, Your Majesty. I can only take orders from my president, so I can't decide now. Please let me check with my embassy. I'll do that right after the performance."

The Tsar stood, ending our interview. He pumped my hand. "Very good, Admiral Wake. I have already spoken to Admiral Rozhestvensky, and he thinks it a splendid idea. You and your aides will be very well taken care of on the flagship. A voyage around the world with the camaraderie of professional colleagues! Europe, Africa, Asia, and then the final battle to avenge our dead and show the world Russia's power." With a shy smile, he then said, "I am more than a little envious of your good fortune. Now . . . let us rejoin your lovely wife."

I tried to tell him not to mention this new development to my lovely wife, but the Tsar was striding out into the imperial reception area. It had filled with people, one of whom was not shooed away from the Tsar and our circle. She was a very beautiful woman in her middle forties, with long auburn hair and sparkling sapphires and diamonds accenting a low-cut dark blue satin gown. The lady's skin wasn't milk-white like the other Russian women around us. Quite a bit darker than María's light olive complexion, it was more of a teak color. Her intense green eyes had an Asian shape to them. Her full lips seemed to be set in a perpetual smile, but I saw a knowing smirk behind that smile. Without a doubt, she knew the effect she had on men.

Nicholas evidently knew her, and their exchange in Russian was friendly. I noticed María tense slightly, though, then step closer to meet the woman. The Tsar explained in English the lady was from southern Turkmenistan, one of his remote southern domains on the Caspian Sea. I didn't know much about that region, except that it was Muslim and long known for slave trading, and that it had been forcibly annexed into the Russian Empire only thirty years before. Nicholas introduced her to us as Maysa Abaev, a minor noblewoman who spoke only Russian and her native language. The Tsar said her given name meant "little flower" among the Turkmen people and pleasantly added that her father had helped his father. He never said how, where, or when, but I got the distinct impression it probably had to do with that bloody annexation.

Even as I took in the intriguing aspects of Maysa, I tried to figure out a way to gently and quietly tell María about the Tsar's plan for me. Everything changed when a hulking general steered directly for the admiral, giving him some sort of cheerless information. The admiral turned and said something serious to the Tsar, whose face went from an amiable expression to a troubled scowl. Rozhestvensky, the general, and the Tsar then disappeared out the doorway. *More bad news from the front? Or was it bad news from the streets of Saint Petersburg?*

María and I were left with Maysa, who made no indication she would depart now that the Tsar wasn't around to hobnob with. We had no way to communicate with her other than apologetic smiles and awkward gestures. In the midst of this, waiters brought us red wine, a merlot type from the Crimea in the south. Maysa seemed pleased with her sip of the wine and made some heartfelt toast to me in Russian. The three of us raised our glasses and I found the wine rather good but the lack of follow up communications disconcerting.

During this lull, I took my wife's hand said, "María, a few minutes ago the Tsar practically ordered me to . . ."

Right then, Edwin Law arrived. I checked my pocket watch—he was right on time. Law whispered his report that Othello, following orders, had gone to the gentlemen's room, where Rork slid a torn shred of paper into his coat pocket while brushing by him, never showing Othello his face. The note was intentionally composed in bad German.

Othello—Go sit in seat 22 in row 9, put invoices under seat, then apologize to anyone there for sitting in wrong seat, return to the gentlemen's room and wait 10 minutes for the reward—Cassio

Law told me Othello was now at seat twenty-two. As soon as the German officer got up and left for the gentlemen's room again, Law would return to seat twenty-two. When the house lights went down for the resumption of the performance, he would quietly put the papers inside his tunic. Once Rork, standing in the back of the house, saw Law give the signal he had the papers—running his fingers over his hair—Rork would drop a valise with the money at Othello's feet in the gentlemen's room.

So far, so good, I told myself. *Only a few minutes more.* I scanned the area again for Harting but saw no sign of him. *Maybe he departed for a bar? He likes to drink—a lot.*

The house lights dimmed and the patrons in the reception room quickly returned to their seats. The guards and staff entourage departed. María suggested we take our wine back to the box and meet the admiral and Tsar there. She started out first, escorted by an admiring young subaltern, followed by the last of everyone else. I delayed long enough to pour another glass for myself. In that moment I realized only Maysa by the wine table and myself were left. Out in the hall I heard applause, then Rachmaninov start playing his Piano Concerto No. 2—the piece everyone was waiting for.

I reached for my glass from the side table just as Maysa leisurely picked up her own glass next to it. I wished her a pleasant evening, which, naturally, she couldn't understand. Her movements were strangely slow, deliberately lingering as she cast glances at me with those exotic eyes and smiling lips.

From out in the main hall, I could hear Rachmaninov's romantic music continuing in a rhythmic rise and fall, like a ship sailing over swells at sea. *I need to go*, I told myself. But instead, I hesitated for a moment.

The corner of my eye saw her passing her glass over my mine. My main attention, however, was focused on the very naughty wink she bestowed on me. Those eyes stayed on me as she softly said something to me in her native tongue, the meaning obvious.

So that's it? Rachkovsky and Harting think I'm stupid enough to fall for a honey trap?

With perfect coincidence, Rachmaninov's romantic melody now rose into a lustful crescendo. And with perfect poetic justice, this was the exact second in time when my smoothly running and efficiently simple scheme came to a rude end.

15
The Ring

Saint Petersburg, Russia
Wednesday, 24 August 1904

Not all my attention was captivated by Maysa's come-hither invitation. I also registered the slight flick of her right ring finger in the hand passing her glass over mine. I'd noticed earlier that the ring on that finger sported a large dark sapphire set into a wide silver band. Now the sapphire setting was hinged open and grayish-brown powder was raining down into my glass of Russian merlot.

I instantly bellowed, "Stop!" and seized her wrist. She might have been a minor noblewoman, but Maysa Abaev was no stranger to violence. The beckoning smile became a crazed animal mask as she twisted her hand free of me, swinging her wineglass toward my face with a piercing shriek. With surprising strength, she started a flurry of punches with her right hand as her other reached into a hidden pocket in the waist of her gown.

My left hand grabbed her left as it emerged with a tiny pistol—a single-shot type with a large muzzle. My other hand was already inside my uniform tunic, holding the Merwin-Hulbert .44-caliber, 6-shot revolver with the infamous "skull crusher" beaked grip.

My left hand pushed that big muzzle away from my face—expecting it to fire at any second—and my right was about to ram the Merwin-Hulbert's beaked grip right into the center of Maysa's beautiful face.

At that moment, I heard María entering the reception room. "Peter, why are you still here? *Oh, my God!*"

A split second later, Maysa collapsed as a heavy candlestick from the wine table crashed down on the top of that coiffed hair. She crumpled down and sideways along the wall. The pocket pistol hit the floor as her body capsized the wine table. With a final gurgling growl, she rolled over on the carpet and lay there silent.

María's face was frozen in shock, both her hands still clenching the candlestick. There was blood splatter on her gown and my white uniform. The wall and floor where Maysa lay had large stains from her bleeding head. I knelt down and pocketed the pistol, then checked the limp body for signs of life. She was still breathing but completely unconscious.

It was not the time to panic. We had to get rid of her fast—people had probably heard her shriek and the guards would come to investigate. Then I heard Rachmaninov begin another piece, a louder one this time, overwhelming all other sounds. It made me realize no one could possibly have heard us over his previous crescendo. I stood up and took María's hands in mine.

"María, you saved my life," I said softly. "Now, we must be quick. Put the candlestick in that small side room over there."

She did as I asked and then returned. Looking at Maysa, then me, she began trembling. She needed to focus on doing something, so I told her, "I need you to set the table back up and straighten up the room. Hurry, we don't have much time."

I put an ornate tablecloth around Maysa's head and dragged her by the shoulders into the side room, trying to minimize the trail of red drops. Fortunately, it was a dark-patterned Armenian carpet, and the stains showed brown. Maysa appeared still unconsciously inert, but I wasn't taking any chances. Using a curtain cord, I lashed her feet together and hands behind her back, leaving her on the floor in the far corner. The tablecloth also served as a gag in her mouth.

I examined the ring. It was an old Afghan poison ring. That made sense—Turkmenistan borders Afghanistan, and Afghans are experts at poisons. There was still some powder inside, which looked to me like arsenic colored with henna so it would mix in with the red wine. Closing the latch tightly, I put the evil thing in my pocket along with her tiny pistol.

In the reception room, María quickly squared away the table, wine bottles, and glasses, wiping away some of the gore and glass shards with a large doily. Rubbing the stain on the floor, she asked with a scared tone, "Is she dead?"

"She is unconscious, but it could be fatal. I just can't predict." What I didn't say was that it would be better for us if she was dead, otherwise she could possibly recover and create a sensational story.

"Are Sean and Edwin all right?" María asked.

"I don't know yet."

They might have been killed too, but our immediately safety came first. I dashed out to the passageway and checked for an accomplice of Maysa. Seeing no one, I returned to the reception room, noticing for the first time a key in the small lock of the side room's door.

María, still on her knees desperately rubbing the carpet, called to me. "Peter, I can't do *anything* about this blood on the carpet."

An unbroken wine bottle on the floor beckoned a solution. "Then we'll make it look like spilled wine," I said while locking the side room door and hiding the key in the melted wax of a wall candle sconce. "Let's empty a couple of those wine bottles onto the blood stain."

We did and the stain spread but seemed marginally less blood-like. María sounded steadier now. "What do we tell people?"

I'd been thinking about that very thing. "We keep it simple: I walked in and confronted two drunken Russian soldiers fighting over stolen wine, then they ran off. My uniform is stained from one of them who flicked his blood on me. Walking back to the Tsar's box, I ran into you. When you saw my uniform, you thought I was hurt and embraced me, getting it on your gown. Got it?"

"Sounds thin, but yes, I understand. But Peter, what really happened?"

"Maysa Abaev is an assassin—but I don't know for whom. I caught her poisoning my wine from a secret compartment in her ring, then she attacked me. She was about to shoot me when you saved me. Now, let's get back to the box. I've got to see if Law, Rork, and Othello are still in their places, then I'll tell the Tsar my story. If they aren't in their places, we'll make a run for it."

"Your story doesn't include Maysa. What about when the Russians see . . ." Her voice faded. " . . . her?"

"At least at first, they'll think the soldiers did it and hid the body."

"What if she lives and says it was us?"

"We'll handle that if it happens. But I don't think she would say that. Assassins, and the spy agencies that employ them, don't want public attention."

We returned to the imperial box. The admiral and the Tsar were engrossed in the concert and nodded when they saw us. Apparently neither saw the stains on us. I willed myself to calmly search the crowd of patrons below us for Rork, Law, and Othello.

To my great relief, I found them in their planned places. Law in seat 22 meant he had possession of the invasion plans. Rork sitting in the back of the grand hall meant he had passed the money to Othello. Our German was in his original seat among his brother officers—now 15,000 imperial marks richer.

I took a breath and assessed our situation. Everyone was safe, at least for now. We had another hour until the end of Rachmaninov's performance. I decided to tell the Tsar my story at the break between the music pieces, making it a humorous and harmless anecdote of drunken soldiers being soldiers until an officer walked in.

Afterward we would go back to Hotel Europa and ready ourselves for a quick departure by steamer in the morning. I would send an apologetic note to the Tsar, explaining that an urgent presidential request demanded my return to Washington, and I would regretfully be unable to accompany his fleet to war. I kept my hand on María's in our plush chairs, and we both settled down, pretending to enjoy the concert.

That is when I saw Arkadiy Harting.

16

Charming the Tsar

Saint Petersburg, Russia
Wednesday, 24 August 1904

Harting was on the far side of the main floor, walking around toward the stairs to the passageway on our side. Notably, next to him was the first secretary of the American embassy. That gentleman was the personal assistant of Ambassador Robert McCormick, who was away visiting Odessa in the south. I'd met the first secretary at the initial reception in Saint Petersburg, but he was so ordinary I couldn't even recall his name. He didn't look ordinary now. His face was grimly tense. Harting's was its usual unreadable mask.

María noticed them also and gave me a worried look. "I believe we will have company soon, Peter."

I tried to sound nonchalant. "Yes, quite an interesting turn of affairs, my dear."

At the next lull in the music, I stood as if to stretch, then coughed loudly—the emergency signal for Law and Rork to come to us. Each rose and began heading our way. María gathered her skirts, ready to move as swiftly as a lady can in a formal gown.

At my coughing, the Tsar looked curiously at me, and I quickly said, "Pardon me, sir," reaching for a glass of mineral water. Nicholas nodded

73

and returned his attention to Rachmaninov. Admiral Rozhestvensky never noticed, apparently admiring a young lady in the first row. Down below us, Harting looked up at me. He showed no recognition of me nor gave the usual polite smile when people's eyes meet. I bobbed my head courteously at him and sat back down, trying to conjure up an escape plan that did not involve shooting. Nothing came to mind.

A few minutes later, as Rachmaninov's piano again rose in crescendo, Harting and the diplomatic secretary arrived in the imperial passageway and were let through by the bodyguards. The Russian spy did a quick glance around the box as he bowed deeply to the Tsar. Harting whispered in Rozhestvensky's ear, then turned toward me with a half bow and said, "Admiral Wake, it has been many years. You may remember me from France back in '93, I am—"

"I remember you very well, Mr. Landesmen," I interrupted, trying to disrupt his chain of thought. In espionage, the best defense is a vigorous offense. "Though these days, I believe you go by Arkadiy Harting, and you work in a high Okhrana position for my professional acquaintance, Pyotr Rachkovsky."

Harting's eyes never reacted to my knowing his current name and position. He shrugged with a shy, insincere smile. "Yes, quite right, Admiral. But as for my position, I am only a simple and loyal servant of His Imperial Majesty's government."

The American diplomat looked discomforted at how things were developing, in front of the Tsar, of all people, and chose that moment to step forward. "Admiral Wake, I am James Gaylord Jordan, First Secretary of the American Embassy. We met several nights ago at a reception. Mr. Harting was kind enough to escort me here so I could let you know an urgent message just arrived at the embassy for you. May we speak privately, sir?"

Jordan and I went out into the passageway, just as Law and Wake walked up. Rork gave me an "Are you all right?" look. I told Jordan to give me a moment.

"We're fine," I quietly said to Rork. "But there's been a messy complication. What about your end?"

Rork knew exactly what "messy complication" signified. We'd had several of those in our missions over the years. "Aye, there's a bit o' a wrinkle on our end as well, sir."

He gestured to Law, who said, "An odd thing's come up, sir. Remember that young German court fellow who was constantly around us at the Kaiser's affair in Hamburg—the one Chief Rork later told us was an operative in German intelligence?"

I nodded and Law continued. "The whole time tonight, he's been sitting directly behind Othello, two rows back, and watching him closely. He saw Othello get up and go to the gentlemen's room and me sit in that seat. I'm not sure, but think he saw me get the, ah, invoices, from under the seat, sir."

"Where is he now?"

"Still sitting behind Othello, sir. The fellow is in plain clothes, and I don't know if Othello knows who he is."

"I see. Well, there's nothing we can do about that now. You still have the invoices, correct, Mr. Law?"

"Aye, sir. Inside my tunic."

"Very good. Now I need a moment with Mr. Jordan."

Jordan and I went a few feet down the passageway. He didn't waste time. "Admiral, an hour ago a message marked urgent came for 'Inscient' from 'Inquinates.' I know 'Inquinates' is 'Instructor,' but do not know who 'Inscient' is. I presumed it is you, sir."

"You are correct, Mr. Jordan. Have you deciphered the message for me?" I said, knowing the answer but wanting to see how he would phrase it.

"No, sir. It's composed of several different codes, and I left it securely locked up back at the embassy and immediately came here for you. I brought a large carriage, should you and your entourage want to go to the embassy now, sir."

I was beginning to respect James Gaylord Jordan, clearly a man who could think on his feet. "Inquinates" was a cover substitute code word for "Instructor," which was President Roosevelt's current code name in State Department cables. "Inscient" was the cover substitute code word for "Integrity," which was my current code name—but Jordan couldn't, and shouldn't, have known that.

Communications between Roosevelt and me were interwoven with several codes from various sources to thwart or at least delay anyone, American or foreign, from deciphering them. And just to make it harder, the code systems we used and the order of decipherment changed every four weeks.

The message presented an opportune excuse to escape the scene of the recent "messy complication" and I told Jordan, "Good thinking. I'll present my regrets to the Tsar and Admiral Rozhestvensky, then we'll all go to the embassy straight away in your carriage."

I went back to speak with the Tsar. Rachmaninov was slowing down, nearing the end of the famous piano concerto. Harting still stood at the rear of the box, his eyes darting over everything and everyone.

I announced to the Tsar and the admiral. "Your Imperial Majesty, Admiral Rozhestvensky, please forgive me for interrupting your enjoyment of the concert, but I must tell you about two events that have transpired in the last few minutes."

They both visibly tensed and studied me. The Tsar worriedly asked me, "Is something amiss, Admiral Wake?"

"Amiss? No, Your Imperial Majesty. Not even an unusual event, but I just want to let you know. A few minutes after the intermission ended, I walked in on two soldiers fighting in the reception room. They were bleeding badly, blood flinging around, and I think they were drunk. I do not understand Russian, but it seemed to me they were fighting over stealing some wine. When they saw me, an officer, walk in, they instantly stopped and fled."

I chuckled and waved my hand dismissively. "The entire thing was minor, sir. Just another example of soldiers being soldiers around fine spirits—we have the very same problems in our army and navy. All armies and navies do. When I returned here to the box, I wanted to wait until the performance was over to tell you, but now something else has come up."

Rozhestvensky's jaw clenched, and the Tsar looked shocked. Harting, however, was coldly evaluating, those eyes boring into me. I knew he didn't believe a word I'd said. *He's trying to figure out where Maysa is right now.*

I resumed my explanation to the Tsar. "An urgent message just arrived at our embassy for me, sir, from my president. Probably my orders in response to your offer. It demands an immediate reply. I am sure you understand my duty is to leave now and attend to that message."

The Tsar's face was clouded with concern. "Yes, of course, Admiral Wake. And I offer my most sincere apologies to you for the behavior of those soldiers.

I am truly appalled at this breach of Russian military pride and bearing. We do *not* allow such conduct in our army or our navy!"

"I am very sure of that, Your Imperial Majesty," I replied. "And now, with your permission, María and I must take our leave. It has been a magnificent evening and I thank you so much for inviting us to share it with you."

"Admiral, our fleet is leaving soon for the Far East. We will have a meeting of admirals and captains in two days, and I want to personally introduce you to them as the neutral observer. I think you'll be impressed with them."

I bowed and said thank you to him, with one eye on my wife. I hadn't yet had a chance to tell her about the observer with the fleet matter, and a flash of irritation crossed María's face as she registered what the Tsar had just said. I groaned inside, knowing there would be hell to pay when we were alone.

Then she recovered her social graces, deftly covered the blood stain on her gown with part of her lace wrap, and curtsied, all the while gazing up into the Tsar's eyes. In breathless French, she told him how much she loved *his* city and culture.

The Tsar responded just as she knew he would—in flawless French—saying the city was even more beautiful now that she was here, and he would forever think of her angelic smile whenever he heard Rachmaninov's music.

At that moment Rachmaninov finished his last piece and the patrons gave him a thunderous ovation. The now-smiling Tsar and Admiral Rozhestvensky walked to the balcony's railing, faced the stage, and stood there applauding the famous musician. Surveying our immediate area, I saw that Harting had disappeared. Down below, so had Othello. And the German intelligence agent's seat behind him was empty.

Our moment to exit had come. María, Law, Rork, and I left the box with Jordan in the lead. Passing the imperial reception room, I caught sight of Harting standing inside, bent over and studying the blood-stained carpet.

Jordan shook his head in wonder and quietly observed, "What an evening you've had, Admiral." I didn't trust myself to reply.

Waiting out front for the carriage to be brought up, Law nudged me. "There's Othello, sir. Walking down the street—and that intelligence agent is right behind him."

Rork leaned close to me. "Want me to take care o' that problem, sir? Methinks Othello can't."

The reader will remember that Rork and Law didn't know about my near assassination, or the bloody aftermath, or Harting's ominous presence, or the Tsar's request for me.

"No, Rork. Othello's on his own now."

17
Translations

Saint Petersburg, Russia
Wednesday, 24 August 1904

As we boarded the carriage, María glared at me, muttering under her breath, "So, when were you going to tell me the Tsar requested you ride with the Russian fleet into battle? And you're going along with it, aren't you? You promised me three years ago those days were over. You *promised* me, Peter. And by the way—you are sixty-five years old. Act like it!"

I softly countered with what I thought was logical, but which came out sounding rather lame, even to me. "It's not my decision, María. It's the president's, and there is more to it than just me. It's a matter of national image, of gaining accurate insight into Russian capabilities, and of dispelling Russian distrust of our country."

Her reply was decidedly not under her breath. "No, Peter, this is a matter of you wanting to play sailor again."

Law and Jordan politely stared out the window. Rork gave me a disapproving look. The ensuing carriage ride was tensely devoid of conversation but mercifully short, since the embassy was located in those days on the "English Embankment" of the Neva River, near the British Embassy.

We all crowded inside Jordan's office and watched as he removed the coded telegram from his safe and put it on his desk, where he invited me to sit.

"Mr. Jordan, do you have anyone here who is fluent in German?" I asked.

"Well, sir, I am," he said. "I just finished five years at the embassy in Berlin."

"Very good. We need some privacy right now to decode the cable. Please return in ten minutes, prepared to translate aloud a confidential German document of the utmost importance. Also, bring the naval and military attachés with you. Tell them to pack their gear for a special assignment that begins in one hour and will last for a month."

Once the door was closed, Law and María sat in chairs as Rork and I stood at the desk and examined the message. The chief and I had twenty-five years of experience with various codes, memorizing many of the most important cover and substitute code words and phrases in several cipher systems so we could understand them at sight.

Memorization is a crucial skill in intelligence work. I fully admit it had gotten more difficult for Rork and me as the years have progressed.

Before leaving the White House, Roosevelt and I had agreed on using multiple code systems inside each of our communications—messages made up of several different code systems, which had number sets standing for real words. To the average person, the cable that lay before us seemed to be meaningless gobbledygook:

XXX—44419—44467—X—44415—00290—23231—34089—88934—
88914—88951—XXX

"Short message," opined Rork approvingly. "The fellow can get a bit long-winded."

The first two sets of numbers designated the sender and receiver, using the 1899 State Department Code System, the only one Jordan could understand. They translated into the words "Integrity" and "Instructor"—which meant President Roosevelt and Admiral Wake. That would change at the end of the month when other code words would be used for Roosevelt and me. The sequence order of the different code systems inside the message would also change.

I dredged up the sequence in my mind, then said it aloud. "Let's see, Rork. This is Integrity's third cable to us, so the proper sequence of code systems should be Scott's 1892 Code for the next number, and that makes this number stand for 'Affection,' correct?"

"Aye, sir," he said, then paused for a moment before solemnly adding, "Which really means 'We accept'—so President Roosevelt approved the Tsar's request." Rork glanced nervously at María, who was staring at an unlit fireplace.

I ignored her. "Next code is what?"

"Anglo-American 1894 Code, sir."

"Right, and that means this number set stands for 'Advocation.' Do you agree, Rork?"

"Aye, sir. An' that translates to . . . 'Act immediately.' Guess that makes it a direct order," he said in a cheerless voice.

I felt damned cheerless too at that point. "Yes, Rork. It does."

María began drumming her fingers on the arm of her chair. Neither Rork nor I dared look directly at her. Law began studying the fireplace.

I forced myself to concentrate on my memory. "All right, the next number set should be from McNeill's 1895 Code and that makes it mean 'Phalangium.'"

"What in hell is that?" wondered Rork. "Sounds Latin."

"It is, for some kind of garden spider, if I recall rightly. I imagine Theodore probably knows all about the damned thing. Anyway, I remember it's McNeill's code word for 'You must ship.' What's next?"

"These final three number sets're all from the '99 War Department Code, sir. Looks like 'Meelkist, Meerbottom, an' Meerkiefer,' sir. Ooh, what drunken soldier made up *those* beauties!"

I chuckled. He was right, the army code used strange foreign combinations of words.

"It's Dutch, I think. Something about a flour box, a lake bottom, and some other thing I've forgotten. Theodore would love them, of course. His family was Dutch." After writing the code words down next to the previous ones, I looked up and met María's eyes glaring at me.

My memory went completely blank. "Oh hell, Rork. I can't remember anything about what the code words mean except they have to do with the Russian navy," I admitted.

He had to ponder the words for a moment, then tapped his temple. "Aye, sir, I've got 'em. 'Meelkist' stands for 'Naval expedition.' 'Meerbottom' stands for 'Russian Navy,' an' this last one, 'Meerkiefer,' stands for 'Carefully avoid violation of neutrality.' Can ye believe that? Methinks it'll be bloody damned difficult to be *neutral* when the Japanese battleships close in on the Rooskies."

María grumbled, "Exactly . . ."

That was the final straw for me. This discord needed to end. Even Rork was sounding like María. I informed him, "Chief Rork, you are wrong. We are *not* going into battle with the Russians against the Japanese. The orders are only to go with the fleet on the transit, an 18,000-mile voyage. You, Captain Law, and I will be gone from the fleet long before the Russians ever meet up with the Japanese. This is a presidential order, and we will carry it out. Period. So stow the gundeck whining and get yourself a proper naval attitude."

He held up his right hand in submission. "Sorry, sir. I meant no disrespect . . ."

"Very well. Now, let's all finish what we originally came to Europe for."

María rose from the chair, opened the office door, and in a tired—or was it mocking?—voice said, "You may come in now, Mr. Jordan. We need your assistance to finish what we originally came to Europe for."

Jordan and a worried-looking naval lieutenant entered. The lieutenant announced his name, that he'd done two years at ONI in Washington, that he'd been stationed as attaché in Saint Petersburg for only a week, and that he had his seabag packed for special assignment. A moment later the army military attaché arrived, an equally nervous captain, carrying a heavy valise. It was his first foreign assignment. I bid both to sit down in the guest chairs and warned them that everything they were about to hear and do was highly confidential and, thus, repeatable to no one outside their respective intelligence units.

Rork went to the window and pulled down the shade. "We don't want the Krauts or the Rooskies to see us workin' too late, do we? Might get ideas on what we're really doin' here."

"Good thinking, Chief Rork," I said. "This is dangerous, and each of us has to be extremely careful. Captain Law, the plans, please."

Law pulled a large, thick manila envelope from inside his tunic. The outside was embossed with the coat of arms of the Imperial German Army. I opened it, withdrew the stack of papers inside, and laid them on the desk. Jordan sat down opposite me and began surveying them silently, page after page, his countenance morphing from pleasant curiosity into grim comprehension. He then read through it again.

After several minutes, he looked up at me. "Admiral, this is a German plan for the invasion of the United States!"

18

Amerikanischer Invasionseinsatzplan III

Saint Petersburg, Russia
Wednesday, 24 August 1904

I checked my pocket watch, then explained to the diplomat, "Yes, I know that, Mr. Jordan. Now listen carefully everyone. We don't have much time, and there is still a lot to accomplish tonight. Mr. Jordan, please start at the beginning of the document and translate it aloud to us."

He straightened up in the chair and began a dispassionate recital of the material before him. He explained it was titled "American Invasion Plan III," compiled by the Imperial German Army General Staff only ten months prior, in November 1903, and signed off on the front page by none other than Othello's nemesis, Major General Johann von Sonnenblume.

The first main section of the document consisted of summaries of the initial invasion plan, the second version, and the third and final product. The first plan was done by naval Lieutenant Eberhard von Mantey, German naval attaché to the United States, during the winter of 1897–98. It was based on his visits to naval stations and coastal fortifications on the East Coast. He called for a major naval attack on the U.S. Atlantic fleet, then a bombardment of the large U.S. naval station at Norfolk and another attack at Portsmouth Naval Station in New Hampshire. He recommended against attacking New York City because the coastal fortifications were too powerful. Other German warships were to roam up and down the East Coast, bombarding ports and causing public and financial panic. That would pressure the leadership in Washington to negotiate with the Kaiser and meet his demands for a German naval base in the Caribbean. This plan was shelved when the Spanish-American War resulted in American victory.

The second plan was done in March 1899, also by Lieutenant Mantey. This one didn't just have naval actions—it was an actual invasion plan with the German army capturing Boston and New York City, and subsequently holding them as ransom until the United States provided the Germans with a naval base in either Cuba or Puerto Rico. Victory over the American fleet, surprise landings, and speedy advance over the land were essential to overall success.

The attack on Boston involved a landing at Cape Cod and a march of 112 miles to the city. On the New York City attack, after vanquishing the U.S. Navy at sea, the German navy would concentrate their main bombardment on forts Hamilton and Tompkins at the Verrazano Narrows, then shell the city itself, all while the army landed at Sandy Hook and marched 50 miles around to Manhattan. This was an invasion on a massive scale. Over sixty troop transports would be needed to carry the army just for the Boston campaign. Approximately forty cargo ships were needed to carry the army's equipment and supplies. The entire German navy would be used to defeat the American navy, convoy the transports, and provide gunfire for the landings.

There were senior official approvals and addendums to this plan. In December 1900 Kaiser Wilhelm changed it, basing the operation out of a captured port in Cuba, rather than the entire effort coming all the way from Germany. Some senior German naval leaders thought their navy could defeat the U.S. Navy in a quick, decisive battle, especially since the American fleet was divided between the Atlantic and Pacific coasts. General Alfred von Schlieffen (whom I met at the Kaiser's recent stilted soiree in Hamburg) said he would need 50,000 men to capture, defend, and operate a base in Cuba and that he could take Boston with 100,000 men. He did not estimate how many for New York. Sonnenblume signed off on this plan also but, like the first, carefully made no indication of whether he agreed with it.

The third and current plan was compiled by another naval attaché, Lieutenant Hubert von Rebeur-Paschwitz, between August 1901 and the end of 1902. He changed the Boston attack, having the troops land at Manomet Point near Plymouth, capture the 120-meter-high Manomet Hill as an artillery base, and march forty-five miles into Boston within two days. An auxiliary landing would be done out on Cape Cod and a decoy attack done at Rockport, north of Boston. I noted with dismay he used the congressional report of a U.S. Navy captain, my longtime friend Charles Train, that detailed weaknesses in our coastal defenses around Boston to be addressed.

Lieutenant Wilhelm von Büchsel contributed modifications to the third version of the plan in 1902. By this time Cuba had become independent, and he amended the plan to include creating a base of operations for the invasion at Culebra Island near Puerto Rico. The plan was submitted up the chain of command in the spring of 1903. Von Schlieffen's assessment of this plan didn't seem as enthusiastic as Admiral Alfred von Tirpitz's, who I surmised wanted revenge after the 1902 Venezuela showdown.

I also noted the final plan came *after* the Venezuelan crisis in the fall of 1902, when President Roosevelt sent fifty-four warships under Admiral Dewey to the Caribbean as a blunt warning to Germany, Italy, and Great Britain not to attack Venezuela in return for her failing to pay off her debts. The Brits and Italians rapidly departed the area, but the German navy did attack Venezuela, then suddenly stopped and returned to Europe once Dewey arrived in the Caribbean. I knew Roosevelt wasn't bluffing then. He never did. Dewey had been ready to go into action. The Germans were lucky they came to their senses.

The plan's next main section covered logistics for the Boston operation, much of which was written by Othello, and was quite illuminating about German efficiency. To load a ship at German ports, I discovered it takes fifteen minutes to load 100 men and all their gear, one minute per horse, and ten minutes for each cannon. The embarkation ports would be Bremen and Hamburg; the Hamburg-America Line and the North German Lloyd Line would furnish the sixty passenger liners to be converted into troop transports (the conversion taking one week); and railroads would bring the troops to the ports, where it was estimated it would take four days to load four infantry divisions simultaneously and a fifth day for the cavalry division. With the attending artillery and support units, that would make 100,000 soldiers—half that to capture the base in the Caribbean, or the entirety to capture Boston.

Loading the supplies on board the cargo ships would take two weeks. Obviously, none of this could be done without detection by the public. Thus, deception as to the reason and target was critical to maintain strategic surprise. That deception as to reason and target would be accomplished by naming the entire effort a training exercise to simulate an expedition to the German colony at Tsingtao in restless China. It would be preceded by political debate as to the necessity of Germany maintaining the national ability to reinforce colonial garrisons. In reality, twenty-five to thirty days after leaving Germany, they would land in Massachusetts.

Though there was no detailed section on the New York City attack, my quick mental extrapolation based on the Boston attack plan indicated the Germans would need 200,000 men, or about twice the number of attackers used for Boston. Sea transport for the New York target would need another 120 passenger ships and 80 cargo ships. The German merchant marine, second largest in the world, could do that, but it would be using all the available oceangoing hulls. As for manpower, 350,000 men would be needed for the entire campaign in Culebra, Boston, and New York. That was a strain but doable for the German Imperial Army since its total regular duty strength was half a million men. They had another million in reserves and militia. But all that worked only if Germany's eastern border with Russia was peaceful, which it had recently become as a result of the Kaiser's deft manipulations of the Tsar.

There was a third main section on the American army's strength, which was soberingly accurate. Of the 65,000 men in the regular army, it was noted that only 30,000 are stationed inside the United States (most of those outside North America are fighting that jungle war in the Philippines), and of those at home 10,000 are in scattered small units on Indian country "occupation duty" out west, at least 2,000-railroad miles from Boston. There were no large combat formations in the New York or Boston areas, the coastal forts only had caretaker units, and it was estimated that it would take the U.S. Army at least a week to get sufficient troops to the invasion area to begin to contest the invaders. The report stated the state militias were untrained and underequipped, and useless against modern European soldiers. Significantly, there was no mention of utilizing the services of German émigrés living in America. I guessed that factor must be covered by another, even more highly confidential intelligence report under separate cover.

My heart pounded. The plan was everything President Roosevelt and I had feared.

19
A Very Terrible Feeling

Saint Petersburg, Russia
Thursday, 25 August 1904

Jordan ended his translation with a sigh. Stunned silence fell over the room. Suddenly, a knock sounded on the door. It was opened slightly by a clerk, stating he had just deciphered a state department telegram to the ambassador originating from the president. Jordan and I studied it.

XXX—INSTRUCTOR TO EMBASSY RUSSIA—X—RENDER ALL ASSISTANCE TO ADM WAKE EMBARKING WITH RUSSIAN FLEET—X—HAVE WAKE CABLE ME REF INVOICES IMMEDIATELY—XXX

Jordan instantly offered, "How can I help you, sir?"

I checked my pocket watch. It was already five minutes after midnight and there was much to do before dawn.

"At this point, Mr. Jordan, we need to move fast. Take the two lieutenants and Mrs. Wake to our rooms at Hotel Europa, gather her belongings, and get all three of them post haste to the SS *Botnia*—a Danish cargo-passenger ship lying at the western docks of the city. There are two staterooms already booked for them. *Botnia* is due to get under way at dawn for Copenhagen."

The reader will note this was a last-minute alteration of the original plan of embarking on a British steamer, changed when that ship was forced by mechanical repairs to remain in port. We'd discovered this on a last-minute confirmation check at the docks while en route to the theater. Fortunately, *Botnia* was moored nearby and had cabins available. Such are the challenges that need to be overcome as clandestine operations unfold. But there was a positive side—*Botnia* was far more inconspicuous and improbable than a large British liner.

"Also, the cover story for everyone here at the embassy, and for consumption of the Russian government and public, is that Mrs. Wake has taken ill and is heading to the spas at Vichy in France to recover her health. The officers are her escorts to the spa and will return here afterward.

"Mr. Jordan, you will not communicate anything about the German plans to *anyone*. That includes the ambassador. Everything understood so far?"

He curtly nodded, "Yes, sir."

I turned to the lieutenants, who straightened up in their chairs. "That is the cover story, gentlemen, and both of you really will escort Mrs. Wake to France by train. But . . . at the main transfer station in Paris, you will not board the train bound south for Vichy. Instead, all three of you will board the westbound train for the rail ferry over to England. In Liverpool, the three of you will take a Cunard liner home to New York and thence get to Washington by train without delay. I estimate three days steaming time to Copenhagen, another three on the rail journey to Liverpool, six days to cross the Atlantic, and another two days by train down to Washington, which makes a total of fourteen days from right now. Therefore, you should be presenting these plans to the president on September tenth."

The lieutenants did their best to hide their surprise at the pleasant news they would be home in two weeks, via first-class travel. I then gave them the unpleasant news.

"You two officers' real responsibility will be couriering the German invasion plan back to President Roosevelt. You both will be armed at *all* times, staying in your stateroom, even for meals, unless needed by Mrs. Wake. You will not partake of any alcohol during the entire transit from here to the White

House. Also, the plans will be hidden on the person of one of you at all times, including when asleep."

I paused, then said, "Trust no one. If the Germans find out you have the plans, all three of you will be targets the entire way. The Germans will stop at nothing."

Their bright attitudes dimmed somewhat at this dash of cold water. *Good, I thought, they need to look at this seriously.* María groaned and looked at the fireplace again.

I continued. "Upon arrival at the train station in Washington, Mrs. Wake will separate from you and go home to Alexandria. You two officers will immediately go to the White House and deliver the plans directly to President Roosevelt, who will be awaiting them. After you do that, you will walk to naval headquarters at the State, War, and Navy building next door and inform the commander of ONI, Commander Schroeder, that per my orders you've brought the plans back and the president has them. You will *never* speak of them to anyone other than President Roosevelt and Commander Schroeder. Do you both understand your orders, and are you ready to get under way right now?"

They piped up in unison, "Yes, sir."

"Ah, what about you and your aides, sir?" asked Jordan. "The word will get out about your observer role with the Russian fleet. These Slavic fellows are fundamentally incapable of keeping a secret, and everyone knows the warships are leaving in a few days."

With Jordan's question, María's face hardened. I looked directly at her and said, "Captain Law, Chief Rork, and I will stay at the Europa until we embark with the Russian fleet. And now, gentlemen, my wife and I need to say goodbye . . ."

Rork led the others out of the office. Pulling up a chair to María's, I reached for her hand. It was limp. I looked into her eyes. She just stared at me.

My heart sank. We'd had arguments before, but this was different. She was cold and distant. "María, I'm sorry. You know I don't *want* to go with that fleet—but for a man like me, there is no other option. I cannot disobey a presidential order. And the consequences of me not going involve national disgrace."

Her expression never changed. "You've said all that before. It is really quite simple—you could have stood by your solemn promise to me and said no to the Tsar, then said no to Roosevelt. You didn't. Just now you talked about me, your *wife*, as if I was cargo. Or a subordinate who has been given their orders."

I needed to soften her somehow, get her to see my side of things. "You're right, and I'm sorry. I didn't mean anything to come out that way, María. Decisions had to be made, and I was trying to make them quickly. With everything that's happened tonight, we need to get you and the plans out of Russia right away."

"The staterooms on *Botnia* were supposed to be for us, Rork, and Law to get the plans out of Russia and back home. Now you've got two youngsters carrying the plans and I have to leave for home without you." Emotion emerged and she shook her head in disgust. "Do not try to fool me or, even worse, fool yourself, Peter. You want to go with the Russian fleet. I can see it in your eyes."

I started to plead that she was wrong, but María stood, her expression returning to frigid indifference. "Don't worry, Peter. I know you have a lot to do, so we won't delay this any longer. Goodbye."

I stood and desperately embraced her. "I love you, María. Please don't worry about us. We'll leave the fleet, at the very latest, in about two months down at South Africa, long before they get anywhere near the war zone. It'll take me a month to get home from there, then you and I can escape the northern winter and go down to Florida for a while, like we used to do." I then added, with a hopeful smile, "Remember our times at the bungalow?"

She pushed me away as a tear descended her trembling cheek and pent-up feelings trembled her voice. "I will worry, Peter, because I love you so much. I have a very terrible feeling about you going away with the Russian navy. If—no, *when*—you get home from this latest war of your life, then yes, of course a trip to Florida would be nice. We need time alone again. Away from war, from the Navy, from Washington, and from that damned White House."

Despite María's sad eyes, there was no mistaking the anger in her next words.

"In the meantime, you need to know I am completely *done* with Theodore Roosevelt, espionage, violence, and all the other horrors surrounding us, which you seem to thrive on. I am tired of it all, and absolutely sickened by my role in it."

The last was a dagger into my heart. María had been through so much in her life. Losing her first husband to work stresses, her firstborn son murdered, and her other son wounded in a war with America. She had endured nursing work in an American war-zone hospital in Cuba, then distrust by the naval elite and humiliation by society matrons back in Washington. And for marrying me, an American Protestant, she had suffered the disaffection of most of her Spanish Catholic family.

Now, instead of making my love's life easier and more comforted, I had made it more horrific. I tried to say something, anything, healing and redemptive.

Through my own tears, I murmured, "María, I'm sorry . . ."

She nodded gently. "I know you are, Peter. And that is the pathetic part. But always know that I love you."

Then she walked away.

20
Plausible Deniability

Saint Petersburg, Russia
Thursday, 25 August 1904

At our seven o'clock breakfast in the suite, Rork reported he'd watched *Botnia* get under way at dawn. I breathed a little easier. *Thank God María and the plans are safely out of Russia.*

Law handed me a blue and silver envelope that had just been delivered to the suite. It was embossed with the Russian Imperial Navy crest. Inside was a personal letter in English from Admiral Rozhestvensky, welcoming me to the Russian fleet.

The admiral went on to say an admiralty carriage would be at Hotel Europe at ten o'clock to transport me and my entourage to the officers' landing, where we would board the admiralty harbor steamer for the fifteen-mile trip to the main naval base at Kronstadt Island, where the assembled fleet lay at anchor. I knew they had been fitting out for months with no apparent urgency, but the letter said they would get under way on their voyage the next day.

Law then handed me a nondescript envelope, which had also been placed under the suite's door. As I read the note inside it, my unease returned.

My dear Peter,   *11:48pm 24 August 1904*

I will be stopping by your suite in the Europa at 8am in the morning to discuss what happened tonight with you at the Maryinksy Theater. It appears to be a most unusual situation.

P. I. Rachkovsky
Chief of the Okhrana

This didn't look good at all. It was on Okhrana stationery, and he'd signed it officially, not personally, in the informal Russian manner of a friend. I also registered the date and time—it was written at his office just as we'd been reading the German war plan and making decisions.

After María, the lieutenants, and Jordan had left, I'd briefed Law and Rork on what happened with Maysa Abaev and the alibi I presented to the Tsar and Rozhestvensky. Rork shook his head. Law was silent, contemplating the causes and consequences.

Now they looked grim, especially Rork. "That Rooskie weasel's up to somethin' an' there's nary a bit o' good in it. Better be ready for anythin', lads."

The previous night I'd given Jordan a short cable to send to Roosevelt from the embassy first thing in the morning—once I telephoned him in the morning after knowing the "invoices" were en route. In plain text it said, *Inscient* to *Inquinates—Abounding.* Those code words translated to: *Wake to Roosevelt—Anchor recovered and reshipped.* Reading that, Roosevelt would know that the German plans had been obtained, had left Russia, and were on their way to Washington.

When the Okhrana chief arrived at our door, all three of us, including Rork for the first time on this mission, were in full dress uniforms, sitting around a table in the suite's parlor, which overlooked the street below. The tableau we constructed was one of pleasant nonchalance—sailors enjoying a leisurely Russian breakfast of omelets, cheese dumplings, black bread slathered with butter, and Turkish-style coffee before going to sea.

Rachkovsky entered with genial brightness. I watched him register the breakfast table, the piled seabags, the dress uniforms. "Peter, I am so delighted our beloved fleet will have such an esteemed naval hero to observe them in action!"

In action? Hmm . . . I thought it would be only while in transit. "Thank you, Pyotr. Please sit and help us eat all this breakfast."

He sat at the table, and Rork served him tea and a plate piled with food, which he dove into right away, grunting with savory appreciation. "Ah, the Europa is still living up to her reputation! Such an excellent way to start such a momentous day."

The man certainly could eat, especially when I (or, rather, the U.S. government) was paying for it. Several more mouthfuls were filled before he gulped down tea and finally spoke.

"I was distressed to hear that your beautiful lady felt ill last night and has left for France this morning. A long way to go, but at least she has two young attaché officers for an escort, as befitting the good lady of an honored admiral, of course. But really, she didn't have to go on that little Danish boat. One of the big German liners is in port. Much more comfortable and fitting for a lady of her station. In any case, I truly hope she will feel better soon." He frowned. "Of course you know, Peter, she never had to leave us at all. We have very good doctors right here. The Tsar would have insisted your wife use his personal physician. He likes you both."

From long experience, I knew how Rachkovsky's mind worked. There was always a deniable double-meaning in his words. Plausible deniability is an essential part of conversations in despotic countries, where paranoia, betrayal, and violence insidiously lurk just below the cultured façades of the elite. The Russian spy's comments were a thinly veiled warning that he knew far more than what I'd thought. I had no doubt there would be threats, once he got around to what happened at the theater.

"Pyotr, María didn't want to impose on the Tsar. She's had these sorts of episodes before and wanted to go to the spas at Vichy as soon as possible. The German liner isn't leaving until later. The Danish steamer was convenient and fast."

Rachkovsky showed a sly little smile. "Yes, Peter, and it was so fortuitous the staterooms were booked so late in the day, just before the theater, in the event she might feel ill."

"She'd been feeling a little off earlier in the day," I countered, with a slight shrug. "I'm afraid Russian food doesn't agree with her sometimes. So, we booked them on the way to the theater to be sure, just in case. Women can be so frail."

His head bobbed in feigned agreement. "I suppose that lamentable incident last night also aggravated her nerves."

"Yes, Pytor, I have to say it did," I said ever so sadly, presenting my own expression of concern. "Your note said you had some information about that?"

"Yes, the admiral and the Tsar were shocked and quite humiliated, as you know. My man Harting immediately investigated, of course, and discovered some remarkable things."

"Really, such as what?" I asked, my brow furrowed in rapt attention.

"The dead body of a Turkmenistan woman, Maysa Abaev, was found. I believe you and your wife met her in the reception room, introduced by the Tsar, who knew her father. It was murder, but she tried to fight her assailants. The right side of the woman's head had been crushed from behind with a candlestick, and her right wrist had large bruises on it, apparently from a large hand crushing around it. Quite a struggle."

He paused as I looked appropriately shocked. "Good Lord! How awful."

I also began wondering. *So, Maysa Abaev did die before they found her. Or . . . did somebody kill her after they found her? That would've been Harting. But why would he finish her off?*

Rachkovsky resumed. "It appeared that one right-handed male assailant grabbed Abaev's right wrist, and another right-handed assailant hit her from behind, so there must be two perpetrators. The body and candlestick were hidden in an adjoining small conference room, which was then locked. That was the same room where you and the Tsar had your private conversation."

"Did those soldiers do all that?" I exclaimed. "No wonder they ran away when I walked in on them."

He paused, as if musing over something in his mind, then said, "As you can imagine, Harting was very motivated to look into everything. Within the hour, every soldier on duty at the theater was *thoroughly* interrogated and their uniforms inspected. The results were interesting. None had any sign of blood or damage on their uniforms, none had any wounds or bruises, none smelled of any alcohol, none confessed to fighting over wine or murdering the woman, and none said they encountered a lone American naval officer."

Rachkovsky then swept his eyes over the front of my uniform, which still had faint stains I'd been unable to remove during the night. He looked at me but didn't say anything, waiting for me to speak. It's an old interrogator's technique. I played for time, seemingly stunned by the news.

Rork, as a veteran servant should, had been standing at parade-rest behind Rachkovsky's chair. Now he brought his false hand around to the front and loosened it for fast removal, then looked questioningly at me—*should I kill him?* Law's face was impassive, as a junior officer is expected to be, but his eyes were on me also. Both were tensed and ready for action.

I shook my head in apparent amazement of Rachkovsky's news—but also to signal my men not to attack—and quietly asked the Russian, "Pyotr, then tell me who could've killed that woman?"

21
Layers of Lies

Saint Petersburg, Russia
Thursday, 25 August 1904

Rachkovsky's right eyebrow rose slightly, then the knowing smile returned. "There was another curious event last night that might provide a clue, Peter. Did you know there were several visiting German staff officers attending the performance?"

"Yes, I saw them down in the audience and wondered why they were in Saint Petersburg."

"Just a routine professional visit. However, after the performance ended and the patrons left the theater, one of the officers was found dead by gunshot in an alley two streets away. Small caliber pistol shot to the rear of the right temple—another right-handed assailant from behind.

"Witnesses said the victim had left the theater carrying a small valise, but when his body was found there was no valise, and his pockets were empty. I thought he was probably robbed by a street villain, tried to resist, and was killed. But Harting thinks otherwise. Please understand this next part is highly confidential, gentlemen. I must have your word not to repeat it." He looked at each of us.

"Of course," I said. "You have my word for all of us." Rork and Law nodded their acknowledgment.

"Harting thinks the officer was assassinated by one of his own. Another German was seen following the victim down the street. Young man, medium height, strong, with close-cropped blond hair, slight fencing scar on the cheek, dressed in civilian attire. He is no civilian, though. We know he is an agent in the German army counterintelligence section—the Abteilung IIIb. He has been known to us for some time. Occasionally we and the Germans have found ourselves looking at the same people of . . . extreme interest. I think you understand."

I did. In the dark world of secret intelligence operations, that quaint euphemism meant assassination targets—usually anarchists. But Rachkovsky wasn't talking about anarchists.

The Russian continued. "Harting believes that agent had the woman killed too. For what reason, we are not exactly sure. There are theories but nothing substantiated yet. Perhaps that German officer was thought by the Abteilung IIIb to be a traitor selling secrets, and the woman was thought to be his Russian contact . . ." He stopped, watching me digest that notion.

I gestured in disbelief. "Pyotr, this is all so fantastical. A German assassin inside Saint Petersburg? They are your allies, here to help you. The Kaiser told me that himself when I was in Hamburg. If the woman I met was a Russian spy, she must be working for you."

His response was just a split second too delayed. "No, Maysa Abaev doesn't work for us, but perhaps the Germans *thought* she did. And if the German officer who was killed in the alley was indeed a traitor, what secrets did he give his contact, whoever they were? I am thinking that the Abteilung IIIb made Abaev's death appear like drunken Russian soldiers did it—a classic false-flag assassination. Can you imagine that, Peter? A foreign false-flag operation right here in Saint Petersburg, at the same theater where the Tsar was attending a performance? A murder in the same reception room where he had just met with an American dignitary! What an evilly bold scheme, or a better description might be *reckless*. You are a professional. Don't you agree it was reckless, my friend?"

"Yes, Pyotr. I agree it does seem reckless when the consequences are considered. Violence is always a sign of an operation's failure. This could get politically messy."

Rachkovsky spread his hands in a gesture of pleasant resolution. "Well, perhaps not. It is over, none of it is known by the public or the press, and I don't see a necessity for further action on our part. What would that accomplish? The woman wasn't one of my operatives or even an informant, just another minor social climber visiting the city from the outer reaches of the empire. None of Russia's secrets were taken. And, of course, our relations with Germany are very important right now."

I nodded my understanding. "The Tsar must be alarmed, to say the least."

"The Tsar has not been told about the murders or our conjecture on motives. It would only make him very upset. He has tremendous responsibilities conducting the war and doesn't need the stress of this additional burden, much less any complications with the Kaiser. By the way, just so you know, that German agent is also no longer in the picture. He boarded the German liner this morning."

Rachkovsky and I locked eyes as he told me, "So, my dear American friend, the logical conclusion to this incident is that apparently those two soldiers you saw were probably German immigrants living in the city, criminals paid by the Abteilung IIIb agent-assassin to be impostors and killers. They wore our army's uniforms to get inside the theater's security perimeter and go after Maysa Abaev, who had somehow become an Abteilung IIIb target. Perhaps they are also on the liner this morning with their leader? In any event, they will never be found because we have no idea of precisely who they are."

I found it amazing to see how Rachkovsky's devious mind worked on closing off loose ends. The man was efficient. I gave him another understanding look, one spy to another.

Then he wrapped up those ends with Heavenly praise. "By unlucky coincidence, you happened to walk in on the end of their murderous plot and were very fortunate to escape with your life. No wonder your lovely wife grew ill at the mere thought of such a grisly deed. I find your survival a truly Divine miracle, Peter. And thanks be to God our cherished Tsar was not the target and will live on to guide our nation to victory over the Japanese."

"Yes, it was a miracle, Pyotr," I dutifully agreed. "What happens now?"

His smirk returned. "I will have Harting write a secret report, which will be held in the vault at Okhrana for a long time. No one, not even the Tsar, will know the details. Only you, Harting, and I will know what really happened last night within close proximity of the Tsar himself. After all, we intelligence professionals cannot have this sort of thing get out, can we, Peter? What would people think? The press would howl. The Tsar would be enraged. The Kaiser would vehemently deny everything. Military confrontations would ensue along the border. No, better to let it rest quietly in the vault."

Rachkovsky was covering this entire mess up, but not for free. There would be a future price for it. I slowly nodded my acquiescence to this new status quo.

"I see your point," I said. "Better to not take a chance on a diplomatic crisis erupting in this fragile time."

Rachkovsky nodded approvingly, rose from his chair, and straightened his jacket.

"Exactly, Peter. I had no doubt that you would understand the entire situation and its consequences completely. And now, things are looking up for you. For the next several months you will be blissfully away from the cesspool of European politics, a pampered guest on a naval cruise around the world. Such an interesting respite, almost a reprieve, from your recent stressful diplomatic work. Everyone needs a *reprieve* at some point, but so few get one. Well, I must go attend to other duties. Good day and adieu, my old friend. I think it may be a while before we have the pleasure of meeting again."

With that, he gave me a bear hug, a bone-crunching two-handed shake of my hand, a hard slap on the shoulder, and was out the door before I could figure out a suitable reply. I just stood there, my head pounding with the import of what had just been said, and what was really meant. I had just been given notice of the secret official story but still had no answer to the overwhelming questions in my mind.

Why did Maysa Abaev try to kill me, and for whom? Why is Rachkovsky covering up our killing of her? How much do the Germans know about our false-flag espionage mission? Why did Rachkovsky orchestrate my installment as neutral naval observer with the Russian fleet? Who will come after me next?

Part 2
The Fleet

22
Preparing for War

Kronstadt Naval Base, Russia
Friday, 26 August 1904

Exhausted by the tension, chaos, and heartache of the previous twenty-four hours, I would have much preferred eating a quiet meal in the senior officers' wardroom on board the flagship *Knyaz Suvorov* or, even better yet, my quite comfortable quarters. But that option was trumped by nothing less than an imperial command summons to attend a formal dinner party at the posh Kronstadt Navy Club ashore.

There was no way to thwart Tsar Nicholas's desire to personally show off to me the twenty admirals and senior captains who were seated around the table, all bedecked with baubles and trinkets and gold lace. Catching sight of the dozens of bottles of wine, champagne, and vodka lined up on the side tables, I could tell it was going to be a long, wet, tiring night.

After a groaningly huge meal consisting of unrecognizable but delicious food in six courses, the Tsar made a wonderful introductory speech about me. Admiral Rozhestvensky welcomed me as a brother naval officer and admiral, and I gave the obligatory brief guest speech, translated by a junior officer into Russian with greater gusto than I had employed in English.

During the entire evening, my tablemates peppered me with polite questions about my career in their rudimentary English. I responded vaguely with humble humor, trying to stifle conversations early so I could go back to the flagship and sleep. They asked many questions about the "cowboy president," whom I described in glowing terms of manliness they appreciated. Notably, none asked about my wife or children. It was almost as if they didn't want to be reminded of their own families back home.

The best part of the evening was the vodka, which I will fully admit tasted good—far too good. Accordingly, I paced myself in its consumption. As the evening wore on, however, it appeared I was the only one doing so. In these male-only kinds of conclaves, Russians are raucous back-slappers, bear-huggers, and shoulder-punchers. Especially when drunk, which by the fourth course most were. Russian after Russian declared to me with thunderous braggadocio what would happen to the Japanese when the fleet got there.

Both the Tsar and Admiral Rozhestvensky steadily drank but somehow maintained their decorum, indulgently ignoring the increasingly loud debates and jests amongst their lesser companions. Instead of erupting at such borderline wild behavior, the Tsar and the admiral merely looked over the gathering with paternal patience.

I knew why, for I'd seen it before in my career around the world. The men at that table knew this was their last night to enjoy themselves. In the morning, they were starting their long journey to the other side of the world, where many actually expected to die at the hands of the so far undefeated Japanese fleet.

I found the whole thing to be an ominous sign. *If this is the attitude among the senior officers of the fleet—what are the junior officers thinking? What about the petty officers, on whom every warship depends to maintain morale and discipline? And what of the common sailors? Just how bad is the morale fleetwide at every level?*

It was late when I finally caught the launch out to the ship and trudged through the passageways to my stateroom. I found the cabin servant standing by the turned-down bed at attention, a cloud of vodka fumes emanating from him. He spoke passable English and asked if I needed his assistance to shed my heavy uniform. I declined and suggested he go to bed himself. He looked relieved and slowly made his way out.

The steward was not alone in his inebriation. From what I saw upon my return, it appeared the entire crew was drunk, quite a few to the point of insensibility. All this made me wonder just how Rork and Law had made it through the evening down in the senior petty officers' and junior officers' messes. I knew that Capt. Edwin Law, USMC, was a stalwart one-drink man who prided himself on stoic military decorum, but in these surroundings, who could resist?

Chief Sean Rork, USN, was anything but a one-drink man. Fortunately, there were no women in the ship—at least I thought not—so I figured he probably couldn't get in too much trouble. But still, if the Russians kept up their drinking on this voyage, I knew there was no way Rork, Law, or even I could say no indefinitely. *Would we become like them? And by the way, where the hell do they store all this vodka, wine, beer, and brandy on a warship?*

At last, I ended the evening in the lumpy bed at two o'clock, eight long hours after that damned dinner began. Suffering from half a dozen bruises, a slight vodka-stimulated dislocation of my equilibrium, and an upset stomach, I also had a profound sense of dread. We would be getting under way in three hours, and I knew I would be expected to stand in a place of honor near Admiral Rozhestvensky on the bridge. I groaned at the thought and then mercifully passed out.

And thus we all, thousands of Russians and three Americans, prepared to go to war.

23

Spies and Torpedo Boats

Skagerrak Straits, Denmark
Monday, 17 October 1904

In the weeks after joining *Suvorov*, I learned just how busy Harting was on his crucial primary assignment. Admiral Rozhestvensky explained that Harting had responsibility not only to eliminate Japanese espionage against Russia in Europe, but also to make sure the fleet's entire transit to the Far East was devoid of Japanese sabotage or torpedo boat attacks—a daunting task, to say the least.

To oversee security for the initial segments of the voyage, Harting was now working out of the famous Phoenix Hotel in Copenhagen, using the names "Abram Garting" or "Mr. Arnold." Garting, as we shall now call him, controlled Russian agents and local informants in five separate networks on the coasts of the Baltic Sea, North Sea, English Channel, and Bay of Biscay. He provided a constant stream of information to Admiral Rozhestvensky, conveyed by telegraph to the nearest port and thence by hired fast boat out to the flagship or, if close enough, by Marconi wireless telegraph, the newfangled receiving and sending apparatus installed in only a few Russian ships.

Garting's efforts were considerably enhanced by the complete cooperation of the Danish military, lighthouse service, and secret police. No wonder on that, for their eighty-six-year-old sovereign, King Christian IX, was Tsar Nicholas II's doting grandfather. The Royal Danish Navy even provided an escort squadron for our passage through Denmark's narrow straits of Kattegat and Skagerrak.

One may question the actual ability of the Japanese to mount a torpedo boat attack so distant from their home waters. I certainly did, but the doubts I had upon first hearing of this fear from Russian staff officers ended when the admiral shared some of that constant stream of intelligence to me. His staff thought the Japanese could charter several European freighters, load torpedo boats on them, send them from the Pacific to various remote bays on European coasts, and use them for a night attack on the transiting Russian fleet when least expected.

In addition, Garting's spies soon started reporting mysterious Japanese men seen along the Scandinavian coasts, and sightings of strange cargo ships and small craft began coming in. The Japanese consul-general was forced to leave Copenhagen, and two of his countrymen in Denmark were arrested on suspicion of being spies and recruiting locals.

It needs to be explained that the admiral's unusual confiding to me of such information was the product of the close bond that grew between us over those initial weeks. As the fleet steamed from Kronstadt to Reval, thence to Libau (our last Russian port) for final training exercises, repairs, fuel, provisioning, and an imperial sendoff by the Tsar on board his yacht, the nationalistic political boundaries between the admiral and me were overcome.

This was understandable. Rozhestvensky had no one of his rank and experience on board the flagship with whom to discuss his responsibilities. He had subordinate admirals in his fleet on other ships, but some he despised, and none had my constant proximity. Command is always a heavy and lonely burden, but especially so for the commander of a fleet of twenty-five vessels (and due to increase) embarking on such a momentous task.

I was a contemporary of Rozhestvensky (we both started our naval careers in 1863) and found myself stuck in a very alien culture and language. The common bond was ships, the sea, and senior command rank. During the progression of shared meals, vodka, night watches on the bridge, and inspection tours of the ship, we entrusted each other with professional observations and opinions. This progressed until the admiral shared intelligence only he and the Tsar had seen. Thus, my neutral status was maintained officially, but personally I became a friend and our private conversations were between Peter and Zinovy.

That is how I found out late one night, after a meal of borscht and vodka in the admiral's luxurious stateroom, that a month earlier Garting's people had broken the Japanese code and read a cable message from the embassy in Holland to the foreign minister in Tokyo. From that cable, the Russians now knew that the ever-efficient and elusive Colonel Akashi's own network of paid lookouts and informants on the coasts were providing continuous updates on the fleet's location, and that they were "taking measures to prevent" the fleet from getting to Asia. The Japanese message ended with the assurance that everything that could be done would be tried.

"So, you can see our torpedo boat fears are not that far-fetched, are they Peter?" Rozhestvensky said. "We must be vigilant, especially at night. Fortunately, we have very good searchlights."

"Even good searchlights burn out the bulb after a couple hours," I said, then suggested the old-fashioned remedy. "Sometimes young eyes are better at night, Zinovy. We're leaving the protection of Denmark's waters. Will you be setting up your own cruisers in a screen around the fleet for the rest of the voyage?"

"Yes, now that we are in wider waters. And as you know, we are arranged in four separate divisions, with forty miles, and sometimes less, between them. Since this division, with the most modern battleships, is in the rear of the fleet, we can speed up and support the others without having to turn around and rush to the rear in the event of an attack."

I brought up another scenario. "You know, if I were the Japanese, I wouldn't even try to do an attack in Europe. It's enough to spread the fear I might. You are waiting and ready for that. But over time, being on constant alert has its efficiency degraded."

"And so, if you were the Japanese, what would you do?"

"Using the Black Dragon Society spy network, I would ascertain your fleet's route and progress, then position chartered freighters at a remote bay on the African coast, off-load the torpedo boats, wait for you to go by, and launch a night attack. In a remote bay on the African coast there would be fewer people to see their arrival and preparations, very scarce cable communications to sound an alert, and therefore they would have a much greater chance of tactical surprise—just as you Russians thought the worst threat area was behind you in Europe."

"Valid theory, Peter. But I have not yet decided whether to go by way of rounding Africa via the Cape of Good Hope, taking the short cut via the Suez Canal, or steaming around Cape Horn and across the Pacific. We may never see the African coast beyond a short coaling stop at Tangiers."

"The Black Dragons are everywhere, Zinovy. Even in South America, where there are many remote coastal bays."

He ruefully wagged his head. "Ah, yes, the Black Dragons are formidable, and their reach is indeed everywhere along any of our possible routes. But first, we have to get out of Europe. Remember, my country, and particularly our monarchy, has many enemies among European anarchists who would love to assist the Japanese. And we must guard against not only the radicals. Scandinavians have centuries-old animosity against us. The British are close allies of the Japanese, built their battleships, trained their officers, and are actively helping them with intelligence. An attack could come in the North Sea or English Channel in a clandestine launch from the British coast. There are so many scenarios to consider, Peter."

The admiral exhaled slowly and took another sip of his vodka. "And all of them have bad endings. The main fact of the matter is that we Russians are all alone on this voyage. The French are our allies but are afraid to help, for it might alienate the British or Japanese. The Germans are our friends only as long as they make money off coaling our ships on this voyage and we lose soldiers and sailors fighting the Japanese. And, of course, everyone believes you Americans are cheering for the Japanese. It is well known your president admires them."

"He admires their country's rapid modernization in the last thirty years. It was a phenomenal accomplishment."

"I agree. And their army and navy—what does he think of them?"

I kept my answer neutral, without revealing Roosevelt's worries about the Japanese in the future. "My president respects their abilities. They have proven them in the war against China nine years ago, the Boxer Rebellion four years ago, and during this current war against Russia."

"Many wars in a short time." The ghost of a smug smile showed on his face. "What do you think Japan's next war target will be when this war is finished?"

"Zinovy, you have a formidable fleet. If the Japanese navy is defeated in battle by you, their country would lose this war. If not, they will still have an exhausting and very expensive war to continue, probably ad infinitum, which would drain them of money and men. So either way, I think any predictions of postwar Japanese policies have no validity at this point."

He clinked his glass to mine. "A thorny topic artfully evaded, Peter. May this fleet be as skilled in evading torpedo boats."

I sipped my vodka. "Everyone knows the first destination is Tangiers, but have you decided the fleet's course to get there? The shortest would be the English Channel. Or you could go northwest through the North Sea, go around Scotland and out into the Atlantic, then south past the west coast of Ireland. That way you would stay away from land, avoiding any more European maritime bottlenecks and their potential torpedo boat menace."

He didn't agree. "The Atlantic option would use too much fuel and the slower, smaller vessels would have difficulties. And we would be spotted by the British while passing the Orkney or Shetland islands anyway. No, we will go south through the North Sea and the English Channel. Riskier but faster and worth it."

A few nights later, Zinovy Rozhestvensky's words proved ironic.

24
Morale?

Dogger Bank, North Sea
Friday, 21 October 1904

Shortly after that intriguing conversation with Admiral Rozhestvensky, he assigned an officer to be my personal liaison. Thirty-seven-year-old Commander Vladimir Semenov was a recent addition to the admiral's staff, but one without an assigned responsibility and thus available for additional duties. He was fluent in English, a specialist in torpedo boat defense and offense, and, quite surprisingly, one of the few Russian naval officers in Rozhestvensky's fleet who had actually fought against the Japanese already in the war. Most of his fellow combat veterans were dead, invalids in hospitals, prisoners of war, or still stuck in the Far East.

Semenov was a man driven by what he'd endured over the previous seven months. Having just returned to European Russia from the Far East, he briefed the idle brass dilettantes at naval headquarters in Saint Petersburg about the real war situation. Discouraged by their lack of comprehension and bureaucratic inertia, Semenov then demanded to immediately join Russia's Baltic fleet about to steam around the world.

There were no ship commands available, so he submerged his ego and embarked at the lesser position of staff supernumerary at the first port beyond

Kronstadt. He wanted other officers to learn from what he'd seen and not make the same mistakes, so he briefed them on tactics, even when this upset some officers' preconceived notions about Russian invincibility. The ruffled officers studiously ignored his presence, but I paid very close attention whenever Semenov shared a battle experience or made an observation of the current fleet's readiness.

The reader must now be wondering about my American naval companions. So far in the voyage, Law and Rork had spent most of each morning in my stateroom. After we separately had breakfast in our respective messes, we met for an assessment of the ship, officers, and crew. Junior officers were discussed by Law presenting his opinion of their training, skills and efficiency, leadership and relations with the crew, morale among themselves, complaints about supplies and maintenance, and general abilities. Rork would present me with a similar report about the senior petty officers as well as his opinions on the lower ranks. These were one-sided discussions—I did not share my view of the senior Russian officers with Law and Rork.

The afternoons were spent with Law and I minutely inspecting the ship, which was completely new and boasted several modern apparatuses in wireless telegraphy, interior telephone communications, engine turbines, and gun layer optics. Rork used the time to further know the crew.

Semenov and I ate in the senior officers' wardroom, several of whom spoke passable English. Perhaps once or twice a week I would be invited to dine with the admiral privately. At each level, these meals were windows into the officers, men, and machines of the fleet, and we Americans found that uncommon candidness among the Russians was the rule. Also their serious and incessant consumption of alcohol.

From the beginning, my colleagues' assessments of the situation were disturbing.

The lower ranks were largely illiterate, unwashed, frequently unskilled and inexperienced in their naval responsibilities, and sullen. Many were peasant conscripts from rural areas, and this was their first ship or sight of water bigger than a river. Some were from distant parts of the empire, didn't even speak Russian, and were constantly ridiculed by their shipmates. Several quietly spoke about the revolutionary ideas spreading ashore in Russia. An unnamed few were rumored to be fervidly anti-monarchy and pro-anarchist.

The petty officers, especially the senior ones, were grizzled thugs who acted more like prison guards than leaders. They kept an iron-clad discipline based on abject terror. Proficiency was secondary. Morale was dismissed as a sarcastic joke. Rork's reports revealed a lack of training and experience in using weapons, no attempts to improve accuracy, and no sign of caring about operational deficiencies. Shiny brass, scrubbed decks, and gleaming paint work seemed to be the main goal.

Law informed us that the junior officers were either naïvely fresh from the academy or already unenthusiastic products of a navy that virtually closed down when the harbors froze over in the winter months. During those many months, officers would huddle in front of fireplaces in barracks ashore and drink themselves insensible or flee to their rich families' mansions where at least there was some form of heat and much better liquor. Navigation, tactics, steam plant engineering, international law, meteorology, gunnery, and foreign languages were taught at the academy, but many officers had no follow-on courses or little application of the subjects at sea, and very few had sailed beyond the Baltic or Black Seas.

It seemed that all ranks had the general opinion that Admiral Rozhestvensky was Russia's greatest admiral after Makarov, who had been killed in battle by the Japanese months earlier. But there was something else about Rozhestvensky I learned from these conversations with officers, something profoundly troubling. In tense moments when things were going unanticipatedly wrong, he was known to completely lose his temper, fly into a caustic tirade, and even severely beat subordinates, both officers and men. I hadn't seen any of that, but I realized many around me were constantly on edge, waiting for him to erupt.

Semenov sensed my negative reaction to all these things and tried to mitigate it with a rousing portrayal of the strength and stamina of the average Russian sailor when roused in battle. His attempt, accompanied by humor and vodka, didn't sway my opinion. In modern warfare, morale is a needed addition to naval skill—not a substitute for it. There was no way to sugarcoat my realization that the professional and personal state of the officers, petty officers, and men on board the Russian flagship—and the rest of the fleet as well—was dismal in every regard.

Contemplating all this wasn't conducive to sleep when I stretched out on my bunk at a quarter to one in the morning on 21 October, as *Suvorov* steamed onward in the murky night through the North Sea. It crossed my mind this was the ninety-ninth anniversary of the momentous British victory at Trafalgar, which had altered the fate of Europe. I lay there semi-dozing and thinking about the 928 men on the ship, each of us shackled inexorably to our own fate somewhere ahead.

Fourteen minutes later, it arrived.

25
Chaos

Dogger Bank, North Sea
Friday, 21 October 1904

Blasted from semi-asleep to wide awake, it took me a moment to realize it was the 3-inch gun just aft of my stateroom firing. The electric lamp's bulb, which had been lit prior, was shattered by the concussion, and the room went black. The duty watch had started shooting. In seconds, a crescendo of rapid fire exploded from the twenty 3-inch gun mounts all over the ship. They were joined by the periodic booms of the twelve 6-inchers and the barking of the twenty Hotchkiss 2-inch guns. It was a deafening cacophony in the dark, and I barely heard the tinny blare of a trumpet repeating the signal for all hands to man their battle stations.

Decades of experience dictated reflexive reactions. First, I struck a match and noted the time by my pocket watch: 12:58 a.m. My stateroom was a mess. The violent rattling from the blasts had opened desk drawers, knocking them to the deck. I lit another match and found a candle to light. Then, amidst this earthquake of gunfire, I pulled on my shoes, uniform tunic, and outer coat (fortunately, I was lying in my trousers and shirt). Next I gathered my personal things from the deck, including my pistol and extra ammunition.

Finally, I stumbled out into the passageway, then forward through the mass of similarly confused men in the dark. Few electric lights were functioning, and only two oil lamps had been lit. Pushing my way through the officers' area, the crew area, and up the starboard ladders four decks, I arrived on the bridge.

Following my instructions about where to meet in the event of an emergency, Law and Rork were already there, standing in the shadows of the starboard aft corner, out of everybody's way. Both looked relieved when I arrived. Semenov came in right after me. There was no greeting among us. We all were consumed by the scene inside the bridge and on the sea around us.

The bridge was bathed in Dante-esque red light from the battle lanterns. A deathly white light illuminated us from the search lights of the ship to starboard. Officers and petty officers were making their reports, their voices on the edge of composure. In the distance other ships were firing, their searchlights sweeping around in all directions. Suddenly *Suvorov* fired a salvo at a ship on the port side a few miles away. A moment later, a fountain of water erupted alongside us.

I tried to make sense of what I was seeing. *These aren't torpedo boats shooting at us—they're large warships. This is a fleet action! How did the Japanese get their fleet all the way here?* I suddenly felt sick. *My God, the Russians have panicked and are shooting at each other.*

I saw Admiral Rozhestvensky manhandling a sailor away from a Hotchkiss gun on the starboard bridge wing, all the while roaring at the top of his voice above the gunfire something in vulgar Russian. The meaning was clear—cease fire!

The captain of the ship, Ignatius, pointed at a silhouette in the water and cried out in a pained voice. The navigator, Flippovsky, shook his head and muttered a report to the captain. A shocked Semenov translated for us. "The captain just said those boats are fishermen, not torpedo boats. The navigator reports we are at Dogger Bank, the fishing grounds. The admiral is ordering all ships to stop shooting but still be on the lookout. The attackers might still be out there."

Gradually, the gunfire slowed. Then ended. I noted the time: 1:08 a.m.

In the quiet tension that now filled the bridge, the admiral stood alone, gazing grimly ahead. The only sound was the steady rumble of the engines and the swish of the bow waves as we continued south. No one spoke in the bridge except the signalman quietly reporting the ships acknowledging the order. Ships began reporting their damage to the flagship, then their casualties. The cruiser *Aurora* reported damage and her chaplain gravely wounded—from Russian gunfire.

I walked out to the side deck and looked out into the mist. There were shapes out there—the same size as a fishing boat. My anxiety increased into dread. *The Dogger Bank is well-known as the fishing ground for British coastal fishermen from the town of Hull, fifty miles to the east. Oh Lord, how many of them were killed and wounded?*

With an impassive face, Semenov pulled me aside and whispered in my ear. "As you know, sir, *Kamchatka*, the repair ship at the rear end of the formation, reported torpedo boats earlier in the evening, but it was nothing. That captain is known to be a nervous type. Then, a few minutes ago, he reported another torpedo boat. Soon after that, the admiral himself saw several darkened vessels approaching on the starboard side. Once he saw one of them was a torpedo boat, he gave the order to open fire. I think many of our ships have hit each other."

"Thank you, Vladimir. You, your admiral, and this fleet, have my empathy. It all seems to be over now, so my men and I are going below now."

I called Law and Rork over and briefed them. "This was a terrible accident. The Russians say they saw a torpedo boat but have fired into a British fishing fleet—and each other. No good can be had from staying on this bridge right now, so we're going back down to our quarters. Sleep in your clothes with your weapons handy. Be ready for anything tonight. Make no comment about this incident to anyone. We'll meet again after breakfast."

As I descended the ladder, I saw Rozhestvensky on the starboard bridge wing, his hands gripping the bulwark as he intently peered out over the sea in the direction of the British coast. No one approached him as he stood there. *Suvorov* and the fleet steamed on as if nothing untoward had happened. No ship stopped to help the fishermen. Our first "battle"—with ourselves and innocent fishermen—was over.

The weather gradually closed in on us—nasty wind and rain, with visibility down to a quarter mile at most. Early the next morning, the admiral decided to forgo his option of a stop at the French port of Brest, which is notoriously dangerous to approach in bad weather. Four rough days later we put into the port of Vigo in northwest Spain.

At Vigo the Russians would learn just how bad the episode at Dogger Bank was, and what the world thought of them.

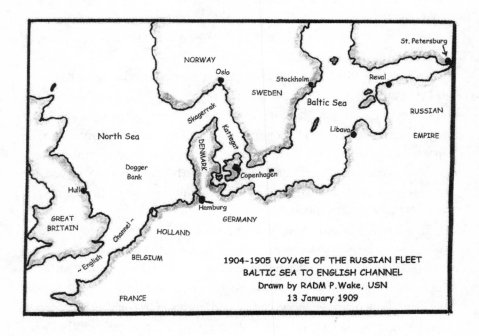

1904–1905 VOYAGE OF THE RUSSIAN FLEET
BALTIC SEA TO ENGLISH CHANNEL
Drawn by RADM P. Wake, USN
13 January 1909

26
Hail Britannia

Vigo, Spain
Wednesday, 26 October 1904

Our first visitors were somber Spanish naval officials who ordered the Russians not to communicate by boat between their ships, nor with the shore, nor with the six German colliers that had just arrived to refuel them.

Behind the Spanish navy launch came boats from the Russian, British, and American consulates, with official telegrams from their home capitals. The Russian consul's eyes were downcast when he came on board. The Brit wore a scowl and looked at everyone defiantly. The American stared nervously at the crew as if they were wild beasts.

He was a little man of middle age, whose Spanish-accented English showed his dual roots. Vigo was a fishing port with minor commercial trade, and he wasn't used to dealing with admirals and weighty international incidents. It plainly made him nervous.

"Welcome to Vigo, Admiral Wake. I am thankful you were not hurt in the terrible, ah . . . the incident . . . at Dogger Bank. Here is a telegram for you from Washington via Madrid."

He thrust it into my hand as if to rid himself of something frightening. I handed the cable to Rork to decipher and returned my attention to the consul. "Any news in the papers about the incident?"

"Oh yes, sir. It seems there was a dreadful mistake by the Russians in iden-tifying the vessels they shot at. There were no torpedo boats. In reality, it was the usual British fishing fleet out of Hull. Several fishermen are dead, several more are wounded. At least three boats are sunk, with several damaged."

"British government's reaction?"

"Completely enraged, sir. Their fleet at Gibraltar has gone on war alert, and this morning three cruisers just appeared on the horizon off the coast to our south. The Home Fleet is sending ships too. It is thought that within three or four days they will have at least twenty battleships and as many cruisers off this port."

"And what of the Spanish government's position?"

"The Spanish government is afraid of the British fleet, especially since the Americans annihilated Spain's fleet six years ago." I noticed he didn't say *we* Americans.

Just then Rork stood and said, "Deciphered, sir."

The consul stepped out to give us privacy and Rork laid the deciphered message on my desk.

XXX—DID YOU SEE JAPANESE WARSHIPS AT DOGGER BANK?—X—BRITISH ANGRY—X—IF WAR BREAKS OUT WITH BRITAIN LEAVE FLEET AT FIRST PORT—X—UNTIL THEN STAY WITH FLEET—X—IS ROUTE CAPE HORN, SUEZ, OR SOUTH AFRICA?—X—IMPRESSIONS OF RUSSIAN NAVY?—X— IMPRESSIONS OF ADMIRAL?—XXX

"Rooskies'll go by the African route," opined Rork. "More German colo-nies along the way where the Kraut colliers can be protected an' refuel the Rooskies."

Law disagreed. "And also British naval bases that entire way, Chief. I think the Cape Horn route is the one the Russians will take. No German or Brit colonies, except Falklands. Once they get into the Pacific, the Russians can stop at their French ally's coal depots at Tahiti, then New Caledonia, then at Saigon and Hué in French Indochina, before making the final dash to Vladivostok."

"Good point, Mr. Law, but I think not," I said. "The westerly winds will be strong against them at both Cape Horn and in the Straits of Magellan. Once in the Pacific, they'd have to go north up the Chilean coast with heavy beam seas to get beyond the latitudes of those winds, at least into the calmer latitudes in northern Chile, before turning west for Tahiti. The Japanese have spies, and maybe saboteurs, amongst their thousands of workers all over that area.

"With the constant mechanical breakdowns among some of these ships, they couldn't steam against the weather down in those Roaring Forties. Even the captains have little experience in that kind of weather. Suez route is through the Med, which is a British lake, so that's out. No, he'll go the African route, which is downwind and in calmer seas most of the way. And in addition to the German colonies in Africa, there are French colonies along that route also. Senegal, Gabon, Madagascar, French Indochina."

"We'll find out soon, sir. Tangiers is the decision point," said Law.

"If the Brits don't sink us first," muttered Rork. Though he'd never lost his boyhood Irish loathing of the British overlords in his county of Wexford, he now expressed a rare empathy with Britain's anger. "But methinks they damn well do have a right to be bloody angry on this. The Rooskies cocked this up royally. Just hopin' we aren't on this tub o' fools when the Limeys start shootin'—those pompous buggers'd love that kind o' bloody easy target practice."

Before I could reply, he lightened up, showing that boyish grin that endeared women to him. "An methinks right about now Tangiers'd be the perfect place for some liberty ashore." He winked at our Marine. "'Tis a Frenchie port, Mr. Law. An' I've fond memories o' those pretty ladies' hospitality from me own time there years ago. *Ooh la la.*"

I remembered too—Rork walking arm-in-arm down the pier with a pair of those ladies over a decade earlier. "Old friend, yes, you had a great time with those French girls back then, but you're an elderly fellow now and couldn't possibly handle them."

His retort was exactly as I knew it would be. "Maybe so, sir, but I'd fancy tryin'!"

It felt good to laugh again.

27

Impressions

We didn't know it at the time, but Tangiers was the Russians' last truly friendly port. The French governor and the Moroccan sultan welcomed the Russians openly and warmly, with formal dinners and balls. The waiting German colliers coaled all our ships efficiently and showed great camaraderie toward the Russians. The town's merchant elite treated us to banquets, receptions, demonstrations of Arab horsemanship, and tours of historical places. Provisions and supplies were loaded on board the ships, and liberty was granted to selected sailors.

Many on liberty ashore came back with exotic trinkets and even more exotic stories. Rork went with his senior petty officer friends and returned to *Suvorov* sporting a devilishly self-satisfied grin, reeking of cognac, and walking down the pier with a bit more sway.

Admiral Rozhestvensky made his fleet routing decision when he got to Tangiers. Late the next day, after spending twelve hours ashore, I replied to Roosevelt with answers to his earlier questions—and more.

—I NEVER SAW JAPANESE WARSHIPS AT DOGGER—X—TANGIERS FRENCH FRIENDLY TO RUSSIANS—X—GERMANS COALING & FRIENDLY—

X—DECISION IS RUSSIAN FLEET GOING VIA DAKAR GABON ANGOLA GERMAN SW AFRICA MAYBE CAPETOWN THEN MADAGASCAR INDO-CHINA OR DUTCH INDIES—X—1 SQUADRON SMALLER SHIPS GOING VIA SUEZ—X—OTHER SQUADRON OLD SHIPS LEAVING ST PETERSBURG SOON—X—HEAR BRITISH WAR SCARE POSSIBLY OVER—X—IMPRESSION THIS FLEET NOT COMBAT READY—X—ADMIRAL VERY CAPABLE—X—MET PERDICARIS NOT IMPRESSIVE—X—SULTAN COLD TO ME BECAUSE PERDI-CARIS CRISIS—X—FRENCH HERE VERY FRIENDLY TO ME—X—GERMANS SUSPICIOUS TOWARD ME—XXX

It was interesting to meet Perdicaris at a reception, and a bit of a letdown. He was an old man with theatrical gestures and flashing eyes, who clearly enjoyed being surrounded by European visitors to Tangiers demanding to hear his rather lurid story of being held hostage by a native bandit. He knew nothing of my role in his incident, of course, and I listened with amusement to his version of the incident, in which he was the star and little was said about the American role. At the end of this performance, Perdicaris announced he was moving his family to England, where such terrors were not common among civilized people. That got a round of applause. I was glad we Americans never ended up bleeding for him.

It was much less pleasant to meet the German consul at the same event. By his posture and forceful manner of speaking, he plainly had a military background, though I saw no dueling scar. I wondered how long he'd been posted in Tangiers but did not ask. He was quite interested in meeting me, asking about my previous interactions with Germans around the world, with an inference that he was already aware of them.

I responded with a smiling blatant lie. "I have many memories of gracious encounters with truly impressive German business gentlemen in the South Pacific, Latin America, and Europe. Your commercial and political expansion around the world is remarkable."

I am sure the reader understands why I thought it best not to include the fact that the Germans shot me in Samoa in '89 and conspired against me in Mexico in '92, and that I had stolen Germany's American invasion plans a couple months earlier. I did emphasize that the Kaiser and I had become close friends in Hamburg in July, and that I looked forward to my next visit with him.

His reaction was a curt bow, clicked heels, and a duplicitous smirk. "Yes, of course it is always a great honor for anyone to meet our Kaiser, even more to meet him again. But, Admiral, that would be well into the future. In the meantime, you will see the African part of our world empire on your coming journey with our Russian friends. Some of it is in very remote and dangerous places which few outsiders ever visit."

"I eagerly anticipate the opportunity to see your African possessions."

"Yes, Africa is fascinating. So beautiful for many, but so very unhealthy to some."

Then he abruptly turned and started speaking loudly to another German. It was a rude gesture, noticed by several of the French attendees who reacted disapprovingly. I walked over to the bar.

Two days after this exchange, Rear Admiral Dmitry Gustavovich von Fölkersam took five warships and several auxiliaries east through the British-dominated Mediterranean toward the Suez Canal. I'd met Fölkersam at Kronstadt and found him to be a very squared-away seaman who had a good reputation. He was definitely Rozhestvensky's best, and most trusted, subordinate commander. As Fölkersam and his captains departed the flagship following the final meeting, I pondered if we would ever see them again.

Two days after that, on the hot morning of 5 November, Admiral Rozhestvensky got the main body of the fleet under way and headed southwest along the coast of Africa, bound for the French colonial port of Dakar, in Senegal. So far in the voyage there had been many mechanical breakdowns, necessitating the entire fleet to stop or slow down to five knots while various ships repaired their engines. Upon leaving Tangiers, this bad luck and the admiral's notorious temper manifested yet again as the fleet weighed anchor. It had been planned as a grand departure and demonstration of naval skill in close-quarters shiphandling. It didn't turn out that way.

A supply ship named *Anadyr* got her anchor hooked on the transcontinental telegraph cable linking French West Africa and Europe. In a disgusted tirade, Rozhestvensky bellowed a blue streak of curses at *Anadyr*'s captain and ordered him to immediately cut the cable. No one on the bridge dared to suggest that might be unwise, and international telegraph communication was cut between the continents. That presented one more incident for politicians to blather about. I belatedly realized it also cut off my cable communication with Roosevelt, a disconcerting development.

An hour later it was the flagship's turn to be humiliated. Her steering engine broke down, jamming the rudder over in a hard-right turn. We barely missed hitting the problem child of the fleet, *Kamchatka*, which had begun the Dogger Bank fiasco. The entire formation was plunged into confusion until the engine was repaired and *Suvorov* could properly resume her position and lead the way. Beyond necessary but muted words, no one on the bridge spoke during this entire time, fearful of attracting unwanted attention, and possible physical attack, from their irate admiral. He stormed off the bridge, but the paranoia still held and no one relaxed. Law and Rork glanced at me to see my reaction to all this.

I did as everyone else and kept my gaze steadily on the sea ahead. However, I did find myself worried about a significant aspect of the upcoming transit. *If the Russians are like this now, how will they handle the tropical heat and humidity of Equatorial Africa and Asia?*

28
Bears in the Tropics

Dakar, French Senegal
Saturday, 12 November 1904

O nce we entered the anchorage, the sea breeze—which had provided a minimum of relief on the voyage southward along the coast—suddenly ended, cut off by the crude town sprawled along a small peninsula curving around the swamp-water-stained bay.

In the deathly still air, the thermometer inside *Suvorov's* bridge read 33.8 degrees Celsius, which meant it was 93 degrees Fahrenheit. The hygrometer measured the humidity at that same number. This combination had immediate effects. Heat radiated up in visible waves from the bay and the ship's weather decks. Cumulus clouds roiled up from the steaming land surrounding us, their bottoms dark gray-blue with rain. Sweat soaked a uniform in five minutes.

With binoculars, I examined the port captain's office almost a mile away. A faded French flag hung from a skinny bamboo pole in limp mockery of European authority. Native people on the waterfront moved slowly. No white people were in sight. Mules stood head drooped, and dogs hid in shade. Even the bumboat peddlers, in most ports annoyingly enthusiastic, rowed lethargically out toward us.

It was a depressing sight for the Russians. They knew they had many thousand more miles to go before leaving Africa astern. Everyone on the bridge, officers and men, loosened their collars and grumbled about the humid heat, comparing it to nostalgic visions of November in their snowy Russia.

I knew their discomfort was going to get worse, for it was only ten o'clock in the morning. *Welcome to the tropics. The bugs will eat your sunburned skin once the sun goes down.*

An hour later it was worse, but not just from the climate. When he finally arrived, the French port captain, attired in his evidently seldom-used formal uniform, had bad news. Gushing that he personally liked Russians and appreciated the visit, he announced that Paris sent a message prohibiting our refueling in French waters. It seemed France was no longer an enthusiastic friend of the Russian fleet, for the Japanese and the British had vigorously protested the provisioning and fueling of the fleet in French colonies, saying it violated international neutrality norms. The joys of Tangiers would be a memory, not a prelude to future French ports.

Looking at five German colliers anchored a half mile away, the port captain shrugged his apologies, saying he disagreed with the policy but was bound to carry it out. He also advised that European newspaper men were in the town, tipped off in advance that the Russians were coming.

The Frenchman did suggest solutions to the coaling prohibition, though: either refuel offshore, outside French waters; or steam to the Portuguese Cape Verde Islands, four hundred miles out in the Atlantic Ocean, and transfer the coal there. The admiral angrily replied there was no place to anchor and refuel outside the territorial waters near Dakar, that their refusal to allow alongside-coaling for Russian ships in the harbor was against international law, and that he had no intention of steaming four hundred miles to try to refuel in the open sea off the Cape Verde Islands.

The port captain said the cable link to Europe had been restored, and he would send a cable to Paris for instructions. The admiral replied that he would send one to Saint Petersburg. The port captain, with further profuse apologies, then departed, no doubt to give the reporters ashore an enhanced version of the conversation.

Rozhestvensky invited me out to the starboard bridge wing. His mood was considerably lighter as he asked, "Peter, do you see any French gunboats or modern shore batteries?"

"No, just that old crumbling wooden fort with what appear to be century-old cannon, which I doubt work." By the glint in his eye, I caught his intentions. "It appears there is no military force here to compel you to leave. And I suppose the authorities in Paris and Saint Petersburg will have several days of political consultations between the capitals."

"Exactly, my friend. And yet, right over there are the German colliers, patiently waiting for us. We'll start coaling in a few minutes and be gone before anyone in Europe decides what to even say in a cable to Africa."

I couldn't help grinning. "I like the way you think, Zinovy. And happy birthday."

"Thank you, on both accounts. Please come to my gathering at noon."

When I arrived at the birthday luncheon, I found an unusual surprise. Rozhestvensky's extramarital paramour was in attendance—Natalia Sivers was a beautiful thirty-year-old, blue-eyed, blonde nurse from the fleet's hospital ship, *Orel*. I'd heard of her presence and role and was surprised she was widely known and tolerated, even by the Orthodox priest-chaplain.

Semenov introduced me to her, and I found her charming, though a bit too giddy. With electric fans providing air movement and a string quartet playing balalaikas, the luncheon was a relatively pleasant affair, in spite of the heat. The most appreciated feature, apart from Natalia Sivers, was the consumption of gallons of ice-cold kvass, a favorite Russian beer-like drink. I had three of them. Outside the admiral's cabin, the German colliers were coming alongside and the entire crew, including all officers, was being mustered to load coal as fast as they could.

After the lunch, I met Rork and Law on the signal deck to watch the proceedings. We volunteered to help but were refused, citing our neutral status. All the Russians, even the admiral, were down on the deck helping, shoulder to shoulder with common sailors. It was a remarkable scene: badly sunburned, grunting Russians on dozens of ships in a sweltering African bay loading coal rocks, with clouds of suffocating black dust hovering around them; shouted orders in German and Russian; the clanking of cranes, and squealing of blocks and tackle. Equally remarkable was the rate of transfer: 120 tons an hour. In fact, the entire fleet coaling operation, 30,000 tons worth, was accomplished in twenty-nine brutal hours.

The toll was also significant. Coal and coal dust filled every nook and cranny of the ship. Food, drink, clothing—everything and everyone was turned black. Breathing through the cotton-waste stuffed into our noses and mouths was labored and sometimes impossible. Many sailors collapsed of heat exhaustion and several died, along with one lieutenant, a young noble who had a heart attack. His father was Russian ambassador to France. His mother was the patron of the *Orel*. The sailors were buried at sea. The lieutenant got a funeral with full naval honors at sunset, his body shipped home by the sympathetic port captain.

Throughout all this, the Russians never slowed in their loading—a phenomenal demonstration of strength and stamina. I began to understand Semenov's declaration about how the fleet would react when facing the Japanese in battle. They had little skill, but the sailors' courage and strength were indisputable. My estimation of Russian combat capabilities went up.

A few days later the fleet weighed anchor and headed south into the back of beyond.

29

The King, the Pygmy, and the Correspondent

Near Libreville, French Gabon
Saturday, 26 November 1904

The "port" of Libreville is just inside the nine-mile-wide mouth of the Gabon River. Though there is deep water in the river close to the town, we never brought our fleet into it. When we were still offshore, the French colonial governor sent us a written welcome, gifts of fruits and vegetables—and a prohibition from entering the Gabon, or even the colony's territorial waters. So we ended up anchored over three miles away from the river's mouth, out in international waters, where the water was still only sixty-feet deep. The German colliers, punctual as ever, anchored nearby. Coaling began, transferred this time by boats between the ships, a much slower process.

There was a cable connection in Libreville, but no cable reports or orders from Russian naval headquarters were waiting for us. However, there was war news. The Russian army in the Far East war zone had a new commanding general, the fighting still raged along the frontlines everywhere, and the defenses of Port Arthur were barely holding out. On the other side of Africa, Admiral Fölkersam's squadron had made it through the Med and the Suez Canal and was now in the Red Sea, heading for the French colony of Djibouti. A small detachment of the Black Sea fleet was in the Med, heading for Tangiers.

A new squadron was being formed back in Kronstadt of older and slower ships. This was the brainchild of Commander Nicolai Klado, a naval intelligence officer on Rozhestvensky's staff. Klado had been sent from Vigo, Spain, to Saint Petersburg to explain the Dogger Bank fiasco.

Once he arrived at the capital, he became a favorite strategist for the press, for which he wrote articles under the pseudonym "Priboi," promoting the idea that all Russian warships, even the slow and obsolete ones, be sent to reinforce Admiral Rozhestvensky, who should wait somewhere until all were united before steaming as a grand naval armada to the Far East to do battle with the Japanese. "Priboi" described in some detail the deficiencies of Rozhestvensky's fleet and his need for reinforcements, causing consternation among the readers. This angered naval leaders to the point that Klado was arrested, but the clamor over that was even worse. Eventually, he was released, had an audience with the Tsar, and, amazingly, convinced him to back the idea.

In my opinion, shared by Rozhestvensky, this idea was ludicrous. The fleet we had was the best in the Russian navy, but that wasn't saying much. Yes, our ships were in bad mechanical shape, and the progress of the fleet was frequently slowed to five knots by incessant breakdowns and repairs. But why would Russia send an even worse collection of elderly vessels? And how long would that take? Every day of delay enabled the Japanese to repair and refit their warships.

The admiral clenched his teeth and his fist but did not go further in his opinion. After all, that decision had been the Tsar's, and Rozhestvensky was a monarchist to the core. In any event, he had other problems, including several new intelligence reports of Japanese activity in the areas ahead of us. Some of these, the more general in nature, he discussed with me.

Were these discussions a skirting of my neutral status and a potential breach of Russian naval secrets? Yes, somewhat. But as the admiral explained, I was literally in the same boat, and my life on the line as well, so he thought I would be interested and might even offer a useful opinion because of my experience.

One report from an agent in South Africa said that a Japanese rear admiral named Sionogu had sailed a flotilla of Bombay-built fishing schooners armed with torpedo tubes to Durban, where they were cruising offshore, waiting for our arrival. This report was assessed to be entirely possible and quite deadly.

With threatening coincidence, the next day a cable arrived from Saint Petersburg informing the admiral that the British cautioned the Russians there was a large fishing fleet off South Africa and sarcastically warned there should be no repeat of the Dogger Bank disaster.

Rozhestvensky was not intimidated in the least. He sent a reply in plain language (so the Germans, French, British, and Russians along the international cable links could see it) that advised Saint Petersburg to ask the British to immediately warn all fishing boats in South African waters to stay out of the way of the approaching Russian fleet or they would be "sunk without mercy."

If nothing else, his message improved morale. When word got out among the fleet's officers and men, it was overwhelmingly greeted by roaring approval.

Another morale boost was the permission to finally visit ashore. Once the Russians actually came ashore, what they found didn't match their expectations. Libreville was a backwater collection of shanties, crumbling government shacks, and indolent people, both black and white. Nothing happened between ten in the morning and four in the afternoon. Even the local trollops were unappealing to the sailors. The place made Dakar look modern and gay.

The highlight ashore for the officers was a journey, in which we three Americans joined, by local steamboat up the river to the "palace" hut of a local African potentate, self-styled as a "king." This drunken oaf presented quite the majestic image: wearing various parts of an old British admiral's uniform, lounging about with his naked wives, and posing for photographs. While all this was going on, his retainers quietly begged money for the "royal household's treasury."

The Russians treated it like a visit to the zoo. Edwin Law's sensibilities were offended by the gratuitous nakedness. Rork was mildly amused by the absurdity. I thought it all a horrendous waste of time. Then, to top off the day, I encountered the Pygmy and the correspondent.

It was at the dock in Libreville while impatiently waiting for the steamboat to take us back to the ship. A short native wearing a burlap loincloth and feathers in his hair paddled his dugout past us down the river current. Suddenly, he pointed at me, laughing for a moment before shaking his head pensively and intoning some sort of chant.

"Ignore him, monsieur," offered a local black gendarme in the small crowd that had gathered to study us foreign *blancs* (whites), so different from the usual French *blancs*,

I was surprised by the policeman's English and asked, "Who is *he?*"

"Just a Babongo Pygmy, come down the river to the town from his tribe in the deep forest. He is a Bwiti shaman, high on iboga bark. It is nothing."

I had no idea what any of that meant, but the gendarme's tone seemed deceptively dismissive. There was something he wasn't telling me, so I insisted, "Very well, but what is he saying about me?"

The gendarme took in a breath, then said, "You have a death face, for you will soon die at the hands of another foreign *blanc* who is hunting you."

That made Rork angry. "Bloody awful hell, this whole place reminds me o' that damned Haiti. Let's get out o' here. Even that Rooskie tub is better than this."

The Babongo and his dugout were quickly swept out of sight around a curve. The gendarme walked away, as if he didn't want to be near us anymore. Suddenly, the three of us were standing there alone—or we thought we were.

Rork spotted him first, a pot-bellied white man in sweat-stained linen suit and disheveled straw hat, lurking behind a shack and watching us. His face was a vivid beet-red, with a week of beard. I noted the coat's right front pocket sagged with something heavy in it. Probably coins; maybe a weapon. He saw us observing him and waved. I didn't wave back. He approached.

"Hello there," he called out in a guttural English, which betrayed his German roots. "I am Richard Birke, a correspondent. You must be Rear Admiral Wake, of the American Navy. This is a great honor for me, sir."

I instantly went on alert. *How does he know who I am? Most locals think I'm Russian.*

"What newspaper do you write for, Herr Birke?" I asked, as Rork nonchalantly sauntered around to the rear of the German. Law closed up ranks beside me.

Birke didn't show surprise I recognized his nationality. Instead, he wiped sweat off his face. "I write for whoever pays me. Yes, I am German, but I write for French and English newspapers too. Right now, I am writing a story about the Russian voyage along the coast of Africa for *B.Z. am Mittag* in Berlin."

"Ah, a famous newspaper. Congratulations, Herr Birke. You must be well-connected and respected in the business."

He showed a small artificial smile. "Thank you, Admiral. Yes, I have worked for them before and know their leaders well, so they trusted me with this important assignment."

I nodded pleasantly in recognition of his achievement. "And how is their famous owner, Leopold Ullstein, doing these days?"

"Doing very well, Admiral. Very nice man. Likes my writing. Do you know him?"

Ah, ha! Got you. "Yes, I did—back when he was alive. Leopold died five years ago."

His fake smile disappeared. I went on. "So, now that we have established you are a liar and certainly are not a correspondent, exactly why are *you* here in French Gabon?"

His eyes darted quickly around the area. Then he made the mistake of reaching into that sagging coat pocket. From behind him, Rork's right hand seized Birke's, crushing it. The left arm's spike went up against the German's spine. Law pinned the man's left arm as Rork lifted a small revolver out of the pocket and jammed its muzzle into Birke's ear.

"Answer the admiral, Herr Kraut," murmured Rork. "An' be *very* careful to tell the truth."

I could smell Birke's terror as he said, "I swear . . . I am . . . just . . . a journalist. I did not know Ullstein died. I was reaching for my cigar, not my pistol."

"Captain Law, would you please search him, closely," I said.

He did and reported, "No cigar, sir. Just extra rounds for the revolver. Thirty-two caliber, some sort of French ladies' gun."

That was unusual, to say the least. "What kind of *German man* carries a French ladies' gun?" I wondered aloud to everyone.

"Not the self-respectin' kind," opined Rork with a disgusted shake of his head.

Law continued his inventory of Birke's pockets. "No note pad, or pen or pencil, sir. Some German and French money. Receipt from the Hotel Impériale in Libreville, dated yesterday for a Fritz Vogel. Ah, and here is a cable to Fritz Vogel in Libreville from the German consulate in Tangiers, dated yesterday.

The message is in five-digit numeric code. There is nothing in his pockets containing the name Richard Birke."

Germans used five-digit numeric codes. I shook my head. "Not very good tradecraft, Herr Vogel. Should've had something with the cover name on it. Who sent you this cable and where is your codebook?"

Rork pushed the spike in a bit more. Vogel was near tears. "I don't know. They are anonymous. I do not have a codebook—they gave me four different number groups to memorize. The real message in a cable is just the last two number groups. Everything else before that is false to mislead."

"Gendarme's coming back over here, sir," warned Law.

We didn't have much time. "What did the two different number groups in this cable mean in plain language, Fritz?"

I held the cablegram up to his eyes. He squinted, then said in a shaky voice. "The first one means 'Wake.' The second one means 'watch.' The other two number groups are not in this message."

As Law stepped away and headed for the gendarme, I asked, "What were those other two number groups and their meaning?"

Vogel almost collapsed. Rork held him up and whispered in his ear. "Fritzie, I really fancy killin' your ugly Kraut arse right here an' now. So answer the admiral, you bloody little bastard."

His answer was a desperate blubbering whine. "Nine two four six one means 'accidental.' Four five zero seven nine means 'death.' Please do not kill me. I am only a cargo broker who is out of work and needed money to get passage home. I only want to go home."

Law was now chatting with the gendarme, steering his attention away from us and toward some girls. I patted Vogel on his shoulder and said gently, "I want to believe you, Fritz. Who gave you these instructions? Describe him. And when and where was it?"

He took a deep breath. "In Tangiers, at some cheap hotel bar a week ago. It was a German I had never seen before. Small man in his fifties, moustache, spectacles, gray hair. He gave me no name. Just the four number groups, their meanings, and some money. Then he dismissed me. Please, in the name of Jesus do not kill me, sir. Please . . ."

Rork gave me an inquiring look, then glanced at the swift-moving Gabon River. It was the same thing I'd been thinking. Fritz Vogel was going to be lucky. We wouldn't kill him. But we would neutralize his effectiveness for a while. I nodded.

Vogel was abruptly propelled to the dock, Rork telling him, "We won't kill you, Fritzie. But we hope you can swim."

There was a splash. I saw him surface fifty feet down current. Then he was swept around the river's bend.

While Rork was screwing his India-rubber hand back over the spike, he mused, "How do ya figure that Pygmy fella knew a foreigner was comin' after you?"

"No clue, Rork. Maybe he's got some mystical Irish blood in him."

That got him laughing, and when Rork laughs, it's impossible not to join in. The inside joke is that Rork is "Black Irish" from County Wexford, with very diluted African Moorish blood from the Spanish Armada, the survivors of which landed there three centuries ago.

In a much better mood, we set off for Law and the gendarme. "The steamer won't be back for an hour. Let's buy this gendarme a drink, Rork," I suggested. "Suppose this dump has a decent watering hole?"

"Well, sir, if it does, sure as hell that copper'll know it. An' aye, I'm a wee bit glad we didn't kill that Kraut fool."

"Why Sean Aloysius Rork, I do believe you're getting sentimental in your old age."

He grinned. "Aye, sir. Must be the Irish in me. Suppose they got any decent rum here?"

The filthy bar didn't. And the next day we went back to sea, where it's much cleaner.

30
Portuguese Bravery

Great Fish Bay, Portuguese Angola
Tuesday, 6 December 1904

Forty miles south of Gabon, we crossed the Equator, always a day of celebration on a ship, especially warships. The Russians were no different, and on that day King Neptune, who looked suspiciously very much like the sailmaker, the oldest man on board, appeared on the flagship's bow, walked aft and up to the bridge, and formally seized the ship from the admiral. Then Neptune and his royal court marched around the ship. They included garishly made up, half-naked male concubine impostors, jesters, courtiers, devils, tritons, and a horrendous orchestra of clangs, off-tune horns, and drums.

Every pollywog (the Russians even used that English word, but it came out "polavog"), or sailor and officer who had never crossed the Equator before (including the chaplain-priest), was rounded up. Hundreds of them were subjected to mock trials and sentenced to humiliations. The final ordeal was being thrown blindfolded into a large canvas basin of seawater on the main deck, filthily clogged with galley slops. Afterward, Neptune's devils turned fire hoses on the entire assembly, Admiral Rozhestvensky being the first victim and me the second.

Then the eating and drinking began. As the reader by now knows full well, that is something the Russians have turned into a monumental test of strength and stamina. It was an exhilarating and exhausting day, and I saw the highest morale of the voyage among our sailors. The next day, the chaplain got his revenge, with Orthodox Christmas seasonal fasting and impossibly long-lasting full-dress-uniform High Masses, hymn singing, and chanting—all done in steaming tropical heat.

A thousand miles later, we entered southern Africa's coastal temperate zone of cooler temperatures and coastal deserts, arriving at the well-protected and fifteen-mile-long Great Fish Bay in Portuguese Angola. The admiral anchored the fleet out in the middle of the bay near the six-mile-wide entrance, a decision I did not understand at the time. German colliers were already there, and the calm waters were perfect for them to come alongside for rapid coaling. Signals were exchanged to begin that operation in an hour.

Surveying our surroundings with binoculars showed the only sign of human habitation was a small fishing village three miles away on the western shoreline. The terrain was nothing but sand desert; however, it did have one notable asset—many pink flamingoes along the beaches. The place was remote and sheltered. Perfect for our purpose.

It also had a man I would soon respect greatly: First Lieutenant Silva Nogueira, commanding officer of the tiny Portuguese navy river gunboat *Limpopo*. Within minutes of our hooks dropping, *Limpopo* set a large national ensign and steamed from the village, through the fleet, and right to the flag-ship. As the senior Portuguese officer present, he was received on board with honors and shown immediately to the admiral on the bridge. The ensuing conversation was conducted in that common language of the sea, English. After introductions and respects were made, Nogueira got right down to business.

"Good afternoon to you all and welcome to Portuguese Angola, sovereign territory of our gracious and beloved Carlos Fernando Luís María Victor Miguel Rafael Gabriel Gonzaga Xavier Francisco de Assis José Simão, King of Portugal."

All the Russians respectfully bowed their heads for a moment and the lieutenant went on.

"As you know, sir, Portugal is neutral in your war with Japan, and you have anchored in our territory. So it is with regret and with respects, I must order you to leave right now. I cannot permit loading of fuel, water, or provisions. You have my best wishes for a safe voyage, sir."

Rozhestvensky bestowed a paternal smile on the lieutenant and gently said, "I beg to differ, Lieutenant. We are not anchored in Portuguese territory. We are more than three miles from the shore in any direction."

Nogueira didn't like being toyed with and raised his voice. "But sir! You are anchored in the middle of our bay!"

The admiral maintained his calm. "In this respect we can only thank the Lord that He made the entrance of the bay wider than six miles, and in that area between the two strips of Portuguese territorial waters—the neutrality of which is, of course, sacred to me—the good Lord has placed a narrow strip of international sea, open and accessible to all seafarers."

Smoldering, Lieutenant Nogueira puffed up his chest and informed the admiral that, in that case, he would be compelled to expel the Russians by force, if necessary. Several officers barely repressed open laughter at the thought of *Limpopo* and her 3-pounder gun shooting at the Russian fleet.

The admiral was more kind. "I appreciate your visit Lieutenant, and if you really insist, we look forward to your attack. Good day."

Nogueira's last words were, "I shall return with reinforcements!" Rozhestvensky shrugged. The young Portuguese officer executed a left face and marched off the bridge. Ten minutes later, his little gunboat was steaming the 250 miles south to Mossâmedes, the nearest place with a telegraph station.

After watching *Limpopo* receding in the distance for a moment, the admiral said, "That lieutenant is a brave and honorable gentleman. I hope he has a successful career."

Then he turned to his staff captain and gave orders, which a delighted Semenov translated for me. "Begin coaling at once. We will weigh anchor tomorrow and steam south to German South West Africa, where they should be considerably more friendly!"

With a lighthearted wave to his men, the admiral left the bridge. The spirits of everyone around me rose to the point of glee with the prospect of finally entering a port friendly to the Russian sailors, for Germany was their friend.

I, however, wasn't smiling.

31

Teutonic Africa

Angra Pequena (Lüderitz), German South West Africa
Sunday, 11 December 1904

After slogging against massive southwest swells and gale-force winds for a thousand miles over four days, we arrived at the German colony under a noonday sun. Amazingly, there were few mechanical break-downs en route—in those conditions, they might have been much more dangerous. Since the latitude was twenty-six degrees south of the Equator, we were emerging from the tropics and the Southern Hemisphere weather was spring-like, clear and warm. Lüderitz was a change from our previous ports, in many more ways than just the weather. Large whales swam near us, an albatross flew overhead, and penguins watched from shore, these alien animals in such an alien land enchanting the Russians.

The fleet anchored in the middle of Angra Pequena Bay, a four-mile-long by one-mile-wide stretch of water the gale was making very rough. The outer bay is separated from the calm inner bay of Robert Harbor and the small settlement of Lüderitz by a peninsula improbably named Shark Island. The shorelines around us were thirty- to fifty-foot rocky cliffs, which then morphed into gray-brown inland rock-sand desert. I saw no quaintness or charm in the stark vista around me.

The first thing I noticed ashore was an absence of trees, the color green, and black people. Then I surveyed Shark Island and saw a group of a hundred or more African natives staring out at the Russian fleet filling the bay. Closer scrutiny showed the Africans were women and children surrounded by barbed wire and armed guards.

Admiral Rozhestvensky's staff captain, who had gone ashore to meet the local authorities, walked into the bridge at that moment and saw me looking at the shore through binoculars.

"Concentration camp," he informed me. "From the war against the natives, the Hereros. The Germans told me there will soon be thousands in there. They are going to either exterminate or exile them."

His comment brought to mind a *New York Times* newspaper account I'd read back in May, describing the German colonial war against the natives in far-off Africa. It turned out the natives were more sophisticated than originally estimated and were winning the conflict against the local German militia until Berlin sent thousands more regular troops under a commander who promised there would be no quarter given and the Hereros would cease to exist.

Beside me, Rork glared at the camp and muttered, "Like the Limey camps for Boers four years ago, an' the Spaniardo camps for Cubans six years ago. Imperial bastards'll never learn—they're just makin' generations o' permanent enemies."

The chief of staff wasn't used to petty officers commenting to senior officers on such matters. With a disapproving harrumph, he switched topics. "The senior German officer of this remote area is only a major, but he is very pleasant and hospitable."

"Well, that's a nice change after the last couple of ports," I offered.

He chuckled. "Yes, quite a change, Admiral. The major said that he is just a soldier, knows nothing about naval matters or international law, and cannot even see us from his office in Lüderitz. He also has no warship, or even a patrol boat, and therefore he cannot do anything about us even if he knew what to do! So we are free to do anything and enjoy the town. Yes, indeed, a very agreeable chap. So different from our supposed friends and allies, the French! I invited him for lunch tomorrow." Then he was off to report to his admiral.

The German colliers had anchored close by, and coaling by small boat commenced at once, a slow and dangerous job in that rough anchorage. The next day the Russians greeted the slightly seasick major with all the pomp and ceremony due an imperial viceroy, complete with gun salute, and ushered the overwhelmed fellow into the admiral's quarters with great flourish. I had not gone ashore for reasons obvious to the reader, but Semenov insisted I attend the luncheon on board.

Rozhestvensky's inner sanctum was decorated with German and Russian flags, the ports opened to allow cool air to ventilate the room, and the place was filled with the thunderous bonhomie only Russians can provide. Now on his third vodka and recovered from the boat ride, the major basked in it all, happily conversing in German and English with his Russian hosts.

Then he saw me and stopped cold.

I recognized him too. His face was indelibly imprinted in my mind. He was the artillery lieutenant I'd had in my sights—at a range of only ten feet—in the fight at Fugalei Swamp in Samoa fifteen years earlier. As I let him walk past my ambush, he spotted me and our eyes locked, but we opened fire on the rest of his column before he could raise an alarm. I'd thought he was shot in the melee and probably dead.

The major recovered his wits before I did and stepped up to me. "Ach, I heard there was an American naval officer with the Russians. Come ashore for lunch and we can talk of Samoa."

The Russians, ignorant of my hidden past with the major, thought this was an outstanding idea and back-slapped both of us. But the German wasn't acting cheery anymore. He stood there staring at me, waiting. At that moment I realized his plan: to challenge me to a duel when we were alone ashore and kill me. The Russians sensed something was wrong and grew quiet.

"I think not, Major," I replied. "I still have bad memories of Samoa, but I am glad you survived. In fact, I am no longer hungry now, so I will leave all of you to your merriment. I insist you have a wonderful time! Good day, gentlemen."

As I exited, the party started up again. It went on all day and a very drunk German major rode that launch back to shore at sunset, to the sounds of the band playing the German national anthem and the crews cheering him from aloft. Very heady stuff for an officer stuck in the back of beyond. The next morning in the senior officers' mess the major's party was the talk of the table. Spirits were up. The Germans were true friends. The fleet was getting more efficient. We would soon be around the bottom of Africa and in yet another exotic place most Russians had never visited, French Madagascar in the Indian Ocean.

Then a British steamer anchored in the bay and a recent newspaper from Cape Town was sent over. It had the latest war news, which circulated around the ship like wildfire.

Port Arthur, and the few remaining Russian ships there, had been heavily bombarded from Japanese positions atop Vissokaya Hill, which overlooked all the Russian positions. Thinking of his comrades still there, Semenov quietly said that was that—now that Vissokaya was in Japanese hands, the forts, city, and ships were doomed. It was just a matter of time. The other news was that Admiral Fölkersam's squadron had been attacked by Japanese warships in the Red Sea. Damage and casualties were unknown. The war news had a sobering effect on everyone.

Full of coal again, we got under way a few days later. From behind the barbed wire, the Africans of Shark Island prison camp silently watched us steam out of the bay. Those faces still haunt me. Rounding the point, the fleet plunged back into those large cold seas from the southwest, bracing itself, literally and figuratively, for whatever lay ahead.

Admiral Rozhestvensky invited me to dinner that night. After the dessert of medovik honey and sour cream sponge cake, accompanied by a very nice French cognac, he regarded me with a bemused expression. "So Peter, were you and our friendly German major foes once? I do not recall America and Germany ever fighting a war."

A little truth was called for, but not much. "Yes, Zinovy, we were foes many years ago, on the far side of the world. And no, it was not in a formally declared war. Beyond that, I cannot go further."

He smiled sympathetically. "In your days as a secret operative in the shadows?"

What does he know? I shrugged, changing the subject. "Madagascar is about 2,500 miles away. Will you refuel in Cape Town or Durban?"

"I know you planned to disembark at our intended stop at Cape Town. Of course, you want to go home to your lovely wife—and having met the lady,

I completely understand that. But our plans have changed. We have enough coal and will press on, past the British spies at Cape Town, the clandestine Japanese torpedo schooners at Durban, and your chance to go home. Do you understand the operational necessity?"

"Yes," was all I could muster right then.

The Russian sighed. "My dear friend, war is a cruel master for men like you and me."

His philosophic comment didn't help a bit, for my heart had sunk. *María . . . What will she think?*

Following the dinner, Law and Rork met me in my stateroom. Law reacted to my news in his usual quiet deadpan manner, simply saying, "Aye, sir," albeit a bit pensively as his mind chewed over it over.

Rork's response was anything but deadpan. "Bloody friggin' hell! The Nips've got spies every damn place in the Indian Ocean. They'll sure as hell find these Rooskie tubs at Madagascar. This fleet's bollocks up the whole operation somethin' fierce an' it's gonna be a bloodbath when the damned Nips do find it. We need to get our wrinkled *old* arses off this ship an' head back home!" He took a breath, then added calmly, "Me achin' bones're seventy weary years old, sir."

I knew he was really seventy-three but didn't mention it. Rork was sensitive on the subject, afraid of being thought too old and useless. The Navy officially listed him as sixty-three. When conversing with ladies, he usually gave his age as sixty.

"I'll figure out a way, Rork," I said, having no idea how. Madagascar had been officially French for only a few years—they were still fighting the locals to "pacify" them—and had very few modern services, and no regular steamer service connecting it to Europe or America, or anywhere else. And since the Suez Canal had opened forty years earlier, even the South African steamer route had dwindled.

I didn't want us to be stuck in, of all places, Madagascar.

32
Stunned Silence

Sainte Marie Island, French Madagascar
Thursday, 29 December 1904

It took two weeks and a miserable, storm-racked voyage to the south, the east, then around to the north toward Madagascar. On the twenty-fifth, off the southern capes of Africa, the three of us (the only non-Orthodox Christians on board *Suvorov*) celebrated Western Christmas with dinner in my stateroom. We invited Semenov, and the four of us gathered for a storm-tossed meal of stew and vodka.

I began by intoning the first verse of *The Sailors' Hymn*, which I thought quite appropriate in the circumstances, with water sloshing across the deck as the ship crashed and shuddered every minute or so as she collided with the next mountainous wave. "Eternal Father, strong to save, whose arm hath bound the restless wave. Who bidd'st the mighty ocean deep, its own appointed limits keep. Oh, hear us when we cry to Thee, for those in peril on the sea . . ."

After dinner, there were vodka-augmented toasts to Tsar Nicholas II, President Roosevelt, and Admiral Rozhestvensky, all which we wisely drank sitting down in the American and British custom.

For the finale, Rork shared a traditional Celtic blessing for the future. "May God go before you to defend you, come behind to protect you, and go beside you to befriend you. May God go beneath you to uphold you, rest above you to bless you, and dwell within you to comfort you." Then, with the bottle gone, my guests slowly made their way back to their quarters.

That was our Christmas of 1904. The whole time I thought of María at our home, alone.

Four days after our Western Christmas celebration, the fleet dropped anchor off the old pirate lair island of Sainte Marie, on the northeast coast of eight-hundred-mile-long Madagascar in the Indian Ocean. We were now back up in the hot, humid tropics. This was where the squadron under Admiral Fölkersam, or survivors of it, were to rendezvous with us. But they weren't in sight. In fact, the only thing that was in sight was a native village with an unpronounceable name on the jungled shoreline. That was it. No German colliers, no real town, and not even a calm anchorage. We sat there and slowly rolled in the swells.

Obviously, the French government in Paris, which had assigned this out-of-the-way locale to the Russians, wanted them out of view and mind. From *Suvorov*'s navigator I learned the original destination was to be Diego Suarez, an excellent protected anchorage at the northern end of Madagascar, but the French had bowed to British and Japanese pressure and changed us to a place nobody in the Russian fleet had ever seen, heard of, or had a chart for.

Saint Petersburg had bowed to the French decision. An irate Rozhestvensky sent the fleet tug *Rus* to the nearest place with a telegraph station, Tamatave, over eighty miles away. His caustic message home to the armchair strategists would get attention, but I doubted it would get action.

The next day was a blur of activity. *Malay*, one of the most problematic of the ships, finally arrived after many breakdowns. The hospital ship *Orel*, with the admiral's paramour on board, arrived from Cape Town where, because the vessel was a noncombatant, she was treated civilly. Two colliers arrived the next day and began transferring coal by boat.

Rus returned with quite a lot of war news. Fölkersam's squadron was fine—there had been no attack—and was heading for the island of Nosy Be on Madagascar's northwest coast by order of naval headquarters in Saint Petersburg. Admiral Rozhestvensky received orders from Saint Petersburg to also head for Nosy Be immediately, meet Fölkersam's ships there, and wait for the obsolete Baltic squadron still forming in Russia under Rear Admiral Nikolai Nebogatov, which wouldn't be departing for several weeks. He was also informed that a Japanese squadron of eight cruisers and twelve torpedo boats had been sighted passing Ceylon on a course for Madagascar.

But even more disturbing news was shared. Port Arthur had fallen to the Japanese, with 23,000 more Russian soldiers now in prisoner-of-war camps. Worse still, open rebellion was sweeping across Mother Russia, and chaos reigned everywhere. Both disasters were almost incomprehensible to many of the officers on board *Suvorov*. They sat at dinner that evening in stunned silence, no one daring to speak aloud what was in their hearts.

Two days later, the fleet began the six-hundred-mile voyage to the other side of Madagascar and the badly charted island called Nosy Be. Rozhestvensky was in a foul mood, indeed, as he grudgingly followed his Tsar's orders.

33

Our Descent into Hell-Ville

Hell-Ville, Nosy Be Island, French Madagascar
Monday, 9 January 1905

On Saturday, January seventh, the fleet was halfway around the top of Madagascar. That day was Russian Orthodox Christmas, and all ships slowed to fire a salute, observe Christmas Mass, and assemble for their captains' speeches.

On board *Suvorov*, Admiral Rozhestvensky emerged from his previous state of ill temper with a gracious smile for everyone. A hush came over the flagship as he began to address the officers and crew. Standing on the after upper deck and looking down in semi-divine benevolence on us all on the after deck, he started out in a level baritone, gradually building in volume and inflection.

As he spoke I surveyed the Russians around us. Every one of them was intently listening to every word from the admiral. All showed respect, most reflected devotion, many had tears. Even those few rumored to be anarchists were enthralled. Their trust in *their admiral* was obvious. The Tsar was a distant figure. For these sailors, *Rozhestvensky* was Russia.

Semenov translated the admiral's final words for me: "Our task is heavy, our goal is distant, and our enemy is strong. But always remember the whole of Russia is looking upon you with confidence and firm hope. May God help us to serve her honorably, to justify her confidence, not to deceive her hopes. *To you, whom I trust! To Russia!"*

Rozhestvensky picked up a glass of vodka in his hand and gulped it down, then held it high over his head. The men roared. It was a deep throated, menacing crescendo such as I've seldom seen. Caps were thrown into the air and the mass of men pushed forward to be nearer their admiral. Voices called out, "Lead us!" "We will do it!"

Semenov turned to me, his usually chiseled face filled with emotion. "Oh, if only we could go into action now."

All hands got a double ration of vodka a few minutes later at their eleven o'clock issue (and again before their evening meal), the upbeat mood staying strong as we picked up speed and steamed toward our Russian comrades at Nosy Be.

Rork told me after the speech, "This Rooskie admiral did it up right. A real sailor talkin' to real sailors, sir, an' the lads knew he meant it. 'Twas worthy o' Nelson afore Trafalgar."

That was rare high salty praise, indeed. Unfortunately, the flagship's elation only lasted another day at sea. By the time fleet arrived at Nosy Be on January ninth, Admiral Fölkersam's detachment had been anchored there for two weeks. The contrast between the two groups of sailors was blatantly apparent.

In that time, the island and inhabitants had been completely transformed from sleepy backwater village to raunchy liberty port offering every kind of vice dreamed of by sailors. It made Naples and Hong Kong look tame. It was the kind of place captains have dreaded for hundreds of years, where good crews descend into surly mobs.

Prostitutes from across Madagascar had made their way to Nosy Be, along with gamblers, liquor brokers, trinket sellers, dope peddlers, thieves, exotic animal dealers, meat and vegetable contractors, coal salesmen, and all other manner of piratical shysters and camp followers. The shanties of the village were now surrounded by hastily put-up bamboo huts adorned with signs in French and even Russian Cyrillic, promising discounts on everything—and everyone—inside. The increase in people had not been accompanied by the necessary sanitation; the stench was nearly gagging.

To top it all off, the main village was called Hell-Ville, after some aristocratic French admiral half a century earlier whose name actually was Anne Chrétien Louis de Hell.

Fölkersam had made a major mistake, allowing liberty for a mass of white uniformed men who lurched from hut to hut along the waterfront, native girls in brief attire clinging to them (and their money). The entire throng was a cacophony of raucous shouts and laughter, strange music, donkeys braying and cattle lowing, and shouts from officers, to which nobody paid attention. Several sailors appeared comatose or dead on the ground at the main dock, and a fight broke out at one of the larger huts. The bay was covered with parasitical bumboats.

I learned that Fölkersam had been ill for a while and the junior officers had lost control of their liberty parties early on. Fölkersam's captains were mainly focused on repairing and refitting their ships after the 10,000-mile ordeal to get there. Engines, boilers, and shafts were disassembled for maintenance, and none of the ships were ready to get under way.

Rork shook his head in wonder at the scene ashore. "Oohee, a better named place I've never seen in all me days. An' if *Suvorov*'s lads ever get ashore, they'll lose all their naval discipline an' morale they got from the admiral two days ago."

Law's face was grim. "A platoon of United States Marines would straighten out that mess in ten minutes, sir."

I tried to sound optimistic. "Admiral Rozhestvensky will put an end to all this."

It would be another week or two, at least, before Fölkersam's ships would be able to steam away from Nosy Be. That was the optimistic estimate. Others thought it could be a month. Meanwhile, the entire newly assembled fleet would stay at Hell-Ville—deteriorating from lethargic humidity, lack of gunnery and maneuver practice, tropical and venereal diseases, wounds from fights ashore, and general breakdown of discipline.

There were also rumors that, now that Port Arthur was gone, the fleet was not going to head to the Far East but would stay in the Indian Ocean and await peace negotiations, or just head home to Saint Petersburg. No one knew for sure.

I, however, had no intention of us staying with them, whatever their plans. A plan had been germinating in my head, but it would require a couple of days to implement.

My men and I met for our daily discussion of developments with the ship, officers, and crew. After what we saw from the main deck that morning, I could see Rork and Law probably anticipated a discussion of discipline and efficiency, but today's topic was going to be different.

"We will be leaving the fleet here. But it will be difficult," I started. Their eyes lit up. "There is no regular steamer service anywhere in Madagascar, so we can't count on that. I do have an idea about transport, though. It's . . . unconventional."

Rork looked at the Marine with a grin. "Oohee, Captain Law. Methinks there's skullduggery an' maybe larceny afoot, an' we're just the lads to pull it off!"

I resumed. "Yes, well, more about that in a moment. We haven't been able to send a cable to Washington since Dakar, and we're long overdue, so the first thing we need to do is update the president on our situation, and request permission to leave the Russian fleet. The only cable station with overseas contact is forty miles south of here, at Majunga. It goes to Portuguese Mozambique in Africa. In two hours, Admiral Rozhestvensky is sending the tug *Rus* there to send his reports to Saint Petersburg, and I have permission to send mine along also. Rork, please encipher this right away and get it to Semenov."

XXX—GERMANS APPARENTLY KNOW ABOUT INVOICE—X—GERMAN TRIED KILLING ME AT GABON—X—GERMAN AT LUDERITZ REMEMBERED ME FROM SAMOA & TRIED LURING ME ASHORE—X—ALL WELL THO—X—FLEET BETTER BUT NOT COMBAT READY—X—NOW AT HELLVILLE ON NOSY BE ISLAND IN MADAGASCAR—X—FOLKERSAM SHIPS IN BAD REPAIR—X—ENTIRE FLEET ORDERED WAIT FOR OBSOLETE BALTIC SQUADRON MONTH OR MORE—X—RUMOR NEXT PORT IS GERMAN EAST AFRICA & FLEET WILL GO HOME WITHOUT BATTLE—X—USELESS TO STAY WITH FLEET—X—UNLESS OTHERWISE DIRECTED WILL CARPE DIEM INNOVATIVE TRANSPORT TO SINGAPORE AND HOME—XXX

I had no intention of waiting for presidential permission.

34
Carpe Diem

Rork and I went ashore in shabby, cheap suits that afternoon, the better to blend in with the locale. Since our first view of Hell-Ville from the flagship, I'd had a feeling a certain type of entrepreneur could be found there. Almost every seacoast has them.

Portraying ourselves as just two more of the newly arrived villains on the island, we started having a drink in various "establishments" along the farthest edge of the waterfront. At the fourth place, a rickety bamboo hut with the grandiose sign "le Club des Messieurs" (The Club of Gentlemen), we hit paydirt, hearing about just the sort of entrepreneur we needed.

Over our second rotgut fake brandy we learned his name was Allard Martin and that he lived in a hut on the beach at Baie des Voleurs—Thieves Bay—three kilometers to the east, under the brooding mantle of Lakoba Mountain.

We set out walking on the path that circles the island. The air was muggy with the scent of coming rain, and before long the journey became an ordeal. Rork began to complain until I reminded him the brandy we had hadn't helped and, by the way, we were old men now. The windless deluge of warm rain, with perfect timing, arrived at that point. An hour later it was gone and the land around us steamed. Two very long hours, and far more than three kilometers, after that we finally spotted the hut on the beach, in reality a thatched lean-to, maybe forty feet from the water. Sitting cross-legged in front was a shaggy-faced man dressed in a rag shirt, trousers cut off at the knee, and a palm-weave hat. He was gazing out at sea like some sort of Hindu maharishi, apparently in a trance.

While Rork studied the surrounding jungle for threats, I walked up to the man and politely asked, "Monsieur Martin?" No answer. I tried again. "Parlez-vous anglais, monsieur?"

He abruptly came out of his spell and stared up at me. "Of course. Those pompous Angie bastards made us speak English back in Quebec."

He spoke with the quaint accent and resentful tone I remembered from French Canadians I'd met during my youth on schooners along the coast of New England, New Brunswick, and Nova Scotia. I remembered the "Angie" epithet for English Canadians, too. And the fact that Québécois didn't much like us Yankees either.

I ignored his latent anger. "I want to take passage in your schooner to Mauritius."

"What schooner? Why do you think I have a schooner?"

"Françoise at the club told me. She said you make *unofficial* trips to other islands."

"Which one? The young pretty Françoise, or the old haggy one?"

That was a trick to see if was bluffing. I never saw a pretty girl at that bar. "Older one."

"She talks too much. Why you want to go?" he growled, remaining seated on the sand.

"I need to leave Nosy Be quietly and get to Mauritius where I can catch a steamer to Singapore. There will be three of us. I want to leave in four days."

"Four days, eh? Next run is in two weeks. Them two others Yankees like you?"

"Yes."

Martin scrutinized me carefully as he said, "That voyage is very rough—nine hundred miles against the southeast trade winds. That is a two-week run at least. Also, this is the worst time of cyclone season here. Extremely dangerous. The waves and wind will be very high. You will be violently seasick. Maybe you will die of seasickness. I will not care if you do."

"No, we won't be seasick."

He harrumphed. "Ha! Even I will be sick! Only the dead are not sick on that voyage. The cyclone danger makes the price go up. The price will be very high."

"How much?"

He kept me in his sights, clearly gauging my worth. This was a game I'd played many times with scoundrels around the world. The trick is to wait without flinching, eyes and voice totally without emotion. He finally announced, "250 British pounds each, in gold sovereign coins. Up front, because I do not trust you."

"You are far too rich for me, Monsieur Martin. The usual cost would be 50 a man. I can pay $100 for each man in ten American $10 gold coins. That's thirty gold coins in total. Fifteen when we start the voyage and fifteen when we arrive. If that is too low for you, I can go elsewhere. Perhaps Capitaine Morisseau on the other side of Nosy Be Island would like to make some money? I will go ask him now."

I, of course, had never met Morisseau. It was merely a name mentioned to me in one of the bars as a possible man who could help me. But my ploy struck a nerve.

"Morisseau is a fool," said Martin. "He will take your money, then sink halfway there. How do I know you are not in the payment of the French authorities?"

"You won't—until we get to Mauritius and I give you the final fifteen gold coins."

"It takes preparation for such a voyage. A gold $10 coin now, for goodwill and to show you really have them. Then, you pay $125 per man. All paid when we set sail."

"A hundred twenty per man is my limit. Three hundred sixty is the total. Half is eighteen coins when we get on the schooner and set sail, and the last half when we arrive at Mauritius. One American coin now—a $1 coin—for goodwill. My time today is short for such squabbling over prices, so decide now or I will visit Morisseau."

Martin shook his head, his bushy beard waving back and forth as he theatrically moaned up at me, "You are very cruel to an old man." Another moan. "Very well, Yankee, I agree to the deal, and will be glad to see the last of you at Mauritius. What is your name?"

I kept my face impassive. "John Smith."

Martin let out an evil little laugh. "Oh yes, and mine is Allard Martin." Then he rattled off the details. "I will meet you at that club in two weeks at ten o'clock on Tuesday evening, the thirty-first of January. Bring only what you can carry in your hands, and be ready to get wet. Very wet."

"Good. Two weeks. See you then. Au revoir, monsieur." We did not shake hands. Instead, I put the dollar in his hand and walked away.

Rork trailed behind me, still carefully watching Martin and the area. When we got back to the path and turned around for a last look, we saw Martin use two sticks to slowly raise himself up off the beach, then hobble over to his hut.

As we walked away, Rork muttered, "Damned if he ain't a nasty little bastard to trust our lives with."

That's what I was thinking too. It was a long walk back to Hell-Ville.

35
Bad News

Hell-Ville, Nosy Be Island, French Madagascar
Wednesday, 25 January 1905

As we Americans quietly bided our time over the next two weeks, Admiral Rozhestvensky descended into an ever-worsening temper. His frustrations and rage boiled over frequently with his officers and men. Everyone, including me, avoided him. But the litany of bad news couldn't be hidden from the admiral, or anyone else.

First, the heretofore efficient German colliers of the Hamburg-America Line never arrived. It seemed a regional manager refused to off-load their coal to Russian ships anywhere in the Indian or Pacific oceans, due to the cancellation of insurance because of the war risk. A flurry of telegrams flew back and forth to Saint Petersburg and Hamburg. The company released colliers already contracted to head for Nosy Be. Future collier contracts were "being considered," and the price was going up.

Nebogatov's contingent of Baltic ships had been separated into two divisions. The first division's departure from Saint Petersburg had been delayed again, and they didn't leave until the twentieth of January, with an estimated time of arrival in Djibouti in mid to late February, and in Nosy Be in early

March. The second unit of ships would not leave Russia until May. Thus, Rozhestvensky's fleet would sit waiting at Hell-Ville until April at least.

Fölkersam's ships were still not ready. The estimated time of availability was now mid-February. I suspected intentional work slowdowns among the crews and maybe the officers. It was suggested by some they should limp home to Saint Petersburg instead, since they considered the war already lost.

Rear Admiral Fölkersam's illness was worse than originally thought, and the doctors didn't think he would get better. In fact, he was deteriorating. It was a heavy blow for Rozhestvensky to realize his most competent subordinate admiral would not be able to take over if he fell in battle. He tried to keep the seriousness of Fölkersam's condition quiet, for that would further decline the fleet's morale.

Rozhestvensky himself had suffered some sort of stroke from the stress and was now trying to rehabilitate. He looked much older, haggard really, and slightly dragged his right foot. He again asked Saint Petersburg for a replacement to be sent out immediately, suggesting two candidates he thought could lead the fleet. His request was declined by order of the Tsar.

After Rozhestvensky's arrival at Nosy Be, Fölkersam's crews had been restricted from shore leave, the gambling parlors and most bars were closed, all locals were banned from ships. Only a few of Rozhestvensky's most trusted men were allowed ashore—where they still got into trouble. On the ships, there was resentment over the lack of liberty ashore. Drunkenness and open surliness increased. Several vessels were on the verge of mutiny.

The climate rapidly sapped energy and morale. Tropical diseases spread. *Orel*, the hospital ship, was valuable in isolating and treating the sick. But by now the relationship between Rozhestvensky and Natalia Sivers was commonly known and resented by many.

And, finally, the fleet's French hosts were growing more and more ungracious. Paris made no attempt to hide their worry over how long the Russians were staying, constantly suggesting they should head to German East Africa instead. But the Germans there, surrounded by British colonies, didn't want the Russians either.

On a personal note, a letter from María, dated two months earlier in November, arrived in the fleet's mail bag. So far she'd gotten none of my six letters mailed from Vigo, Tangiers, Dakar, Gabon, Lüderitz, or Hell-Ville. María's summary of happenings between our last communication by cable in early September and November was extensive, but notably without her usual number of personal endearments.

Dear Peter,					*28 November 1904*

Did you get my letter from 15 September, written right after my arrival home? Or my seven letters after that? Why do I not hear from you? The newspapers tell us the Russians are in various places in Africa. Are you sick somewhere? Are Sean and Edwin well and still with you? Please send a letter or cable when you get this.

Theodore won his election. The press says it is the most overwhelming election in U.S. history. I still do not understand the electoral college voting, but that seemed to be paramount and Theodore won in a "landslide." Theodore says that gives him a lot of political influence to get things done in Congress. He and Edith have had me over for dinner at the White House three times since my return from Hamburg, and each time he tells me how very valuable the German plans were in formulating foreign policy and updating U.S. defenses and thanks me profusely. A little too profusely. I think he feels bad for ordering you to go with the Russian fleet. He told me you would soon be home from Cape Town, and said he had received cable reports from you in October from Africa. But he said he had not heard anything for a month. He looked worried, then quickly said all would be well. Why have I gotten nothing at all this whole time?

Autumn has been cold and wet so far, and the farmers say it will be a frigid winter. I fixed the gutter myself and also piled and burned the leaves. The flowers are all gone now and the trees getting bare and forlorn-looking. I feel the same way.

Our family cheered me up. We gathered for a nice Thanksgiving four days ago. Useppa, Mario, and little Peter and Linda took the train up from Tampa. Our son Sean was transferred to Washington in October and assigned to the ordnance depot at the Navy Yard, He came to dinner with his delightful wife, Filipa (remember, she is from Cebu, in the Philippines), who announced she is going to have a baby in May—the family is growing!

My Juanito had been assigned to the Spanish embassy to Canada and was en route there via Washington, so he also came to the big dinner.

It was a grand afternoon, with the girls helping (with no argument from me!) cook the turkey and all the side dishes. Everyone said the family prayer you usually lead, and added you, Sean, and Edwin to it. The weather here in Alexandria was blessedly perfect on that day (it is raining today), so we all sat on the porch for our pumpkin pie dessert (I made three and they were all eaten), and several bottles of very nice California Bordeaux, as we watched the children and dogs play in the garden. But there was a big hole in the celebration—you were gone. Everyone asked about you when they arrived. I could not tell them anything. Sean looked very surprised and concerned when I said I had no idea of where or how you were, other than the newspaper reports on the Russians.

What am I to think, Peter? I am worried sick, lonely, and wanting to live our life again. I want to live my life again—with you.
Love, María

The letter was painful for me. I cursed myself for sending letters to her instead of cables, out of a misplaced sense of privacy. I resolved to immediately send her a telegram upon arriving at Singapore, the nearest place with a reliable cable connection—if we got there.

A few nights later, I arrived for a private dinner with Rozhestvensky in his quarters. I wasn't looking forward to it.

36
Proshchay, Moy Drug!

Hell-Ville, Nosy Be Island, French Madagascar
Monday, 30 January 1905

Rozhestvensky looked worse than ever. Once I saw him, I decided to delay telling him until after we ate. The man was completely worn out—his eyes sad and tired, the uniform draped limply from his thinned frame, and that right foot was dragging even more than before. He was the very image of all the many disappointments, obstacles, and failures on the voyage. The sheer magnetic will and strength, the epitome of Russian manhood, demonstrated in his Christmas speech just weeks before, was gone.

He cast a wan smile and bid me to sit, apologetically explaining that the dinner reflected the dwindling supplies of true Russian cuisine on board. Many ingredients were also past their best time: odd-smelling tinned caviar, watery borscht soup, tired stroganoff. But there was very good fresh sourdough rye bread, albeit with rancid butter, and nice baked sweets for dessert. And there was, naturally, a copious volume of vodka and the Russian version of brandy.

For the entire dinner, we spoke of things other than the current situation: our families, our early careers, worst and best ports visited, loves won and lost (he didn't mention Natalia Sivers), and plans for retirement. Two hours later, during a pensive lull, I broached my topic.

"Zinovy, the reality is that you will be here at Hell-Ville for months more. By the time you are allowed to leave, the war will be effectively over, if it isn't already. Both countries cannot maintain the present level of action—and, yes, I know full well Russia has more peasants for cannon fodder than Japan, but Russia also has other major problems at home. So, my friend, I urge you to take your ships and go home now. Save the lives of your men. They will die of diseases here. Those who don't, will lose their fighting spirit and skills, becoming useless as sailors. Or, worse, mutinous."

"That is true, Peter." He woefully wagged his head. "But my Tsar's direct orders are the opposite—remain here until the Baltic reinforcements arrive. Then go, do battle, and get to Vladivostok." He looked me in the eye. "Would *you* violate the direct specific orders of your president?"

He had me. "No, I wouldn't."

My Russian friend nodded in empathy. Then, with a quiet sigh, he told me, "I could tell you were caught unaware by the Tsar that night at the theater. You did not want to come with us. Yet you did because your president ordered it. Oh, yes, do not look surprised, Peter. I knew the Tsar had maneuvered you into coming with us. Probably by the suggestion of the Okhrana, though why I do not know. You always thought this a doomed mission but knew you would be gone from us at Cape Town, at the latest. And now I can tell you are leaving us here in Madagascar. When will you disembark?"

Emotion welled up in me. I felt like a craven deserter confessing my crime. "Tomorrow night, Zinovy. Schooner to Mauritius, steamer from there to Singapore. Then home."

"Ah, a long and difficult voyage." His face eased into a smile. "I will give you two bottles of my best vodka for medicine to keep the tropical fevers at bay. I think you have come to enjoy vodka, my friend."

"I've come to enjoy many things about the Russian navy, Zinovy. But I think it needs to be rebuilt, and I know you are the man to do it. Bring your ships and sailors safely back to their homeland. It won't be long until Russia will need a strong navy against the Germans in the Baltic and their Ottoman partners in the Black Sea."

"Yes, that is true," he admitted, then changed the subject. "I want you and your men to get home safely as well. Semenov will be sad at your leaving.

You have many acquaintances on this ship, Peter, but Semenov and I are true friends for you. And true Russian friends are friends forever."

I raised my glass and said what was in my heart. "To Mother Russia, and my Russian friends."

We downed the vodka, smacking the glasses down on the table. Rozhestvensky filled them again and raised his. "To America, leader of the New World."

Then we stood. It was time to say goodbye. With a resurgence of his famous strength, the admiral gripped my hand and looked into my eyes. "Proshchay, moy drug."

I knew what that meant. *Thank you, my friend.*

The next day at lunch I said goodbye to a moist-eyed Vladimir Semenov, who proceeded to hug me and kiss my cheeks, wishing the very best for me and my family, and insisting that we would meet again in Mother Russia. He said he had special abilities in foretelling such things. I was not alone in my sentiments about the Russians. Rork and Law had tearful farewells with their messmates also.

That evening, we three Americans departed *Suvorov* with deep melancholy. There was no ceremony or gaiety on the quarterdeck when we descended the ladder in our plain clothes, lugging our sea bags. The two fancy bottles of vodka—ornately decorated in Cyrillic calligraphy—were in mine, securely cushioned by socks amidst my underclothes. Once on shore, none of us looked back at the magnificent warship. We were no longer the naval personages known as Wake, Law, and Rork.

Now we were Smith, Jones, and Murphy, shysters who needed to get away from Madagascar for shadowy reasons. There was no time for sentiment anymore.

The way ahead was too dangerous.

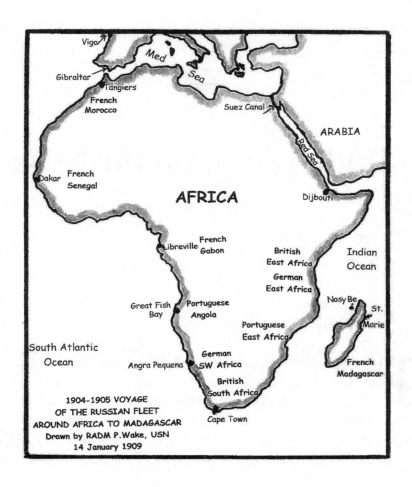

Viga

Med
Sea

Gibraltar

Tangiers

French
Morocco

Suez Canal

ARABIA

Red Sea

Dakar

French
Senegal

AFRICA

Djibouti

Libreville

French
Gabon

British
East Africa

Indian
Ocean

German
East Africa

Nosy Be

Great Fish
Bay

Portuguese
Angola

Portuguese
East Africa

St.
Marie

South Atlantic
Ocean

Angra Pequena

German
SW Africa

British
South Africa

French
Madagascar

Cape Town

1904-1905 VOYAGE
OF THE RUSSIAN FLEET
AROUND AFRICA TO MADAGASCAR
Drawn by RADM P.Wake, USN
14 January 1909

37

Trade Winds on the Nose

Southern Indian Ocean
31 January to 17 February 1905

The meeting at the cigar-smoke-filled "club" was tense and quick. Martin again tried to get all his money up front, then tried to get the first half before we got to the schooner. Several of his cohorts were in the bar eyeing us malevolently, but we made it obvious that Smith, Jones, and Murphy were well armed. I had no doubt every desperado in the place was armed, but, not desiring a bloodbath, Martin backed down his demands with an exaggerated huff and a toss-down of rum.

A moment later he slowly led us on his walking sticks out of the shack and a quarter mile down the road to a dinghy on the shore. Two trips in the dinghy got us all on board the schooner, which lay hove-to off the beach. She was about seventy or eighty feet of filthy decks, patched sails, cracked spars, and badly spliced rigging. Her name currently was *Denise*, according to a sloppily painted sign at the stern. To my surprise, Martin was not the captain, though he stayed on board to guard his investment after I gave him the first half of the payment upon stepping on deck.

The captain turned out to be his supposed competitor, Morisseau, a tall, muscular, and shrewd-looking black creole fellow of indeterminate age who growled orders at the four-man Lascar crew in some mysterious patois stew of Malagasy, French, Hindi, and English. We got under way immediately under a full moon with double-reefed sails. Rounding the point, we were soon out at sea, heeling hard over and smashing into seas and wind.

For the next seventeen days, we three—disdainfully referred to by all else on board as "*les riches américains*"—stayed armed at all times, even when trying to sleep. One of us was always on duty, guarding our three sea bags full of personal possessions (including uniforms, weapons, and ammunition) and each other.

The food on board was some sort of vegetable mush served twice a day and an occasional tidbit of unknown meat. Once we got some rotted bananas. The only drink was cane liquor (not even up to the low standard of rotgut rum), for we dared not ingest the slimy water in the cask. Such was our nutrition. I saved the admiral's vodka for a successful arrival. And after the third day, I began to doubt that would happen.

Martin was right. He got seasick. The three of us got sick also, though for us it was probably a dysenteric consequence of the lousy food and drink. Morisseau and the Lascars never seemed to be sick and made fun of the rest of us. I did note, however, they avoided speaking to or about Martin, frequently casting furtive glances in his direction. I wondered what he had done to them in the past.

The trade winds were the strongest I'd ever seen anywhere in the world, and the wind and seas never let up a bit from a constant near-gale. Days became a blur of struggling to stand, struggling to eat, struggling to sleep in the twenty-foot waves, gale winds, and incessant rain squalls that soaked everything, everywhere. The most basic of human needs were done out on deck and were a test of determination and acrobatic coordination.

The cabin was tiny, the berths were planks, deck leaks poured rainwater and seawater down on us, and it lacked a table or headroom. It was a dark, dank, wooden cave that stank of cigars, urine, sewage, and rotted food. The cargo of illegal French brandy in the holds just forward of the cabin constantly clanked and shrieked as it rubbed and rolled, and periodically shattered, adding yet another odor.

Of course, the cabin wasn't the only thing that leaked—so did the hull, to the point where she had to be pumped at least six hours a day. The ship's bilge pump, situated just forward of our sleeping planks, was an ancient relic from some other vessel. Its worn valves and pipes squirted water in our faces with every draw. The handle took two men to seesaw it up and down, bent over and grunting in pain, all the while staring at each other's suffering. Everyone on *Denise* took turns on this exhausting duty with half an hour each, except crippled Martin. Law and I were partners. Rork pumped with Morisseau.

In extreme situations like these, even friends have occasional clashes of personality. Law focused his analytical mind on estimating how much water we were pumping overboard. He reported it to be approximately a gallon a minute, which meant 360 gallons in our daily six hours of working the damned apparatus. That meant, he proudly added, we pumped overboard 2,520 gallons of bilge water every week. He also shared his important calculation that *Denise* collided with a wave every two minutes, or 2,880 waves each twenty-four-hour period, or 20,160 waves a week. Law made these announcements as we were trying to rest our sore bodies, and Rork used the last bit of naval discipline inside him, very politely asking Law to please shut the bloody hell up.

With more than fifty years at sea for comparison, I concluded this was the most miserable voyage I'd ever endured. Rork concurred. He also pronounced our fellow shipmates "the most evil-hearted, piratical bunch o' bloody cut-throats outside o' them stone-faced Malay bastards we fought in the South China Sea back in '83." I thought that summed them up pretty well.

The end of the ordeal was anticlimactic. It came two in the morning. We "rich Americans" were wedged into our sleeping positions on the pitch-black cabin's lee side, unconsciously holding on with tensed arms and hands as the schooner smashed her way forward in the huge seas.

Suddenly there was no more pitch and roll. No more thunderous shudder of hull hitting wave. The cabin leveled out. The incessant din of squealing metal and groaning wood stopped. We woke from our exhaustion (it wasn't really sleep) and peered through our gloom.

I didn't know where *Denise* was—Morisseau would never tell us our position and I began to worry he didn't know himself—but my mental dead reckoning had us somewhere near Mauritius and the Mascarene Islands. Now we were obviously in smooth water, a bay of some sort.

I staggered up on deck with Rork. Law stayed below with our gear. In the dark ahead I saw the loom of hills against a clear starry sky. The scent of flowers and tropical forest floated in the air. In the water around us were darting splashes of luminescence. The shoreline was devoid of lights.

Morisseau grunted, "You get off now."

38
Smugglers?

Noire Bay, Mauritius Island
Friday, 17 February 1905

"Where are we?" I asked Morisseau as his eyes swept along the shoreline.

"Noire Bay," was the gruff answer. I'd never heard of that place. "Are we at Mauritius? How far away is Port Louis, the capital?"

Morisseau ignored me, ordering his crew to quickly open up the main hold. Words among them were hushed and sparse, as one would expect of practiced smugglers on a dangerous coast, for time and silence were of the essence. No one got the dinghy in the water and I wondered how we would get ashore. Then four rowing skiffs came alongside.

Morisseau pointed to a skiff, snarling to me through bared teeth, "Go now. Off ship!"

I heard a click, clack of sticks thudding the deck behind me and turned around.

Martin hissed, "Not so fast, Smith. You owe me money."

In his hand was a revolver, pointed at me

"Yes, I do, Martin. Here," I said, reaching into my trouser pocket and the hidden pouch sewn into it. "The last half, as agreed."

His other hand took the coins, which he held up close to his face to examine in the starlight, biting several. The revolver was still aimed at me. "Our expenses rose a bit on this voyage, Smith. I need ten more of these."

Morisseau and the Lascars ignored all this drama, evidently used to such last-minute coercion. Instead, they concentrated on quickly getting crates of bottles out of the hold and over the side to waiting natives.

Rork and I had our hands on our weapons inside our coats. Martin sneered, "I know you have ten more, Smith. I just heard them jingle in your pocket. Give them to me now. Or . . ." He gave out a mocking sigh. "I can just kill you and take—."

Martin's head was crushed from behind with the butt of my 1883 Martini-Henry rifle in the hands of Captain Edwin Law, United States Marine Corps. As Martin collapsed to the deck and his sticks clattered down, Law executed a perfect parade-ground backward rifle twirl while snapping the bayonet in place and bringing the rifle up to the point-shoulder position, squarely aimed over my shoulder at Morisseau ten feet behind me. Rork and I joined, spinning around with our revolvers aimed at the crew.

Morisseau and his Lascars stopped hoisting brandy crates and stared wide-eyed at us. So did the crews in the boats alongside. They'd never seen *this* sort of thing happen.

"Permission to kill them all, sir?" asked Law in a frighteningly dispassionate manner. Most of our targets didn't understand the words, but Morisseau did. He raised his hands in surrender, quickly followed by the others. Morisseau, glancing between the dead man on the deck and me, murmured, "No want fight you. No want more money. You go now."

"Mr. Jones," I said to Law. "Kill them if you think they make a threatening movement. Mr. Murphy and I will get the gear in the skiff."

The pirates understood that meaning clearly, too, and stood in a motionless tableau for the next two minutes as we three were rowed away from the ship by a terrified pair of natives. Morisseau picked up the gold coins scattered on the deck, then ordered his crew back to unloading the brandy.

"Well done, Mr. Jones," I offered to Law. "That rifle drill was particularly impressive."

I saw him grin in the starlight. Rork's mind was on more practical matters. "Where are we headed now, sir?"

"Port Louis, the capital, but I have no clue how to get there from here."

Rork gestured toward the nearest rowing native, an old leathery man in tattered clothes, terrified by Rork's malevolent demeanor. "Oh, methinks this fine lad'll help us out on that. By the by, are we still incognito, sir?"

"I think that might be wise whilst we're around these fellows, Mr. Murphy."

Once on the beach, "Murphy" used pidgin-lingo and pantomime to learn the directions to the governor's house which, ipso facto, would be in the capital. The old man ran back to the dinghy when it was over. Other native smugglers on the beach gave us a wide berth. Following the old man's directions, we started walking north.

A few minutes later, Rork mused aloud, "Oohee, methinks we should stop an' have a wee taste o' that vodka, just to celebrate gettin' all the way here on that hell-ship from Hell-Ville."

"Good Lord, Rork—you've become a Russian. Let's get father away from these smugglers before we start celebrating."

He muttered something and we kept trudging along the dark road. Ten minutes later, we heard gunshots back at the beach. Before I could say a word, a man called out to us in British-accented schoolhouse French, "Arrêtez, vous êtes en état d'arrestation!" That was followed by, "Stop, you are under arrest!"

"Bloody hell an' damnation—what now!" uttered Rork.

A tall, lanky white policeman in a dark uniform stepped out of the jungle. Around him were four dark-skinned men in uniforms, all with rifles aimed at us.

I heard more shots at the beach. The policemen looked scared. Their fingers were on the triggers. I tried to calm the situation and spoke to the white man, who appeared the senior. "What have we done wrong, officer? We're just heading to Port Louis. And sorry, but I didn't get your name."

"You're *Yanks*? Didn't think Morisseau had Yanks in his crew. I'm Inspector James Green of the Constabulary." Then he commanded, "Stand absolutely still—my men are going to search you for weapons and stolen goods."

I continued. "There is a completely understandable mistake here, officer. We're not smugglers. I am Rear Adm. Peter Wake of the U.S. Navy. This is my aide, Capt. Edwin Law, U.S. Marines, and our assistant, Chief Sean Rork, U.S. Navy. We're headed for Port Louis to see our diplomatic consul and then visit the governor. Please take us to the U.S. consul's office immediately."

"There is no Yank consul at Mauritius, or for two thousand miles in any direction."

"Then I demand to see the governor right away. He will want to see I am shown every courtesy."

Green came closer, and I could see in his face that he didn't believe a word I'd said. Admittedly, it sounded far-fetched. In our disheveled, soaked, ripped, and stained civilian clothes, and with no shave in over two weeks, we didn't look naval at all. In fact, we looked, and even smelled, exactly like smugglers or pirates. Our filthy seabags were taken. Our coats were removed, exposing our revolvers, causing great consternation and solidifying their suspicions. The weapons were quickly taken from us.

I tried again. "Those are for personal protection, as is standard for naval and army officers around the world. In my seabag you will find my uniform."

Green grumbled something derisory in return. That's when the searching got far more physically rough. I told my men to just go along with it and not say anything. Our shirts, trousers, and underwear were removed until we stood there naked. The man searching the bags saw my vodka bottles and announced we possessed some of the smuggled liquor. Then he saw all our long guns and ammunition and gasped, shouting in Creole. I got the gist of it—we weren't smugglers, we were revolutionaries landing to overthrow the government!

"No, no!" I barked at him. "Look at our uniforms in the bags!"

He rummaged around but didn't seem to see any of them. I started to head over to the moron so I could pull out my uniform, but a rifle muzzle stopped me. I got back in our naked line, sure that they would see the uniform at any moment.

Seconds later we were told to put on our underwear, then handcuffed tightly behind our backs. That led them to discovering Rork's false hand and the spike underneath—which led to further gasps and speculation as to precisely what type of monsters they had found. They couldn't handcuff Rork, so they stationed a man behind him with the rifle muzzle at his spine. He murmured a Gaelic curse, and I knew what he was contemplating.

"Not now, Rork," I whispered. "These fellows are on edge, and you'd never make it."

A group of men with a lantern approached from the beach: more policemen escorting the Lascars and Morisseau, and two locals. When Morisseau passed by us, he sneered at me, then added, "So, Smith, you arrest for smuggle too. And murder of Martin, too?"

"What murder was that, Jonathan?" asked Green of his white counterpart with the other group.

"Found one of these scum bludgeoned dead on the deck. This lot says your blokes did it."

By the light of the lantern, Green knelt down to my seabag, lifting out a large oiled-muslin waterproof wrapping. Opening it up, he found my folded working uniform coat and trousers and shoes, then my dress uniform tunic and trousers, complete with medals. Unfolding each and holding them up for close inspection, he finally turned and stared at me.

"Good God, you really *are* an admiral!"

39

A Day Late, in the Middle of Nowhere

Government House, Port Louis, Mauritius Crown Colony
Saturday, 18 February 1905

What a difference a uniform makes. Smugglers, murderers? Never heard another word about that. In fact, Sir Charles Cavendish Boyle, Governor of the Crown Colony of Mauritius, welcomed us with figurative open arms later that morning, even though we were still in our wild state of appearance: rags, stench, and a desperate need for a decent bath, shave, and haircut.

However, within hours of our arrival at the magnificent Government House on the hill overlooking Port Louis, all of those personal necessities had been supplied, our uniforms had been cleaned and pressed, our weaponry and valuables were in the vault, and we were sound asleep in real beds with linen sheets. Rork asked if we could celebrate with the vodka yet. My answer was no—it certainly wouldn't do to show up already drunk for our first evening with such high-ranking hosts. He moaned something that sounded like a Russian epithet.

At five o'clock, Law and I descended the stairs to the sunset veranda for drinks and dinner. Mauritius is a Crown Colony of His Majesty King Edward VII, and a certain decorum is expected for drinks and dinner, even for those recently suspected of being smugglers. And since February is summertime in the Southern Hemisphere, dress whites were the norm.

The governor was resplendent in all his bemedaled and sashed regalia. His assembled guests were positively elegant, especially the ladies, who were quite fetching and very attentive to their American guests. Evidently, Yanks were quite a rarity. Of course, our odyssey from Russia to Mauritius was the main topic, and I narrated it with considerable redactions for reasons of both security and delicacy—not to mention a few awkward legal aspects.

There was one moment, however. As I vaguely described our arrival at Noire Bay, an uncommonly sober artillery captain with a hyphenated double name interrupted rather insistently, "I'm a bit confused. How exactly did that scoundrel Martin die, Admiral?"

"A blow to the head, Captain, in the midst of all that barbarian terror. Thank God above!"

That got a round of applause. I diverted the conversation to the wine at the table and proposed a toast to Anglo-American friendship. The captain never asked another question.

Meanwhile, downstairs, Rork was treated to dinner in the wine cellar with the senior butler, his equal in relative rank. The decorum down there lasted three drinks—all of about twenty minutes—at which time sea stories and army tales emerged. It turned out the butler was a retired sergeant major, having done twenty-eight years in India and Egypt. The good rum was opened, and Rork's usual antipathy for Brits was submerged in gratitude and camaraderie.

Five hours later in the gentlemen's smoking room topside, over our final, final, final cognac of the evening, I remembered to ask my new friend Governor Boyle when the steamer for Singapore was arriving, for we would need passage on board.

He laughed. "Why, you missed it yesterday, old chap!"

"What? When's the next one!"

He wasn't laughing now, for he'd caught the worry in my voice. "Peter, there won't be another steamer here for at least a month. Maybe not even then—it's cyclone season, you know. It looks like we'll have the wonderful pleasure of your company for many more weeks!"

I tried to clear my groggy mind and think of options. "Do any of your local sailing vessels head east to Australia or the Dutch East Indies, or at least the Cocos Islands?"

Boyle, who was ten years my junior in age and a bachelor, replied with genuine paternalistic concern for me. "Peter, old boy, listen to me. The Cocos are two thousand miles away. Australia and the Dutch islands are three thousand miles. So is India to the north. Nobody here even tries such a thing under sail against the trades in the cyclone season. I'm afraid you and your men are here until the next steamer."

I took a breath. "I see. I need to send a cable first thing in the morning."

His brow furrowed and my heart sank. "Peter, there is no cable connection right now, and we don't know where the break is. The cable repair ship is busy at Ceylon and won't be here for months. So, I'm afraid I have no joy for you on that subject either, my dear man."

And so, we three Yanks sat and waited amid comfortable opulence, incommunicado in the middle of nowhere, the luxury ruined by mounting guilt while my wife and president were consumed with worry about our disappearance. As far as they might possibly know, we were last seen in a brothel-bar full of cutthroats in a place named Hell-Ville.

40

Drinking Rum in a Whisky Bar

Raffles Hotel, Singapore, Straits Settlements Crown Colony
Thursday, 6 April 1905

Governor Boyle and the Brits of Mauritius were gracious and elegant hosts, but I was worn down by the full-dress nightly dinners (Sir Charles insisted every night—he thought it all great fun), the artificial gaiety, and incessantly repeated conversations and opinions by the time the passenger-cargo steamer *Clotilda* arrived on 15 March 1905.

Clotilda was a rusting hulk of around 1,200 tons, incapable of more than nine knots. Her builder and age were unknown for certain, but there were many rumors—none of them complimentary. What *was* known by everyone in the Indian Ocean was the wretched vessel had plied this dismal route for twenty years, all while nourishing vast communities of bedbugs, cockroaches, ants, and rats.

She carried fifteen white passengers in the "first-class" cabins on the upper deck, one hundred native "second-class" passengers somewhere in the nether region below decks, and seven hundred tons of cargo (mainly European finished goods outbound via Mombasa in British East Africa, with sugar cane and Asian goods on the return). A majority of the second-class people were Muslims from the East Indies returning from their life's sacred Hajj pilgrimage to Mecca during the Holy month of Dhu al-Hijjah. Their inner peace was reflected in their gently smiling faces. Nothing human or oceanic could bother them now, for God appreciated their tremendous effort. Their devotion and tranquility provided the only inspiring part of the voyage.

Mauritius was *Clotilda*'s first stop after Mombasa, then she put in at the Chagos Islands, Cocos Islands, and Christmas Island before passing Krakatoa Island (which I last saw in 1883, when the famous volcano blew) and through the Sunda Strait to stop at the Dutch East Indies colonial capital of Batavia. Once departed from that notoriously disease-ridden port, we steamed on to Singapore, where God answered my prayers and we arrived on the sixth of April.

At customs, my rank solved the initial serious difficulties about our weapons. I told the officious-acting immigration officer we were on leave and heading home, assuring him of having no urge to dally on the public dole. After the British Empire's numerous bureaucratic needs were all duly satisfied and recorded, rickshaws took us to the Raffles Hotel. We quickly headed to our rooms in the new addition, which boasted running water and electricity. The first imperative was to soak in tubs and scrub away our grime and parasites, while having all our nonlethal possessions disinfected, cleaned, and pressed.

While soaking, I wrote out an invitation to the American diplomatic consul—whose name I did not even know—to join us for drinks and dinner later. I needed his help with several crucial needs: cables to María and Roosevelt, funds to pay the hotel bill (I was completely emptied after bribing the smugglers and five weeks of the high life with Sir Charles), steamer passage home to America, and news of the war (the steamer's captain apologized that vermin had devoured his recent newspapers from Mombasa).

Four hours later, we wore civilian attire and met the consul in the far corner of the hotel's busy Long Bar (actually just a veranda with a line of tables) in Cad's Alley, overlooking bustling Bras Basah Road. Around us were rubber planters and shipping brokers in wilted linen suits and Panama hats, nursing their gin or whisky and commiserating over their lot in life. The buzz of conversation centered around falling prices, wives' extravagance, lazy natives of various nationalities, imperial bureaucracy, bad weather, and broken-down machinery. Fortunately, the bar's electric ceiling fans, a major draw for the place, worked flawlessly.

Consul James Benjamin Hustwayte was an English (Devonian) gentleman of the old school who'd been in Asia for fifty years and seen it all. In the 1890s he'd become a naturalized American citizen (I thought that mysterious) and been our diplomat in Singapore for five years. He drank gin or whisky like everyone else, of course. I dislike gin and scotch whisky and ordered Australian Bundaberg Rum for me and my subordinates.

That caused a stir more than anything else about the Yank strangers. Several planters frowned at us, and the Malay servants whispered disapprovingly. Hustwayte explained that rum, especially Aussie rum from that continent's wild Banana Coast, is considered the drink of low-class blackbirders, roustabouts, and ne'er-do-wells. Rork grinned.

As far as our needs, Hustwayte informed us that he would take my messages straightaway to the cable station. Since our convoluted multiple-code sequence with Roosevelt was now well out of date, I kept both messages brief. Roosevelt's would be in standard state department code, which meant any U.S. diplomatic post along the way could read it. María's was in plain English. Both said the same thing. *Left Russian fleet in Nosy-be. Now in Singapore and heading home.* Hustwayte said he could pay the hotel bill, miscellaneous expenses within reason, and the deposit for a passenger steamer—all to be reimbursed by navy voucher upon our arrival home.

Though Singapore is the crossroads of the British Empire in Asia, American flagged-ship connections with California were limited and getting fewer. The next passenger ship heading east across the Pacific would be the last one for the Occidental and Oriental Steamship Company, which was folding soon due to commercial pressure from rival Japanese shipping companies. But we were in luck. The 4,300-ton *Coptic* was due at Singapore in a week, and Hustwayte said he could get us passage to San Francisco on her last run from here to there.

Hustwayte then told us the news from around the world. None of the Russo-Japanese War news was good for the Russians. In Manchuria, the Russian army was losing ground all along the front and defeated at someplace called Sandepu, with 12,000 men killed, wounded, and captured. But there was far worse: The Russians had lost the critical rail junction of Mukden in a massive battle against a smaller number of Japanese troops. There, the defeated

Russians had 88,000 men killed, wounded, or captured. Their army's morale was shattered, and the general was sacked in disgrace.

There was an intriguing development with Admiral Rozhestvensky. Nine days earlier he abruptly left Hell-Ville, heading east into the vastness of the Indian Ocean. This happened *before* the Tsar-ordered rendezvous with Rear Admiral Nebogatov. Did his orders change? Was he ignoring his orders from the Tsar? No one knew where Rozhestvensky's fleet was at the moment. Nebogatov's ancient relics were at French Djibouti in the Red Sea, heading east also. Meanwhile, the Royal Navy had stationed two cruisers at Singapore and sent two more from Hong Kong as reinforcements—should they need to protect British territorial waters.

Naturally, the Japanese navy had not been idle during all this. Cruisers were scouting from Formosa to Java to Ceylon. Togo, the victorious admiral who had humiliated the Russian navy several times already, was expected to force the Russians into battle somewhere in the South China Sea, or the Dutch East Indies, depending on the Russian admiral's route.

Back in Russia itself, the revolution halted normal commerce and transport in many places, Grand Duke Sergei Alexandrovich Romanov was assassinated by a bomb, troops were diverted from the war to "pacify" rebellious areas, and the Tsar very reluctantly agreed to allow a national consultative legislature (the Duma) and some limited increase in individual liberty.

In Europe, Kaiser Wilhelm was stirring up more trouble, this time with the French over Morocco. Having just left Greece on his imperial yacht, the Kaiser intended visiting Sultan Abdelaziz to discuss German assistance to the sultanate. The French were not amused. The Germans took umbrage about the French being so touchy. Both sides darkly hinted at war.

Theodore Roosevelt had a busy new year so far: designating wildlife refuges, enjoying a magnificent inauguration after his historic landslide election, inspecting new weapons for the army and the navy, crafting legislative regulations on food safety and corporate greed, and giving away his beloved niece Eleanor in marriage to a distant cousin named Franklin.

At long last, we and Hustwayte left the bar and parted ways—he to the cable office and we to our rooms for more rest. In a few days I would get a reply from María. In a week, we'd be heading home on *Coptic*. In two months, María would be in my arms at our cottage in Alexandria. I felt the tension ebb away. I slept soundly for the first time since Port Louis.

We were finally going home.

41
The Brethren

Singapore, Straits Settlements Crown Colony
Friday, 7 April 1905

The next morning, still in plain clothing, we visited the Wesley Methodist Church on nearby Coleman Street, offering up profound thanks for our deliverance to a civilized and peaceful locale. Afterward, Law and Rork wandered about the town like tourists. I relaxed at the Long Bar, reading the local newspaper, the *Straits Times*. I found the local news delightfully mundane and normal as I sipped a glass of orange juice, looking out over Singapore's European elite in their fancy carriages along Bras Basah Road. The tranquil scene led me to lean back and smile. The war, Roosevelt, and German agents all seemed far away and unreal.

Right at that instant everything changed.

A wild-eyed, bushy-haired man in a pressed linen outfit suddenly appeared and sat down at my table. My hand was inside my coat and on my revolver in an instant, but he smiled and said in a strangely accented rasping voice, "Please pardon my intrusion, Admiral. My name is Davit Kasabian and I mean no rudeness or offense, but we have mutual friends around the world. One of them asked me to see you. I see you have traveled to the East."

It took me a moment to get my wits. I let go of my weapon, looked at his shining black eyes, and shook his hand, saying, "I have traveled to the East. I am now traveling to the West."

The reader may be puzzled by this exchange, for the second part was not entirely true geographically. I had, of course, come east from Africa and was continuing east across the Pacific to America. But that is in the conventional sense of those statements. I knew this was not a conventional discussion, for Kasabian's unusual opening had a special meaning. So did the style of his handshake. They connected with an event in my life seventeen years before.

In 1888 I was on a clandestine mission to find and rescue Cubans held by the Spanish secret police in Havana. I had a personal obligation, for they were operatives in my intelligence network inside Havana. I received crucial assistance when I was designated a "Friend of Freemasonry" by my dear friend, the famous Cuban Master Mason and revolutionary leader José Martí.

To be clear, I am *not* a Freemason, only a "Friend." But in my work around the world since then, I have periodically been the beneficiary of that friendship, frequently when I didn't even realize I was in desperate need of it. It now appeared this was one of those times and Davit Kasabian was one of my "Friends."

His statement let me know that. My reply let him know I understood. *Traveling to the East* meant "seeking knowledge." *Traveling to the West* meant "spreading that knowledge."

Kasabian then replied in the manner I thought he would. "I am here to help your travels, for there are unseen dangers to those without knowledge."

"Thank you," I said. Then I added a seemingly simple and divergent question. "How old is your grandmother?"

"Seven hundred and forty-eight years old," he said without hesitation.

Since I am only a "Friend" and not an actual Freemason, I do not possess any of their truly confidential knowledge, which is encyclopedic, but I do understand some basic ways to determine with whom I am speaking. While walking back from the Methodist Church, by habit I'd noted a Masonic lodge on Coleman Street. It was the Zetland of the East Lodge, #748. Kasabian had answered my question correctly, giving me his lodge number.

As I rapidly processed the information, more subtle links presented themselves to me. There has long been a small but thriving and influential Armenian community in Singapore. Kasabian is an Armenian name. Right across the street from the Masonic lodge is the Armenian Apostolic Church of St. Gregory the Illuminator. By articles in the *Straits Times*, I knew that the owners of Raffles Hotel, the Sarkies brothers, were members. Catchick Moses, the newspaper's founder, had been also. Other Armenians were involved in banking and shipping. The man in front of me was connected in at least two ways to very powerful people in the region.

"Who sent you, Davit?"

"A very wise and accomplished Brother who knows both you and the birdcall of the Antillean Goatsucker. He wants you to have level-headed resolute men of action you can trust in this time of impending decisions for you."

The bird name told me. Theodore Roosevelt is a Mason, a gifted ornithologist, and prefers men of action. "I understand, Davit. Thank you for the help. So, what is the situation?"

"In an hour, a dinner invitation from Governor Sir John Anderson will be delivered to your room here at Raffles Hotel. The dinner is tomorrow night. As usual, the colony's social elite will be there. But there will also be British, Japanese, and German intelligence officers there. The German officer, Gerhard Weber, has been asking about you and your plans. I suggest you go to the dinner, be very careful of what you eat and drink and say, and gracefully retire early. Your driver will be a Brother."

"Anything else I should know?"

"An hour after the dinner invitation arrives, you will get two reply cables delivered to your room by Consul Hustwayte. One you will treasure, the other you will resent."

I knew better than to ask how he had all this information. The Brethren never divulged such confidential things, not even to a "Friend."

Kasabian stood and reached down to shake my hand. "Soon you will make a choice between them. Either way, we will be standing beside you."

He turned to go but stopped. "Oh, and a British customs officer told Major Yoshida of the Kokuryūkai about you. I think he will target you for recruitment in their subtle ways."

The Kokuryūkai was the Black Dragon Society. Obviously, the Japanese wanted information about the Russian fleet. "Tell me about Yoshida."

"Yoshida has been here four years, is very polished, and well entrenched in the social scene. He'll be at the governor's dinner. Ostensibly, Yoshida is a wealthy businessman who owns thirty-two Japanese barber shops and three restaurants here. He also runs 109 Japanese brothels, the Karayuki-san. Both groups are excellent sources of blackmail, funding, and intelligence for the major. Beware of the honey trap, friend. And now, I am on my way."

When Law and Rork arrived an hour later, I briefed them on developments. Rork summed up his opinion with, "So much for relaxin' 'til the bloody ship comes in. Now we've got the Krauts an' Nips an' Limeys all on us. Hmm, methinks surrenderin' to those Nip girls sounds like the best course ahead, sir."

I couldn't help but laugh. "Somehow, I knew you'd say that, Rork."

Hustwayte was on time and Kasabian was right. María's cable was a treasure.

> XXX—THANK GOD YOU ARE SAFE—X—I LOVE YOU—X—CAN'T WAIT FOR YOU TO HOLD ME—X—COME HOME SOON—XXX

Roosevelt's was not. Hustwayte delivered a deciphered version.

> XXX—THANKFUL YOU ARE SAFE—X—STANDBY IN SINGAPORE UNTIL FURTHER ORDERS—X—FUNDS TRANSFERRING TO CONSULATE—X—NEW DEVELOPMENTS ARE REASON FOR NEW ORDERS—X—WILL EXPLAIN DELAY TO MRS W—XXX

Damn it all.

42
Amazed and Dismayed

Singapore, Straits Settlements Crown Colony
Saturday, 8 April 1905

The next day, as I was readying my full dress whites for the dinner later, I got two shocking pieces of news, delivered personally by a nearly breathless Hustwayte in white tie and tails.

"The Russian fleet is here! Look, just beyond Raffles Island lighthouse!"

I dashed out and looked to the south. There they were, about five miles away. Steaming at about ten knots with flags flying, they were in a perfectly spaced and aligned double-column fleet parade formation, looking magnificent. Other guests came out on the veranda and stared at the sight, buzzing with excitement at the miles and miles of Russian warships so far from home.

Rork and Law showed up from their rooms and took in the sight.

I stood there in awe. "Amazing! Zinovy actually pulled it off—he got through the Malacca Straits undetected and unopposed. He'll be in the South China Sea soon. Well done!"

"Probably stopping at French Saigon for more fuel before the battle," opined Law.

Even Rork was impressed. "Damned if the Rooskies aren't lookin' pretty friggin' squared away! Aye, I wish the lads luck. They'll be needin' it against the Nips." Then he looked up at the sky. "An' thank you dear Jaysus *we* won't be with them for *that*."

Hustwayte cleared his throat and stepped closer to me. "Ah, well . . . about that, sir. Another cable just came in from the President. Had it deciphered for you." He handed me a telegram decipher sheet. Skipping the routing information, I read the message aloud.

XXX—REJOIN RUSSIAN FLEET ASAP IF THEY STOP AT SINGAPORE OR SAIGON—X—NEED YOU ON BOARD WHEN THEY ENGAGE JAPANESE— X—NEED DETAILED EYEWITNESS ASSESSMENT OF JAPANESE TACTICS, SHIPS, COMMANDERS—X—NEED ANY INTEL ON JAPANESE PLANS IN ASIA & PHILIPPINES—X—JAPANESE WARSHIPS & INTEL AGENTS SEEN IN SOUTH PHILIPPINES—X—POSSIBLY RECON TO ASSIST MOROS—X—JAPAN POSSIBLY ALLIED WITH CHINESE REVOLUTIONARIES—X—KEEP FUTURE COMMS THROUGH TIGER CODE—X—SEND FROM EACH PORT WITHOUT FAIL—XXX

"Tiger Code" was yet another private code moniker between Roosevelt and me—and an example of his ornithological humor. It referred to the tiger shrike, a small predatory bird in Asia. The name was merely a ruse to deflect the curious, however, for the code was a simple one that used a simple cipher wheel. Each progressive day after you started, you advanced the substitute for the letter "A" five places. Since Roosevelt's cable was sent on 8 April, the substitute for "A" was the eighth letter, or "I." The next day it would be five places beyond "I," or the letter "N." This sort of code was not impregnable or even difficult to break but was fast and easy to remember and use in ever-changing situations.

The cable reflected concerns Roosevelt had long held about the Philippines and China. The Muslim Moros had successfully resisted American "pacification" for five years, being slaughtered in the process but never giving up. I doubted they ever would. We'd already lost thousands killed, wounded, and disease-sickened in the fight. I assessed the Japanese factor. *If I were the Japanese, I would urge on the Moros and foment unrest against the Americans across the Philippines. Then I would "liberate" the people from the American barbarians.*

The Chinese intellectual, medical doctor, and revolutionary Sun Yat-sen had been calling for the dissolution of the Manchu imperial dynasty leaders in China and the establishment of a republic. His movement was growing across China, in the southeast of Asia, and even in Japan. I knew he was an uncertain factor in the Chinese situation. *Roosevelt's worried about America's "Open Door" policy in China. I imagine the revolutionaries are probably in Singapore also, with its large Chinese population. Are they among the laborers in the American West, too?*

I looked at Rork for his reaction to the cable. "'Tis a direct order . . ."

Law quietly asked, "What now, sir?"

I tried to keep the dismay out of my voice. "We follow orders, Captain Law."

Hustwayte asked, "Is there a reply for me to send, sir?"

I thought for a moment, then said, "Yes, just say 'Orders received.' Send it in State Department code."

43

The Bear, the Lion, and the Black Dragon

Singapore, Straits Settlements Crown Colony
Saturday, 8 April 1905

The dining room at Government House was impressive. Marble floored, ornately chandeliered in cut glass, with a dais at one end displaying a large trompe-l'œil-style mural of black orchids in a colorful tropical garden, it was worthy of a royal palace. Fifty people sat at the polished tamarind heartwood table topped with the finest silver, china, and crystal. Ladies in glittering gowns and men in bemedaled and sashed uniforms and white-tie evening dress were silently served by three-dozen tall Sikhs, impassive in their *dastār* turbans and red-coated livery.

Most of the talk and shocked gasps were about the great event of the day—the sudden appearance of the Russians, long the traditional enemies of the British, at this Far East bastion of the British Empire. With the courage of several gins in him, one wag loudly opined, "Seems that moth-eaten old Bear has done a bloody bang-up job of teasing our ferocious Lion."

With Rork in plain clothes off loitering among the drivers outside and Law dutifully trailing behind me in his dress blues, Hustwayte took me around to be introduced to various notables before we were called to dinner. He started with the governor. Sir John Anderson was less enthusiastically welcoming to me than his bored and lonely gubernatorial counterpart, Boyle, at far-off Mauritius. I next met the bland captain of the Royal Navy cruiser at anchor in the harbor, who had nothing of interest to say, or apparently even to think.

Hustwayte then introduced me to a man who clearly did have interesting thoughts, though he kept them concealed. Major Akito Yoshida—most likely an alias—was a handsome man in his forties with graying hair at the temples, trimmed moustache and goatee, wearing a Savile Row suit and speaking impeccable British English. He suavely deflected my subtle inquiries about his work, then invited me to his home for a Japanese-style dinner the next evening. I less than suavely deflected the invitation. In addition to a potential honey trap, I could tell Yoshida wasn't going to be a source of any usable intelligence, for the man lived by the Bushido code of honor. Lesser Japanese beings might part with information, but never a man like Yoshida.

Next on my social presentation list was the assistant secretary of the German consulate, an old and reliable bureaucrat now uncomfortably filling in for his recently deceased superior, the beloved doyen of the diplomatic set in Singapore. The secretary called over "a visiting businessman from Hamburg," who turned out to be none other than the mysterious Gerhard Weber, recently arrived at Singapore.

Weber had an obvious military background. He was also as charming as one can be, from the brusque, saber-scarred cheek, stiff-necked Prussian culture, where even a chuckle can sound menacing. Within minutes, he suggested I join him for lunch the day after tomorrow. It came out as more of a challenge than a suggestion. His carriage would come by Raffles at noon and take us to a little place he knew of on the North Coast that had excellent satay cuisine.

I was more inclined to accept this offer, and not just because I happen to greatly enjoy satay, which I'd first had when in Cambodia and Vietnam twenty years earlier. Unlike the Japanese spy, this one just might be penetrable and come up with answers about the various murky perils I'd survived lately from German intelligence. Of course, when a Prussian spider invites a fly into his parlor, that fly better be damned lethal himself. I fully intended to have Rork and Law follow us and remain just outside the restaurant.

Those were the interesting guests; the rest bored me. The French consul spent most of his time trying to impress the ladies. The Spanish fellow brooded over brandy in the corner. The smiling consul from Siam seemed to be joined at the hip with the wary-eyed consul from Japan, who never spoke with Yoshida. I noticed one major country's consul was not there—Russia's. Hustwayte explained that Consul Rudanovsky wasn't invited. It would be too "delicate."

Almost three hours later, after a far more intriguing and pleasant evening than I'd anticipated, I was sleepily preparing for bed when a knock on the door turned out to be Kasabian.

He stepped inside and lost no time with pleasantries. "Admiral, you need to leave Singapore. Now. There is a French freighter getting under way before dawn for Saigon, where you will arrive in three days. The Russian fleet might still be there then, if that is where they are going. The freighter captain is a Brother and allowed me to book three passenger cabins for you.

"We are all going to the ship *right now*, under cover of darkness. There will be no exit formalities with the authorities, or the hotel. We will carry the bags ourselves down the back stairs and not check out at the desk.

"Leave a note for Hustwayte with me and I'll see he gets it. He can sign and pay the hotel bill for you later. Also, if you want to, seal whatever telegram messages you want to send in an envelope, and I will give them to Hustwayte as well. But time is short, so we need to hurry."

Kasabian saw my doubting look. "Admiral, there are two reasons for you leaving now. Yoshida's Black Dragon people have already bribed the doorman here to let one of their girls into your room in the morning. Much worse, Weber cabled Berlin tonight, saying you will no longer be a problem as of tomorrow. A Brother has heard the plan. Instead of his personal carriage, Weber will be sending a local cab to take you to the restaurant. In reality, Weber is not going. All three of you Americans, and the cabbie, will be killed en route by local gangsters. It would be just another local crime, without any apparent German connection."

"Do you know why they are doing this?"

"There is a rumor a German you met in French Gabon was found drowned in a river. But I think there must be more than just that."

So did I. *If Vogel did drown, they wouldn't care two cents about him. No, this is because of Othello, and they know about that because Rachkovsky did a deal with them.* "Davit, thank you for the help. We'll get under way now."

I dashed off a brief note to Hustwayte and sealed it in an envelope. *Thank you for your considerable help. Must go to Saigon immediately, please handle hotel and send the two messages via cable, the first in State Department code, the second in plain.*

My first cable message was to the president: *Heading to Saigon. Will cable from there.* My note to María was as simple: *I love you. Heading to Saigon where I will send detailed cable. We are all well, but things have changed.*

And with that done, I hurriedly packed my gear while Kasabian told the others.

44
Pulling Rank

Saigon, French Indochina Protectorate
Wednesday, 12 April 1905

Our little French steamer, *Emma Louise*, arrived at Saigon's river docks at high noon on the twelfth of April. The Russian fleet wasn't there, only the Russian cruiser *Diana* (Semenov's old ship), interned by the French a year earlier after she'd escaped from the Japanese near Port Arthur.

The voyage from Singapore wasn't that bad, with good food and clean, though small, cabins. The steamer would take four days to discharge the cargo, and her Masonic captain very kindly let us stay on board. Theoretically, if the Russians were ever coming to Saigon, they would arrive in the next day or two. If they didn't, I had no idea of where they would go for provisions, communications, and coal.

The captain also saw to it that my two sealed envelopes with messages were delivered to the French cable office for transmission to the United States. Since it was now four days since the Tiger Code had started on the eighth, the cipher wheel substitution in my report to the president had advanced twenty letters, which made the message appear thus:

XXX—UDZR CUMOGH—X—DACCMUHC HGB NQDQ—X—HG GHQ KHGYC
YNQDQ—X—HG MHPG UTGAB LUFC QXSQFB IUHW TJUSK RDUOGHC

MHBQV UOBC MH CMHOUFGDQ—X—JMKQYMCQ SNMHQCQ DQZ
ODGAF—XXX

The reader will note it is not in artificially contrived five-digit groups, part of its simplicity. In plain, it said: XXX—ARVD SAIGON—X—RUSSIANS NOT HERE—X—NO ONE KNOWS WHERE—X—NO INFO ABOUT JAPS EXCEPT MANY BLACK DRAGON INTEL AGTS IN SINGAPORE—X—LIKEWISE CHINESE REV GROUP—XXX

Writing my clear-language cable to María was torture for my heart, but I tried to make it sound hopeful. XXX—ALL SAFE IN SAIGON NOW—X—ORDERED BY TR TO REJOIN PREV FRIENDS—X—UNK WHERE OR WHEN—X—WILL PROVIDE HOMEWARD BOUND INFO WHEN I KNOW—X—MAYBE FROM CHINA—XXX

Communications having been sent off and with nothing else to do, we now waited for developments. Rork and I hadn't been to Saigon since 1883, so we all relaxed in a shady spot on the upper deck, recounting memories for Law as the sun lowered over the twin spires of the Notre Dame Cathedral of Saigon. The city had become pleasantly more French and agreeable in those twenty years, and our afternoon was quite enjoyable.

As we were about to go to dinner, a surprise arrived. *Orel*, the white-and-green Russian hospital ship with Natalia Sivers on board, steamed around the bend in the river and moored just astern of us. Because she was not subject to the same neutrality restrictions as warships, Rozhestvensky had used *Orel* in Africa and Madagascar for sending and getting dispatches, discovering local information, obtaining provisions, and doing sundry other errands.

I quickly got into uniform and walked over to the other ship, where the quarterdeck watch passed the word to the captain that a foreign admiral wanted to visit. That gentleman, whose impossible name I regret I cannot recall, recognized me. I was instantly invited to dinner on board. Minutes later I was in the captain's stateroom for a private dinner with three nurses, Miss Sivers, Miss Klemm, and Miss Pavlovskaya (gossip said she was Admiral Rozhestvensky's niece), and a young Russian in plain clothing. He spoke excellent English and introduced himself as Commander Polis.

With yelps of delight, the nurses remembered me from dinners on board *Suvorov*. Natalia's English was good, so she translated for the other two girls, each time eliciting a flurry of giggles that began to grate on my nerves. Polis had just arrived on *Orel* and didn't know me, but I knew of him—Rozhest-vensky's intelligence operative in Batavia, watching Japanese activities in the Dutch East Indies and reconnoitering the Sunda and Lombok straits in case the admiral chose that route. The admiral had alluded to his reports several times in conversations with me, though I didn't dare let Polis know that.

After dinner, the young ladies, who treated the evening as a great lark, retired to their quarters. The captain, the commander, and I retired to the afterdeck for digestifs. This entire time, the war hadn't been discussed. Now it was, with fatalistic resignation on their part. I asked where the fleet was, explaining I'd been ordered to rejoin it. Obviously, it wasn't Saigon. The two Russians glanced sideways at each other, and I knew what they were think-ing—could they trust the Yank with such a secret?

There was a pause, then Commander Polis said, "We are leaving Saigon tomorrow morning to go meet the admiral. He's not far. I can take him a message, if you like."

It was plain they weren't going to tell me Rozhestvensky's location. I didn't blame them at all. I deduced it must be somewhere close, probably one of the many bays on the Cochin or Annam coast of Vietnam.

This was the decisive point for me. Should I not press the matter, report back to Roosevelt that I couldn't get to the fleet, and find passage on a steamer bound for home? Or should I push these two officers into taking me to the doomed Russian fleet?

Roosevelt needed information about the Japanese navy's combat ability. There was really only one way to do that. Observe it directly. So my choice was clear. Watch the battle and the Russians surrender.

I decided it was time to pull rank on my Russian hosts. "Commander Polis, I am under presidential orders to rejoin the fleet. The Tsar himself authorized it originally. Therefore I, along with my aide and petty officer, am going along with you to Admiral Rozhestvensky. The admiral will be very pleased to see me again, and very angry with *you* if I am delayed."

The captain was not pleased but said nothing. Polis held up a hand. "Admi-ral Wake, with respect, sir, this is not your navy and—"

"I know that far better than you do, Commander Polis. The matter is settled. I will be back in one hour with my aide and my petty officer, and our gear. Don't worry, we travel light. By the way, I know this coast far better than any of you, from *another* war that wasn't mine, so I can help you on that."

He thought for a moment, then quietly said, "Yes, sir. One hour."

The next morning at dawn *Orel* cast off and steamed down the Saigon River with me on her bridge. Two days later we entered Cam Ranh Bay, where thirty-five gray warships sat at anchor, accompanied by several German colliers and one French cruiser.

Rork and I knew the place.

45
Déjà Vu and a Warning

Cam Ranh Bay, Annam, French Indochina Protectorate
Saturday, 15 April 1905

As the two of us stood on the main deck in the morning sun, I could see it in Rork's eyes. Memories of twenty-two years earlier had ignited the phantom pains in his missing left hand. He looked over at the French cruiser *Descartes*, anchored near the mouth of the bay, and rubbed his India-rubber hand.

"You all right, Sean?" I asked him quietly. "Some salve for your stump might help."

"Nay, sir. It'll go away. Just the sights an' smells around here, an' lookin' at that Frenchie cruiser. It all makes me think o' that Frog surgeon cuttin' the damned thing off."

He studied his left arm as if it was a strange animal. "Gangrene-rotted as hell, an' stank like a Timbuktu tart—remember that awful stench? Had to come off, though, an' now me rubber hand does just fine, not to mention me spike. Now *that* saved us a few times, didn't it?"

"Yes, it surely did, my friend. More than a few."

Rork changed his gaze to the Russian fleet and let out a long sigh. "So now we're back in it, for the friggin' duration . . ."

"I don't think it'll be that long, Rork. After those months of waiting at Madagascar, the French'll kick the Russians out of here pretty soon. So Rozhestvensky will top off his coal and steam north, meet the Japanese fleet, lose some ships, and be forced to surrender—or dash into a Chinese port to be interned. Then we'll go home, and the president will get a detailed assessment of the Japanese warships."

Rork's head slowly wagged in the negative. "Admiral, you know I appreciate a good rah-rah, but really, we both know that Rozhestvensky 'tisn't the sort to surrender. Aye, the gentleman doesn't want to do this—but he will do it 'cause Russian honor demands it. An' methinks it'll get ugly as hell, so we three Yanks best be watchin' out for ourselves when the time comes."

He was right, of course, but before I could come up with a suitable reply, his eyes suddenly lit up. "Hey, you know what? Let's broach that fancy vodka now, an' celebrate our return to the Rooskie fleet!"

Hmm. It was far too early in the day for me—or him. I countered with, "Let's save our fancy vodka for after we're finally home—it'll mean even more then. But let's drink the *Russians'* vodka later today, once we get on board *Suvorov*."

And that is precisely what we did at lunch with our respective messmates in the flagship. I lunched with Rozhestvensky and Semenov in the flag cabin, both of whom were elated to see me. At the start, the admiral teased me about my method of return.

"Polis complained to me that you *ordered* him to take you here. He said he thought that far too much for a foreigner, even an admiral, but went along with it. I complimented him for his decision."

That evening, I had dinner in the admiral's quarters with him and Semenov. There was another guest, Rear Admiral Pierre de Jonquières, commander of the French Indochina naval squadron, whose flagship was *Descartes*. It was a full-dress affair, with medals and all the regalia, and Semenov and I both wore our French Legion of Honor medals. They brought an approving nod from the Frenchman upon our introduction. Jonquières turned out to be a jolly fellow in his mid-forties who loved Russians, heartily despised the Japanese, and was a fountain of information about espionage in the region. He had no Russian but was conversant in English, which became our common language.

Jonquières was worried about the near future. He predicted that as soon as the war with Russia was over, the Japanese would attack French Indochina next, with the help of their close allies in Siam, where the minister of war was a Japanese army officer, and the wife of the heir to the throne was a Japanese princess. The French army was busy handling revolts in Tonkin, and the navy didn't have the assets in the area to properly defend the colonies' coastline from seaborne invasion.

He pointed a warning finger at me. "After us, they will go after you in the Philippines."

I asked about what he knew of the Black Dragon Society.

"The Black Dragons are the insidious Japanese vanguard spreading across Asia. It is discounted by most colonial authorities because, after all, the Japanese are only Orientals doing menial or disdainful jobs. Actually, the menial occupations are a very useful subterfuge. Many Black Dragon leaders are actually army and navy officers on foreign assignment, and the rank-and-file common members are held in line by the iron discipline of the code of honor they call Bushido. And they are funding other groups across Asia, like Sun Yat-sen and his Chinese liberal intellectuals, and the Muslims in Manchuria and China. Black Dragons have penetrated everywhere. Their planning is complex and long range."

"Where all are they located?" I pressed.

"Every place in Asia that has Japanese running barbershops, laundries, dry goods stores, vegetable markets, taxis, stevedores, restaurants, brothels, tourist hotels, or bars. And yes, Admiral Wake, that includes your Manila and Honolulu and our Saigon, Phnom Penh, Hué, and Hanoi."

"Admiral Jonquières, how is it you know all this?"

He gave a Gallic shrug. "Our Deuxième Bureau has informants, but only low-level workers who are kept out of important functions—only officers do those. It is very difficult for whites to obtain intelligence, or even true identities, on Black Dragon middle or high ranks. By the way, do any of you know what the Black Dragon refers to?"

None did. Jonquières gave Rozhestvensky a knowing look. "The Amur River, which is called the Black Dragon in Chinese."

"*Our* Amur River?" exclaimed Rozhestvensky.

The Frenchman nodded. "Yes, your border with China. The Japanese named their secret society that to symbolize Pan-Asian strategy. Their work to control all of Asia from Siberia to Singapore is already well under way."

I wondered how many in Washington knew about all this. Particularly Theodore Roosevelt, a famous admirer of Japanese culture, who I knew had lately been very concerned about Japanese expansion. "Thank you for this warning, Admiral Jonquières. I need to pass it along to my leadership. Where is the nearest cable station?"

"Ah, the nearest functioning one is down at Saigon, where I happen to be heading tomorrow. Since you are a neutral, I can deliver your message to the cable office there."

"Thank you, sir. That is very kind. And now I must beg everyone's pardon so I can go to my quarters and compose it immediately."

Little did I know it would be my last cable message out to the world.

46
Waiting for Unwanted Help

Van Phong Bay, Annam, French Indochina Protectorate
Sunday, 14 May 1905

A week later, on 25 April, Jonquières returned to Cam Ranh Bay. After a heartfelt personal apology, he gave Rozhestvensky bad news. Paris had ordered the Russian ships to leave French territory within twenty-four hours.

Given the French government's attitude about the Russian fleet's presence at other colonies, this news was somewhat expected, but it capped a frustrating week for Rozhestvensky. Training mishaps among his ships, newly verified sighting reports of Japanese scout cruisers along the coast prior to our arrival, and mysterious wireless signals in our immediate area all led to the rise of apprehension about the future. One positive accomplishment was that the Hamburg colliers' contract was restored, and with their usual efficiency, the fleet was now completely coaled, even to the point of extra bags being carried on the weather decks.

Rozhestvensky complied with the expulsion the next day, taking his entire fleet out into the South China Sea under the sad but watchful eyes of Jonquières and two French cruisers. They duly reported the Russians were last seen steaming northeast, toward Japan, then the French steamed south toward Saigon.

Rozhestvensky had other plans, however. Late that evening we came about and returned to the coast. The fleet entered secluded Van Phong Bay, sixty miles north of Cam Ranh Bay and, most importantly, possessing no connecting road, rail, or telegraph. Once again at anchor, final preparations resumed for the ultimate battle.

But as remote as Van Phong was, fate intervened. A large coastal fishing vessel saw us and then quickly fled for Saigon. Four days later the French district administrator twenty miles away at Nha Trang was instructed by the governor at Saigon to order us to leave within twenty-four hours. That poor soul didn't arrive until May second, exhausted and disheveled from the jungle journey. Admiral Rozhestvensky again complied and led the entire fleet to sea. Our departure was witnessed by the now well-fed and rested French bureaucrat, who then returned to Nha Trang. The newly returned Jonquières also reported to Saigon that we had left. Once again, the French admiral exited the area, assuming he'd seen the last of us.

The next day, Rozhestvensky returned his ships to an empty Van Phong Bay. But our location was soon learned again by the authorities on May seventh, courtesy of passing vessels. We also got word that Admiral Nebogatov and his Baltic relics had passed by Singapore and were heading our way. Unfortunately, the press—and therefore the Japanese—knew as well. The amusing game of hide and seek was ending. We all knew that soon the world, and the war, would descend on Van Phong Bay.

On the morning of the eleventh, a wireless message was received from Rear Admiral Nebogatov. By three that afternoon, his ships were anchored in the bay. Two hours later he was in a closed-door conference with Rozhestvensky. When he departed the flagship, I noticed Nebogatov's face looked ashen.

The next morning, Jonquières reappeared with the usual expulsion orders, this time more pointed. Time was running out. Then, at half past eight on Sunday morning, the fourteenth of May, Vice Admiral Rozhestvensky took the entire fleet out to sea on a northeast course toward Japan. This time there was no thought of delay or turning back.

Each ship was at battle stations.

1904–1905 VOYAGE OF THE RUSSIAN FLEET
INDIAN OCEAN TO EAST CHINA SEA
Drawn by RADM P.Wake, USN
15 January 1909

47

Peering into the Rain and Mist

East China Sea
19 to 26 May 1905

The mission was no longer to engage and defeat the Japanese fleet, as the Tsar had repeatedly insisted for a year. Now the mission was to evade the enemy and get through to Vladivostok, where the modern ships of the fleet could be used for raiding in the Sea of Japan, or at least to be a fleet-in-being to tie down the Japanese fleet. A major problem, confided by Rozhestvensky to very few, including me, was the recent report that Vladivostok did not have enough food or medicine for another 10,000 men, or fuel, supplies, or repair facilities for our ships. That made the entire mission a futile beau geste to fulfill Tsarist honor. I found it sickening.

On 19 May the sun came out and a gentle warm breeze blew from astern. The Tsar's birthday was celebrated with extra vodka for all hands, while tense lookouts scanned the clear horizons for smoke. There was no way to hide our fifty ships covering ten square miles, smoke funneling into the air, from the enemy on a bright sunny day. The first side to spot the other would gain a mortal advantage.

After many slowdowns from ships' machinery failures, we finally got everyone up to eight knots and in a risky decision passed Japanese-occupied

Taiwan through the adjacent Straits on 20 May. Late that day the weather became overcast with high clouds. Several cruisers were sent off in various directions to raid and confuse the enemy. Most of the supply ships had been ordered away, but a few remained with us.

The battle fleet consisted of Rear Admiral Enqvist's scouting cruiser squadron, Rear Admiral Fölkersam's battleship squadron, Vice Admiral Rozhestvensky's personal squadron of the newest battleships, and Rear Admiral Nebogatov's squadron of ancient hulks. Trailing behind was the hospital ship *Orel* and some Russian colliers.

There were three options for routes toward Vladivostok. Go east into the vast Pacific, circle the Japanese home islands, then go through the narrow, shallow, current-swept, and foggy La Pérouse Strait between the northern Japanese island of Hokkaido and the desolate Russian Sakhalin Island—a navigational nightmare. Second was also to circle Japan to the east, then dash west through the twelve-mile-wide Tsugaru Strait between Hokkaido and Honshu islands, but any element of surprise would be forfeit in those very crowded Japanese home waters.

That left the Korea Straits between Korea and Japan, otherwise known as the Tsushima Straits, which led from the East China Sea north into the Sea of Japan. They were wider and thus easier to navigate in fog and rain, and much shorter and quicker, being the direct route to Vladivostok, at the northern end of the Sea of Japan.

Rozhestvensky explained to me he intended to take the Tsushima Straits. He watched my reaction carefully. "Zinovy, it's even more audacious than your route through the Malacca Straits and passing so close to Taiwan. You know, of course, that Admiral Togo has a base at Busan on the Korean coast, less than a hundred miles away."

"I do, Peter," he said. "But is Togo there? Or is he somewhere in the East China Sea, looking for us? In this weather, we could slip by him and be at Vladivostok in three or four days after passing Tsushima."

I admitted he had a thin but valid point. "It *might* work. And make history."

His next words emerged solemnly. "History will judge me. And history is never kind."

That wasn't Rozhestvensky's only bold decision. His new order on succession of command, should he fall in battle, was also unusual, causing a stir among all ranks. None of the subordinate admirals would take over. Command would instead devolve upon the senior battleship captain still alive and capable. Rozhestvensky never told me directly, but from our conversations over time, I knew what he thought of his admirals: Enqvist was a political climber posing as a sailor, Nebogatov was a soft inexperienced dilettante, Fölkersam was competent and respected but sickly and near death.

On 23 May the weather was calm, with low-hanging clouds. We stopped in the open ocean to coal the ships in a long lazy swell. Everyone knew it would be our last chance to fuel. We were exposed to attack during this, and all hands began working feverishly. They accomplished it in one day—quite a feat—and we resumed steaming late that night.

The next day the weather deteriorated completely, with a rising wind from the northwest, scudding low clouds, and rain. This was a hopeful development since the low visibility would help to hide us, but navigation would be much more difficult with no celestial sights to fix our position. Because of the slower ships, we were still steaming at an average of eight or nine knots at most. The Japanese fleet, well maintained and supplied, had clean hulls and routinely cruised at almost double that speed.

On 25 May the last of the colliers were sent to Shanghai, 90 miles to the west. By my dead reckoning estimate, we were only 450 miles from Tsushima Island in the middle of the straits. Vladivostok was another 600 miles north of that. We had five days steaming until reaching our destination. Everyone was amazed the Japanese hadn't found us and attacked. Or maybe, suggested some officers, they were just waiting for the right moment.

Rear Admiral Dimitry Fölkersam died that day. Rozhestvensky ordered Fölkersam's flag to remain flying on *Oslyabya*, his flagship, so as to not demoralize the sailors. Few were fooled.

The sky cleared with a southwest wind on the twenty-sixth, eliciting foul remarks by the officers and doubled intensity by the lookouts. How could the enemy not see us? That night the overcast returned, accompanied by appreciative comments on the bridge. But all was not rosy, for no less than seven Japanese wireless stations were picked up on *Suvorov's* apparatus, though the exact content of their messages could not be determined.

As we moved north, Rozhestvensky grew more quietly confident in his manner, which influenced others. After nine exhausting months and 18,000 miles, everyone seemed ready to get it over with, one way or another. Gone was the nervous repartee, drunken boasts, or even the muted fear. There were no more illusions, no discussions of grand strategy, no complaints about the navy's abysmal logistics, no morose lethargy—only a grim determination to make personal and professional preparations for the inevitable Armageddon.

After dinner on the twenty-sixth, all officers and men were called to their battle stations. At dawn we would enter the eastern side of the Tsushima Straits and with any luck be through them before the Japanese found us. Rork and Law moved their seabags into my cabin, the easiest to access from the weather decks, should we have to abandon the ship. Our plan was to stay together at all times, starting at dawn. Both of them then returned to their own bunks.

At three o'clock on the morning of the twenty-seventh, my nervousness got the best of me. I took a turn around the deck. Everywhere, the men stared into the dark. On the bridge, Admiral Rozhestvensky dozed in a deck chair. The wireless officer told me they heard the Japanese transmitting close by.

The wind had veered northerly and was cold, with heavy mist almost completely obscuring the quarter-moon rising in the east. The cold air and mist calmed me, and I went back to my quarters, suddenly too tired to worry anymore. In minutes I fell asleep, dreaming of María.

Rork and Law woke me less than two hours later. Both were in their duty uniforms and openly armed with pistols.

Rork simply said, "Time to get up, sir. The Nips've found us."

48

Fate Arrives

Tsushima Straits
Saturday, 27 May 1905

O nce up at the bridge, I noted the wind was strong from the southwest, swells were at about six to eight feet, and the sky was thick with a humid haze. Everyone, including me and my men, was wearing bulky life jackets, standard practice for battle stations. All the officers and men were in their best working uniform. The officers quietly conversed. The petty officers maintained their watchful silence in the eerie glow of the red battle lanterns.

Rozhestvensky, the only man not wearing a life jacket, beckoned me over to him out on the starboard bridge wing. "A Japanese cruiser spotted our hospital ship astern and sounded the alarm by wireless. No sign of Togo yet, but he is out there. I can feel him. They are all out there."

Law and Rork stood in the back corner of the bridge, staying out of the way. I excused myself from Rozhestvensky and rejoined them. We watched as a stream of reports came in from the lookouts and also the wireless room: Japanese ships were sighted and heard in all directions.

Semenov joined us, asking, "Is there anything I can do for you and your men to make sure you are ready for *any* eventuality, Admiral?"

I knew exactly what he meant. "No, we are ready, Vladimir. Thank you for asking."

Rork then uttered what I was thinking, "Been here an' done this before, haven't we, Admiral? Aye, but methinks that last time was a piece o' cake compared to this friggin' mess."

He was referring to being prisoners on the bridge of a Spanish cruiser at the Battle of Santiago seven years earlier. We knew what it was like to be on the hopelessly losing side, on a foreign ship being destroyed by high explosive shells, watching the crew die around us.

"We'll handle it, Rork—if we stick together."

My old friend shrugged. Law, busy recording battle events in a small note-book, looked up. "Aye, aye, sir." Then he went back to writing.

To the east, the mist was lightening somewhat. Dawn was coming. An urgent report came in, followed by another. Semenov translated for us. "The enemy cruiser *Idzumi* has been spotted several miles off to starboard. A wireless has been heard to the north. They think it is Togo's fleet from Busan, heading this way."

At eight o'clock the after 12-inch guns swung around to fire at *Idzumi* five miles away, but she sheered off back into the haze. Minutes later, another five enemy cruisers were seen steering a parallel course to us on our port bow. From the rear of the fleet, the hospital ship *Kostroma* reported four large Japanese warships behind her. Japanese wireless signals constantly filled the ether, reporting on us to their fleet commander. We were surrounded.

At this point, Rozhestvensky told the captain something, who then gave an order to the officer beside him. In seconds, junior officers bustled about, and the senior signalman dashed outside to shout to his colleagues above us at the flag locker. The Russians smiled at each other.

Semenov explained, "It is the Tsar's Coronation Day, so flags are being raised by all ships in celebration. Everyone gets a bit of vodka."

"Now *that's* a capital idea, an' might actually help steady the lads," suggested Rork. "By the by, sir, you do still have our special vodka, right?"

Our special vodka? I ignored his appropriation of my gift from the admiral and replied with mock subservience. "Yes, Chief Bosun's Mate Rork. It's stowed amidst the underwear in my seabag, in proper naval fashion and fully secure for your future enjoyment."

His retort was deadpan serious. "Well done, sir. Methinks we'll be needin' more than a wee nip o' it afore this day's done."

At ten o'clock Rozhestvensky ordered the fleet to form a single line at noon, speed up to eleven knots, and steer course "NO 23"—023 degrees, or north-northeast—the direct track to Vladivostok, now only 500 miles to our north. If the fleet could really maintain eleven knots, it was only three days away. I could see that every man on that bridge did the calculation: after 18,000 excruciating miles circumnavigating the world, safety was only three days away.

At 10:20 a.m. our lead battleship, *Zhemchug,* fired some shots at an enemy cruiser crossing ahead of the fleet, which promptly fled. At 11:20 another battleship near us fired an accidental discharge, immediately apologizing by flag signal. But that shot led to other Russian ships firing blindly into the haze. The admiral didn't explode with a tirade. Instead, he calmly signaled all ships, "Do not waste your ammunition."

At noon the fleet changed formation to a single line ahead and sped up even more. Then the admiral ordered the fleet's crews to lunch, including that extra coronation tot.

Admiral Rozhestvensky's demeanor that day was unlike any I'd seen by him before. Deliberately calm, professionally calculating, compassionately polite—gone was the volatile anger, withering rebukes, physical bullying. I've seen that happen before in combat. Personalities are changed. The nervous uncertainty is over. All that is left is to function. His subordinates took the cue. There was no panic, hesitation, or fear shown by anyone on that bridge.

After the men ate and had their vodka, the officers quickly did likewise, for they knew there wasn't much time left. Semenov and I went to the wardroom, where a toast was raised by a senior staff officer, with Semenov putting it in English for me.

"On this, the great anniversary of the sacred coronation of their Highnesses, may God help us to serve with honor our beloved country! To the health of the Emperor! The Empress! To Russia!"

Everyone tossed down their vodka and cheered in a deep roar, then went back to their battle stations. We saw the Japanese sending cruisers and torpedo boats to cross ahead of us.

That concerned Rozhestvensky, who now gave the order to change the formation again, this time to line abreast. He called me over and explained, "They might be thinking of a torpedo attack. This will be better to enable all twelve of our battleships to concentrate fire on their line."

I concurred. "Very good idea, sir." I didn't add that it would work only if the fleet executed the complicated maneuver perfectly.

Suvorov and two other battleships did just that. The fourth in line, *Alexander*, misread the signal and turned in the wrong direction. Others behind *Alexander* were confused, some following her move, others taking the opposite move. The result was a conglomeration of warships in two vaguely parallel columns steaming toward the Japanese ahead. The four new battleships were heading the right column, the older ones were in the left.

I saw that each column prevented the other from engaging the enemy if they attacked from the other side. Fortunately, the Japanese cruisers and torpedo boats ahead of us did not attack. Instead, they withdrew farther off.

Rozhestvensky didn't curse or shout at his officers. In a measured tone, he ordered his fleet to return to the previous line ahead, squadron by squadron—Enqvist's cruisers in the lead, followed by our squadron, next the deceased Fölkersam's ships, then Nebogatov's, and lastly the hospital ships. Semenov and I conferred, figuring that sorting out the fleet would take, at the very least, half an hour. It appeared the Japanese cruisers' withdrawal would provide enough time.

We were dead wrong.

Three minutes later, at 1:20 p.m., Togo and his main battle fleet of four battleships and eight armored heavy cruisers in column ahead appeared. They were seven miles away to the northeast, on our starboard bow. Soon, many more emerged from the haze.

Fate had arrived.

49
Crossing the "T"

Tsushima Straits
Saturday, 27 May 1905

We were now halfway through the Tsushima Straits, still steaming north-northeast at eleven knots. The low mountains of northern Tsushima Island could barely be seen about eight miles to the west of us. Honshu Island was somewhere off in the haze, thirty miles to the east. The unseen small Japanese island of Iki was ten miles to the southwest. The day had grown warm, the wind slightly diminishing but still from the southwest, and the haze thinning somewhat, with sea horizon visibility increasing to about seven or eight miles.

Rozhestvensky stood on the open forward bridge, studying Togo's flagship *Mikasa* and the Japanese fleet through his binoculars. He ordered his staff and the captain into the armored conning tower, but he stayed out in the open. My men and I remained in the back of the bridge's wheelhouse, watching the proceedings unfold. Law was still busily scribbling details, now many pages into his chronicle of the day.

Periodically, Rozhestvensky would glance back at his fleet, still trying to reconfigure into a line ahead. His face would tense, as if he was struggling to not curse at their lack of skill. Or maybe it was at his own decision to execute a relatively complicated change of formation just as the enemy approached. Either way, he refrained and returned his gaze toward the Japanese ships. They were in a line ahead formation crossing from east to west, four or five miles in front of us.

It was a classic naval tactic—the "Crossing of the T." We were the vertical part of the "T." The Japanese were the horizontal part, which meant that all of their main and secondary guns on their port side would bear on our lead ships, but only our few forward main guns could fire on their ships.

However, there was an adjunct to Togo's advantage. It was temporary, especially if the Japanese were steaming fast, and they were. I estimated they were moving across our front at fifteen knots. That would give them ten to fourteen minutes to accomplish maximum destruction to the Russian ships. After that, Togo's ships would only have their stern guns bearing on us, or they would have to turn their column around and attack again. In that turn they would be slowed down, vulnerable to confusion, and exposed to the concentrated fire from our fleet crossing *their* "T" from behind them.

But beyond a few random shots, they weren't firing. Evidently, Togo wanted us to get closer before unleashing salvos at us. *He'll have to turn back across our path soon*, I calculated.

Sure enough, minutes later Togo had his ships turn 180 degrees to come back across our front. But he ordered it done not *simultaneously* but in *succession*, the slowest and least confusing method but one that also exposed them to our fire longer. I wondered why.

As the first two Japanese ships, *Mikasa* and a cruiser, turned at 1:49 p.m., Rozhestvensky gave the order to commence firing. *Suvorov* fired her first shell at Togo's *Mikasa*. It exploded only twenty yards astern, an outstanding first shot at a range of 6,400 yards, or three-and-a-quarter miles. Follow-on salvos bracketed Togo's flagship. I was surprised and impressed—the Russian gun crews had had minimal practice due to the scarcity of ammunition for training.

Beside me, Rork exclaimed, "Bloody good shootin' by our lads!" More subdued, Law observed, "Good firing rate, too." But Semenov, a gunnery expert, warned, "There is something wrong."

Mikasa held her fire as the fountains of water rose all around her. But in spite of these near misses, there were no decisive hits, no explosions on board, and no major damage to Togo's flagship. Unfortunately, only the three lead Russian ships—at least they were the new battleships—could fire, all aimed at *Mikasa*. The others behind were still maneuvering into formation or were masked by their colleagues ahead of them.

Then, at 1:52 p.m., the Japanese opened fire. Grossly wide of the mark—*us*—at first, within five minutes they started zeroing in. Rozhestvensky was still out on the open forward bridge, studying the enemy's direction and speed, and noting the fall of their shot nearing us. He was accompanied by an aide, some young prince, keeping a record of the admiral's observations. Around us the water boiled with very close near misses, unleashing a hail of shrapnel. The Japanese had our bearing and range and were firing incessantly at us—a mind-stunning volume of blast and noise. Several rounds hit the port side, *Suvorov* shuddering from the concussions.

Dashing out to Rozhestvensky, I shouted into his ear, "Zinovy, this fleet needs your decision-making. Get in the armored conning tower. *Now*, my friend."

He turned toward me. His physical transformation was complete—gone were the slumped shoulders, tired expression, and dragging foot of the past several weeks. The man before me was Vice Admiral Zinovy Petrovich Rozhestvensky, the hope of all Russia, standing tall and speaking firmly, his penetrating eyes showing no doubt or fear.

A strange calming sensation swept over me: I realized that all of Rozhest-vensky's life—and all of *my* life—had led us to this exact place on earth and point in time. I had become part of his destiny. He would never surrender. He would die here on this ship.

We were all going to die together. Here, in the Sea of Japan, so close to a port of safety. So far from our homes and families.

50
The Tower

He did a slight bow to me. "You are right, Peter. And you and your men are coming in the armored tower too. Let us go."

The admiral led the way. I gestured for Law and Rork to follow me, and we all went aft through the hatch into the crammed tower. At that moment, a Japanese shell hit the open forward bridge where we had stood. The young prince was still there, writing. The blast destroyed the entire deck area. Two stretcher bearers rushed over and took the bloody mess away.

As before, in the tower we Americans stayed out of the way, shoulder rubbing shoulder in the back. Rozhestvensky squinted through the tower's narrow observation slits at *Mikasa*, now only three miles away. Another round hit just outside the tower. Then another. The shower of thudding shrapnel against the steel became constant.

By 2:15 p.m., *Suvorov* was being pummeled under the fire of several ships but taking it—still level and still steaming forward. Most important, I could still hear and feel her big 12-inch main guns firing back. Inside the ship, communications were still working via the voice tubes and telephones. Semenov provided a stream of information to me from the reports being given to his admiral.

Looking through the viewing port, Rozhestvensky bellowed a question. "Signal officer, what is that signal of Admiral Togo's? Is it in plain words?"

"Yes, sir, it is in plain signal flag code for," the lieutenant quickly replied, then read off verbatim from his signal book, "The Empire's fate depends upon the outcome of this battle. Let everyone do his best."

A faint smile crossed the admiral's face as he glanced at the signal lieutenant.

"How very Nelsonian . . . Admiral Togo trained with the Royal Navy. He learned well. I would like to meet him one day. In a Russian prison!"

The lieutenant laughed and his admiral returned to the viewing slit, but soon put down his binoculars. "Too much smoke and flame outside. I can't see a thing."

Semenov muttered to me, "Shimose—that new Japanese explosive they put in their shells. It has an incendiary effect as well as blast. The reports say we are on fire everywhere."

He'd explained it to me before. In his previous battles with the Japanese offshore of Port Arthur, their shells had literally burned the Russians' ships up. After the initial blast, the paint used on Russian ships fed the Shimose flames and spread them quickly. Suddenly, I could feel the heat increasing inside the tower. Smoke began streaming in through the slits.

Just then the forward main gun turret just ahead of us was hit. A wave of shrapnel thudded against the tower, several of the shards ricocheting into the tower from its top. Several petty officers at the helm and a senior staff officer collapsed, dead. The signal lieutenant screamed in pain. An officer took the wheel.

"Design error," said Semenov. "The fools back home put an overhang on it, and the shrapnel is coming in through that gap."

At 2:19 p.m., another round struck the ship near the conning tower; this hail of shrapnel hit Rozhestvensky, wounding him slightly but killing several others. The deck inside the tower had bodies everywhere. The footing was slippery from the gore.

"Dammit to hell!" blurted Law. I looked over and saw his notebook was soaked in Russian blood. His hand holding it was shaking.

I put a hand on his shoulder. "Steady on, Captain Law. You'll just have to memorize the time and events from here on. It's *important* for us to learn here, for when *we* have to face the Japanese. Can you do that?"

He was still shaken. "Yes . . . yes, sir. Sorry."

Rork nudged him with a shoulder. "Hell, Mr. Law, you're solid as a rock. I'm the one who's bloody friggin' scared!"

Then another round hit. This one got Rozhestvensky in the head and legs. He collapsed into a chair and a sailor wrapped a filthy towel around his head. A flag lieutenant, the last one of them left alive, held the towel. I went to see if I could help my friend.

In the dim red haze from the sole remaining battle lantern, I felt the wounds, which were bleeding badly. None was mortal—if he got medical help. "You need the doctor to dress these wounds right away, Zinovy."

"They are a bit busy, Peter—"

Another explosion interrupted his answer. The ship's captain was hit in the head, his scalp peeled back to the bone. He was laid on the deck. A lieutenant commander reported all the voice tubes and telephone lines wrecked and sent the last available messenger to the engine room for information.

I realized the ship was listing heavily to port. We seemed to be stopped. The flames were all around us now. The tower was filling with thick oily smoke. They dragged away the bodies to open the hatch to the vertical ladder that led to the deck below.

"Admiral first, then everyone else climb down," Semenov ordered. He was the senior man left standing. Right after I helped to lower Rozhestvensky down into the ladder way, there was another blast. Rork fell down on me. I was still kneeling, and we ended up in a heap on the deck, his leg draped over my shoulder.

Law staggered over and dragged him off me, stretching him out on the hot deck, then sat down next to him. I rolled over to check Rork.

His face contorted in pain, he gasped, "Bloody damn sorry, sir. Me old pegs're actin' up."

I looked. Rork's trousers were in shreds and soaked in blood.

51
Blood and Smoke

Tsushima Straits
Saturday, 27 May 1905

Law and I ripped the trouser legs away. There were small gashes from ankle to thigh—from metal splinters.

Rork tensed again, grunting out, "How's . . . me . . . jewels, . . . sir?"

I examined him. "Fine, Sean. Damn near virginal, right Edwin?"

Law caught my drift. "Well, I don't know about the virginal part, sir, but everything appears to be in proper working order."

Rork groaned, "Fine bloody time . . . for jokes, . . . *sirs*. Damn, this deck's hot."

It was, and getting hotter fast. With grunts and groans from all three of us, Law lowered Rork down the ladder, where I took his waist while Law climbed down. I looked around for Semenov, but he was gone. So was everyone else. The lower deck had been abandoned too. The deck was canting more. We had to get out, but how? In the smoke and chaotic noise, I was disoriented. Law went through a side hatch and found a way out to the boat deck. By supreme effort, Rork walked on his own with his arms around our shoulders. We ended up out on the boat deck, forward of where the forward funnel had been. It was completely gone. There was no fresh air—though it was three o'clock in the afternoon, the sky was dark with thick black smoke.

I looked around us, shocked at the sight. The entire ship was wrecked.

Masts and funnels were gone. The list was at least ten degrees. Charred bodies were strewn across the deck. Everything wooden was aflame, and the painted steel had completely peeled and buckled, with jagged smoking holes everywhere. The main guns forward and aft were wrecked and silent, but several 6-inch guns were still firing on the starboard side. We descended a ladder to the main deck, starboard side, and made our way aft.

Somehow, *Suvorov* was still moving, maybe four or five knots, and turning out of the line of Russian battleships in a wide circle to starboard, toward far-off Japan. Obviously, our rudder was jammed. The ships astern began to follow us in the turn, then *Alexander* straightened up and resumed the fleet's original course to the north. I guessed that her captain, Rozhestvensky's old friend Bukhvostov, had realized *Suvorov* was no longer functioning, and he was now leading the fleet, as per the succession of command orders.

The remaining battleships steamed past us to the north toward Vladivostok. But I knew none would make it—each was heavily damaged. Astern of us, *Oslyabya*, the dead Fölkersam's flag still flying over the ship, was rolling over on her port side and capsizing. At 3:20 p.m., twenty minutes after *Oslyabya* sank, *Alexander*, smoke gushing from stem to stern, turned out of the line. *Borodino* took the lead. She was instantly hit all over.

At that demoralizing moment, Rork piped up, "Feelin' a bit stronger in me pegs, an' the bleedin's slowed. Aye, nary a worry for me, sir."

His timing was perfect, but his veracity wasn't. As Law and I set Rork down on the deck, he groaned in pain. And he was still bleeding through the rag bandages wrapped around his legs. Law propped his legs up on a bollard to reduce the bleeding.

I asked passing Russians where Admiral Rozhestvensky or Captain Semenov were. No one knew. Unless I spoke directly to them, the blank-faced Russian sailors ignored us, trudging by on their tasks. Law volunteered to brave the flames and smoke, get down to my quarters, and bring out our seabags. He came back half an hour later, dragging the three partly charred bags, and collapsed in exhaustion next to us.

The enemy battleships were still busy destroying the remaining Russian battle line, the big guns echoing somewhere to the north of us. *Suvorov* was on her own now. Japanese cruisers arrived and fired slowly into her as they circled. *Suvorov*'s lone still-functioning 6-inch gun, and few remaining light guns, shot back at the enemy cruisers, more a gesture of defiance than anything effective. I was amazed the ship was still afloat. I heard no talk of surrender from the Russians, seaman or officer. They just kept trudging by, doing their work.

At 4:15 p.m. a thick fog mixed with the ship's roiling smoke. The sun completely disappeared, the horizon vanished, and I couldn't even tell our direction of movement. At first, I thought this smoky fog might provide some concealment to abate the enemy bombardment, but a few minutes later several Japanese torpedo boats attacked. The stern exploded from a torpedo impact. Normally, that would have been a serious blow, but now it was just another catastrophic hit. The torpedo boats pulled back into the fog as the cruisers resumed their unhurried firing into us. I knew what they were doing. Rork put it into words.

"Those Nip bastards're usin' us for gunnery an' torpedo practice."

52

Nyet!

Tsushima Straits
Saturday, 27 May 1905

A t a little after five o'clock, a lone torpedo boat approached. I braced for another explosion, but someone midship on *Suvorov* yelled something above the din in Russian, which sounded hopeful.

"*Buiny*! Idi syuda istro!"

Then I saw what they were talking about. The boat flew a flag with the blue "X" cross on a white field—the flag of the Russian Imperial Navy. It was *Buiny*, and the flagship's officers called for them to come alongside to starboard.

"Peter! Thank God you and your men are alive!"

I turned and saw a man limping toward me, a dark silhouette against the flaming ready ammunition and guns of the stern 6-pounder guns. He got closer and I could see his once-immaculate uniform was torn and bloody, with burned sleeves. His face was covered in soot and grime, and the eyes were full of tears. It was Vladimir Semenov. His left leg barely moved. Law and I rushed toward him as he stumbled over a body.

"Sit down, Vladimir. Here with us."

"No time, Peter. *Suvorov* has no boats left. She will be gone soon. The torpedo boat has come to take off the admiral and staff to another ship, to continue command of the fleet. You and your men must come too. The admiral will insist."

Buiny stopped fifty yards away. Officers on both vessels yelled back and forth for several minutes. *Buiny* moved closer, then finally came alongside forward of us, the metal grinding and shrieking as the hulls crashed. Several *Suvorov* officers jumped on board the torpedo boat; others were gathered in a group on the battleship's main deck. I realized they were carrying Rozhestvensky, who I could see was wounded even more badly. The admiral was giving orders, but the men didn't seem to be listening.

Semenov left us and went forward to join the others. "Come *now!*" he shouted back to us.

"All right, let's go, men," I managed to croak out of my dry, choking mouth. "This is it, our only chance. I'll take Rork. Edwin, you get our bags."

It took a while for the three of us to stand up. Law, still memorizing the facts, glanced at his pocket watch and announced to himself, "At 5:38 p.m., disembarking *Suvorov* to *Buiny.*"

Up forward, they were trying to get Rozhestvensky over to the torpedo boat. There was no ladder or gangway left. We would all have to jump. Normally, that would be a considerable drop, but the battleship was so low in the water she was nearly level with the torpedo boat. The problem was the swell, grinding the two vessels, then pulling them apart.

The officers carrying Rozhestvensky jumped en masse. They made it to the torpedo boat's deck, some of them falling to their knees but saving their admiral. Semenov jumped over and almost fell between the hulls. He ended up sprawled on *Buiny*'s deck but didn't get up. A burly sailor dragged him to a hatch cover and left him. Officers on the torpedo boat started yelling for the other staff officers to hurry. Several were about to jump, then hesitated.

Buiny's crew began pushing away from the battleship with poles. More shouting. We staggered faster toward the jump off place. The torpedo boat engines suddenly rumbled.

"*Nyet!*" I gasped as loud as I could.

Nobody heard me. The torpedo boat began moving away.

"Oh bloody friggin' hell . . ." growled Rork, then dropped to his knees. Both of us fell to the deck. One step ahead of us, Law turned around to help. But just at that moment, time ended.

A blinding flash of white and an ear-splitting roar stopped everything.

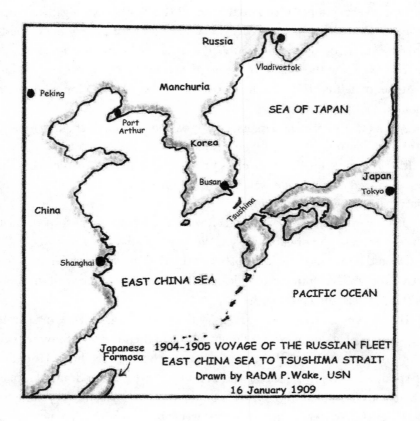

Part 3

Mother Russia

53
Back to Reality

Tsushima Straits
Saturday, 27 May 1905

I have no idea how long we lay on the hatch cover. Grotesque sounds and sights faded. I wasn't there anymore. I was with María.

Suddenly, I was jarred out of my memories and back into our deadly reality. Close by, a Japanese rapid-fire gun began firing its rhythmic thudding. Several more joined in. They were attacking again.

Law's eyes were still swollen shut. "Are they Russian?"

Rork answered. "Nay, they're Nips. Our ship's done for now."

He and I watched the Japanese torpedo boat squadron coming right at us in line-abreast formation, their white bow waves like maniacal smiles in the gloom. I heard the whoosh of compressed gas as torpedoes were fired at short range. Explosions rippled along *Suvorov*'s port side. The torpedo boats rushed by us, their wakes washing over the hatch cover as we three held on for dear life.

"An' there she goes, the poor bastards . . ." murmured Rork. "God bless 'em all."

Suvorov began a roll over to port, disappearing in a funereal hiss of steam and huge roiling air bubbles. The Japanese cruisers stopped firing. The torpedo boats never returned. Everything went quiet, and without the glow of *Suvorov*'s flames, the sea and sky were dark.

Rork broke our silence. "Hey, that fella's movin'." He pointed to a dead body floating next to the hatch. The body had a life belt and was holding on to several canvas floats. It sputtered something in Russian, lifting up a head to stare at us.

I reached out for him in the dark. He reached back. Young and strong, he grasped my hand, then my arm, pulling himself over to us with sheer desperation. He was also big, and I couldn't lift him.

"Law, I know you can't see him, but just grab his shoulders and pull when I tell you. Rork, once we get him up a bit, pull him all the way on board. Now!"

The man seemed to understand our intent. With profane grunts in English, Gaelic, and Russian, we all heaved. It took a while, but we got him on board. Everyone just lay there for several minutes, catching our breaths. The floats the Russian used were drifting away.

They looked familiar to me. "What the hell—those are our seabags. They're floating!"

"Yes, sir," said Law, his head swiveling to turn toward our voices. "I put some life belts in yours' and the chief's seabags. Figured they might keep them up if we sank. Only enough for two. Guess mine's gone. Not much in it anyway."

"Sorry for the loss of your seabag, Mr. Law, but damn well done on the other two," I congratulated him. "They've got our weapons. I'll go and bring them back."

I swam over to them. Rork hauled them and me on board. In the dark, I didn't dare open them and lose something, but they felt as if still full of our weapons and belongings.

The Russian said something to me. I tried to remember the little Russian I knew, but my mind went blank. "Hell, I can't even remember how to say hello."

The Russian abruptly said, "Hello, sir. Lieutenant . . . Sergei . . . Dyvoryanin. I learn . . . English . . . at academy. I at . . . battleship *Borodino*. Gone now. You . . . Americans with . . . admiral at *Suvorov*. Gone now. All ships gone now . . ." His voice faltered.

He put his hand on mine. "Spasi menya . . . you help . . . me."

Sergei paused for a moment. Then he put his face closer to me.

"Thank . . . you."

54
XGE

Sea of Japan
Sunday, 28 May 1905

Dawn arrived in a miasma of acrid smoke, fog, and the stench of death. My acuity was slowed by a mental haze of uncertainty and fear. Where were we? Presumably somewhere to the north of where we had been, propelled by the current, which I recalled moved at about a knot. That meant about twelve miles, well out in the Sea of Japan.

There was no wind. The swells had gone down. One by one the others awoke, Law first. Scanning the obscure horizons, we saw nothing. But we did hear the rumble of engines. Sergei identified them as Japanese cruisers or battleships.

Rork's shrapnel cuts had closed somewhat with the saltwater immersion, so my first task was to examine Law's eyes. I am experienced at gunshot, stabbing, and burn wounds, but eyes? I had Rork hold him down while Sergei stroked his forehead and made reassuring sounds in Russian. I knew enough to bathe his eyelids but had no fresh water. The high alcohol percentage of the vodka in my bag would most certainly not do. The seawater was filthy with lubricating oil, coal dust, and debris. That left my spit, of which I had little. Rubbing it on his eyelids, I pulled them apart as gently as I could. Law gritted his teeth and never made a sound of distress, but it was obviously painful.

I saw no obvious damage to the eye itself, but they were blood red. Perhaps the oily seawater had inflamed them? I didn't know.

"I can see a little bit, sir. Shapes, but no detail," Law said. "It's too bright for me to focus on anything."

I had Sergei provide some shade for Law's eyes. "How about now?"

"Better, sir!" he exclaimed. "It's getting better!"

"Good, then we're going to put a cloth around your eyes to shade them, and have you open them every hour. You can use your own spit to moisten them."

"A wee nip o' that vodka could help the lad right about now too, sir," suggested Rork, with a remarkably straight face. Sergei perked up at that word. Even Law stirred a bit.

"No, not yet, men," I said. "We're dehydrated. Alcohol would be very bad for us."

Rork damn near pouted. Sergei took his cue from Rork and laid back down. Law unenthusiastically said, "Yes, sir."

We lay there for hours while I carefully inventoried the bags. It was good news. Our weapons, belongings, and the fancy vodka were all still there, most in good shape due to our waterproof wrappings. There was no fresh water, but there was a sadly small tin of expensive caviar. We shared it slowly, each having a sip of the briny water from the tin as well. Then we laid back down and waited. For what, we didn't know.

At 8:32 a.m., Sergei suddenly sat up and turned to the east. He gestured for us to be quiet. Then I heard it, a higher pitched rumble than the others.

"Russkaya . . . torpednyy," he said to himself, then told us, "Russian . . . torpedo boat."

And there it was, heading at fifteen knots from east to northwest. It would pass at least a mile from us.

"Everyone, stand up as best you can and wave everything you've got. I'll keep firing my shotgun to get their attention."

None of us could really stand, so all hands knelt and waved shirts, rags, and a Russian navy flag from my seabag, which Vladimir Semenov had given me as a memento one drunken evening. I fired the shotgun—my Spencer pump-action .12-gauge—at the distant torpedo boat every twenty seconds. After several minutes of this bizarre effort it seemed useless to me.

Then they slowed and turned toward us.

We redoubled our exertions. They sped up. Five minutes later they came alongside. In seconds, we were brought on board, where everyone was amazed at seeing Americans. Dozens of other survivors were collapsed all over the decks. The skipper told Sergei he was heading north to the fleet to put all the survivors on a larger ship. The first thing we did was drink a liter of water each, followed by a glass of the wardroom's vodka.

The skipper said the Japanese were all around us, and within moments of resuming the course northward, we saw plumes of funnel smoke everywhere, especially to the north. On ahead of us, a heavy-caliber cannonade began between the two sides. Two hours later, we saw the remnants of the Russian fleet, Nebogatov's ships. There were battleships heading south, some of which didn't look that damaged, but the skipper took us alongside the nearest ship, the light cruiser *Izumrud*, where we were quickly herded up and onto the cruiser's deck. Then the torpedo boat sped off to the northeast.

Having heard of my arrival on his ship, *Izumrud*'s captain came down to the main deck to meet me. "I am Captain (second rank) Hans William Freiherr von Fersen. Yes, I speak English, for I had the honor to be our country's naval attaché at Washington from 1899 to 1902. We met there. Do you remember me now?"

I did, indeed, remember him. Fersen was a Baltic-Russian of German heritage, like so many other officers in the Imperial Russian Navy, and highly regarded in Washington as an intelligent and charming naval officer. "Hans, I do remember you, and we are *very* glad to see you!"

"Admiral, you and your men will be taken care of right away. And you and I have much to discuss later. But for right now, there are more pressing matters. Vice Admiral Rozhestvensky is mortally wounded. Rear Admiral Nebogatov is in command of the fleet now."

He cast a disgusted glance at the battleships, then looked at me. "I am told he has just hoisted the XGE signal. Our other ships are repeating the signal."

XGE is the international signal flag code for "I am surrendering." In the far distance I could see Japanese battleships coming toward them. That Rozhestvensky was dead or dying didn't surprise me from what I saw on *Suvorov*'s deck. But the captains of all the new battleships in the vice admiral's squadron were dead too? Nebogatov had taken command of the fleet? We were only a few hundred miles from Vladivostok—the fleet's destination. Nebogatov's battleships were old and slow, but some of the cruisers weren't. Why not have them at least try to make a run for it?

I asked him: "Will you obey Nebogatov's order to surrender?"

"What signal, Peter? At the Battle of Copenhagen, Horatio Nelson accidentally put the telescope to his blind eye and couldn't see his admiral's signal to disengage—and he won the battle. I don't seem to be able to see Nebogatov's signal either. Must be the haze."

"What are you going to do?"

"We're heading for Vladivostok, as Rozhestvensky had ordered. We will not win this battle and we may die in our escape, but we will die as *free* Russians! I am sorry you must share our fate, though. You may end up in the water again."

Fersen then returned to the bridge, for enemy cruisers were reported heading our way. I thought about how his decision affected us. If Fersen had surrendered, the Japanese *might* have treated Americans with courtesy and arranged our transport home. But Fersen didn't—couldn't—surrender, and so Rork, Law, and I were tied to the Russians' destiny.

After we were quickly attended to by the ship's medical men, the four of us (we Americans and Sergei) were shown our quarters—a cramped junior officer's cabin. I told them to get some rest while they could. Full of nervous energy, I stood out on the main deck as *Izumrud*'s engines spun up. Within minutes, black smoke poured from her three funnels and we were steaming northeast toward Vladivostok at twenty-two knots, faster than any Russian ship I'd yet been on board. For a moment it felt exhilarating.

Then the Japanese cruisers opened fire.

55
Decisions

For hours, as *Izumrud* steadily outdistanced her pursuers, the Japanese never gave up their chase—until the fog blessedly returned in the mid-afternoon. By miraculous timing, a steam pipe burst in the boiler room just *after* the fog arrived. It caused an immediate loss of speed and some other problem degraded the steering engine. We heard the enemy cruisers pass us to the west and then back to the south.

The crew repaired the problem, but now the liability was coal. *Izumrud* had used up so much of her 522 tons during the battle and escape that she had only enough left to steam north at thirteen knots. This we did for the next two days, all alone but expecting to see the Japanese squadrons searching for us at any moment.

During this time, Fersen changed his mind about Vladivostok. He reasoned that the enemy had probably already arrived there in strength to cut off any escaping Russian ships, so he decided to head for the remote bays to the north of there. Either Vladimir Bay or St. Olga Bay would serve his purpose, for he knew them both. Both were deep and shielded from view by enemy ships at sea. There he could arrange for coal to be delivered to the ship by land, then leave before the Japanese searched the coast for us.

When he explained this to me, he ended his comments with a laugh and some dry Russian wit. "Admiral, I have decided that you will not be with us when we finally get the coal and get under way. Oh, yes, I know that by this long time you must love Russian ships and sailors so very much that you never want to leave us. But, no, my friend. You must go overland to Vladivostok when we first arrive at the bay. I am assigning Sergei to be your guide and assistant. And there in Vladivostok your men will be treated by their army doctors, and *you* will be treated very well by the admirals and generals. You are a fellow admiral, after all!"

I wondered if Vladivostok was even still in Russian hands but didn't bring that up. I simply thanked him, never letting on how relieved I was to be getting ashore. Hopefully, I could use my rank to get a cable sent back home.

We never did see the enemy this entire time, though several smoke plumes were seen over the horizon. As we approached the Russian coast on the twenty-ninth of May, we had only sixty tons of coal left in our bunkers. Fersen decided Vladimir Bay would be best.

There was no time or coal to wait for daylight. At one o'clock in the morning of the thirtieth, *Izumrud* went in under cover of darkness—the last quarter of the moon being obscured by the ubiquitous fog of that area, which is even thicker near land. Everyone on board, from captain to cook, was excited and emotional.

They had survived the grueling nine-month voyage, the catastrophic battle, and the sea chase by the enemy—and now they were finally home at land belonging to Mother Russia. We passed between the two high-ground headlands and entered the bay, turning to port to anchor in the deeper southern part.

But Fersen turned in the fog twenty seconds too soon.

Izumrud suddenly crashed to a stop, throwing everyone off balance. Her bow was inclined up and the hull canted slightly over to starboard. We'd hit the rocks by the headland. On an ebb tide. A cliff loomed up on the port bow. I looked around us, peering into the dark, then checked the chart and with a sinking heart found my suspicion was correct. Come dawn, *Izumrud* would be in full view of any enemy ship who passed by offshore.

Fersen immediately tried backing off, but we'd slid up on the rocks at eight knots. Fully a third of *Izumrud* was lodged on and between huge black boulders. And the ebb tide was pressing broadside on us. Engineers reported cracks in the hull and shattered interior piping. All night he tried. Much later in the morning the flood tide started, but at its height it didn't help—we were too far onto the rocks.

Visibility improved somewhat as the day unfolded and the fog thinned, but that just made our dire situation more apparent. His face a study in exhausted frustration, Fersen asked for opinions from his officers. They said the ship was immovable. The choice was to wait for the possibility that a large ship from Vladivostok could come and pull *Izumrud* off—not a certainty by any means—or scuttle her by explosions to prevent the Japanese from salvaging and using her.

Fersen decided on blowing up his ship, stating that as a proud Russian naval officer and man of honor, *he* would never surrender a Russian warship to the enemy—a clear and derisive reference to Nebogatov's surrender.

Izumrud's boats were making constant runs up the bay to a small village, and we Americans and Sergei Dyvoryanin were sent to the village after our lunch. The goodbye with Fersen on the quarterdeck was as emotional for me as that with Semenov and Rozhestvensky. He wished us luck for our long trip home, saying at least we would be away from the war and safe on dry land. I told him I thought his decisions to be the difficult but correct ones. Then I wished him good fortune in the future.

And with that we went ashore.

56

Expensive Vodka from Grimy Glasses

Vladivostok, Russia
Friday, 2 June 1905

What we found at Vladivostok was not the oasis of peace and culture I'd been led to expect in the last month by my *Suvorov* shipmates. Instead, it was a sullen place ravaged by riots and vandals, starving for food, and dreading further disasters in the war. It expected to be cut off from the rest of Russia at any time—its sole tenuous link being the single track of the Trans-Siberian Railway and the Manchurian rail extension that wound to it through that mountainous region from Vladivostok. This peril came not from the Japanese enemy, however. They were certainly getting closer to the rail line, but the immediate danger came from Chinese bandits and Russian revolutionary mutineers.

I had been without news of the land war or the unrest sweeping Russia since Saigon. It had gotten far worse. An hour after arriving in the city, Sergei Dyvoryanin heard all about it from an army major on the street and then passed it on to me.

The Japanese armies had overrun much of Manchuria to the west, Chinese mounted bandits in the pay of Japan were raiding supply depots along the railway, and mutinous Russian troops were periodically robbing officers on trains and generally disrupting schedules. Several army units in the city and surrounding fortresses and defensive lines had balked at following orders or openly refused. Many displayed red flags of revolution. Fierce-looking Ussuri Cossacks had been brought in to restore discipline and order.

Only three ships of the Russian fleet at Tsushima made it to Vladivostok. *Izumrud* had *almost* made it, of course, but fully thirty-six ships had been destroyed, captured, or surrendered. After Vice Admiral Rozhestvensky had transferred off *Suvorov*, not one officer or man of the over 900 still on board survived the battle. There was some good news, though. The admiral and Semenov were slowly recovering from their wounds as prisoners of war in Japan. The vessel to which they transferred from the torpedo boat ended up surrendering to the Japanese—against Rozhestvensky's orders as he lay semiconscious in a bed down below.

There was no grand flag-rank reception for me in Vladivostok, which was fine by me. The military and naval commanders were overwhelmed by the war, and social functions or hospitality had long since ceased. I wasn't in mental or physical condition to deal with that anyway. My companions and I were exhausted by three days of rough travel in a crude ox-cart, pulled by an openly mutinous mule, across three-thousand-foot mountains to get to the city.

We went to find the army telegraph office. They were inundated with message traffic, there being only one line still functioning—and that frequently downed. Sergei explained to me only official cables could be sent, so my message to María stayed in my pocket. What was sent to the U.S. Embassy in Saint Petersburg was this: XXX—WAKE ET AL SAFE IN VLADIVOSTOK—X—FORWARD TO POTUS—XXX.

It was my first communication home since Saigon. With the magnitude of the Russian disaster now known to me, I worried that everyone back home assumed Rork, Law, and I were among the thousands of dead. María and my family would be devastated. I trusted that once Theodore got the cable, he would let María know we were safe.

Immediately after that task was done, Sergei and I took Rork and Law to the naval hospital. Once I saw the filth and disorder, I instantly took them out of there. There was no space for us at the naval barracks, so we got the last room available at the only "hotel" left open, really more of a flophouse. Through Sergei's efforts, I paid for a doctor and his attendant to attend Rork and Law.

Rork's lacerations were beyond the stage where they could be sutured properly, and most had turned into dozens of livid purple scars, beneath which the shards of shrapnel still lay. Some were still open and infected, the yellow, black, and red colors warning they were getting worse. The doctor cleaned out the wounds and bandaged them. He gave me more bandages for use later but said that was all he could give since they were running low. Neither could the doctor remove the painful embedded shards that impeded Rork's walking—they were also low on surgical antiseptic. *Izumrud*'s carpenter had created a pair of crutches for him. It now appeared he would have to use them for some time.

The doctor said Law's still-swollen eyes were probably the result of the Shimose incendiary component in the Japanese shells. The flash of the explosion had burned his eyelids, which might get better if frequently bathed in a salve he gave us. Law could see now, but his sight remained a bit blurry. The doctor could make no prediction regarding the eyesight getting better.

After the doctor left, Rork insisted we broach the fancy vodka, that it would improve our morale. He had a good point, but I suggested an improvement on his plan. "Let's drink one bottle only, leaving the other for when we emerge out of this mess into someplace more civilized."

That met with unanimous support and during a lull in the frequent rain we all retired to the roof at sunset. There we took in the depressing vista of the city, a rather anemic rainbow in gray sky, and drank the expensive vodka from grimy glasses.

Halfway through the bottle, Rork let out a long sigh and turned to regard me ruefully.

"Methinks there's a damned hellish trend in our lives. Spain back in '74, Peru in '81, Vietnam in '83, Samoa in '89, the Spanish cruiser in '98, an' now this totally bollocks'd up mess—we're always in the bloody midst o' the friggin' fightin' on the *losing side*. You know, we're actually gonna get *killed* if we keep doin' this sort o' thing. An' oohee, me tired bones're too damned old to get killed. They want to die in me sleep after a decent romp."

"Rork, you're right, yet again. Once we get home, no more of this adventure stuff for us. Just paperwork in a dull office. We'll die of boredom . . ."

He nodded approvingly and resumed his drinking.

57

The Straightforward Russian Method

Vladivostok, Russia
Saturday, 3 June 1905

I thought about Rork's comment later that night while trying to decide how to get us home. There were no neutral ships in Vladivostok on which to book passage away from the war zone. That left three options. Go east to Japan, south to China, or west to European Russia.

Which was the least likely to involve combat? Even though we were neutrals, nobody stops for legal niceties in the midst of a heated battle. The fighting on both land and sea was far too intense to somehow get to Japan by boat. The route to China, by sea or land, was also cut off by the fighting. That left the final option: get to European Russia on the Trans-Siberian Railway.

Westbound trains only carried sick and wounded Russian soldiers. Because they carried no fresh reinforcements or valuable cargo, they were less harassed by bandits or mutineers. I talked it over with the others. We all agreed, the railway was the best way to get out of the danger area. However, I knew that to get us on board one of those trains, we would need transit orders signed by a senior Russian army or naval officer. That might prove difficult since I knew none of them, they had not reached out to me, and most probably thought I was pro-Japanese because of my nationality.

The next morning, Lieutenant Sergei Dyvoryanin handled that problem as well, employing the straightforward Russian method. Using a few of my gold U.S. coins I obtained at Singapore, he bribed a senior clerk at naval headquarters to provide him the proper forms for each of us. Then he filled them out in Russian Cyrillic, making up an admiral's name and scrawling the approval signature on each form. He explained that with a little additional pecuniary lubrication—two more gold coins—the train guards wouldn't look too closely at the transit passes. Besides, he added with a grin, half of them couldn't read and none had any idea who the real admirals were.

The next morning, we lugged our seabags and a few scrounged loaves of stale bread to the depot. As predicted, the guards slid the coins into their pockets and waved us through, not even looking at the passes. We were assigned to a dilapidated former passenger train car, now filled with moaning and wailing wounded soldiers. The four of us crammed together on a wooden bench seat made for three at the front end of the car and waited.

At Sergei's recommendation, we all wore plain overcoats outside our uniforms. Of course, we were armed to the teeth with pistols and knives, our long guns ready in the seabags at our feet. Our plan was to be quiet, try to blend in, and be respectful. These wounded were mostly uneducated peasants and, like their class in every country, were very wary of anything foreign. With luck, we might gain their confidence, or at least tolerance.

There were no medical people for the wounded other than two slightly wounded soldiers, who were to tend the others. Sadly, I saw they had no medicine or bandage supplies for the three-week journey. A friendly conductor tended a steaming samovar at our end of the car and offered us some tea, then offered some to each wounded man.

An hour later the train began chugging through the city. It consisted of three passenger cars and fifteen cargo cars, some of them lacking any shelter. It was pulled by a straining locomotive somehow still running from the 1860s. People in the streets looked up at us with a mixture of pity for the wounded and envy at our escape. A few cast scowls at us.

Sergei, normally pretty cheerful, grew increasingly pensive as he gazed out at the street scene, then at the wounded around us. He knew what was ahead of us, having done the trip in the opposite direction three years earlier. But that had been in peacetime.

"Trip not easy," he said in his improving English, which had been clearly, and badly, influenced by Rork. "Remember, we bloody bastards must always stay together on bloody damn train. Very important."

Rork, naturally, grinned at his linguistic protégé, but I realized Lieutenant Sergei Dyvoryanin, Imperial Russian Navy, would need some additional refinements in English from me during the journey—*before* he encountered any Brits or Americans at the European end. Then he told us the Russian nickname for the six-thousand-mile-long single-track Trans-Siberian Railway.

The Long Thin Ribbon of Iron.

58

The Long Thin
Ribbon of Iron

Manchuria, Russia
June 1905

Back home in America in this modern new century, trains travel at an average of forty miles per hour. Not so in the Russian Far East. None of my train experiences around the world prepared me for the Russian rails.

We'd started out on that single track from Vladivostok on June third. Over the next two and a half days we averaged ten miles an hour, constantly swaying like a top-heavy vessel in a beam sea. We frequently stopped for boiler repairs, fuel, water, and to change the train crew; sidetracked to let eastbound trains loaded with troops and munitions through to the front; and stopped to change ancient locomotives every several hours. Many times, we stopped to just sit there on the tracks, with no reason given. There seemed to be no overall plan and no one in charge. None of the Russians on board seemed surprised or angry about this inefficiency.

I discovered there were some army troops on board to guard the train, mostly perched atop the cars in sandbagged revetments, some with machine guns. They were special transport troops, which Sergei said were usually derided by frontline combat soldiers. Nobody derided them now, for they were the only defense between the unarmed wounded passengers and the surly groups of armed men seen all along the route near towns. In several groups I saw homemade red flags. Sergei pronounced them all anarchist deserter cowards and said they should be shot on sight. I suggested he calm his rhetoric since some of the wounded seemed to be of the same mind as those outside. I noticed several smiling and waving at them.

We got to Harbin, the capital of Manchuria, on June sixth. This area was close to the fighting, and I noted Cossacks guarding the railroad bridges and depots. I also noted a mob of armed men in the plaza near the train station staggering around wearing disheveled parts of different uniforms. They were not disorderly, only drunk, and the Cossacks left them alone.

Rork whispered to me, "That's not good at all, sir. Those boyos're screwin' up the courage to do somethin' nasty. Hope we get under way soon."

We stayed on the train while Sergei went to ascertain news of the rail line ahead. An hour later he returned. The crowd was starting to turn ugly, he said, but also reported good news. The train had just been given priority to get under way, for a senior army commander's private car had been attached. Sure enough, minutes later we started lurching forward, and I thought we might actually get some distance accomplished. That hope was illusory, though, for we traveled a half mile to the edge of the city and stopped. I imagined the general's rage would soon get things going again. But no, we stayed put. The train guards climbed down from the roof and looked around. They were nervous.

Sergei was told by the conductor there was a problem with a curve just ahead. Repairs were needed to the track, the bed of which had been washed out from a hard rain. From one of the train guards he discovered the truth. It was sabotage from mutineers—the track connectors had been pounded into useless metal lumps and the rails dumped down into a gorge.

The train backed up toward the station, then suddenly stopped and moved forward, back to where we initially stopped. We halted again. The conductor returned from speaking with the engineer and smilingly informed Sergei that another special train had been sent for us from the other side of the curve. Everyone would walk to the other train, and then we'd be on our way. The new train had an even better locomotive, and the cars were more comfortable, he said.

Prior to this moment, we Americans had tried to stay quiet and deferential among the wounded soldiers. I decided, and Sergei agreed, that this would be our chance to cement relations with our train-mates by helping them walk the quarter mile to the other train. After all, we did have a bond with them: Rork and Law were plainly wounded and I was limping from my strained knee. Our companions in the car knew we were American navy by then, and that we had been hurt at the Battle of Tsushima. They all had heard the story of the battle, and Admiral Rozhestvensky had become a hero to them, having been grievously wounded alongside his men.

I had a growing feeling we'd better have these men on our side because sooner or later we foreigners would be targeted by mutineers, bandits, or bureaucrats. So each one of us helped a wounded Russian soldier plod through mud and rocks to the other train. Even Rork, on his crutches, had a soldier hanging on to his shoulder. Law, dragging the two seabags with his right hand, had his left arm around a soldier. I supported a grizzled sergeant, and Sergei carried a man on his back.

I thought it curious that the important senior army officer with the private car was nowhere in sight during our walk. Sergei discovered from a train guard lieutenant that the general wasn't coming to the new train. He'd returned to Harbin for his safety.

When we arrived at the new train, we found that the conductor had lied about its condition. He had also disappeared. Far more importantly, we found a much stronger bond had grown with the wounded men. The soldiers were astounded when we helped them walk—their officers would never do such a thing. From that point on, the wounded always doffed their hats and smilingly referred to us in their quaint term for an officer: *vasha cheist*. Your Honor. I could tell it wasn't done out of the usual abject fear a Russian soldier or sailor has for an officer, but out of genuine respect.

As our new transport began to roll way from Harbin and out of Manchuria, I began to feel marginally better about our chances.

59
The Siberian Sea

Siberia, Russia
June 1905

We crossed from the mountains of Manchuria to those of Siberia three days later, stopping at each village along the way for food, fuel, and water for the boilers. Villagers provided free food and drink to the wounded (and us), their language beyond me but their compassion clear.

We pulled into the large city of Chita on 12 June—six dismal days to travel the 1,500 miles from Harbin. During the confusion in Harbin, Sergei had said I would like Chita. He was wrong.

Sergei went off the train to ascertain the local situation. He returned with a worried face. The situation in the city was "strange." Once I heard the explanation, I thought it worse than strange.

The military governor-general, Kholshchelvnikov, had only a small battalion of dubiously loyal soldiers to protect him from his very unhappy population. The governor very wisely realized his tenuous position and was trying to reach a modus vivendi with the revolutionaries in order to maintain the railway and trains on the sole war supply route to the east. So far he had been successful, but I doubted it would last.

In reality, Chita was in the hands of anarchists. These weren't the intellectual types I'd seen in Saint Petersburg a year before. This was a three-thousand-man army of fully armed, professionally organized deserters; complete with red flags, military discipline, and marching bands playing anti-monarchy songs. Their leaders were veteran army officers who had jumped over to the revolutionary side.

The political high chieftain of the rebels was a notorious European Russian named Victor Kurnatovsky, who styled himself as Chairman of the Soviet of Workers, Soldiers, and Cossacks. Some of his minions were already calling the place the "Chita Republic." Their leader had been a very experienced leader of radical assassins, saboteurs, and rioters for the last twenty years.

There was no doubt Kurnatovsky was the real power in Chita. He knew we were a train full of demoralized soldiers, therefore potential fellow rebels bound for their home areas. He knew these shattered men were ideal for spreading the seeds of revolution—and his own importance—across Russia.

We got a demonstration of his power right away. An hour after our arrival, with an astonishing efficiency I'd never seen in Russia, the wheezing old locomotive was replaced with an apparently new engine, the coal cars were topped off, decent food and vodka were brought on board for the wounded and train guards, and a rebel regiment paraded up to us in perfect order to the sounds of the French revolutionary song *Marseillaise*. In a booming voice, Chairman Kurnatovsky then proclaimed to us that he was personally guaranteeing we would be expedited homeward because we were the true heroes of Russia and all the world!

It worked. He and his army received a rousing roar of approval from everyone on the train. We gringos were no fools, joining right in with our Russian comrades. Sergei stayed mute.

Five minutes later we were under way, steaming west. Twenty-four hours later we arrived in Irkutsk, having done an incredible 629 miles. This place was near the shores of the "Siberian Sea," a giant freshwater lake called Baikal, in the middle of Siberia. The tracks followed close to the southern shore with lovely vistas of water and mountains and little villages nestled in small valleys. Irkutsk appeared to be a relatively neat and orderly town. I saw and heard nothing of the chaos we'd observed so far.

As we slowed to a stop, I allowed myself a moment to take in the tranquil scene. There was even the smell of flowers in the air.

60

The Invitation

Irkutsk, Siberia, Russia
June 1905

We sat at a siding in the railyard all day and into the night. Loyal troops were bivouacked nearby, and we felt safer for it. My men and I began to relax. Then, at one o'clock in the morning of the fourteenth, we had a visitor.

It was a man in a dapper business suit and homburg hat who said he worked for the newly installed governor of the Baikal area. He stood in the doorway and announced himself to Sergei. The wounded soldiers around us grew tense as they listened to him. Sergei and the man spoke in animated words, one of which stood out to me. The man said it when glancing at me. It was *shpion*—spy. Then I picked up another unpleasant word: *Okhrana*.

I nudged Rork and Law awake and whispered the developments. The governor's man waited in the doorway while Sergei came over to us and reported the situation.

"Admiral, man named Igor Ivanovich Kaminsky. Not speak English. Bloody damn bad bastard. Is Okhrana chief for this area. Work for governor. Has bloody damn bad news about you. He get cable from Saint Petersburg Okhrana. Cable say you go west on railway and he must to watch your actions."

Sergei paused and, with embarrassed tone, then said, "He say you maybe bloody damn bastard spy, later tell Japanese bastards about Russian railroad. He say wounded train leave now. Kaminsky say us stay at big damn palace tonight—big honor guest. Big good time. Tomorrow big special train, no stopping, take us to Moscow. Us happy. Okhrana big happy. Governor happy. Kaminsky bastard happy. Americans gone. Everybody here happy."

As he finished, I glared at Rork. "I told you to clean up his language."

He looked sheepish. "Ah, yes, well sir, the lad seems to've latched on to certain words. I'll remind him again they're not to be used in delicate company." His left eyebrow raised devilishly. "Like naval officers an' ladies an' children an' such . . ."

Sergei sat there looking innocent, while Law tried to stifle a grin.

"You're hopeless, Rork," I said, as the car jolted. They were changing the train's locomotive. There was another lurch and a steam whistle sounded. Conductors up and down the line of cars began calling everyone aboard.

I asked Sergei, "Can you send a cable to the head of Okhrana, a man named Rachkovsky, in Saint Petersburg. He is a good friend of mine. Can Kaminsky get that done right away?"

He shook his head. "Conductor man say telegraph no work now. Rebels cut maybe. I ask Kaminsky."

He did, and I could see that my invoking Rachkovsky's name held no sway over him. Sergei returned and reported, "Kaminsky bastard say telegraph broke in storm. Say no bloody damn rebels here. All dead. No bloody problems here. Cable fix soon. Maybe morning. Big damn palace big bloody good time for us. He has wagon."

"Nay, that's all a load of bilge water, sir," muttered Rork. "That copper won't admit the rebs've done the cable in. An' his invite for the night smells to high heaven. The Okhrana ain't our friend these days. I say we stay on this train with the lads we know. An' if Kaminsky makes a fuss o'er that, me spike can take care o' the slimy bugger right now. Nice an' silent."

With a curt nod toward Rork, Law agreed, "Chief Rork's right, sir. This is a trap. I say we kill Kaminsky and stay on the train."

I looked at Sergei for his opinion. "No trust bloody damn bastard Kaminsky. But no kill him. Many see us and Kaminsky. Big damn problems if kill bastard."

I thought for a minute, then told them, "Here's our plan. We are *not* going with Kaminsky, and we're not killing him. Because the cable line is down, he can't wire ahead to stop us. So, therefore, no need to kill him. Understood?"

They all nodded, and I went on. "Good. Instead, we need to deceive him. Sergei, go now and thank him very much for the invitation. Tell him we are very happy to go with him to the governor's palace, but we need to gather our things and say goodbyes to our friends. We will meet him at his wagon at the depot. Now, I want everyone to smile at Kaminsky and look very happy to go to the palace."

We all did. I waved. Kaminsky gave us a little wave and smile in return. The train whistle blasted out and the few ambulatory wounded outside began reentering the car.

"Go now, Sergei and tell him to wait at the carriage—we will be right there. Then get back on board fast."

Sergei's theatrics must have been very convincing because Kaminsky waved to us again, smartly saluted me, and started walking across the tracks to the depot. When Sergei returned, I asked him how it went.

He grinned. "I say you bloody strong big damn man. Want many vodka, caviar, and womans—" Sergei mimed the figure of a buxom woman "—in room at big damn palace. Bastard Kaminsky laugh. Say no bloody problem. Go to telephone, make happen."

The train started moving forward, just as another rolled into the station. We watched, but Kaminsky never stopped or even looked back.

Rork slapped Sergei on the shoulder. "Lieutenant Dyvoryanin, you're a man after me own heart!"

61

Options

Siberia, Russia
June 1905

From Irkutsk to Omsk, the train steamed westbound across the Siberian Steppe, a vast area of relatively flat and featureless grasslands. They were interspersed by broad rivers flowing north somewhere on the Arctic coast, and it was a long way between villages. During this time, from the fourteenth of June to the eighteenth, we averaged twenty miles per hour. Still not fast, but we had no mechanical troubles and so remained almost constantly under way. That kept the air moving through the car—a huge blessing in the increasingly warm summer temperatures.

Arriving at the large and thankfully quiet city of Omsk, I decided we needed to stock up on tinned food as a precaution against what might lay in our future. Sergei dutifully sallied forth on that mission. Two hours later, he returned with tinned meats, fish, and caviar, along with some newspapers from the rail station lobby.

As we loaded the provisions into what little room remained in the seabags, Sergei perused the papers with an increasingly dour face. He said they were filled with news of revolts among soldiers and workers across European Russia. It appeared the closer we would get to that region, the greater the chance of

251

encountering serious anarchy and hatred of anyone tied to the government. And foreigners, he added.

"We must ready leave bloody damn train any time," he said. "No warning, must leave fast, any time."

He had a general map of the train route through European Russia. We all examined it to deduce which direction to go, should we have to flee the train quickly. Sergei, who knew nothing of our troubles in faraway Saint Petersburg, was thinking we would head northwest on backroads to that city, where he had family. He explained that, once we were there, his family would take care of us until we could take a steamship home. I politely acknowledged his suggestion but had no intention of following it. We Americans needed to get as far away from Okhrana headquarters as possible. I had no doubt another alert about us would go out along the rail line—this time with maybe more drastic measures.

Rork counseled a typical sailor opinion. When faced with danger on land, sailors always head for the sea. The nearest large body of water would be the landlocked Caspian Sea to the south. Turkmenistan, home of my femme fatale assassin and her influential clan, bordered that body of water, so I ruled that out.

The nearest real saltwater would be the Black Sea to the southwest. The major port would be Sevastopol, in legendary Crimea. From there we could get a ship to Istanbul and thence to Britain and home. I suggested that escape plan and was backed by Law and Rork. Of course, I wanted Sergei to stay with us to Sevastopol for the obvious reasons. He reluctantly acquiesced to flee southwest instead of northwest, then head home from Sevastopol.

An hour later, with a new locomotive and coal cars forward; fresh food and vodka for the train crew, guards, and wounded; and a private car aft (for exactly whom, we never learned), the train got under way. Soon we were headed west at a good clip toward the setting sun.

The next major stop would be at Chelyabinsk in the Ural Mountains and after that, Samara in European Russia. From this moment onward, we all took turns on watch and slept with our shoes on and weapons ready.

My feeling of apprehension was heightened that first night when Rork shared his longtime arthritic warning while rubbing his left foot.

"Oohee, boyos, methink's somethin' nasty is comin' our way. Damned foot bones're hurtin' bloody fierce—an' you know what *that* means."

Rork's "damned foot bones" had provided valid warnings in the past. Accordingly, while the scenery became more and more beautiful as we traversed the Urals and descended into the valley of the storied Volga River, I succumbed to superstition and kept a close eye on Rork and that left foot.

62
Doing What
Needs to Be Done

Nearing Samara, European Russia
Wednesday, 21 June 1905

Nothing of import came until three nights later, when Rork woke me at 3:23 a.m. I instantly drew my revolver, searching the dark for a target while nudging Law and Sergei awake. They sat up, each with pistol in hand. I couldn't see a problem. Outside, the landscape rushed by in the gloom. Inside, snoring and moaning from most of the men. A man in the middle of the car was grunting loudly in pain, calling out for someone.

Rork explained. "Sir, me sniffer tells me that lad with the mangled arm is in bad shape. 'Tis green as hell, I can smell it from here. Won't make it unless he loses that arm."

"It'll wait until we get to Samara, Rork."

He shook his head. "No, it won't, sir. Has to be done *now.*"

Law was still groggy. "Your sniffer, Chief? What the hell do you mean?"

Rork was already up from the bench seat and heading down the center aisle to the wounded soldier. I answered Law. "Rork smells gangrene. He knows the smell because he had it in French Indochina and lost his arm to it. I smell it too, now. We'll have to amputate that arm right now to save that man."

"*We,* sir?" said Law. "We're not doctors."

"There aren't any doctors here. It'll have to be me and Rork, but you and Sergei can help and learn. You might have to do it someday for one of your men. So, fetch some lanterns and clean cloths, and some boiled water from the samovar. Sergei, you will translate for me as best you can."

Law didn't hesitate now. "Aye, aye, sir." Sergei echoed him, though with little confidence.

The two slightly wounded soldiers detailed to tend the worse-off men had no idea what to do. I decided to leave them out of the operation and told Sergei to have them calm the other men. All hands were now awake and watching us examine their comrade by the light of all four lanterns in the car, held overhead by soldiers.

The patient was a tall, big-boned, skinny man of about twenty-five called Yury who had been brought on board at Omsk. He was in a lot of pain but only occasionally groaned through gritted teeth as we stretched him out on a bench seat. I carefully unwrapped the bulky rag around his arm and forced myself not to recoil from what I saw.

Large chunks of canister shrapnel, much larger than those in Rork's legs, had torn apart Yury's right forearm. One was still in the wrist. What had been a routine—for the Russian army—reddish infection had turned in hours into a suppurating greenish-yellow mess three inches below the elbow. The skin around it was black and dried out.

"Aye, just what I thought, sir," murmured Rork. "No time to wait. Lieutenant Dyvoryanin, can you get a large knife for us? The sharpest you can find."

He looked me in the eye. "You know I can't do it by me self, sir, not one-handed as I am. I'll hold the lad down while you do the deed."

"Yes, of course, Rork. Let's start by giving him vodka, a lot of it. I'll use some of it to wash out the wound area."

A cask of vodka was brought over to us—the trip's entire allocation for all hands in the train car. Everyone in the train car silently watched our every move as Yury started gulping vodka. Sergei returned with a bayonet, just sharpened. I washed it in vodka, then my hands, then the wound.

The vodka didn't faze Yury. Rork gave him more. "Aye, you're a mighty brute o' a lad, ain't ye? Nary's the worry, son, we've enough vodka here to bring down an elephant."

Sergei translated it loud enough so everyone could hear. Several smiled, no one laughed.

Yury looked at me when I picked up the knife. His big eyes locked on to mine. I glanced up at the ceiling. "Lord, please increase my wisdom and guide my hands, so I can help my brave friend Yury live and go home to his loving family. With Your help, Lord, we will do what needs to be done."

Sergei told everyone my prayer and they crossed themselves. Yury, a leather rucksack strap between his teeth, took a breath, growled something, and nodded to me. He was ready.

Rork leaned his body onto Yury's chest so he couldn't see what was about to happen. A soldier grabbed Yury's legs. Law stood beside me with the hot water and "clean" rags.

I placed the bayonet on the skin an inch above the blackened part. Rork whispered, "Nay, sir, a bit higher. Just below the elbow. Got to make sure we get all the bad part off. An' be quick about it when you start."

I moved the blade higher up the forearm and sliced down into the skin at an angle, then turned it straight down as I pulled the blade back and down until I felt bone. Yury's scream was stifled by the strap, but his arm still jolted reflexively, though Rork and the men held its movement to a minimum. I sawed back and forth into the bone, putting all my weight into the effort. It took maybe sixty seconds but felt like an hour. The final part of the bone snapped apart and the blade sank into the flesh on the other side. With a last draw of the bayonet, I felt it bite into the wooden bench. Blood was everywhere.

"Throw the damned thing out!" I bellowed. Law picked up the severed forearm and quickly threw it out the window. "Stay on top of him while I look at the stump."

"Tie off the arteries as quick as you can, sir," Rork reminded.

"I know that, Rork!" I snarled back, instantly regretting it.

Both the ulnar and radial arteries were retreating back inside the meat. I grabbed the ulnar and pulled on it. Blood shot out. Law handed me one of the vodka-soaked shoestrings (we had no thread) we had readied for this part of the procedure, and I tied it around the artery. I barely got the radial out of the meat and tied it off with another shoestring. I called for more vodka and washed away the blood from the raw meat on the stump. The major arteries were tied off, but some of the smaller ones were still bleeding.

Sergei poured the boiling water onto the stump, in effect cauterizing it, and the small blood vessels stopped bleeding and withdrew into the flesh.

"An' now the flap, sir," Rork said gently. "Gotta press down an' bond the two parts so they'll grow back together with no abscess."

"Right," I answered, pulling down the slight flap made from my angled initial cut. It was far from a perfect fit, but most of the stump was covered by it. I held the two parts tightly together while Law lashed another shoestring around them. Rork nodded his approval. Sergei handed me the clean cloths and I wrapped them around the stump into a large bundle.

"Damn well done, sir," said Rork. "You just gave this lad a chance at life now."

I stepped away to our bench seat up in the front. My shirt drenched with sweat and blood, my hands shaking, and my mind reeling with emotions, I sat there overwhelmed for a moment. An older soldier limped over to me, bowed from the waist, and handed me a glass of vodka. I drained it. He smiled and went back to his seat.

Yury was taken to a cleaner bench, given yet more vodka, and laid out. His comrades held him tenderly as he moaned in pain. Outside, the sky was getting lighter. Suddenly I felt completely exhausted by it all—a whole damned year of tension since arriving at Hamburg.

Sergei came over to me and sat down with tears in his eyes. "I never to forget, Admiral. Thank you, from all Russians."

He gave me a bear hug and walked back to Yury. Five minutes afterward, I was asleep.

Two short hours later, everything went to hell.

63
Don't Overreact

Samara, Russia
Wednesday, 21 June 1905

Gunshots through the open windows woke me. All four of us went to the floor and drew our pistols. I quickly peeked out the window and saw we were in a city.

"Samara city, Volga River," Sergei explained.

More shots cracked, closer now. The train slowed. We were stopping. Sergei asked his fellow Russians what was happening. They had an excited exchange. I checked Yury. He was still cradled by friends and in pain, but he saw me looking and managed a smile.

Sergei told us what he'd learned. "Cavalry regiment, now bloody damn rebel bastards. Stop train. Look for very big rich bastard man. He get big bloody money in war."

I remembered the private car at the back end. "Samara is with the rebels now?"

He shook his head and shrugged. "Maybe little. We in poor damn part, near train depot."

The train stopped. Cavalrymen rode up to all the cars and dismounted. These were quite different from the Cossacks I'd seen since Vladivostok. Each of these had a red rag tied around their upper left arm. Definitely revolutionaries, and they didn't look in the mood for conversation.

I surveyed the surrounding area for an escape route. There was a fast-flowing river a hundred yards away on our left. A dozen fishing dories were tied up to a dock. Two old men stood nearby, watching the train.

Sergei saw me studying it. "Samara River. Go eight kilometers to big damn Volga River. Volga go to Caspian Sea. Many bloody kilometers."

Rapid shots came from the rear of the train. Three cavalrymen strutted into our car and immediately spotted us as foreigners. Sergei rose to speak to them and soon there was a heated discussion about the foreigners, with threatening glares toward us from the biggest cavalryman. He shoved Sergei out of the way and stood looking down at me. I rose and faced him.

A head taller than me, he was a big muscular monster. He grunted something at me, obviously an insult. I calculated it would take several shots to his face to bring him down. I slid my hand inside my coat to my revolver. Law and Rork stood up beside me, their faces expressionless but their eyes calculating. I knew what they were thinking.

"Easy men," I gently said to them. "There's more of these fellows outside, so let's try to stay calm. Don't overreact. Understood?"

Just after they murmured their acknowledgment, a predatory sneer came over the brute's face. Fingering the faded gold braid on my coat sleeve, he said something that made his cavalry comrades laugh. A giant paw on my shoulder shoved me down hard onto the bench. He spat in my face and laughed. The sneer turned into pure hate as his fist reared back to hit me.

I saw Sergei moving toward him, but my gun hand was faster and far more efficient.

Three .44-caliber shots from my Merwin-Hulbert went into that malevolent face.

The brute instantly went down in a heap. Sergei turned on the other two, his pistol in their faces. They raised their arms in surrender. Law took their revolvers and leaned the men against the bulkhead. Rork spun around and instinctually leveled his revolver at everyone else in the car. The wounded soldiers raised their arms in surrender. Yury raised his stump. Rork lowered the weapon.

"Bloody good thing we didn't *overreact*," he declared to me. "By the by, nice shot grouping, sir. Full marks for that one. What now?"

One of the wounded said something and all of them swiveled their heads to look outside. A dozen cavalrymen were approaching us on their horses. Several of the wounded made disapproving sounds toward the cavalrymen. Others nodded in agreement.

"We're leaving now for one of those boats. Mr. Law, grab the seabags. Rork, grab some bread. Sergei, ask these wounded men if they will help us by distracting those cavalrymen."

He did so and those who could, including a wobbly Yury, stood up in solidarity with us. Yury brought his remaining hand up to his forehead in a salute. The others followed his lead, holding it until I returned the salute.

I touched my chest and said a very heartfelt "Spasiba" to them all, then dashed out the door on the river side of the car. Law followed, then Rork on his crutches. We hobbled over the tracks toward the riverbank, the train hiding us from the cavalrymen on the other side. I heard Sergei say some final words to the wounded, then run after us.

Sergei caught up and told me, "Wounded soldiers big angry about damn attack on you by horse soldier bloody damn bastards. Make horse soldier bloody damn bastards wait, other train side. Horse soldier bloody damn bastards no see us go to boat. Yury leader man against horse soldier bloody damn bastards. I go now boat man to talk."

He ran ahead. Rork stumbled and I steadied him as he looked tiredly at the boats.

"Sorry, me friggin' pegs're still actin' up. Exactly where the hell are we, anyway? An' how far down the bloody river do we go?"

"Not sure on either, Rork."

"At least we're on water, sir. I'm bloody well done with trains."

64

Volga and Don

The Volga River, the longest in Europe, raced south in full spring flood. When we'd started out in our fifteen-foot boat on the Samara River, I'd figured our speed on the Volga would average eight knots. I was wrong. The wild ride on the river, with very difficult steering, averaged over ten knots. We quickly arrived at our destination, Tsaritsyn, the last major river city on the Volga until the landlocked Caspian Sea, three hundred miles to the southeast. It was just before dawn on 22 June, three weeks after we had arrived at Vladivostok.

Sergei was the navigator during this river voyage, but he only had a vague concept of the region, for he'd never been there. Our sole map was the general one of European Russia obtained at the train station. This made every plan an estimate and every decision tentative. We also looked at our limited food supply (bread, a couple of tins, and some uncooked cabbage) and drink (the ubiquitous rotgut vodka, of course) as emergency rations, to be prolonged as much as possible.

The Big Plan, as we came to call it (Rork, rather derisively), was discussed in detail during our river descent. We would get off the southbound Volga

261

at Tsaritsyn and walk about thirty miles west to Kalach-on-the-Don. There we would take a boat down the Don two hundred miles southwest to the Sea of Azov and cross it to the Crimea and Sevastopol on the Black Sea, from whence Sergei would go north to Saint Petersburg and we Americans would embark on a steamer bound anywhere—as long as it was away from Russia.

At Tsaritsyn, we stocked up on more bread and that damned dried beets and cabbage concoction, which by this point I had grown to hate. We also stocked up on the news. The war was relatively quiet, both sides exhausted and looking across the trench lines at each other. Rumors of peace talks abounded. No one argued against them. Much of Russia was still seething, but Tsaritsyn and the surrounding area seemed to be relatively loyalist and peaceful.

I took advantage of the favorable locale and working telegraph line to send a quick cable to María: XXX—LOVE YOU—X—IN TSARITSYN RUSSIA COMING HOME—X—TELL TR—XXX. With mist filling my eyes, I imagined her poring over an atlas to find Tsaritsyn after reading that. Sergei sent a cable to his family in Saint Petersburg, telling them he would be home in a month. I hoped he was right. I was also worried about Rork trying to walk the thirty miles to Kalach.

Sergei, who the reader knows by now is a very resourceful fellow, found a wagoner who agreed to take us to Kalach that very day with his load of sunflower seeds. He was a pleasant rotund fellow, and the day was nothing less than perfect for a ride through the countryside. As his pair of horses steadied into an easy six-knot trot, the sun filled the powder-blue sky and birds were singing. Southern Russia was such a wonderful difference from foggy dismal Vladivostok; or the moody Steppe with menacing Cossacks; or the smoke-clogged cities filled with anarchist revolutionaries. Our spirits finally brightened. I finally relaxed. We'd escaped.

None were more relaxed or happier than Rork. He thought our mode of travel quite grand as he reclined among the seeds like a pasha waiting for his harem. Helping himself to a handful of seeds, he lubricated his good mood with periodic swigs of vodka. By the time we got halfway there, he was feeling even grander and started in on his Gaelic ballads. By the time we arrived at Kalach he was in full musical bloom, albeit increasingly off-key, according to Law.

The driver thought it funny and hummed along. Sergei completely loved it, pronouncing Rork, "Very bloody good damn Russian!" The passing locals, who couldn't understand a word of it, clearly assessed him, and by extension *us*, as crazy. I didn't care. It was good to see Rork happy, at last. It was even better to be in a land of sunny peace and plenty.

At Kalach, Sergei secured us last-minute passage on a fast riverboat heading downriver to Rostov, the large city at the mouth of the Don River, where we had a real dinner.

Sergei asked around and returned an hour later with a worried face. He'd discovered there were no steamers crossing the Sea of Azov to Crimea. There was revolutionary unrest there, too, and rumors said it was getting worse since part of the garrison had changed sides. By land and sea, everyone was staying away from Sevastopol, the new center of the anarchy, and the Crimea in general. Our spirits sagged.

With a hopeful tone, Sergei said Odessa in the Ukraine was still loyal, and trains from there went north to Saint Petersburg and west to Vienna. By land, it would take at least ten days by road. But with the current strong northeasterly winds, by sea we could sail there in four or five days. He'd found an eleven-meter-long charter sloop ready to get under way immediately. We walked to the docks and met the captain. He looked sketchy, and I wondered why he was so eager to leave Rostov so quickly. His crew was an emaciated sickly youth with dim eyes. I suspected they were opium smugglers. But what choice did we have? Nothing else was moving, so we booked the passage.

By sunset, after an incredibly long day, we cast off. Soon we were on a broad reach under all plain sail, steering south across the Sea of Azov toward the Black Sea and then Odessa to the west. The skipper at least seemed competent, and I allowed myself to unwind enough to appreciate the beautiful copper and pink sunset melting into the gunmetal gray horizon ahead of us.

The stars came out. Ahead of us in the south, Mars was aligned with our forestay.

"So, it seems we're steering for the Roman god of war," mused Law. "Ironic— there's no war in the Black Sea."

Rork pointed directly astern, where Polaris hung high in the sky. Below it was the Big Dipper, otherwise known as Ursa Major—The Big Bear. "No worries, Mr. Law. See that? The Russian bear's finally behind us. We're goin' home to America."

Rork put an arm around Sergei. "An' me dear lad Lieutenant Sergei'll be leavin' us at Odessa to go north to his home, so Admiral, methinks we should broach that last bottle o' the good stuff, an' drain it in proper naval fashion."

Everyone thought that an excellent idea, and the bottle was soon opened and passed around and around. As the crew steered and worked the sails, the four of us naval professionals lounged on deck looking up at the stars as we sailed away from war and death and anarchy.

When it was Law's turn to propose a toast, he raised the bottle.

"To going home . . ."

65
Ismail

Approaching Odessa, Russia
Tuesday, 27 June 1905

After a very fast downwind passage around the Crimea peninsula, Odessa was only fifteen miles ahead to the west. It was two o'clock in the morning, but everyone was awake with anticipation. We'd be dockside in two hours, and our gear was already piled on deck next to us. Elation at nearing our final destination inside Russia turned to wariness, however, when Rork pointed out the odd darkness of the sky over a large city, especially since there was enough high overcast to reflect the city's loom of light.

Given the turmoil in Russia, this was disturbing. Odessa should have illuminated the night sky, but we saw nothing. Parallel to us a couple of miles to the starboard was a thirty-five-mile-long sand-and-rock spit of land called Tendra Spit, forming a barrier to the Gulf of Tendra, to the north. The skipper had seen Tendra's lighthouse, so he knew where we were. When asked by Sergei, he had no explanation for the lack of light loom over Odessa.

Law did. "Odessa's been taken by the anarchists. There is no electricity."

Unfortunately, that made sense. It also meant there might be no trains out of this part of Russia.

The young crewman up on the bow shouted for quiet, cocking his ear to hear something. A vessel was approaching from ahead, he reported—fast, with dim lights. Everyone strained to see something. I heard the throaty roar of steam-turbine engines getting louder.

Soon it became a constant thundering. I saw red and green running lights.

"Hundred yards, dead ahead!" yelled Rork. "They're gonna hit us!"

The skipper tried to slew the vessel around to starboard without broaching, but he was too late. A hull suddenly launched off the crest of a wave twenty feet ahead of the bow. It crashed down right where the boy was on the bow. Our boat instantly went under water as the steel hull and thrashing propellers rushed by us.

I felt warm liquid darkness close around me as I descended. There was no pain, no panic, just the surreal sensation of the absurdity of dying here after all we'd been through. *So, this is the way it ends, Lord? Please watch over María.* Then I felt bubbles on my face, and buoyancy lifted my arms. I was rising.

I still heard the engine sound, but it had diminished to a rumble. My mind subconsciously assessed that factor: *The ship must be slowing.* The rumble sounded closer. *They're coming back.*

Suddenly the liquid darkness gave way to air. A wave washed over me. I choked on the water. Floating up and down with the black waves under the black air, looking for Rork. A light flashed, blinding me. I heard Russian voices shouting.

The light blinded me again. Something in the water bumped into me. Everything was confusing—strange and yet familiar. *I've been here before,* my mind told me. *God, did I die at Tsushima? Am I still there?*

Eyesight returned. The small ship was fully lit up now. She stopped only a few yards away from me, the frightening rumble of her engine right beside me. Spotlights swept across the waves around me. Insistent words in Russian told me they'd seen me. *No, this is different,* my mind said. *No battle.*

I tried but couldn't yell out to them. A boathook poked me, then snatched my shirt and pulled me to the hull. Hands reached down and grabbed me. My arms were rubber. I couldn't help them lift me.

"Sorry . . ." I managed to gasp out. "I need . . . help."

They cursed as the hands yanked me up and dumped me on the deck. I rolled over on my side, retching out water, too weak to even sit up. Somebody gave me hot tea, spiked with vodka. That helped a bit. I tried to figure out where I was. *A warship? Where is Rork, and Law, and Sergei?*

A man knelt down in front of me. "You shout in English. I speak English. I am Lieutenant Pyotr Klodt von Yurgensburg, commander of this torpedo boat, the *Ismail*. We see four men in water. Now on *Ismail*. Who are you?"

I moaned something back at him, then hands lifted me and took me down a ladder and laid me on a table. A lamp swung overhead. Somebody removed my shirt and trousers, then ran their hands over my body, pushing on my bones, moving my arms and legs. I was lifted up again and taken over to a nearby bunk in the shadows. A gruff voice told me something in Russian.

"Where is Rork?" I asked the shadows. "Sean, are you here? Edwin? Sergei?"

Nobody answered.

66
Maggots

Battleship Potemkin
Tendra Spit, Russia
Tuesday, 27 June 1905

My eyes abruptly opened when I recognized a familiar sound: Rork's snoring. The lamp was still lit but not swaying. The vessel wasn't rolling in seas anymore. *It's a torpedo boat*, I remembered. *They ran over us.*

I leaned up on one arm and saw Edwin Law staring at me from another bunk. In the bunks next to him was Sergei and the sailboat's captain, both passed out. Sergei's face was bloody. The skipper's arm was wrapped in bandages. *Where is Rork?*

Law sounded in good shape. "Sir, are you all right?" he asked.

"Yes. You and Rork? Sergei?"

He sat up. "I'm banged up a bit, but nothing bad. The Chief's over there." He pointed to another bunk, where Rork's long lanky frame was laid out. "His leg wounds have opened up again. They gave him laudanum for the pain and he's mostly out of it. Sergei's head has a bad gash and the skipper's arm got crushed, but they can both still walk."

Law got out of his bunk and came slowly over to mine, wincing with every step he took. "You had me worried, Admiral. I thought you might have a bad concussion and brain damage."

"No, other than a headache, I'm fine, Edwin. What's the situation?"

"Not sure, sir. We're on board the torpedo boat that ran us over. *Ismail*, or something like that. I think we're coming alongside a big cruiser or battleship."

"Help me up out of this bunk," I said. "And wake up Rork and Sergei. Let the skipper sleep. Did we save any of our gear?"

"Yes, sir. Both seabags are soaked but saved. The sailboat's bow was sheared off, but the stern where we were was swamped and didn't sink. Good thing, because I took the life belts out of them when we got ashore in Russia. I got the sailors to bring our seabags on board the torpedo boat. They're over there." He pointed to them by the bulkhead.

We woke up the others. I wanted to check my men over and make sure they were all right. Rork grumbled about his mind being foggy, being made to stand, and the Russian navy. He was able to stand using his crutches, also recovered from the swamped boat, though missing the armpit pads. He grumbled about that too, then stopped.

Sniffing the air, he said, "Oh, hell. Bloody friggin' gangrene here too?"

Law shook his head, "No, we're all right, Chief. No gangrene on us."

A waft of air came down the companionway ladder, then I smelled it, too. We climbed the ladder up to the torpedo boat's main deck—a major exertion for all of us—and surveyed the scene around us. In the diffused amber light of dawn, I realized *Ismail* was tied up to a large warship in the open sea, under the lee of a beach a mile away. A line of men on our deck was silently passing along big racks of raw meat up to the main deck of the large warship alongside. I heard a man gag, then another cough. Many of the men had their undershirts pulled up over their noses. The stench was overpowering.

Holding my breath, I scrutinized the nearest hunk of meat. It was crudely ripped apart. I wasn't even sure it was beef, except by the size. The viscera were brown, black, and some were yellowed. Maggots crawled inside and outside it. Hundreds of them. It had gone bad many days earlier.

"Good Lord above," I moaned. "They're loading rotted meat onto that ship. They can smell this stuff isn't fit for consumption."

Sergei was stunned too. "Very bad. Big trouble. Against navy regulation."

Rork whispered in my ear, "These lads are angry as hell. Look at their faces, sir. This is the stuff o' mutiny."

Yurgensburg appeared and greeted me with a smile, ignoring the rancid stink. He inclined his head toward the massive ship next to us. "*Potemkin*, new battleship!"

Seeing our disgust, he shook his head and said, "Not good. *Potemkin* supply officer Makarov and doctor soon in trouble. Buy bad meat in Odessa."

The namesake of that comment arrived on deck, accompanied by the medical officer who examined me. Russian sailors crowding the decks of both ships watched them silently, their hatred apparent. Makarov glared back at the seamen as he and the doctor climbed the ladder up the battleship's side.

Yurgensburg watched the scene unfolding, then gestured to me. "You go now to *Potemkin*."

I climbed the ladder, glad to be off the cramped torpedo boat but worried about what I might find on *Potemkin*. Once we were all up on the battleship's quarterdeck, Sergei introduced himself to the officer of the quarterdeck watch, who was distracted by the transfer of provisions. Sergei used a very long, apparently formal version of his name: Knyaz Leytenant Sergei Ivanovich, vnuk Aleksandrovicha Dyvoryanin, doma Romanovykh. I didn't understand the meaning of all that, but the officer of the watch certainly did. He stood straighter, turning his full attention to us.

Then Sergei introduced each of us to the officer, translating into English as he went. He introduced us as American war observers, but *not* as naval officers. The reader will recall we were not in uniform, so the insinuation was that we were newspaper men. Sergei looked at us meaningfully as he said this, a clear nonverbal request to go along with the façade.

It was obvious the officer was far more impressed with Sergei than us. An ensign instantly trotted off to notify the captain. The second-in-command soon arrived, a trim middle-aged man with delicate face, carefully trimmed handlebar moustache, nervous eyes, and receding hairline. I noted he was armed, with an extra ammunition pouch on his belt. In short order he returned Sergei's salute, ran his eyes over us, said something about the captain being indisposed, and made some comments to the quarterdeck party, who rushed about following his orders. He then curtly bowed his head to Sergei, excused himself, and strode over to a nearby ladder.

A moment later, he was up on the spar deck cursing the sailors who had gathered to watch the proceedings below. They scattered in terror, but I saw others on the ship looking at the officer with undisguised loathing.

"Sergei, what is all that about?" I asked. "He seemed impressed by you."

He gave a little shrug and vaguely replied, "He is Ippolit Giliarovsky. He know my family in Saint Petersburg."

I thought there was more to it, but we were interrupted by a young officer arriving at the quarterdeck. He embraced Sergei and engaged in an animated conversation, which soon turned serious. Sergei explained to us that the lieutenant, whom he called Misha, was an old friend.

Misha gave Sergei the latest news about Odessa. The city was overrun by revolutionaries who had shut down all power, water, and trains. There were also some of them on *Potemkin*. The officers trusted no one below the rank of senior petty officer. Misha showed Sergei a brown-covered pamphlet found in a crew berthing space. Sergei explained it was by a notorious fellow named Lenin, a socialist-anarchist type, titled *What Is to Be Done?* It called for the overthrow of the autocratic Tsar and the entire nobility of Russia.

As for our immediate future, Sergei learned that *Potemkin* was leaving for a nearby gunnery range later in the day, then heading for Odessa the next morning. Once there, Misha would try to arrange rail transport for us.

Following this sobering report of the current situation, Misha led us to our quarters. As we set off, Rork glanced at the sailors around us and quietly said, "Sir, methinks we better all berth close by each other. Look at these poor lads. They're ready to explode. An' it's gonna be damned bloody when they do."

Rork was right. The atmosphere on *Potemkin* was lethal.

Pulling Sergei aside in the passageway, I told him, "Rork will be in my cabin with me. Law and you will be in the next cabin. Talk to Misha and make that happen, Sergei. Right *now*."

He didn't argue or hesitate. "Yes, sir."

The accommodation arrangements were changed, and Misha showed us to two cramped junior officers' cabins, with two over and under bunks in each. I told my men to memorize routes of egress to the main deck, get some rest, stay armed, and be ready for anything.

None of them had to ask me why.

67

Borscht

Battleship Potemkin
Tendra Spit, Russia
Tuesday, 27 June 1905

All of us were so physically and mentally fatigued, we were sound asleep in minutes. Six hours later, I was awakened by a very worried-looking Sergei and Law. Neither was in uniform but both had pistols openly stowed in their belts. I heard angry shouting from the weather decks above.

As I rolled out of the bunk, Sergei lost no time. "Put bad meat in borscht. Sailors say no eat borscht. Mutiny start. Sailors have guns. Misha has boat ready. We go to boat—*now!*"

Rork was already up and on his crutches in the passageway. The shouting from topside was getting louder, throatier, more menacing. It sounded like hundreds of men.

Then we heard a rifle shot.

We ran forward through the passageway, Sergei in the lead. Law carried Rork's seabag. I carried mine, the Spencer shotgun just inside the drawcord opening. At the starboard side midship ladder, sailors were standing there, confused and plainly scared. We rushed past them and up the ladder, Rork growling in pain as hauled himself up. I lugged his crutches, stumbling most of the way.

From the main deck came two more rifle shots. Then a third, then a fusillade. Then continuous shooting. Screaming by individual men. Cursing by the mob.

Already up on the main deck, Sergei called down to us. "Go fast!"

We tried. At the top of the ladder, I saw it was a pump room. A hatchway on the starboard side led to the outside main deck. Just as we were going out, a crowd of sailors, some with rifles, and all with desperately maniacal faces, came in. We backed away from the hatchway. Glaring at us, one of them shouted a threat at us. They all turned toward us.

Sergei tried speaking to them, his Russian sounding calmly respectful, his hands outstretched with open palms. The leader of the crowd spit at Sergei's hand and sneered something, then lunged toward him.

Law's Navy Colt revolver was already up and on target. Two shots went into the man's chest. He fell on the deck.

68

Invoking Tsushima and Rozhestvensky

Battleship Potemkin
Tendra Spit, Russia
Tuesday, 27 June 1905

The crowd froze into a tableau. Rork drew his Colt on the sailors. I brought out my shotgun and leveled it at them. Sergei commanded them to stand aside or die. Though we were still in civilian attire, they knew our naval ranks were superior to theirs. Most now looked frightened, but a few of the older ones showed no fear, watching us with cold eyes. All of them slowly backed away from us, into a corner of the pump room.

Sergei pointed to a midship passageway to the port side and told us, "Go port side boats."

Law and I led the way while Rork and Sergei covered the sailors. When we got to the hatchway, Law made a quick glance outside. "There's hundreds of sailors out there, sir. Couple of boats are in the water and there's a Jacob's ladder down to them. I don't see Misha anywhere."

Several more rifle shots came from the starboard side. The sailors on that side began roaring approval at something. Rork and Sergei got to the hatchway.

"Misha gone. I get boat," Sergei told us, then stepped out on deck. We followed closely behind. No one stopped us. We got to the ladder descending to the boats, a twenty-five-footer and a big thirty-five-foot launch, moored against the side, ten feet below us.

Sergei pointed at the boats, then grimly looked at the sailors milling around on the after deck. Several were now noticing us, calling heatedly to their comrades. The sailors from the pump room were at the hatchway, inciting their comrades on the after deck to rush us.

"You go down," Sergei told us. "I stay here. Go down last."

"Right," I said. "Law first, then Rork. Then me and Sergei. Get in the small one. Easier to row."

Law went down the ladder three steps at a time. Rork tossed his crutches down to Law and slid down the ladder by grasping the sides. I dropped my seabag down to the boat. As I turned back to face the crew, more shots banged out, this time from inside the ship. It didn't sound like a battle—it sounded more deliberate, like executions.

A mass of sailors advanced toward us from the after main gun turret. I swung the shotgun around toward them. They hesitated for a moment, then started inching forward. Some had rifles and aimed them toward us.

Sergei spoke to the mob, again using a calm reasoning voice, pointing to us. I recognized the words Tsushima and Rozhestvensky, and knew he was telling them we'd been with the admiral—the one senior officer they respected—in the battle. The effect was immediate.

The mob stopped advancing. Some made the sign of the cross. Many faces lost their hostility. Rifle muzzles were lowered. Several turned away.

I went down the ladder. Rork and Law were already seated at the thwarts, hands on the oars. I sat down and grabbed two oar handles. Sergei came down to the boat and took another pair of oars. As we quickly rowed away, Rork calling the stroke, there was a commotion on the ship's main deck forward. A large sailor strutted to the railing carrying a body. Triumphantly bellowing, he threw the body overboard. Another sailor dumped a pot of blood-red borscht overboard where the body went in. The sailors thundered their approval.

The dead man was Ippolit Giliarovsky.

69
Broad Reaching

Black Sea
Tuesday, 27 June 1905

Sailors lined the railing and stared at us as we pulled as hard as we could. We were facing aft at the oars and trying not to falter as we watched captured officers being led out onto the battleship's main deck.

Misha was one of them. They were lined up against the stern railing, a line of sailors with rifles standing in front of them. The volley killed them all. I glanced at Sergei. He never slowed in his rowing as Rork continued calling out the stroke.

Right afterward, several rapid-fire guns on the starboard side began shooting at the *Ismail*, which had been drifting a hundred yards away. A white bedsheet went up her halyard and the mutineers cheered.

A half mile later we were beyond the lee of the land and began feeling that northeasterly fresh breeze that had taken us from Rostov around the Crimea. We didn't stop rowing. The farther we went on, the larger the waves grew.

"An' where're we headin' now, sir?" asked Rork. He sounded a bit winded—like I felt.

The boat was headed southwest, but was that where we wanted to go? I conjured up a mental map of the Black Sea. Southwest would be Romania, independent from the Ottoman Empire for the last twenty-five years. It was the closest non-Russian territory, but I wasn't sure of the distance.

"Avast all," I said. Everyone stopped pulling. Then I asked, "Sergei, how far is the nearest port in Romania, and does it have trains to the west?"

"Maybe two-, three-day sail to Sulina. No train there. Maybe three-, four-day sail to Constanta. Big city of coast. Train at Constanta. Go to Bucharest, Budapest, Vienna."

There was a sailing rig—spars and canvas for a mainsail and jib sail—stowed under the thwarts. A rudder and tiller were under the stern sheets. That decided it for me.

"Very well, then—Constanta it is. Drinks are on me when we get there. Rork, you and Law rig the mast and sails. There's no compass in this boat, but just steer downwind and we'll get to Romania. We'll each have two-hour tricks on the helm. Rork first, then Law, Sergei, and me. I see no food or water in the boat, so conserve your energy and try to stay in some shade."

With Law's help, Rork got the rig up and working. Soon the boat was doing all of six to eight knots, the wind on our port quarter. Rork seemed rejuvenated as he sat gauging the seas and swinging the tiller to meet them.

"Sergei, me lad," he asked. "They have any decent vodka in Romania? Aye, I'd fancy a gallon o' that stuff right about now!"

Rork's attempt at improving morale failed to work. Sergei didn't answer. He couldn't. Our Russian friend was staring back at *Potemkin* with tears streaming down his cheeks.

70
Expedited and Incognito

Constanta, Romania
Friday, 30 June 1905

Ve sailed into the bustling port of Constanta at sunset three days later. Disheveled and odorous, we immediately abandoned the boat at the first dock and hailed a cab for the office of the port captain. There we related what had happened to our sailboat en route to Odessa; our rescue by the torpedo boat, which had nearly killed us; and *Potemkin*'s mutiny. I then requested to be taken to the American consulate. Sergei asked to go to the Russian consulate.

The port captain didn't appear to be surprised at our arrival, news, or request. In very good English, he said that there had been a steady influx of wealthy Russians and other foreigners escaping the chaos, bringing tales of unrest in Russia. He assumed we were civilians, like the others. I thought it best to not share with him my rank and profession—no sense in complicating things by disabusing the fellow of his comfortable assumption.

With a grand sweep of his hand, he waived the port fees, import duties, and customs and immigration fees because we were obviously refugees. Then he recommended the best hotel in the city, the Cherica, overlooking the sea. It was too smooth and practiced. I immediately suspected he had some pecuniary interest in the place. It also worked. That's where we stayed.

I did tell the U.S. consul, a pleasant young fellow named Granthill, our profession and rank. His initially disdainful gaze disappeared, replaced by a promise to assist us in any way needed. What we needed right then was a soft bed at the Cherica, but arranging transport was a priority. I asked him to set up the fastest possible rail journey to London, expedited by the American embassies in Bucharest, Budapest, Vienna, Paris, and London. It would be informal and incognito as far as officialdom was concerned—name only, no rank—and I specifically did *not* want any formal recognition, social affairs, or meetings with anybody along the way.

I did not tell him the reason: we were back in German-influenced Europe and I wasn't certain they weren't still after me.

At the telegraph office, I sent a brief plain-language cable to María, my first since Tsaritsyn: XXX—ALL ARE SAFE IN CONSTANTA ROMANIA—X—TAKING TRAIN TO LONDON—X—TELL TR—XXX

Then Sergei met us at the Cherica and we all headed for the soft bed in our comfortable rooms. The next day at our late-morning breakfast, Granthill reported the journey set up as requested. The train to Bucharest would leave the next day, July second. At Bucharest, we would receive the other tickets for the rest of the journey. He estimated the journey to London would take two weeks, at very most. Impressed by his efficiency, I made a mental note to remember Granthill to the president, then handed him a message to cable to María: XXX—LEAVING CONSTANTA 2 JULY—X—ARVG LONDON 16 JULY—MEET ME AT SAVOY HOTEL—X—WE WILL RETURN TOGETHER—X—TELL TR—XXX

Before he departed, Granthill inquired, "Sir, do you have any German friends in Romania, either here in Constanta or in the capital at Bucharest?"

I said no and waited for the explanation, which I already had a bad feeling about.

"This morning the German consul's clerk asked my driver about you, by name and rank. He was rather insistent to gain information about you. My driver deflected the question by feigning ignorance but thought the clerk didn't believe him. I imagine the port captain must have told the Germans about you. He's a well-known gossip. But he didn't know you are an admiral. Is there some trouble?"

I replied reassuringly, "No, no trouble. I'm friends with Kaiser Wilhelm, so perhaps the fellow recognized my name."

Law and Rork smiled benignly at Granthill. He went on his way. Afterward Rork muttered, "Bloody Kraut bastards're *still* causin' trouble. Nary the worry, sir. Me and Mr. Law know just how to deal with the likes o' them."

Sergei, who never knew anything of our Germanic troubles, asked, "What happens?"

I frowned at Rork for forgetting about Sergei's presence. He turned to the Russian and waved away his concern with a grin. "Oh, sorry, me lad. 'Tis all just in good fun. The Krauts lost a poker game an' they're wantin' another chance. Bad losers, that lot."

Sergei accepted that and I changed the subject to trains. The next day we would head west through rugged mountains toward Bucharest. Sergei was joining us for this last passage together. He told us his plan was to go north to Saint Petersburg from Bucharest—a far more complicated, and probably perilous, journey than ours.

Our farewell at the Bucharest station was poignant. We'd been with Sergei four weeks since finding him in the water at Tsushima, but it seemed so much longer. In that tumultuous month, we'd only survived by bonding closely together. Law thought of Sergei as a slightly younger brother. Rork, as a son. Me, as a grandson. With the dry wit of bloodied comrades, we all told him the usual sentiments but no more, afraid to let loose the emotions welling up inside each of us.

Sergei was more open. His final words to us were a heartfelt echo of that night with Yury on the train.

"Admiral Wake, Captain Law, Chief Rork . . . I *never* forget you."

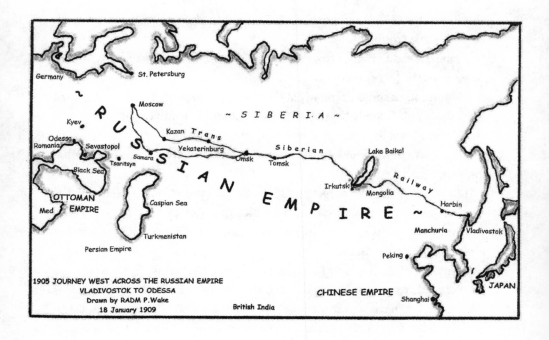

1905 JOURNEY WEST ACROSS THE RUSSIAN EMPIRE
VLADIVOSTOK TO ODESSA
Drawn by RADM P.Wake
18 January 1909

71

Further Instructions

Savoy Hotel, on the Strand
London, Great Britain
Tuesday, 18 July 1905

On Saturday the fifteenth, we pulled into the giant Gare de l'Est train station of Paris. Jostling through the crowds, we climbed on board the westbound overnight train to London. In addition to guiding us amidst this chaos, the embassy's first secretary pressed into my hand a cable message from Theodore Roosevelt (deciphered from Navy Department Code), the first I'd had from him since Singapore.

The message expressed "profound relief" we were alive and well, and confirmed that María was on a Cunard ship arriving at Liverpool on the seventeenth, thence taking the overnight express train to London. A rather troubling addendum said I would receive "another cable with further instructions" when we checked into our hotel in London. *Further instructions? What does that mean? He's up to something . . .*

By two o'clock on the afternoon of the sixteenth, my men and I were very comfortably lounging in our rooms on the fourth floor of the quite posh Savoy Hotel, on the Strand near the Victoria Embankment of the Thames River.

I awaited María's arrival on the eighteenth (or maybe sooner) with joyfully nervous anticipation. *Only two more days . . .* kept going through my mind.

A brief explanation about the coded communications is in order at this point. My cipher wheel had been hopelessly damaged during the ordeal since Saigon, and there was no way I could use "Tiger Code" or any other. When Roosevelt got word through María of our whereabouts, I knew he would be bright enough to understand something was wrong and would send his messages through our embassies. It wasn't privately personal, but it got the job done. Thus, when the additional "further instructions cable" arrived it was deciphered by our London naval attaché, then presented to me.

I pondered this message in uncharacteristically neutral language (he knew others would read it). The president informed me that my mission regarding the Russo-Japanese War was not yet done. María, Law, Rork, and I would rest at the Savoy until the twenty-first, when the entire entourage would entrain for Liverpool, there to embark on a Cunarder—he noted we would all have first-class accommodations—for Boston. We were not to return home to Washington, however, but instead take the local train north to Portsmouth Naval Station, up in New Hampshire. The message ended with the statement that I would soon receive a letter from him with "highly secret instructions for a crucially important assignment."

My patience with Roosevelt's fondness for cloak-and-dagger endeavors evaporated with that dramatic little comment. There had been too much of this sort of thing for too long, and I was tired of it. And I absolutely knew that María would openly revolt at the mere idea of us not going directly home to our cottage in Alexandria for a period of rest and relaxation.

The blood in my head pounded at the very thought of telling her, so I decided to postpone the unpleasantness until the day after her arrival. *Or maybe I should never tell her—just reply to Theodore with a resignation effective immediately? María wants me to retire. This might be the best time to do it.*

That lovely moment I'd been dreaming of for eleven months finally came at five o'clock on the eighteenth. I heard a knock, the manager opened the door to the suite, the porters quickly deposited her luggage, and the staff withdrew, leaving an impossibly beautiful María standing there in front of me.

What do you say—what can you say?—when finally reunited after enduring a year of fear and uncertainty? Especially since our parting in Saint Petersburg was so heavy with anger on her part and shame on mine. I'd fantasized about murmuring romantic verses to her as we finally embraced. But, instantly overwhelmed by the moment, I found myself suddenly unable to move or speak.

I didn't have to—no words were needed. With a wide smile María glided into my arms. Kissing away our tears, we held each other for a long time. The built-up tension inside me disappeared, and I led her to the great soft bed. The only things we needed were the gentle reassuring touches of two people so much in love.

Hours later we awoke as the sun was setting outside our window. María was still smiling, but now she had that delicious naughty twinkle in her eyes. We decided to stay in bed.

Dinner could wait.

72

Breakfast in Bed

Savoy Hotel, on the Strand
London, Great Britain
Wednesday, 19 July 1905

As the sun rose over the Thames, we had a hearty English breakfast delivered to the suite and savored it in bed. Since first embracing, we'd spoken nothing about duty and country, or our suffering through the previous year. Instead, María filled me in on all the good news about our family.

Down in Tampa, my daughter Useppa; her lawyer husband, Mario; their seven-year-old son, Peter; and four-year-old daughter, Linda, were doing well. My son, Sean, and his wife, Filipa, had their baby in May, a boy they named Robert James Wake. Sean was due to take command of a gunboat in Norfolk in six months, so he would still be able to see his wife and son in Washington. María's son, Juanito, was still posted to the Spanish embassy to Canada and enjoying it immensely. All this was wonderful, but she had even bigger news.

My fifteen-year-old daughter Patricia—whose mother refused my sincere offer of marriage and then died in childbirth, and who was raised by her aunt in Illinois—was now living with María in Alexandria. The aunt was seriously ill and did something previously unthinkable for her: asking María for help.

María was delighted, and Patricia came east. The two were getting along very well, and Patricia was enjoying school. I hadn't seen her in years, and María described her as intellectually impressive, very pretty, and fascinated about everything in Washington. She had even been with María to dinner at the White House. I was overjoyed at this development.

I knew that joy couldn't last, however, for I would have to ruin it by broaching the matter of Theodore's last message—or, should I say, new orders. I would mitigate that by also telling her I was resigning. We would be free of obligations to the president, the country, or anything else. We were going to live those dreams. It was time.

As I steeled myself to begin, María took my hand. "You know, Theodore and Edith were very kind to me while you were gone. They had me to dinner quite often. Theodore was very sincere in his appreciation for our work on the German invasion plans. He told me he has learned the Kaiser has ended all planning for an invasion, insinuating it was because the Germans know we have their plans. Theodore and Edith also offered their sympathy for our separation. It was obvious Theodore felt very bad for sending you and Sean and Edwin on that Russian fleet mission. He never actually apologized to me for that—of course—but Edith told me privately how deeply sorry he was. Theodore was scared for you, but never showed it in front of me."

She hesitated for a moment, then continued. "Darling, I'm telling you this because when we parted in Saint Petersburg, I was so angry and said some things about Theodore I now regret. I want to correct that impression for you now. He is not callous, and he and Edith took good care of me. He is still my friend."

Well, I hadn't expected *that* sentiment from her. The legendary Roosevelt charm had managed to melt her anger and restore their friendship. And María wasn't done yet.

"Theodore gave me a very confidential letter to give you. He insisted I read it too, then asked my opinion of it. I think him correct on all points, even though one of them impacts us. Here it is, Peter."

She handed me a plain envelope with no addressee or sender information. The several-page letter inside was handwritten by Theodore himself.

The sinking feeling in my gut grew as I began reading.

73
The Letter

Savoy Hotel, on the Strand
London, Great Britain
Wednesday, 19 July 1905

My dear Peter,   *1 July 1905*
    I am deeply grateful to the Almighty for answering my fervent prayers that you, Sean Rork, and Edwin Law would make it through to safety and civilization in Western Europe. María stalwartly weathered this past year's incessant storm of fear and uncertainty, impressing Edith and I even more than we've always been by her. You are indeed a very fortunate man to have such a remarkable lady as your wife.
    During your difficult mission, your continuing messages about the Russian capabilities were quite prescient and assisted me in making several decisions, two of which will be discussed below. Before addressing that, however, I want to share with you some important confidential information I recently received.
    The Tsar and the Kaiser are forming a non-aggression pact, signatum secreto. This was the idea of Willy, who hasn't an altruistic bone in his body. I know not exactly when it will be concluded, but it will be very soon. It is quite concerning to me. By securing Russia's western border, it will embolden the Tsar to prolong the bloody war in East Asia. By securing Germany's eastern border, it will free

the Kaiser to intimidate France, yet again, on many issues in Europe and Africa. They are threatening war over Morocco now. This will make it worse. And not just for them. The consequences of this covert agreement directly impact our American interests in both Africa and Europe, but especially in Asia.

Now, as to my decisions. First, I have tasked our new ambassador to Russia, George von Lengerke Meyer, to pass along my thoughts directly and plainly to the Tsar. They include the fact that neither Russia nor Japan can sustain war operations, finances, or public support indefinitely, and that now is the time to end the fighting.

Second, in furtherance of the aforementioned, I have again offered my services to facilitate an end to the Russo-Japanese War. This offer has been rejected by both sides for six months, but now the Japanese have agreed—as has the Russian foreign ministry, though very reluctantly. I am told the chief Russian will be former Finance Minister Witte, whom I believe you met at an imperial soiree in Saint Petersburg. The chief Japanese will be Foreign Minister Komura, a Harvard friend of mine whom, as you well recall, you met while he was the ambassador to our country in 1902. It is critical that the war be ended soon, so that Russia will stay in the Far East and thus balance Japan. Otherwise, Japan will have no restraint to her ambitions further south.

Third, in view of Japan's ambitions, I am sending Bill Taft and a congressional delegation (including my daughter Alice) to Japan, the Philippines, and China to see what precisely is going on out there—especially on the part of the Japanese. He is also to try to dampen the growing dispute with us over the Japanese immigrant laborers in Hawaii and California, on which there has been much uproar here, which engenders much anger over there.

My fourth decision involves you. Your mission regarding this war must continue, but not with the combatants. You will be with the peace negotiators, particularly concentrating on the Russians. The Tsar still believes he can win the war. He agreed to these peace talks only to gain time to send more troops to Manchuria. He has no intention of agreeing to anything substantive. I have Meyer working on him. I need you to convince Witte that Russia can't win the war and must accept a compromise for peace. This must be done with subtle confidentiality and plain talk during the evenings, away from observation by the press, other negotiators, and onlookers. I recommend utilizing María's *considerable diplomatic skills—invaluable when dealing with such a personality as Witte's.*

As per the previous cable, you will go to Portsmouth Naval Station immediately upon arrival at Boston. Your rooms will be at the Hotel Wentworth, and you will await the negotiating parties, who also are to be lodged there. Leaving from my home at Oyster Bay, they will arrive in Portsmouth on the new presidential yacht Mayflower *on the eighth of August. The official discussions will be held at the naval station, but the parties will retire each evening to the hotel, which is when and where your work will be carried out.*

These talks must be concluded quickly. I expect daily coded cable briefs from you utilizing cipher wheel code EM. At the conclusion of your mission, you will return to brief me in person on the naval capabilities and tactics of the Japanese at Tsushima and your impressions of both countries' negotiators at Portsmouth.

Immediately after this briefing to me, you will embark on a very well deserved and long-overdue six-month rest leave with María, during which I promise not to bother you.

Good luck, my friend. Burn this letter after reading.
TR

Part 4

The Wages of Peace

74
Night Work

Hotel Wentworth
New Castle, New Hampshire
August 1905

It was going to be a difficult mission. Like so many in service of the Russian autocracy of the Imperial House of Romanov, Witte could spot a spy or sycophant instantly. He erected silent defenses against any opportunity for flattery, inducement, or coercion. But we had María, and she had the shrewdness and charm to penetrate those defenses. She would be the initial conduit to Sergei Yulyevich Witte.

Witte had not even a notional military background, immediately setting him apart from other higher-strata Russian leaders. Instead, he was an intellectual. Raised by minor nobility parents in Russian Georgia, he'd studied and wanted to teach theoretical mathematics at the university but ended up working in rail transport, then in government. He became the consummate court politico, balancing egos off each other, knowing where not to step, all the while producing impressive results in rail transportation across the vast empire. This garnered him both praise and dangerous enemies among the nobility and the governmental bureaucrats. Witte was known as a peace supporter but also as an ardent Tsarist.

His public fame was growing, though, and that is a bad thing in a dictator-ship like Russia. He had the ear and grudging respect of the Tsar, but there was also a growing distrust of him by that insecure man who ruled over Russia. However, the very fact that Tsar Nicholas chose him to go to Portsmouth was an indication of how dire the situation was in Russia.

For our purposes, Witte had a deficit that would prove a tough challenge. He spoke no English. He did speak some German (his paternal family was Baltic German), but his primary foreign language was a fluent and cultured French. My French was not equal to the task of subtle discussions on sensitive issues. I wasn't worried. María's French is perfect.

It took almost a week to penetrate Witte's silent wall of deterrence. María and I appeared on the lantern-lit veranda at ten o'clock each evening to enjoy a leisurely post-prandial digestif—Hennessey cognac for me and burgundy wine for her. Arriving early, we sat in the same rocking love seat, situated mere feet away from our target. Smoking an H. Upmann Cuban cigar while also sipping a Hennessey, Witte would appear ten minutes later to sit alone in his usual rocking chair, gazing out over the dark waters, deep in thought.

On the sixth night María, daintily feigning ignorance of his identity, glanced his way and let out a soft sigh of contentment. "Oh, these are such beautiful evenings here. So very romantic and calming for the soul, are they not?"

Witte looked over at us and smiled. It was a gentle, genuine smile, giving no indication of alarm or vexation. With an apologetic shrug, he expressed sorrow at his lack of English, and explained he did possess French, German, and Russian. "Je suis désolé Madame, mais je ne parle pas anglais. Je ne parle que le français, l'allemand et le russe."

María bestowed her sweetest smile upon him, her eyes lighting up in delight as she proclaimed them both kindred souls in such a beautiful language. "Ensuite, nous sommes des âmes sœurs. C'est une si belle langue."

She went on to explain that her husband possessed no French but had some Spanish, which was her native tongue. In the next ten minutes, Witte learned we were at the hotel for rest and recuperation, particularly me, for I had just returned from an arduous and very long overseas assignment as a naval officer. On his second cognac, Witte explained that he was trying to negotiate peace with Japan. Through a heartfelt translation by María, I expressed deep personal gratitude for his efforts to end war and save lives.

On our third mutual cognac, we spoke of our families and homes. Witte had no children, but he had adopted his beloved wife's children by a previous marriage. I spoke of my love and worry for my two children. María shared the sad story of her two sons, one being wounded in war and the other killed. Witte shook his head in sympathetic sorrow. María translated both sides of the emotional conversation with effortless skill, enabling true sentiments to be easily passed between us.

When he rose to leave at midnight, Witte kissed María's hand and shook mine firmly. María got misty-eyed, which made him squeeze her hand in empathy. I wished him luck in ending the war and saving thousands of lives. He shook my hand again and embraced me in a prolonged Russian hug. When he walked away, I knew we had been successful.

Now came the hard part.

75
Code of Honor

A nother week of late evening pleasantries, which never delved into the peace negotiations with any detail, lowered Witte's initial wariness of us. For the Russian, our tête-à-têtes provided a much-needed escape from the extreme tensions of the day. The few times I mentioned the peace talks, he changed the subject, wishing instead to speak of culture and science.

Meanwhile, the war ground on. The most recent action was the victorious Japanese invasion and capture of Russian Sakhalin, the six-hundred-mile-long rocky frozen island just north of Japan. The place's value lay in its two sea straits allowing northern access to the Sea of Japan and therefore Vladivostok. Russia had held the place since an 1875 treaty between the two countries.

Elsewhere the war was slowed, but not stopped. In Manchuria, four new Russian divisions arrived and were put into the trenches to face fresh Japanese forces reinforcing their lines. Newspaper reporters on the front lines predicted Armageddon would soon erupt on a scale dwarfing that already seen.

During this ominous period, the peace talks descended from awkward introductions into a grim stalemate. Following the strict instructions of his

Tsar, Witte refused to make any concessions on two salient Japanese demands: payment of war reparations and the ceding of Sakhalin Island to them. The diminutive Japanese diplomats weren't intimidated by the giant Russian in the least. They simply gazed up at him and continued insisting on 1.2 billion yen as payment, along with demanding that all six hundred miles of Sakhalin be forever Japanese.

Roosevelt's anger escalated with each day's inaction. I grew more frustrated. María's worry about the impending death toll rose. On Friday, the twenty-fifth of August, things got worse. In the negotiating room, both sides simply stopped speaking, sitting there staring at each other.

On the morning of Monday, the twenty-eighth, the Russians asked for their hotel bills, intimating they would be leaving the next day. I decided to try one more time with Witte that evening. I had an idea, a last-ditch notion that Theodore and I had discussed in our daily coded messages.

Tonight, the conversation with Witte would be very different.

The Russian had a weary manner when he sat down with us on the veranda and picked up the cognac I'd ordered for him. The night was gentle, with a light breeze off the water and stars dusted across the sky. The horrors of war seemed unimaginable in that moment.

He sighed. "It is ending tomorrow," he said to me, through María. "These Japanese want everything, give nothing. We have lost battles, yes—but not the war. They have not vanquished Russia and should not act as if they did."

"Then *you* must give them something first, Sergei," I replied carefully. "You have plenipotentiary powers from the Tsar to make a treaty. Make it."

"What do I give?" he asked heatedly, glaring at me. María's translation echoed his emotion. "Over a billion yen in the war reparations they want? They *started* the war, Peter! Give them Sakhalin Island, which protects Vladivostok, the capital of our Far East? We will never give in on these points. You know it is contrary to our code of honor."

I kept my tone calm. "And concessions are contrary to Japan's code of honor as well, Sergei. But concessions are the way peace treaties are made. Is the problem the money, or the *description* of the money?"

Brow furrowed in sudden interest, Witte leaned back in his chair. "What do you mean, Peter?"

"War reparations is one way to describe the money—a very negative way. Another way is to say there will be a generous amount to care for Russia's thousands of soldiers and sailors now in captivity in Japan. That is not negative at all."

"And Sakhalin?"

"Divide it across the middle, at the fiftieth degree of latitude. Japan takes the south, Russia the north. Japan gets a defensive buffer against invasion and Russia still retains the northern sea passage to Vladivostok."

While he sat there thinking, I added more. "Ambassador Meyers in Saint Petersburg has already talked with Tsar Nicholas about this. The Tsar did not reject it. Why should he? It does not violate or stain Russia's code of honor, nor Japan's."

Witte's eyes bored into mine. "How do you know this?"

"President Roosevelt told me," I replied, then reached out my hand. "You have my word of honor it is true, Sergei Yulyevich. Make the offer tomorrow morning. Do not waste this last opportunity to save thousands of Russian lives."

"Thank you, Peter," he said. Then, without another word, he stood and walked down the veranda into the hotel. I glanced at María. She patted my hand and murmured, "We have tried."

As we rose to go to our room, my eyes took in the table by Witte's rocking chair, seeing an unusual sight. The cognac glass was still full.

The next morning, as everyone around him began preparing for departure from the meeting, Sergei Witte declared there would be no indemnity paid to Japan but offered a considerably smaller amount of money couched as funding to maintain Russian prisoners of war in Japan. He then agreed to divide Sakhalin Island in the middle, at the fiftieth parallel, and share it with the Japanese.

Minister Komura continued sitting in silence. Witte began his nervous habit of ripping small pieces off a sheet of paper, something which annoyed the Japanese and others. This went on for a while until Komura nodded his agreement, saying Japan desired peace. The following week the treaty was signed.

The Russo-Japanese War was over.

Leaders in Washington, Saint Petersburg, and Tokyo breathed easier. In Portsmouth, smiles emerged everywhere, and all parties made their weary way home from the Hotel Wentworth. Chief Boatswain's Mate Sean Rork returned to his quarters in the garret over the Latrobe Gate of the Washington Navy Yard, going back to duty later in the week. Within a month, Capt. Edwin Law embarked in a troop transport for his new tour of duty with a Marine battalion fighting the jungle war in the Philippines. María and I returned to our cottage in Alexandria. I worked at the White House until November, when we went to our bungalow on Patricio Island in Florida for that much-needed six-month leave. I imagine the reader expects the story would end at this point.

But it doesn't.

76

The Wages of Peace

Family Dining Room, White House
Washington, D.C.
Thursday, 3 January 1907

I had a very special delivery to complete—the culmination of a 4,467-mile journey from Kristiania, Norway. It was not an ordinary mission. The entire world knew about what I was to give President Roosevelt.

María and I were in full evening dress when we arrived at the White House gate in the presidential carriage. She, naturally, looked her usual radiantly beautiful self in light-blue silk. I looked, as I always do in full dress, uncomfortable. Rork was also in full dress uniform, carrying the package with great solemnity. Nineteen months after being wounded at Tsushima, the crutches and cane were gone now, but his slight limp was persistent.

Dinner was in the small private dining room upstairs. Besides we three, there were the president and Edith and the Russian ambassador to the United States, Baron Roman Rosen, and his wife, Baroness Elizabeth. Throughout the first courses and main dishes, Theodore was in fine fettle, holding forth on a range of comfortably nonpolitical topics, from manatees in Florida, to the song of a Carolina chickadee, to his latest writing project, the four-volume *Winning of the West.*

Baron Rosen sat next to me and at one point passed a small, sealed envelope to me. "A message for you came in the diplomatic mail pouch from your friend in the Okhrana."

I read the note inside.

Dear Peter,   *1 December 1906*

    Enough time has gone by that I can now be candid with you about the past. Your false-flag ruse worked too well—the Germans were convinced we Russians had gotten their man to spy for us. It caused us many problems and senior Russians were angry you set us up as the scapegoats with the Germans. They wanted you dead in revenge. That is why I convinced the Tsar to get you out of the way in the fleet going around the world. Of course, nobody thought our fleet would be annihilated. And I certainly did not think the Germans would find out what really happened and try to kill you in Africa and elsewhere.

    A recent bit of news may interest you. The main German insisting on your death was General Sonnenblume. Fear him no longer, for he was found suspiciously dead last week, possibly at the hands of his lover, another general and nobleman in the Kaiser's personal circle, though none of that was in the press!

    As an intelligence professional and man of the world, I hope you can understand my actions and further hope that we are still, and will always be, dear friends . . .

    Pyotr Ivanovich Rachkovsky

His plea rang hollow to me. I knew he had set me up with the Germans so they could kill me in an out-of-the-way place. I walked over to the fireplace and slipped the note and envelope into the flames. In any event, it was over.

María watched my behavior questioningly, so I told her, "Rachkovsky says Sonnenblume was the one who wanted me killed—and he was just found dead. One less thing to worry about, María."

She closed her eyes in prayer. "Thank God. Now we can live life."

Rosen showed no sign of knowledge of the note's contents—but then, all diplomats are professional liars—and I returned to the table's conversations and gaiety. After the dessert of chocolate cake and ice cream, it was time to

do my duty. After tapping my wineglass, I stood and asked, "Mr. President,
I believe it is time to complete my assignment. May I, sir?"

He stood also and nodded his approval. Accompanied by Rork carrying
the inlaid rosewood box, I approached the president.

"Mr. President and Mrs. Roosevelt, Baron and Baroness Rosen, ladies and
gentlemen," I began. "Chief Rork, María, and I have carried out our duty in
bringing this rare accolade here. It is now my great honor and pleasure to
present to you the world's prestigious token of their esteem and gratitude
for your skilled and tireless efforts to end the bloodshed of the recent war
between Russia and Japan—the Nobel Peace Prize."

Rork opened the box, revealing a glittering gold medallion reposing in an
etched-glass presentation base. I put the medallion in the president's hands.
Rork then brought over the large diploma that proclaimed Theodore Roosevelt
the Laureate of Peace of 1906. Finally, I laid a gold embossed royal blue envelope
at the president's place on the table. It contained a check for $38,500, the prize
part of the award.

Everyone at the table rose and applauded with radiant smiles. Stewards
and butlers filled the room, joyfully clapping with genuine enthusiasm. It
went on for many minutes as Theodore Roosevelt beheld the medallion with
reverence. Then he looked up at everyone and blinked behind his spectacles.

He spoke humbly. "Unfortunately, my national duties precluded my attend-
ing the ceremony in Norway, and I thank Admiral Wake, Chief Rork, and
María Wake for escorting these wonderful artifacts safely to their new home.
As for my thoughts on receiving such an accolade, I will echo a bit of what
I wrote to the chairman of the Nobel Committee and was read aloud at the
ceremony in Norway . . .

"I am *profoundly* moved by this signal honor. No gift could I appreciate
more. I thank the committee for it on behalf of the United States of America,
for what I did, I was only able to accomplish as the representative of the nation
of which, for the time being, I am president.

"After much thought, I have decided the best and most fitting way to use the
prize money is for a foundation to be established at Washington, a permanent
industrial peace committee. This committee will strive for better and more

equitable relations among our countrymen, both capitalists and wage earners, who are engaged in America's industrial and agricultural pursuits."

The humble tone now faded, replaced by a more insistent energy. "I further hope this award is the first of many such for our compatriots and nation in this exciting new century, which promises so much. The old century and old ways are over. Let us all work to never make the same mistakes of the past. Thank you all so much for sharing this moment with Edith and me."

After the applause faded away, Theodore winked conspiratorially at Baron Rosen. The Russian called for everyone's attention.

Then he faced me.

77

Nobody Does It Better

Family Dining Room, White House
Washington, D.C.
Thursday, 3 January 1907

B aron Rosen spoke with theatrical flourish. "Mr. President and Mrs.
Roosevelt, Admiral and Mrs. Wake, my dear Baroness Elizabeth, and
Chief Rork. First, may I convey the Great Tsar Nicholas the Second's
most sincere appreciation for all that you have done to secure a just peace,
Mr. President—and his congratulations on your history-making award!"

He paused for the polite clapping, then started up again. "And secondly,
I have the pleasure to announce there is another award to be given tonight!
This award was wholeheartedly recommended to His Imperial Majesty, the
Tsar, by Prince Sergei Alexievich Constantinovich Dyvoryanin Romanov,
cousin to the Tsar and a lieutenant commander in the Imperial Russian Navy."

As Rosen paused again for dramatic effect, I whispered to Rork, "*Our
Sergei is a prince?*" He grinned. "Aye, that he must be! An' the boyo did say
he'd never forget you. An' I also see he got promoted."

Rosen resumed, now really warming to the subject. "And so, for saving the
life of Russian sailors, among them Prince Sergei, at the Battle of Tsushima;

and for saving the life of a Russian soldier by performing a delicate surgery while on a train crossing Siberia; and for repeatedly proving by his skill and courage that he is a true friend of all Russians and their beloved Tsar, Adm. Peter Wake of the United States Navy is hereby presented the highest imperial award of the Empire of Russia, normally only given to Russians: the exalted Order of Saint George."

"*Me?*" I blurted out.

Roosevelt pumped my hand. "Of course!"

María joined me and Rosen pinned the medal—a white enamel cross with cameo of Saint George in the center and suspended by gold-and-black ribbon—above the other medals on my chest. Everyone crowded around to congratulate me. María kissed my cheek. Rosen gave me a Russian bear hug. Rork shook my hand, and Theodore thumped me on the shoulder. "*Bully* well done, Peter!"

I stood there in stunned silence for a moment, then managed to say, "Thank you, Baron Rosen. Please extend my deepest thank you to Tsar Nicholas and Prince Sergei. May Russia and her great people have a peaceful and prosperous future."

A steward holding a long box appeared beside the president. Theodore held up a hand and said, "And now it's *my* turn, Peter. This is a symbol of my personal appreciation for your very perilous service to our nation at a critical time in our history. Chief Rork and Captain Law have already received theirs and were told to keep this a surprise."

The box was opened. Inside was a gleaming sword, scabbard, and sword belt. The sword was pressed into my hands by the president, who declared, "I present this sword to a United States naval officer and gentleman, who knows not only *how* to use it but also *when* to use it."

More applause erupted as Theodore quietly said to me, "The war never would've ended, and I never would've been awarded that Nobel Peace Prize, if it hadn't been for your incredible abilities and perseverance, Peter. Thank you for all you did out there around the world, and then up at Portsmouth. Nobody does it better."

He showed me the engraved words on the steel blade just below the golden hilt:

To Rear Admiral Peter Wake, U.S.N.,
with the greatest appreciation
From President Theodore Roosevelt, 1907

Memories flooded my mind—people, places, ordeals, terrors. Emotion welled up inside me. Sensing my discomposure, María kissed me again. This time, we held the embrace while everyone stood there around us, waiting for me to say something.

We let them wait.

Notes by Chapter

Chapter 1: This War Ain't Even Ours

The Tsushima Current flows northeastward up to one knot into the Sea of Japan. It is a branch of the Kuroshio Current, bringing warm water north from the Philippines, like the Atlantic's Gulf Stream brings warm water all the way to the British Isles.

Chapter 2: The Sheik, the Kaiser, and the Tsar

The White House West Wing construction began in 1902. During the construction, President Theodore Roosevelt used a temporary office in the new wing. When the work was done, he moved into the new Oval Office. That temporary office still exists as the Roosevelt Room.

Cipher wheels are an ancient technology from three thousand years ago. Julius Caesar used them, as did Thomas Jefferson. The German Enigma machine of World War II was a series of complicated cipher wheels.

Ion "Jon" Perdicaris (1840–1925) was a Greek American dilettante traveler, writer, promoter, and quasi-engineer who, in the 1870s, convinced a British woman to divorce her husband and afterward marry Perdicaris. In the 1880s they settled, with her children, in Tangiers, where he soon became the leader of the foreign community. Perdicaris and his stepson, Cromwell Varley, were kidnapped from their home, Place of Nightingales, on 19 May 1904 by Sheik Mulai Ahmed er Raisuli, leader of three hill tribes and adversary of Morocco's sultan. During the ensuing Perdicaris crisis, Perdicaris's actual nationality was called into question. It still is. After Raisuli freed his hostages, the Perdicaris family moved to England.

Mulai Abd al-Aziz IV (1878–1943) became Sultan Abdelaziz of Morocco in 1894 at age sixteen upon the death of his father, the respected Sultan Hassan I (whom Wake met in 1874—read *An Affair of Honor*). Deposed by his own family and courtiers in 1908, Abdelaziz did not have the greatest reputation.

Mu'al-lim Sohkoor was the erudite Royal Scholar of the Sultanate of Morocco whom Wake met in 1874 and corresponded with until Sohkoor's death fourteen years later at age ninety-eight.

The 1904 Republican National Convention was held at the Chicago Coliseum just as the Perdicaris crisis entered its most critical stage. Secretary of State John Hay had Speaker of the House Joseph Cannon read aloud to the convention the grammatically flawed but historically famous statement, "We wants Perdicaris alive or Raisuli dead!" It had the desired effect, electrifying the convention and the country. Roosevelt was nominated overwhelmingly.

A **"false-flag" espionage operation** is a common technique where the target is deceived as to the nationality of who he is dealing with, or who runs the operation. A "double cross" (or double agent) is where an agent portrays himself as betraying his own side to help an adversary but is actually working for his own side against the adversary. Russians are masters at this.

Kaiser Wilhelm II (1859–1941), at the age of twenty-nine in 1888, unexpectedly became Kaiser of Germany and King of Prussia after his father, the publicly beloved Kaiser Frederick III, suddenly died of throat cancer only ninety-nine days after his ascension to the throne following the death of his father, Kaiser Wilhelm I, who died at age ninety. Thus, Germany had three Kaisers in less than one hundred days. Wilhelm II was completely unprepared.

Kaiser Wilhelm II's deformed left arm was caused by a traumatic birth delivery, resulting in Erb's palsy, making the arm six inches shorter. Once Kaiser, his behavior became egomaniacal, and he soon rid himself of experienced imperial counselors, surrounding himself with fawning underlings and embarking on a bombastic course of military and naval expansion for Germany. Within five years, colonies had been founded around the world, and by 1904 a naval arms race had begun with Great Britain, France, and Russia. The king of Great Britain at the time, Edward VII, loathed his nephew Wilhelm, as did many in the Royal Navy.

Kaiser Wilhelm was a grandson of Queen Victoria, who grew to despise him in her later years. He also was a first cousin of Russia's Tsar Nicholas II and Britain's King George V (reigned 1910–36)—becoming a mortal enemy of them in World War I and eventually outliving them. Kaiser Wilhelm II lived in exile at Doorn, Netherlands, from 1918 to his death at age eighty-two in 1941. In the 1930s he hoped the Nazis would restore his monarchy, but Hitler thought him an idiotic old man and ignored him.

Tsar Nicholas II (1868–1918) reigned autocratically over Russia from 1894 (when he was twenty-six) until 1917. His grandfather, Tsar Alexander II, was assassinated and his father, Tsar Alexander III, died at age forty-nine of kidney disease. Tsar Nicholas was the opposite of his father and his cousin Kaiser Wilhelm II. Nicholas was gentle, polite, shy, devoted to his wife and family, and terribly indecisive and incompetent at running the massive Russian Empire. He thought the Russo-Japanese War would be quick and easy, ignoring all facts and warnings to the contrary. He also ignored the smoldering rebellion inside Russia until it was far too late. Nicholas and his entire family were brutally murdered by communists on 17 July 1918. Since 1981 Tsar Nicholas and his murdered family have been considered saints by the Russian Orthodox Church.

The Russo-Japanese War had gone on for six months by the time of this conversation between Wake and Roosevelt, with tens of thousands of dead and wounded on both sides. The Japanese had consolidated their positions in Korea and were advancing on Russian-held Manchuria. The great Russian base at Port Arthur was under siege. The morale-sapping litany of Russian defeats ashore and afloat encouraged revolt at home and deflated Russian prestige in the world. It was unthinkable in the not-so-subtle racism of the times—Asians were out-fighting Europeans?

Chapter 3: My Entourage

Hotel Vier Jahreszeiten started with 11 rooms and 3 bathrooms in 1897 and now has 156 rooms, award-winning restaurants, and is one of the most famous luxury hotels in the world.

Wake's previous encounters with the German Navy at Samoa can be seen in *Honors Rendered*, and in the Caribbean in *The Assassin's Honor*.

Deuxième Bureau was the primary French military counterintelligence agency from 1871 to 1899, when its intelligence duties were transferred to the national police. In 1907 they were returned to the Deuxième Bureau. With the fall of France in 1940, the agency ended.

Chapter 4: Othello

"Othello" is the main character in Shakespeare's 1603 tragic story *The Tragedy of Othello, the Moor of Venice*. Othello is a Moorish general in service to Venice, his lover is Desdemona, his trusted second-in-command is Cassio, and Cassio's lover is Bianca.

***Renommierschmiss* fencing scars** were common among university men in nineteenth-century Germany, Austria, and Hungary. The scars were sometimes intentionally inflamed to make them look worse. I learned nineteenth-century saber fencing to be able to write the opening scene in *Honorable Lies* and find this scarring practice idiotic.

Sonnenblume is German for "sunflower." Was this an alias used by Wake to conceal the man's real identity in his memoir? He never said, and we'll never know.

Chapter 6: Repugnant Skullduggery

Vyacheslav von Plehve (1846–1904) was so hated in Russia that his own spy inside the revolutionary group plotting to assassinate him, Yevno Azef, never warned Plehve of the plan.

Okhrana is the common name of the Department for Protecting the Public Security and Order, the Russian Empire's primary secret police counterintelligence apparatus from 1881 to 1917. Operating inside Russia and foreign countries (including the United States), they were particularly effective at infiltrating anti-Tsar revolutionary groups, spreading disinformation, influencing other countries' politics and press articles, and creating chaos. Soviet Russia's subsequent secret police agencies, the Cheka, NKVD, KGB, and current FSB, all use techniques perfected a century ago by the Okhrana. Wake's first encounter with Okhrana was in the Caribbean in 1888, as depicted in *Honor Bound*.

The Socialist Revolutionary Party (1902–21) grew to over one million members by 1917, a very influential antimonarchy political faction. The Okhrana thoroughly infiltrated it and periodically arrested members as they began their activities. In fact, the party's deputy leader, Yevno Azef, was an Okhrana agent who set up the party's leader for arrest. The party's combat organization was not as infiltrated and conducted bombing assassinations of several high government officials across Russia. The party lost its influence with the Bolsheviks and dissolved in the chaos of the Russian Civil War.

Count von Hülsen-Haeseler (1852–1908) was chief of Kaiser Wilhelm II's military cabinet, but he is chiefly remembered for the manner of his death. After a private dinner for the Kaiser's entourage during a hunting trip, a drunken Hülsen-Haeseler entered the room wearing nothing but a pink ballerina tutu and tried to perform a dance for the shocked attendees before falling dead in front of the Kaiser. The manner of death was never revealed to the press. Several members of the Kaiser's entourage were homosexual noblemen and generals, and when the press learned of several unsavory incidents in 1907, it had been Hülsen-Haeseler who had tried to orchestrate a coverup to prevent the public from ever knowing. He succeeded in that the public never knew the Kaiser's awareness.

Prince Philipp of Eulenberg-Hertefeld (1847–1921) and **General Kuno von Moltke** (1847–1923) were members of the Kaiser's entourage who were also homosexual lovers and prominently outed in public during the 1907 Harden-Eulenberg affair.

Chapter 7: The Biggest Pickelhaube

The Imperial House of Hohenzollern began in 1061, ruling Prussia, Germany, and Romania, with nobility in other countries as well. The house split centuries ago into the Catholic Swabian branch and the Protestant Prussian branch, which included Kaiser Wilhelm II. The last monarch to reign was King Michael I (1921–2017) of Romania, who was forced by the Soviets to abdicate in 1947. As late as mid-2019, Hohenzollern family members pressed claims in courts to their ancient castles and property in Germany—to no avail. Interestingly, several properties in Romania have been willingly returned by the government to King Michael's family. King Michael is still beloved by many Romanians. Not so Kaiser Wilhelm II among Germans.

Albert Ballin (1857–1918) made the Hamburg-America Line one of the top shipping lines (cargo and passenger) in world history. Although he was Jewish, and Kaiser Wilhelm and many German elite despised Jews, he became a friend and adviser to the Kaiser—in private locales. By the end of World War I, his company had lost almost all its ships and many of its other assets, and Germany was mired in rebellion. Two days before the end of hostilities, Ballin committed suicide.

A Pickelhaube was the famous German helmet with a spike. When faced with the reality of modern combat in World War I, the Pickelhaube was replaced by the spikeless Stahlhelm (German for "steel helmet"), designed to provide greater neck and head protection from shrapnel. Most western militaries, including the United States, have now adopted that German design. Interestingly, Pickelhaubes are still worn today by ceremonial military units in Great Britain, Sweden, France, Chile, Colombia, Venezuela, Ecuador, Jordan, Bolivia, and Romania.

The Imperial House of Bourbon monarchies began in 1272 in France. Over the next eight centuries it spread to Spain, Navarre, Luxembourg, and Italy. The current king of Spain, King Felipe VI, is a descendant of the Bourbon monarchs.

Chapter 8: The Desdemona Decoy

Alfred Graf von Schlieffen's (1833–1913) last combat was the invasion of France in 1871 during the Franco-Prussian War. He'd been a garrison and staff officer ever since. His "Schlieffen Plan" for the invasion of France was used at the beginning of World War I. A variation was used in the invasion of France in World War II. His plans featured bold, large-scale maneuvers and were studied intensely after the war by most major armies. With poetic justice, the concept was used by American generals Patton and Eisenhower against the Germans in 1944.

Desdemona is Othello's beautiful wife in Shakespeare's play. Othello is devoted to her but believes a lie that Desdemona has committed adultery, so he strangles her to death.

Abteilung IIIb was the Imperial German Army's military intelligence department from 1889 to 1918. It specialized on France and Russia. German naval intelligence focused on Great Britain.

Chapter 9: Undercurrents

Hotel Europa is now the Belmond Grand Hotel Europe and is 140 years old.

The Putilov factory, a major munitions plant, still exists and is now called the Kirov Factory. Notably, it was the scene of revolutionary strikes in 1905 and the scene where the Russian Revolution began in 1917.

Chapter 10: A Siberian Tiger Can Never Be a Vegetarian

Pyotr Ivanovich Rachkovsky (1853–1910?) worked in the Okhrana from the late 1870s until about 1910, when he disappears from historical records. From 1885 to 1902 he ran the Paris station, infiltrating his operatives into exile Russian revolutionary groups across Europe and in New York. He is acknowledged by many intelligence historians to have been a world master of disinformation, infiltration, false-flag ops, inducement, blackmail, and sowing confusion and distrust. In the midst of the domestic revolutionary unrest during the Russo-Japanese War he was brought back to Saint Petersburg to run domestic counterintelligence operations, which he did quite effectively. In 1905 he became chief of the entire Okhrana. No one knows exactly what happened to him in 1910. Some (including me) suspect he simply used one of his many aliases to disappear from Russia and live off his ill-gotten side moneys.

Henri Bint was a French Alsatian counterintelligence agent who was also an Okhrana agent from 1880 until about 1909. Bint initially ran a group of beautiful female operatives out of Paris in 1885. Later he used them around Europe. He rose to become a senior Okhrana agent and trusted operative of Rachkovsky. Like so many others, Bint disappeared from history.

Akashi Motojiro (1864–1919) was the senior Japanese intelligence officer stationed in Europe who ran a complex network of Japanese spies, European informants, and Russian revolutionary saboteurs during the Russo-Japanese War. The Okhrana tried very hard but never found and killed him. He retired as a lieutenant general and died while governor of Taiwan.

Chapter 12: The Hope of All Russia

The Imperial Maryinsky Theater, built in 1860, was the largest in Russia and one of the most famous in the world. This grand dame of the performing arts world still exists.

Sergei Vasilyevich Rachmaninov (1873–1943) became one of the most famous composers and pianists in the world, touring throughout Europe and America. He left Russia permanently after the 1917 Revolution and eventually settled in New York City. In failing health, he moved to California in 1942 but still performed. He became a naturalized American citizen in February 1943, died a month later, and is buried in Valhalla, New York. In 2015 Russia attempted to have his remains reburied there, but his family refused.

Zinovy Petrovich Rozhestvensky (1848–1909) served in the Imperial Russian Navy from 1863 to 1906. When the Russo-Japanese War started, he was already a highly respected Russian naval officer with diverse experience, known for trying to increase the efficiency of the navy. A loyal Tsarist, he did his duty in the war, knowing where it would lead him and his fleet. Sadly, he lived his final years as a recluse in Saint Petersburg, dying of a heart attack at only sixty years of age in January 1909—only two months before his friend Peter Wake completed this volume of memoirs. They maintained correspondence until the end.

Arkadiy Mikhailovich Harting (1861–?) was actually named Aharon Hackelman and born into a Jewish family in Belarus. In his shadowy life, he went from being an anarchist to a senior officer in the Okhrana and trusted colleague of Pyotr Rachkovsky. Along the way he had several aliases but mostly used the name Harting or a variation thereof. He operated throughout Europe and ultimately controlled about sixty operatives, becoming second only to Rachkovsky in power and influence. In 1913 he was awarded a minor Russian noble rank in recognition of his long service. He was last noted working counterintelligence against the Germans in France and Belgium during World War I. As with so many other Okhrana leaders, the circumstances of his end are unknown.

Chapter 14: The Surprise Offer

A **"honey trap"** is an ancient ploy. Sex is offered to the target, commonly when he is under the influence of alcohol or drugs. If he succumbs to the offer, there are three usual outcomes: he unwittingly spills his secrets in bed, he is subsequently blackmailed into divulging secrets, or he falls in love and willingly shares his secrets.

Chapter 15: The Ring

The Merwin-Hulbert revolver, with the "Skullcrusher" beaked grip, was first made in the 1870s and is still highly regarded as one of the stoutest of revolver frames. Wake never goes on a mission without it. Recently, one in perfect original condition sold for $7,250.

Henna is a brown dye extracted from the henna tree and is common in the Islamic world, where it has been used as a decorative tattoo agent for centuries, especially for women. It can be sickening if ingested.

Afghan poison rings are still used today. I have a dear friend with one, but I don't allow her to hold my wineglass.

Chapter 17: Translations

Telegraph codes were used to save money (you paid by the letter) and provide confidentiality. Commercial codes weren't that secret, but government codes were. Combinations of different codes started being used at the turn of the century to make penetrating the message more difficult. I am quite fortunate to have a collection of exemplars from a dozen of those codes, along with a simplified cipher wheel, from my research visits at the NSA museum at Fort Meade, Maryland, a fascinating place, indeed. They have hundreds of codes spanning from 1694 to 1922.

Chapter 18: Amerikanischer Invasionseinsatzplan III

Eberhard von Mantey (1869–1940) served in the Imperial German Navy from 1887 to 1920. He also became a well-known naval historian with half a dozen works to his credit.

Amerikanischer Invasionseinsatzplan III had three phases, increasingly more detailed, of the 1897–1903 German invasion plans. It might seem far-fetched with our 120-year hindsight, but given the Kaiser's bizarre combination of national arrogance, ignorance of the United States, and egomaniacal dreams of conquest, at the time they were very concerning.

Hubert von Rebeur-Paschwitz (1863–1933) was a German naval officer (1889–1920) who commanded German-Turkish naval forces in the Black Sea during World War I. Defeated at the Battle of Imbros in the Aegean on 20 January 1918, he soon retired out as a vice admiral.

Charles Train (1845–1906) was a U.S. naval officer who served from 1864 to 1906. At the time of his report, he was a captain commanding the Board of Inspection and Survey. He died on duty at Chefoo, China, as commander of the Asiatic Fleet and is buried at the U.S. Naval Academy in Annapolis, Maryland.

Wilhelm von Büchsel (1848–1920) was a German naval officer (1865–1916) whose career from 1890 onward was administrative, mainly planning and training. He retired out as a vice admiral.

Alfred Peter Friedrich von Tirpitz (1849–1930) was a towering figure in German history—the dominant force in the expansion and modernization of the Imperial German Navy. After serving from 1869 to 1916, he had a falling-out with the Kaiser and retired out as a grand admiral (equivalent of a five-star admiral in the U.S. Navy). He was a politician afterward, until his death.

Chapter 19: A Very Terrible Feeling

Seaton Schroeder (1849–1922) was a U.S. naval officer (1864–1922) who specialized in hydrography, gunnery, and naval intelligence. He retired out as a rear admiral but was called back to active duty twice (in 1912 and 1917) for his considerable expertise in intelligence work.

Chapter 22: Preparing for War

Kronstadt Naval Base has been the primary Russian naval base for the Baltic Fleet since the early 1700s. It still is. The famous naval cathedral, which tourists now visit, was opened four years after Wake was there.

The battleship *Knyaz Suvorov* (Prince Suvorov), on board which Wake and his colleagues would live for months as they steamed around the world, had just been commissioned in the Russian navy and was the flagship of the Baltic Fleet. Her measurements were 14,415 tons, 397 feet long, 30-foot draft, twenty large boilers serving two triple-expansion steam engines and two propellers, with top speed of seventeen knots and a complement of 782+ officers and men. She was armed with four 12-inch guns, twelve 6-inch guns, twenty 3-inch guns, twenty 2-inch guns, and four 15-inch torpedo tubes. Her armor consisted of seven inches on the waterline belt, two inches on the main deck, and ten inches on the main turrets. She was built by the Baltic Works factory in Saint Petersburg, which still builds merchant ships.

Chapter 23: Spies and Torpedo Boats

The Phoenix Hotel in Copenhagen, site of Russian skullduggery in 1904–5, still exists. It now is even larger, with 213 rooms.

Wireless telegraphy at sea had just begun in 1899 and was still quite unreliable in 1904. Marconi and Slaby-Arco were the leading companies in the field. The new apparatus quickly increased in range and reliability. The Russo-Japanese War was the first time it was used for communication, interception, and deception in combat at sea. By 1907 all major navies used it.

King Christian IX (1818–1906) was a contemporary of Queen Victoria and known as "The Father-in-Law of Europe," since his descendants occupied the thrones of Denmark, Russia, Great Britain, Spain, Greece, Belgium, Norway, and Luxembourg. Tsar Nicholas II was his grandson.

The Black Dragon Society was a secret Japanese paramilitary organization founded in 1901 along the lines of the Black Ocean Society, a secret Japanese political organization begun in 1851. Both had agents across Asia in the 1890s and early 1900s, and both cooperated with Japanese government and military efforts to gather intelligence and stir uprisings in China and European colonies. Both operated behind Russian lines in the Russo-Japanese War, and the Black Dragons helped Colonel Akashi's anti-Russian efforts in Europe. Both were officially disbanded in 1946 by the American occupation forces of Japan—however, some vestiges are thought to remain even today.

Chapter 24: Morale?

Vladimir Ivanovich Semenov (1867–1910) was a respected Russian naval officer, torpedo and gunnery specialist, ship captain, wounded combat veteran, and author of a renowned two-volume memoir of the Russo-Japanese War, which was published shortly after the war.

The Dogger Bank Incident was a terrible stain of Russian honor. Three British fishermen died, six were wounded, and three trawlers were sunk. The Russian government paid sixty-six thousand British pounds to the fishermen and their families. Well over five hundred rounds were fired by the Russian ships, mostly at each other in the chaos. Two Russian warships were damaged, and a chaplain and sailor were killed. Another sailor was wounded badly. In 1906 a memorial to the fishermen was erected in their home port of Hull, England, and it still stands.

Chapter 26: Hail Britannia

The Roaring Forties is the traditional seaman's term for the very dangerous latitudes between 40 degrees south and 50 degrees south, where high winds and seas from the west are prevalent.

Chapter 27: Impressions

Baron Dmitry Gustavovich Fyolkerzam (1846–1905) (a.k.a. Fölkersam) was a Baltic-German Russian officer in the Russian navy (1867–1905) and well respected by both officers and sailors. He was the only subordinate flag officer in the fleet heading to battle the Japanese that Vice Admiral Rozhestvensky trusted. Unfortunately, he was very ill with cancer and, as the reader will see, will be greatly missed at the battle.

Chapter 28: Bears in the Tropics

Kvass is a favorite Slavic fermented drink made from rye bread and usually served cold. It is very popular in Russia, where even Coca-Cola makes its own brand of kvass. I've had some and didn't like it.

Chapter 29: The King, the Pygmy, and the Correspondent

Nicolai Laurentievitch Klado (1861–1919) wrote two books about the war, but neither were as well received as Semenov's. Klado's career stagnated until after the 1917 Revolution, when he convinced the new leaders he had been a victim of the Tsar. They gave him command of the naval academy until 1919. He retired out as a captain and little is known of what happened to him afterward.

Babongo pygmies are known as the "forest people" of the Gabon River region. They follow the spiritual discipline of Bwiti animism beliefs and ingest the root bark of the Iboga bush as a hallucinogenic intoxicant. Babongo shamans interpret the spirit world for the tribe in the form of warnings of things to come and explanations of things that happened.

B.Z. am Mittag was a well-known newspaper in Berlin, started in 1877 as *Berliner Zeitung*. In 1904 the name was changed to *B.Z. am Mittag*. It was owned by Leopold Ullstein from 1878 until his death in 1899. During the Nazi years it was taken over and "Aryanized," but in 1953 it reappeared and is now a daily tabloid called simply *B.Z.*

Chapter 30: Portuguese Bravery

João Carlos da Silva Nogueira (1872–1954) was a Portuguese naval officer (1888–1942) specializing in hydrography who became famous in his country for his honorable behavior in this incident. He retired out as a vice admiral!

Limpopo, named after the local river, was small, indeed: 288 tons, 124 feet long, 21 feet beam, 7-foot draft, twin screws, eleven-knot speed, and armed with one quick-firing 3-pounder and one 5-barreled Nordenfelt machine gun. British built in 1890 and immediately commissioned into the Portuguese navy, she served in Africa for fifty-three years.

Chapter 31: Teutonic Africa

Penguins in Africa? Yes, they are Cape penguins, about two feet tall and eight pounds.

Shark Island Concentration Camp kept approximately six thousand Herero and Namaqua prisoners of war (including women and children) from late 1904 to 1907. About three thousand died.

Chapter 32: Stunned Silence

Eternal Father, Strong to Save has been the U.S. Navy Hymn since Wake's friend Lt. Cdr. Charles Train was the choir master at the U.S. Naval Academy in 1879. Also known by many in the world as *The Sailors' Hymn*, it is widely recognized by mariners everywhere.

Chapter 33: Our Descent into Hell-Ville

Anne Chrétien Louis de Hell (1783–1864) was a French admiral and colonial administrator most famous for serving in the Indian Ocean French colonies. The village of Hell-Bourg on Réunion Island (originally Isle de Bourbon) is named for him also. Hell-Ville on Nosy Be Island in Madagascar still exists but now has a population of 39,000.

Chapter 37: Trade Winds on the Nose

Lascar is the old Portuguese-Persian term for native South Asia sailors or militiamen working on European ships or colonies in the Indian Ocean area from the sixteenth to the twentieth centuries. Eventually all the European colonists and Americans used the term. It is not widely used today.

Chapter 39: A Day Late, in the Middle of Nowhere

Sir Charles Cavendish Boyle (1849–1916) was born in Barbados and served the British Colonial Office all his life, including as governor of Newfoundland, Guiana, and Mauritius. His bachelorhood ended at age sixty-five in 1914 when he married a woman twenty-five years younger, Judith Sassoon. Sir Charles only lived another two years.

Chapter 40: Drinking Rum in a Whisky Bar

Raffles Hotel was built in 1887 with 10 rooms and now has 115. It has an iconic place in Asian history. I've been there a couple times, always spending time and money in the famous Writer's Bar, where I sit in Somerset Maugham's chair and channel Maugham, Joseph Conrad, and Rudyard Kipling. I urge you to visit—it's worth the money.

Brits spell it "whisky" and wonder why Americans can't get it right. I, too, have drunk rum (Bundaberg) in that whisky bar.

The Occidental and Oriental Steamship Company, commonly called the O&O Line, was famous for fast Pacific crossings. By 1905 they had it down to twelve days between San Francisco and Japan. Their last voyage was in 1906.

Chapter 41: The Brethren

The Zetland of the East Lodge, #748, the Wesley Methodist Church, the Armenian Apostolic Church of St. Gregory the Illuminator, and the *Straits Times* still exist and function in Singapore.

"Friend of Freemasonry" is a moniker I am proud to have held since 2010. Theodore Roosevelt became a Mason in 1903. Many of his policies, like giving Americans "a Square Deal," were rooted in Masonic teachings.

Chapter 42: Amazed and Dismayed

The American-Philippine/Moro wars dragged on incessantly in the southern Philippine jungles from 1899 to 1913, with over 6,000 American and pro-U.S. Filipino troops and 20,000 enemy troops killed. Hundreds of thousands of civilians were killed, many in atrocities perpetrated by both sides.

Sun Yat-sen (1866–1925) was a Chinese Christian physician, philosopher, and political activist who led the 1911 revolution that overthrew an ancient Qing Dynasty imperial regime. The first president of the Republic of China, Sun is still revered today in both Communist China and in Taiwan.

The Open Door Policy was an 1899 American state department effort to assure free trade inside China for the U.S. companies while promising to respect Chinese sovereign territoriality. Many Chinese revolutionaries wanted all foreigners out. Most Europeans in China didn't support the American policy.

Chapter 43: The Bear, the Lion, and the Black Dragon

Government House still exists and is now called the Istana, which functions as the official residence of the prime minister. The dining room has been restored to its historic magnificence. The impressive changing of the guards ceremony is open to the public on the first Sunday of each month.

Chapter 44: Pulling Rank

Commander Polis was in charge of Okhrana operations in Southeast Asia, focusing on the Dutch East Indies (now Indonesia), in case the Russian fleet went into the Pacific via those islands.

Cam Ranh Bay is a large, deepwater bay that has been used as a naval base by the Russians (1905), French (1910–54), Americans (1965–75), and the Russians again (in the 1980s). Now it is a Vietnamese navy base. Wake was in that area in 1883, as depicted in *The Honored Dead*.

Chapter 45: Déjà Vu and a Warning

Pierre de Jonquières (1859–1919) was not only an amiable sort—he was very successful, making vice admiral in 1907 and chief of the naval staff in World War I.

Chapter 46: Waiting for Unwanted Help

Nikolai Ivanovich Nebogatov (1849–1922) had a routine career up until the Russo-Japanese War. He was not highly regarded by Vice Admiral Rozhestvensky or the rank-and-file sailors. The squadron he brought out to join the Russian fleet consisted of obsolete ships, and Nebogatov made ludicrous suggestions for tactics and strategy. Rozhestvensky mostly ignored him.

Chapter 49: Crossing the "T"

Tōgō Heihachirō (1848–1934) was one of the most famous Japanese naval officers in history. Tōgō served for fifty years, during which he was trained in Great Britain for seven years, fought in four wars, and was widely regarded in the West as the "Nelson of the East." He retired out in 1913 as a marshal-admiral—the highest military rank in Japan—and as a count in the imperial court. From 1914 to 1924 he was in charge of the education of Prince Hirohito, who was emperor from 1926 to 1989.

Chapter 50: The Tower

Shimose was a Japanese naval gunpowder used after 1893. Generating increased heat and blast effect but with decreased smoke, it was similar to British lyddite and French melinite in the same time period.

Chapter 54: XGE

Hans William Freiherr von Fersen (1858–1937), yet another Baltic-German Russian in the Imperial Russian Navy, had a routine career until this battle. He is one of the few officers to emerge from the battle with reputation enhanced. Directly afterward, he was promoted to captain first rank, commanding ships in the Baltic Fleet until World War I, when he was a senior officer on the naval general staff. He retired out as a vice admiral in 1917.

Chapter 59: The Siberian Sea

Victor Kurnatovsky was a chemical engineer with a murky past. Even his age is not exactly known. Friend of Lenin in exile, he became a radical revolutionary and was arrested several times but kept escaping. After helping to lead the 1905 revolution, he was imprisoned for life but in 1906 escaped the prison yet again and fled Russia. In 1910 he surfaced in Paris and reunited with Lenin. He died in France in 1912.

"Soviet" is the Russian word for *council*, usually used in the political-governmental sense.

Chapter 64: Volga and Don

Tsaritsyn has had several names: Tsaritsyn from 1589 to 1925, Stalingrad (yes, where over a million died and were wounded in the horrendous World War II battle) from 1925 to 1961, and Volgograd from 1961 to the present.

Chapter 65: *Ismail*

Pyotr Klodt von Yurgensburg (1864–?) was the grandson of Tsar Nicholas II's favorite sculptor, who specialized in horses, with many statues still existing in Saint Petersburg. The family was Baltic-German Russian nobility out of the Russian province of Finland. We don't know what happened to him later.

Ismail was built almost thirty years before, 127 feet long, with a full speed of about sixteen knots, a crew of twenty-one, with a couple of revolving quick-firing 1-pounder guns and two torpedo tubes.

Chapter 66: Maggots

The battleship *Potemkin* was a new (in service only three months) pre-dreadnought type of 12,600 tons, 378 feet long, twenty-two boilers, sixteen-knot speed, complement of 731, four 12-inch guns, sixteen 6-inch guns, fourteen 3-inch guns, six 2-inch guns, and five 15-inch torpedo tubes.

Ippolit Giliarovsky (1865–1905), son of an Orthodox priest from the Russian province of Estonia, was second-in-command of *Potemkin*. After thirty-two years in the navy, he had the reputation for being brutal to his sailors.

Evgeny Golikov (1854–1905), son of Moldovan nobility, had been in the navy since 1872 and never distinguished himself in combat or naval skills. But he did serve in the Tsar's various yachts for twelve years, currying favor and friendships among the gilded imperial elite of Russia. In June 1905 he'd been in command of *Potemkin* for eight months, overseeing her completion and commissioning. He complained to peers and superiors about Giliarovsky's brutal ways, but nothing changed. Golikov was completely incapable of controlling Giliarovsky, keeping revolutionary anarchy out of his crew, or handling the eruption about to happen.

What Is to Be Done? was written by Vladimir Lenin in 1902 and widely distributed in the Russian army and navy. Lenin (1870–1924) was originally named Vladimir Ilyich Ulyanov, but changed his name after his brother Alexander's execution in 1887 for revolutionary violence. The word "lenin" in Russian implies the person is from the Lena River region in Siberia, which he was not.

Chapter 70: Expedited and Incognito

Hotel Cherica was built in the 1890s and still exists, the oldest hotel on the Romanian coast and famous for its elegance.

Chapter 71: Further Instructions

The Savoy Hotel was opened in 1889 and is still (in my humble opinion) the premier hotel and dining experience in London. Plus, they have a great piano bar.

Cunarder refers to the passenger ships of the famous Cunard Line (operating since 1841), which is still the epitome of luxury and service at sea. I have been fortunate enough to be guest author on board *Queen Mary 2*, *Queen Elizabeth*, and *Queen Victoria* all over the world, and heartily recommend them.

Chapter 73: The Letter

Signatum secreto means "secretly signed" in Latin. The treaty was indeed signed in secret on 24 July 1905, when the Kaiser and the Tsar met at a fjord in Finland on their yachts, the German *Hohenzollern* and the *Polar Star*. The treaty was Kaiser Wilhelm's idea, and the two governments' senior leaders were not consulted, becoming very angry when informed of it by their monarchs afterward. Neither government ratified it—extremely unusual at that time. France was irate.

George von Lengerke Meyer (1858–1918) was a remarkable public servant. Born into a patrician Boston family of German immigrants, he became friends with Theodore Roosevelt at Harvard. When Roosevelt became president, Meyer served the United States as ambassador to Italy, then Russia. In the subsequent Taft administration he served as postmaster general and secretary of the navy. He was widely regarded as having done a very good job in Russia.

Sergei Yulyevich Witte (1849–1915) was a Baltic-German Russian raised in Russian Georgia. A brilliant mathematician and administrator, he ran Russia's railroads for twenty years. For eleven years he was finance minister. A financial conservative, he was moderate on most other topics and did not think the Russo-Japanese War the right course for Russia, resigning his post in 1904. Scandalously married to a divorced Jewish woman, he had many enemies in society and government. Witte had a somewhat contentious relationship with the Tsar, who nonetheless valued his abilities and asked him to return to government to try to defuse the revolutionary chaos in 1905. He was successful to a degree and was then asked to negotiate an end to the war.

Baron Komura Jutarō (1855–1911) was born into a samurai family in Kyushu, Japan. He became an internationally famous and well-respected Japanese diplomat who served in that capacity from 1880 to 1910. He was known for his humble manner and fluency in several languages, including English. When he led the peace talks, he was visibly ill and would die of tuberculosis a few years later.

William Howard Taft (1857–1930) had by this point been a highly respected lawyer and then superior court judge in Ohio, federal solicitor general, a U.S. circuit court of appeals judge, and governor-general of the Philippines. In the next few years after 1905 he would be governor-general of Cuba, U.S. secretary of war, president of the United States, and chief justice of the U.S. Supreme Court. Taft and Theodore Roosevelt were best friends until Taft became president in 1909 and subsequently neglected or undid many of Roosevelt's most heartfelt and famous programs. Their falling-out was legendary, ending with a poignant reconciliation in 1918, only seven months before Roosevelt's death.

The dispute over Japanese and other Asian immigrant laborers in the western U.S. grew in the 1890s and early 1900s into outright racist state laws and national organizations, such as the 1905 Japanese and Korean Exclusion League. It was known at the time as "the Yellow Peril." This prompted increasing international tension between the United States and Japan. Canada had similar issues.

Hotel Wentworth was built in 1874 as a grand hotel resort across the water from the Portsmouth Naval Station. It still exists and is still magnificent.

Sagamore Hill was Theodore Roosevelt's home at Oyster Bay on Long Island, New York. Now a wonderful museum, I urge you to visit it to learn more about this fascinating American.

USS *Mayflower*, a former private yacht built in 1896, served as a warship (and for other duties) for the U.S. Navy from 1898 to 1929. Roosevelt made her the presidential yacht in 1905, a status she held until decommissioned by President Herbert Hoover in 1929. She was in various private hands in the 1930s and returned to U.S. Navy and U.S. Coast Guard warship service from 1942 to 1946. She then returned to private ownership until 1948, when she was a clandestine ship bringing holocaust survivors to Israel. She stayed in the Israeli navy until 1956, when her remarkable life of service finally ended, sixty years after it had begun.

Chapter 76: The Wages of Peace

Kristiania, Norway, was called Oslo from its founding in 1040 to 1624, when it was destroyed by fire. The rebuilt city was named after King Christian IV and called Kristiania until 1925, then it went back to the original name.

$38,500 in 1905 dollars would be about $1 million in 2020. The industrial peace committee was never started by Congress, so in World War I Roosevelt gave the money to war relief funds.

Chapter 77: Nobody Does It Better

The Order of Saint George award was begun by Empress Catherine the Great of Russia in 1769. It was awarded until four years after the 1917 Revolution, when it was considered bourgeoisie by the Soviet Union and stopped. With the fall of the Soviet Union, it was reinstated in 2000 and is still awarded now and quite prestigious. There are four classes of the order, with the highest three usually reserved for Russians. As a non-noble foreigner, Wake would've been awarded the fourth class.

The engraved sword given to Wake in 1907 by Theodore Roosevelt may be familiar to longtime readers (the beloved Wakians). It is the same sword discovered in the Vietnamese emperor's trunk from 1890, which was found in the attic of Agnes Whitehead's home in 2007. That story is depicted in Wake's seventh volume of memoirs, *The Honored Dead*. And thus another clue emerges about the sword, the trunk, and Agnes Whitehead's connection to Peter Wake.

Acknowledgments

I am blessed with a diverse crew of sources for intriguing and hard-to-find information. A heartfelt thank you goes to Richard Rolfe for his translation and explanation of difficult German government and media documents, both historical and contemporary—*Danke mein Freund.* The National Security Agency Museum's Rob J. Simpson has my enthusiastic thanks for yet another entrée into the "historical code vault" and the eleven sets of extracts of American and British code books in use during 1904–5. The delightful Mary Thomas is recognized for showing me the malevolent wonders of an Afghan poison ring. Thank you to Mike Woodgerd and Marci Woolson, who offered me their tranquil subterranean hideaway to start writing this book. I am grateful to Dr. Paul du Quenoy, a true gentleman of the world, for introducing me years ago into the fascinating culture of imperial Russia, remnants of which still exist today—*moya blagodarnost'.* Ted Connally has my thanks for helping me understand the origins and depth of Freemasonry around the globe. Sincere thanks go to Sidi Goudimi Ahmed of the Kingdom of Morocco who, during our 1,100-kilometer trek from ocean to Sahara in 2005, immersed me into the mesmerizing culture, cuisine, and landscape of that beautiful place—*Salaamu 'lekum, Sabbi. Shukran bezzef.*

For over thirty years, I've been a proud member of the United States Naval Institute, the highly respected forum of all things naval and maritime. The Naval Institute Press has been wonderful to work with on my last three books, which they've published—professional, pleasant, and proficient every step of the way. Everyone in the Naval Institute Press crew has my sincere gratitude for it all.

As many readers know, the brilliant Nancy Ann Glickman has long been my expert for the fascinating subject of historical celestial events, some of which are in this book. She also is my business manager, an exhausting duty she does with incredible efficiency. More than all that, she is my wife and the love of my life. Thank you for all that, and for your patience with my absences into the absorbing world of 1904–6.

And as always, I thank my readers, the legendary Wakians! You are the very best readers an author could hope for, inspiring me for over twenty years.

Onward and upward!
Robert N. Macomber
Distant Horizons Farm
Pineland Village, Pine Island
Florida

Bibliography of Research Materials

Most historical novelists do not append their research bibliography. I do, however, out of respect for my readers, for many enjoy delving further into the remarkable personalities, places, and decisions that are connected to the events depicted in this book. It is, after all, the story of how our current state of geopolitics came to be. Just look at today's headlines to see the relevance.

Theodore Roosevelt

The Arena, vol. 95, no. 2, Newsletter of the Theodore Roosevelt Association, March/April 2015.

The Autobiography of Theodore Roosevelt, 1920 ed., Theodore Roosevelt (1913).

The Bully Pulpit: Theodore Roosevelt, William Howard Taft, and the Golden Age of Journalism, Doris Kearns Goodwin (2013).

Colonel Roosevelt, Edmund Morris (2010).

Grover Cleveland: The 24th President 1893–1897, American Presidents series, Henry F. Graff (2002).

New York Times, 1897 and 1898 newspaper articles (website), http://spiderbites .nytimes.com/free_1897/articles_1897_02_00001.html.

"The Right of the People to Rule," 1912 Roosevelt campaign speech recording (recorded by Thomas Edison), Vincent Voice Library, Michigan State University.

The Rise of Theodore Roosevelt, Edmund Morris (1979).

The Rough Riders, Theodore Roosevelt (1902).

Theodore Rex, Edmund Morris (2001).

Theodore Roosevelt, William Roscoe Thayer (1919).

Theodore Roosevelt's Naval Diplomacy, Henry J. Hendrix (2009).

William McKinley: The 25th President 1897–1901, American Presidents series, Kevin Phillips and Arthur M. Schlesinger (2003).

General U.S. Intelligence Work

A Century of U.S. Naval Intelligence, Capt. Wyman H. Packard, USN (Ret.) (1996).

Espionage and Covert Operations: A Global History, Vejas Gabriel Liulevicius (2011).

The Friedman Legacy: A Tribute to William and Elizebeth Friedman, United States Cryptologic History, Source in Cryptologic History Number 3, Center for Cryptologic History, National Security Agency (1992).

Masked Dispatches: Cryptograms and Cryptology in American History, 1775–1900, Series I, Pre–World War I, Vol. 1, Ralph E. Weber, Center for Cryptologic History, National Security Agency (2nd ed., 2002).

The Office of Naval Intelligence: The Birth of America's First Intelligence Agency 1865–1918, Jeffery M. Dorwart (1979).

Practice to Deceive, David Mure (1977).

Secret Servants: A History of Japanese Espionage, Ronald Seth (1968).

Secret and Urgent: The Story of Codes and Ciphers, Fletcher Pratt (1939).

Turnabout and Deception: Crafting the Double Cross and the Theory of Outs, Barton Whaley (2016).

Twenty-Five Years in the Secret Service: The Recollections of a Spy, Henri Le Caron (1892).

The World That Never Was: A True Story of Schemers, Anarchists, and Secret Agents, Alex Butterworth (2010).

Imperial Russian Intelligence and the Okhrana

"The First War on Terror," Brian Doherty, review article in *Reason Magazine* (2010).

Guide to the Registry of Okhrana Records, 1883–1917, Hoover Institution Library & Archives.

A History of the Russian Secret Service, Richard Deacon (rev. ed., 1987).

The Illustrious Career of Arkadiy Harting, "Rita T. Kronenbitter," CIA Historical Review, Studies in Intelligence 11, no. 1 (declassified 1993).

The Ochrana, the Russian Secret Police, A. T. Vassilyev and René Fulop-Miller (1930).

Okhrana: The Paris Operations of the Russian Imperial Police, Ben B. Fischer, History Staff Center for the Study of Intelligence, CIA (1997).

The Okhrana's Female Agents—Part I—Russian Women, "Rita T. Kronenbitter," CIA Historical Review (declassified 1993).

The Okhrana's Female Agents—Part II—Indigenous Women, "Rita T. Kronenbitter," CIA Historical Review (declassified 1993).

The Paris Okhrana, 1885–1905, "Rita T. Kronenbitter," CIA Historical Review (declassified 1993).

Russian Military Intelligence in the War with Japan, 1904–05: Secret Operations on Land and at Sea, Evgeny Sergeev (2007).

"Russia's Naval Intelligence in the 19th and 20th Centuries," Vitaly Belozer, *Military Thought Magazine* 17, no. 4 (October 2008).

A Secret Agent in Port Arthur, William Greener (1905).

"Siberia and the Exile System—Russian Police," George Kennan, *Century Magazine* 37, no. 6 (April 1889).

The Third Section: Police and Society in Russia under Nicholas I, Sidney Monas (1961).

Military and Naval Operations in the Russo-Japanese War

Admiral Togo, Georges Blond (1960).

Admiral Togo: Nelson of the East, Jonathan Clements (2010).

Battle of the Sea of Japan, Capt. Nicolai Klado, Imperial Russian Navy (1906).

Brassey's Naval Annual, Thomas Allnutt Brassey (1902).

"A Century of Japanese Intelligence," LCDR W. M. Swann, Royal Australian Navy, *Naval Historical Society of Australia* (December 1974).

Coaling, Docking, and Repair Facilities of the Ports of the World, Office of Naval Intelligence, U.S. Navy (1909).

Conway's All the World's Fighting Ships 1860–1905, Robert Gardiner, ed. dir. (1979).

From Libau to Tsushima, Eugene S. Politovsky (1906).

Kaigun: Strategy, Tactics, and Technology in the Imperial Japanese Navy, 1887–1941, David C. Evans (2012).

Maritime Operations in the Russo-Japanese War, 1904–1905, Vol. 1, Intelligence Division of Admiralty War Staff, Julian Corbett (1914; reprint, Naval Institute Press, 1994).

Maritime Operations in the Russo-Japanese War, 1904–1905, Vol. 2, Intelligence Division of Admiralty War Staff, Julian Corbett (1914; reprint, Naval Institute Press, 1994).

The McCully Report, the Russo-Japanese War, 1904–05, Lt. Cdr. Newton A. McCully, USN (1906; reprint, Naval Institute Press, 1977).

A Modern Campaign, or War and Wireless Telegraphy in the Far East, David Fraser (1905).

Official History (Naval and Military) of the Russo-Japanese War, Vol. 3, Committee of Imperial Defence, Great Britain (1920).

"Prisoners and Spoils of Port Arthur, a Heavy Total," *Straits Times* (Singapore), 9 May 1905.

"Reach Vladivostok and Tell of Battle—Cruiser Almaz and Destroyer Grozny Escape," *New York Times,* 31 May 1905.

Red Mutiny: Eleven Fateful Days on the Battleship Potemkin, Neal Bascomb (2007).
Report of the International Commission of Inquiry—Incident in the North Sea (Dogger Bank Case), 1905.
River Gunboats: An Illustrated Encyclopaedia, Roger Branfill-Cook (2018).
Russia and Japan, and a Complete History of the War in the Far East (1904), Frederic William Unger and Charles Morris (1904).
The Russo-Japanese War, Part I, The General Staff, British War Office (1906).
The Russo-Japanese War at Sea, 1904–5, Vol. 1: *Port Arthur, the Battles of the Yellow Sea, and Sea of Japan*, Capt. Vladimir Semenov, Imperial Russian Navy (1907).
The Russo-Japanese War at Sea, 1904–5, Vol. 2: *The Battle of Tsushima and the Aftermath*, Capt. Vladimir Semenov, Imperial Russian Navy (1907).
"The Slaby-Arco Portable Field Equipment for Wireless Telegraphy," A. Frederick Collins, *Scientific American*, 28 December 1901.
A Staff Officer's Scrapbook during the Russo-Japanese War, Vol. 1, Maj. Gen. Ian Hamilton, British Army (1905).
"Terrorised in St. Petersburg, Scenes connected with Sunday's Massacre," *The Graphic* (London), 28 January 1905.
The Tsar's Last Armada: The Epic Voyage to the Battle of Tsushima, C. Pleshakov (2003).
"Wireless Telegraphy for the Navy," *Electrical Age*, July 1904.
With Russian, Japanese and Chunchuse: The Experiences of an Englishman during the Russo-Japanese War, Ernest Brindle (1905).

The Trans-Siberian Railway

The Great Siberian Railway, M. Mikhailoff, *North American Review* 170, no. 522 (1901).
The Great Siberian Railway Accommodations, London advertisement (1906).
Guide to the Great Siberian Railway, A. I. Dmitriev-Mamonov and A. F. Zdzidrski (1900).
A Ribbon of Iron, Annette M. B. Meakin (1901).
Trans-Siberian Handbook, Bryn Thomas and Anna Cohen Kaminski (2014).

Background on Russia and Europe in the Early Twentieth Century

By Order of the Kaiser: Otto von Diederichs and the Rise of the Imperial German Navy, Terrell D. Gottschall (2003).
Caviar and Commissars, Capt. Kemp Tolley, USN (1983).

Dreadnought, Robert K. Massie (1991).

A Gentleman in Moscow, Amor Towles (2016).

George, Nicholas, and Wilhelm: Three Royal Cousins and the Road to World War I, Miranda Carter (2010).

History of the Imperial Russian Navy, Fred Thomas Jane (1899).

"The Kaiser's Secret Negotiations with the Tsar, 1904–1905," Sidney B. Fay, *American Historical Review* 24, no. 1 (October 1918): 48–72.

Letters from the Kaiser to the Czar: Copied from Government Archives in Petrograd Unpublished before 1920, Frederick A. Stokes (1920).

Nicholas and Alexandra, Robert K. Massie (1967).

Operations upon the Sea: A Study, Baron Franz von Edelsheim, German Imperial General Staff (1901).

Outline of the History of Russian Freemasonry, Boris Telepnef (1928).

The Riddle of the Sands, Erskine Childers (1903).

"St. Petersburg, Russia's Capital," Augustus I. C. Hare, *Bay View Magazine*, October 1904.

The Tale of the Next Great War, 1871–1914, ed. I. F. Clarke (1995).

"Text of the Treaty; Signed by the Emperor of Japan and Czar of Russia," *New York Times*, 17 October 1905.

Tidings from a Faraway East: The Russian Empire and Morocco, Paul du Quenoy, *International History Review* 33, no. 2 (June 2011): 185–203.

The Willy-Nicky Correspondence: Being the Secret and Intimate Telegrams Exchanged between the Kaiser and the Tsar, ed. Herman Bernstein (1918).

Africa and Madagascar

Blurring the Lines: Ritual and Relationships between Babongo Pygmies and Their Neighbours, Julien Bonhomme, Magali De Ruyter, and Guy-Max Moussavou (2012).

Living with the Babongo Pygmies of Central Africa in Gabon: A Life in the Margins of Society—Foraging, Hunting, Dance, Music, Spirituality, Poverty, and Discrimination, Ramdas Iyer (2019).

Singapore

Ah Ku and Karayuki-san: Prostitution in Singapore, 1870–1940, James Francis Warren (2003).

Maps and Charts

Carte du Theatre de la Guerre Russo-Japanese (Map of the Theater of the Russo-Japanese War), *Le Petit Parisien* magazine (1904).

Colonial Africa and Madagascar (1910).

Encirclement of Port Arthur Fortifications, Imperial Japanese Navy General Staff (1909).

German South West Africa (1886).

German Tsingtao (1906 bird's-eye map).

Hamburg City Map (1905).

International Transoceanic Cable Systems Map, Eastern Telegraph Company (1901).

Korea and Manchuria, U.S. Army General Staff, Supplement to the *National Geographic Magazine* (March 1904).

Kronstadt (1899).

Kronstadt (2019).

Japanese Coast Defences, Col. A. M. Murray, British Army (1907).

The Japanese Empire and the Russo-Japanese War, Cambridge Modern History Atlas (1912).

Manchuria and Korea, Imperial Russian Army General Staff (1904).

Mongolia, Korea, and Manchuria, Madrolle Guide Book (1912).

Moscow, in *Handbook for Travelers in Russia, Poland, and Finland*, Col. A. M. Murray (1893).

Northern China, Madrolle Guide Book (1912).

Northern Part of the Yellow Sea (China, North Korea, South Korea), nautical chart by the National Geospatial Intelligence Agency (2011).

Port Arthur, Madrolle Guide Book (1912).

Russia, National Geographic (2012).

Russian Asia (1904).

Sea of Japan, University of Texas (1911).

Singapore (1905).

Sketch Map of the Theatre of War, Showing Positions of Russian and Japanese Forces at the beginning of February 1904, Weller and Graham (1904).

St. Petersburg, Russia city map, by Joseph Meyers Bibliographic Institute, Germany (1905).

Tran-Siberian Line/Ural Line/Baikal-Amur Mainline/Trans-Mongolian Line/Trans-Manchurian official route map (2015).

Trans-Siberian Railway route map (1903).

Vladivostok, Pacific Russia, Madrolle Guide Book (1912).

Vladivostok and Port Arthur, Imperial Russian Army General Staff (1904).

About the Author

Robert N. Macomber is an award-winning author, internationally acclaimed lecturer, Department of Defense consultant/lecturer, and accomplished seaman. When not trekking the world for research, book signings, or lectures, he lives on an island in southwest Florida, where he enjoys cooking the types of foreign cuisines described in his books and sailing among the islands.

Visit his website at www.RobertMacomber.com.

The Naval Institute Press is the book-publishing arm of the U.S. Naval Institute, a private, nonprofit, membership society for sea service professionals and others who share an interest in naval and maritime affairs. Established in 1873 at the U.S. Naval Academy in Annapolis, Maryland, where its offices remain today, the Naval Institute has members worldwide.

Members of the Naval Institute support the education programs of the society and receive the influential monthly magazine *Proceedings* or the colorful bimonthly magazine *Naval History* and discounts on fine nautical prints and on ship and aircraft photos. They also have access to the transcripts of the Institute's Oral History Program and get discounted admission to any of the Institute-sponsored seminars offered around the country.

The Naval Institute's book-publishing program, begun in 1898 with basic guides to naval practices, has broadened its scope to include books of more general interest. Now the Naval Institute Press publishes about seventy titles each year, ranging from how-to books on boating and navigation to battle histories, biographies, ship and aircraft guides, and novels. Institute members receive significant discounts on the Press' more than eight hundred books in print.

Full-time students are eligible for special half-price membership rates. Life memberships are also available.

For a free catalog describing Naval Institute Press books currently available, and for further information about joining the U.S. Naval Institute, please write to:

Member Services
U.S. Naval Institute
291 Wood Road
Annapolis, MD 21402-5034
Telephone: (800) 233-8764
Fax: (410) 571-1703
Web address: www.usni.org